BODILY HARM

RACHEL BILLINGTON

BODILY HARM

MACMILLAN
LONDON

First published 1992 by
MACMILLAN LONDON LIMITED
a division of Pan Macmillan Publishers Limited
Cavaye Place London SW10 9PG
and Basingstoke

Associated companies in Auckland, Budapest, Dublin,
Gaborone, Harare, Hong Kong, Kampala, Kuala Lumpur,
Lagos, Madras, Manzini, Melbourne, Mexico City, Nairobi,
New York, Singapore, Sydney, Tokyo and Windhoek

ISBN 0-333-57828-7

A CIP catalogue record for this book is available from
the British Library

Typeset by Intype Ltd, London
Printed by
Billing and Sons Ltd, Worcester

To Nat

PART ONE

CHAPTER
ONE

I SHALL begin my story at the Turkish baths.

The Turkish baths were a habit, a drug. Even on that summer's afternoon I longed to feel my naked body in hot steam, to feel my skin opening up and releasing all the dirt and grime of the city. I might have preferred rain outside but the placid blue sky, the liquid yellow in the air could not deter me. Other people might head for the park, the tennis court or the tables outside pubs but I needed my cleansing process, my purification. Besides, I was about to start my independent life in London and I wanted to be in an area where I could think on my own and in peace. Privacy and order had always been very important to me.

'Six pounds, please.' The woman in the kiosk slid across a ticket. I paid my money and went through to the main upper hall. The baths were, are still, in a grand building, although in the last years it has become very run down. Then it was truly splendid, designed in the thirties with a lavish use of marble, pillars, gold paint, panelled wood, art-deco lighting, the lot, if you like that sort of thing.

I did. I accepted the towel and a wrap – a length of blue and white squared cloth like a tablecloth – from the attendant and went to my red-curtained cubicle. How secure I felt there! Ridiculous, in retrospect. Yet it seemed to have the safety of an old-fashioned British Rail sleeper, of a world where order prevailed.

I undressed, wound myself in the tablecloth and went down the curling marble staircase, more suitable for a palace than a council baths. I glanced at the ice-green waters of the cold plunge. When I was hot enough I would swim the four strokes across its length, if not with pleasure, at least with bold enthusiasm.

3

Some days the baths were too full but that afternoon, my last afternoon, as I came to think of it later, they were gloriously empty. I could lie naked along the wooden planks in the steam room and stretch my arms above my head. Soon sweat began to break on the surface of my skin and my muscles, taut from end-of-term parties and clearing up my books, began to relax.

I loved my body then, not, I would like to say, in a narcissistic or conceited manner. I was perfectly aware that my figure was nothing out of the ordinary, neither fat nor thin, neither long nor short, but it had the firmness and clean lines of a twenty-one-year-old. Perhaps it was more accurate to say I was comfortable with my body, it was an acceptable expression of what I felt myself to be, still relatively new, untried, but prepared and hopeful for the future.

Unusually, I suppose, judging by what you read in the papers, I was still a virgin. This did not seem so strange to me. I had plenty of boyfriends, plenty of men in my life, at lectures, classes, working on the university newspaper.

The truth is that I had never been in love. Perhaps that showed too much of an urge for self-protection, although I thought of myself as romantic. I've talked all this over with my psychiatrist since and thought about it so much and yet I'm still indefinite. What more can I write? I was a virgin. There it is.

When the sweat was rolling off my body, I knew it was time to take a quick shower and then head for the plunge. Ah! The numbing shock of it, then the delicious pain – so delicious that I couldn't resist turning round at the end and swimming back.

When I allowed myself to walk up the steps my body was scarlet and trembled. I was like frosted glass, encasing fiery spirit. I felt as if I had swallowed half a bottle of vodka. I smiled in self congratulation and then rushed back to the steam room.

Unfortunately a cluster of overweight Arab girls had arrived in my absence. They were using scouring pads to roll off their dead skin. This is a healthy practice – I had it done professionally at the end of my session – but it is revolting to watch and since the dirty whorls of skin are brushed off onto the floor, it made walking with bare feet a disgusting experience.

I removed myself for a shower but there, to my dismay, an Indian girl was shaving her pubic hair. Again, I have nothing against this in principle but in public view, with the hair dropping to the floor, it is an offputting sight, so I headed off to the Hot Rooms. These are an interconnecting series of three rooms each one becoming hotter until the third, smaller than the others, reaches a blistering one hundred and twenty degrees.

I settled in the second room, lying in a wonderful old-fashioned, blue-and-white-striped deck-chair, and pretended I lay beside a pool in Marrakesh. This made me feel more charitable towards the Arab ladies who were only behaving in a racially appropriate way. I shut my eyes and felt the sweat begin to roll again.

'And then she said I could fucking well shut up or get the hell out of her office.'

Although there are notices requesting SILENCE, whispering, by general consensus, is acceptable. Unfortunately, I have exceptionally good hearing. The noise came from two English girls, fair-skinned and busty, clearly settling in for a good gossip.

'I didn't like the job anyway.'

'It was well paid though.'

'Money isn't everything.'

Actually those girls were all right. I found their voices soon drifted away and by the time I was ready for the steam room again, I'd almost forgotten their presence. The Turkish baths had that effect on me – everything became a little bit remote, a little bit blurred.

Usually I took the three full hours to do the rounds – steam, plunge, hot, steam, hot, plunge – but that afternoon I presented myself for the body scrub a mere hour and a half after my arrival. Perhaps I wanted to get outside before the beautiful sun went down.

The body scrub is a strange experience but very effective. You lie naked on a marble slab, the sort of slab on which a

5

butcher lays out meat, and then a girl in a bathing suit attacks you with loofah and brush and basins of water. In my day the girls were usually out-of-work actresses.

'Hi, Lydia.' They knew my name.

'Hi, Patti. Busy?'

'Not too bad considering the weather.'

Sometimes Patti complained about her very fat clients. It was so much more work but she wasn't allowed to charge more than the standard couple of pounds.

By the time she had finished me with a touch of massage and a slap around to tone the skin, I was ready to wash my hair and then return joyfully to my cubicle.

'Anything to eat, dear?'

I always ordered the same from the attendant, whatever the time of day. 'A cup of black coffee, a poached egg on brown toast and an orange, please.'

This was the purely sybaritic bit. I still do not understand why being clean should make one feel virtuous.

I spent half an hour cooling off in my cubicle while I carefully creamed my body and made resolutions about how I would approach this new beginning to my life.

The sun was fairly low when I came out onto the street and the yellow in the air had turned to a deep gold. Even such a dingy part of the world as Westbourne Grove was illuminated by its colour and the softness of the air. I felt as if I had been born only a few minutes ago, so tender was my skin and my disposition. I walked the crowded and dirty pavements with a sense of invincible goodness. It was then that I remembered a friend telling me about a shop in that area, which specialised in cut-price kitchen equipment.

I could not remember the name but I wandered along keeping an eye open. I had a job in prospect and also a flat – hardly a flat, more a bed-sit, but it had a separate little kitchen.

I suppose it was nearly six by now. Of course I know it was nearly six but, although these hours have been raked over so often, and the panic is nearly gone, I still have a tendency to avoid precision as the moment draws nearer.

I saw the shop from a side-street. 'The Cutting Edge', it

was called, which the press picked up afterwards. To me it was only a weakish pun indicating that they specialised in good French knives at reduced prices.

It was a pretty shop, glazed and coloured pottery in the window, copper pans, glass jugs, rows of mugs hung in a circle. But when I pushed the door, it would not open.

Here Fate showed herself inexorable for, under normal circumstances, I would have gone away obediently, not the sort of person to force myself where not invited. But I was feeling so light-headed, light-hearted, light-bodied, that when I saw a figure moving in the back of the shop, I knocked on the door. He must have only just locked up, I told myself, for I could see a clock inside, saying two minutes past six.

So a young man came forward and opened the door. He was tall, well over six feet, with well-washed fair hair that flopped over his face. I noticed that because I used to like men with fair flopping hair. I did not notice his face so particularly, I think because although quite darkly sunburnt it had no strong features, just palish eyes and a slightly prominent chin. It was the sort of face I'd grown up with all my life, a nice English face.

When he opened the door to me, I felt nothing for its keeper except to be pleased he'd let me in.

'Thank you very much,' I said. 'I was recommended your shop and I just happened to be passing.'

He mumbled something, perhaps, 'That's all right,' and I turned eagerly to find what I needed.

'I'm fitting out a new kitchen,' I said and again he murmured a response, before leaving me and going back to the counter.

Taking this as an invitation to prowl, I began to shimmer about the shelves. There was a pile of baskets for smaller items and I had soon filled one with beautifully designed tin-openers and cutlery and whisks and spatulas and painted wooden spoons. I took it to the counter where the young man seemed to be contentedly totting up some figures and returned to the fray.

'This is such fun!' I called over my shoulder. 'But I promise

7

you I'll be as quick as I can. You just have such a terrific selection.'

This time there was no response at all, unless I was too carried away by my shopping to hear it. But certainly I felt no atmosphere of irritation or impatience. He seemed quietly occupied and after all, I told myself, I was bringing him a good sale.

I soon found a stack of Mexican earthenware cooking pots which I especially liked. I began to sort out the sizes, ranging them on the floor in admiration.

'I need four, I think!' I cried, picturing how pretty they'd look on the shelves of my newly painted kitchen. 'The big one with the two handles, the medium with the long handle and then two smaller.' Having settled that, I spent a little more time cheerfully trying to decide whether the flowers painted on the biggest were more effective when blue or yellow. It was only when I had realised the yellow would go better with my kitchen walls that I realised it was slightly cracked near the rim.

'Oh dear.' I took it to the counter, now convinced it was the one I desired above all. 'I really love this one but it's cracked.'

The young man slipped off his stool or chair or whatever he was sitting on and peered at the pot. 'Yes, it is.'

'You don't have another, do you? I'm terribly keen.'

He looked towards the stack vaguely but I interrupted his thought. 'I've been through that lot already.'

I turned back and brought the other three to the counter. 'You see. I do need a bigger one.'

Perhaps I did become aware then that he was more silent than normal but before the thought got very far he said quietly, 'I suppose there might be some more in the back.'

'Oh, that would be wonderful!'

'I don't know really. I'm only temporary.'

'It's the big one with two handles and the yellow flower, not the very biggest . . .' I encouraged him.

'Why don't you go and look?' He stood aside and showed me the door behind the counter. I went eagerly, imagining further rows of delightfully decorated pots. Perhaps there would be something even more magical than the Mexican ones. I had always liked the treasure hunt element of shopping, feeling, I think, that new purchases made life new too.

But the room was disappointing, boxes of what seemed to be plates, piles of knives, a shelf of heavy Le Creuset pans, nothing glowingly Mexican. 'It's rather dark,' I said, sensing the young man had come in behind me.

The room was dark since it had only one narrow window which was covered by a Venetian blind. It was small, too, and airless, more like a cupboard than a room. I turned to go and at that moment, with no warning, no sense of danger, no sudden sound or scream or abuse, I felt a heavy blow on my back.

Instinctively I turned and saw him already raising the knife again. It was a long wide Sabatier, obviously picked up from the pile beside him.

I screamed, 'No! No!' raising my hands in front of my face. Of course I wanted to run but the space was so small that all I did was knock against the shelf on which the Le Creuset pans were balanced. As he cut about my defending hands, I fell and as I reached the ground, I felt a stunning blow on my head. From that moment I was partly unconscious but not enough to avoid all awareness as the knife came down again and then again.

At last, everything, the fury, the noise (although he was silent), the pain, reduced to black.

CHAPTER
TWO

I woke up very early the day my story started. There was a blackbird outside that was making a god-awful racket but it was nothing compared to the racket going on in my head.

I knew Nell was still asleep because even after five weeks of marriage I had learnt her breathing pattern, her snorting,

9

her turning, her sighing, her suppressed farting, her kicking. It's extraordinary how present a not particularly substantial girl can seem in bed. Then there were my rollings and snoring and gaspings to add to hers. Of course I am not giving an objective view of what went on in our fresh down bed. If it had been in reality how it felt to me then our neighbours would have been knocking from below and above – unless, of course, they, too, were taken up by their own animal physicality.

So I woke on a peaceful summer morning with my young bride quietly sleeping beside me and my head banged and clattered with anxiety. The noise was too loud and too painful for me to be able to think. I just lay there suffering, waiting for it to be time for a cup of tea. As soon as possible I would leave the flat for work.

'I'm sorry, Pat.' At about seven, Nell woke and touched my hand with hers.

I immediately leapt up and went to our little kitchen. The relief was intense as I made ordinary household noises. I even brought an early piece of toast to Nell – as a kind of peace-offering, perhaps. I was able to kiss her on the cheek now I was out of bed and even smile.

'It's so sunny,' I said. 'Do you want me to draw back the curtains?'

She smiled too. It was fairly unbearable this smiling, but better than crying – or screaming. 'Yes. Draw them. I need waking up.'

She was pretty in the sunlight, in her white nightdress, rosy, skin sunburnt from our honeymoon in Turkey. She drank her tea and nibbled at the toast while I went into the bathroom. The sounds in my head had started again and I wanted to drown them with rushing water. Also, I wanted to be dressed. When I took off my pyjamas I rolled them up and put them under the sink.

It was a shock when she followed me into the bathroom. I was shaving and cut myself slightly, the blood welling up in a thin line. I smoothed it off with my finger and she, as if sensing something, went out again without speaking. I supposed she wanted to go to the lavatory and by a great effort of will, I managed to call out, 'Won't be a moment.'

'No hurry.' Nell had never been insensitive. We would never have married if she had been insensitive but there was a naturalness about her which put her always in the right. That was a kind of insensitivity because, without meaning to, she put me in the wrong. Now I could imagine her crunching more toast, this time thickly spread with honey. She has a sweet tooth. She had loved the heavily sugared Turkish coffee while it had put my teeth on edge.

'I love you.' I came out and said that, standing in the kitchen doorway with a towel round my waist. It was a shocking lie. I said it all the same, hoping, I suppose, to placate the God of Love.

She turned round, looked at me for a moment and then came over and kissed me. Before she had got very far, even though I had invited her, I extricated myself saying, 'I mustn't be late.'

'Certainly not,' she responded cheerfully. 'Nor must I.' Nell had an interview. We had both finished college in the summer. That's where we met. Now I had a temporary job and she was still looking.

I dressed quickly in our bedroom; it was going to be another hot day. There had been so much sun in Turkey that I had looked forward to English greyness and rain. But ever since we'd been back London had sat under hard blue skies which caked the dirt on the walls and pavements and turned the trees dark and lifeless. There was no freshness or moisture anywhere.

'Don't you want any breakfast?' Nell realised I was preparing to leave.

'No, thanks! See you at six!' She put down her toast and looked up at me. Although fairish, her eyes were brown, speckled like a hen's. I turned away and almost ran from the flat.

I was too early. If I caught a bus now I'd be at work by eight thirty. So I decided to walk. The Uxbridge Road was as noisy and unattractive as ever. Since we'd only just bought our little flat, I had the prospect of getting to know this ugly great thoroughfare intimately.

I walked fast until I noticed sweat was starting on my forehead. My direction was straight, no hope of relief from a crescent here or an avenue there. It was a six-lane highway with a barrier down the middle. After fifteen minutes I had reached Shepherd's Bush and a new flux of people and cars was coming from every direction. For a while I had to concentrate fully on negotiating the crossings. For a moment or two I even felt a fearful exhilaration at so much noise and energy. I was an explorer faced with a thundering waterfall, a vast canyon, an electric storm.

Once past Shepherd's Bush Green I passed under the roundabout, following a trail of sheep through a subterranean passage. Any reassuring nursery connotations were defaced by explosions of Arabic graffiti.

After the roundabout the road continued straight again; now it was fringed by large elegant houses and the side-roads retreated into avenues of prettily painted villas. Even the main road, although as congested with traffic as ever, was lined with tall trees. I knew that Holland Park was just to my right and, to my left, garden squares alternated with blocks of houses. In one a couple was playing tennis – not very well but energetically and letting out sudden shrieks of laughter. Their gaiety made me feel uncomfortable because I could not believe it was real.

The road began to rise quite steeply upwards so I slowed down further. I realised I was already exhausted at eight forty-five in the morning. At the top of Notting Hill a breeze blew, enough to flap the waste-paper on the streets. I bought a pastry from a patisserie under a tall building and ate it as I walked. A little further I stopped again and bought a Diet Coke. At last I had passed all the shops and the tube station which seemed to suck in people like peas into a drain and Kensington Gardens was running along the right-hand side of the road. I was beginning to look forward to the end of my journey.

The only drawback was that I would have to speak to Larry, my cousin, who was owner of the shop, but it would be cool and peaceful inside, an escape into darkness. I imagined the little shop as a safe burrow where I could shut my eyes.

I turned down a side-street. The pretty villas had long disappeared, now replaced by red-brick blocks, a mosque, rows of houses too large to be family homes and showing, by their rows of bells and peeling paint, that they had been converted into bed-sitters and small flats. It was a depressing area leading into the cosmopolitan untidiness of Westbourne Grove. The Cutting Edge lay just off it, its window a bright spot of pots and pans.

'Hey. You're the early bird.' Larry was looking up from the desk, nicely enquiring in his Australian way. He was about thirty, rugged-looking, no one's idea of a shopkeeper.

'I walked all the way.'

'Good on you. How long did it take?'

I looked for my watch but I had forgotten to put it on. 'I started soon after eight.'

'About three-quarters of an hour. Not bad.'

Larry was interested in exercise. Back in Australia he'd owned and run a gymnasium but he said the people were too difficult. He preferred cutlery. He had inherited money from his father, my uncle, who died when he was fifteen and had already tried several different ways of using it. The Cutting Edge was the latest venture.

'So you'll be all right on your own?'

'Fine.' I knew he was going to meet the owner of a local newspaper who might want to sell. Another venture. Larry was so adventurous.

'It's a miserable day to be stuck inside.' He grabbed his jacket and peered out of the window.

'I don't mind.'

'You're a saint.' He patted me on the back and left the shop briskly without looking back.

The moment he'd gone I let out an enormous breath. I felt as if I had been holding it all the time we'd been talking. I walked slowly round the shop, breathing deeply in and out. I had to sort myself out before a customer came in.

But every few moments, just as I was beginning to cool

off, calm down a little, the picture of Nell as she'd been in bed last night came into my head and I could feel the tension building all over again. To take my mind off it, I plugged in the kettle and prepared to make myself a cup of coffee.

Luckily no one came in before ten and by that time I had been able to sit down quietly for half an hour.

'Can I help you?' They were two women, very alike, grey-haired and stringy.

'We've bought a house in the French countryside.' They wanted to tell me their story. As they laughed and exchanged glances I began to feel uneasy again. Two old women should not be giving out an aura of sexuality. It was abnormal. I needed the normal so much on that particular morning – although I hardly knew what I meant by it.

'It's taking coals to Newcastle, I expect.' They fingered the heavy pottery.

I forced myself to break my silence. 'Those pots are made in Mexico.'

'Oh, good!' They laughed again. 'We met in Mexico.' I noticed one of them had an American accent. That clinched it. I went back to the desk and left them to it.

After they had departed, taking with them an extraordinary amount of stuff, there was another period of calm. The shop was stuffy and although I knew Larry usually propped the door open, I didn't feel the urge to be so welcoming. On the contrary.

Half an hour later I was visited by another couple. The girl was about eighteen, although she could have been much younger under all the make-up, and the man was at least sixty. He was bulky, well dressed, the businessman type you imagine eating too many lunches.

'Pipkin! Pipkin!' she cried. 'Pipkin, there're such sweet things here!' Everybody used to be thrilled by the Cutting Edge's stock; it was different, they all said, original.

'Oh, Pipkin, we must have this little painted jug! And just look at this soup bowl shaped like a water-lily!' He didn't say much, just looked as she darted round the shop, like a dragonfly in light black cotton leggings and a patterned T-shirt. He watched her and I imagined where his pudgy old

14

hands had been all the night before. They made their relationship only too obvious.

'Just think how pretty my kitchen will be with this jug!'

In the end he was hardly generous, buying only a couple of small items, but I was so hot by the time they left, head beginning to throb and eyes to ache, that I reluctantly left the door open. This encouraged a few prowlers who never looked as if they might buy anything. I didn't mind them because they needed no attention.

It was around lunch time that the third couple came in. Two young men. At least, at first I thought they were young but when they came closer and began to ask intense questions about oven-proofing and dishwasher viability, I realised that they were both over fifty and one was nearer old than middle-aged. Yet even from a few yards away, the fresh pinkness of the skin, the shine and bounce of their hair, one dark, one fair, the slim jean-clad hips and the straight neat backs made them seem much younger. It was only in and around the eyes you saw their ages, a smudged weariness of the spirit. I found it distasteful and looked away, even blushing.

'We'll have a set of the terracotta plates,' the older of the two said and as he turned his bare arm touched mine. I jumped back hastily but not before our hairs had risen together.

I needed some space after these two left so I gave myself a lunch break and closed the shop for an hour. For a while I sat on the floor under the desk where no one could see me but then I changed my mind and decided to get some fresh air. But the air was no longer fresh. Two o'clock is always the hottest time of day, I should have known. Walking briskly along Westbourne Grove, I could smell all the odours that humans produce when they live in too great numbers in too great proximity. The dirt, the cheap food, the car exhaust, the dog shit.

I remembered reading about a blind writer whose sense of smell became so acute in compensation that he could no longer bear to walk down a city street. I felt like that man. There was not a whiff of purity. I began to sweat hard and my head became so bad with the noises of lorries and buses and vans and cars and motor-cycles that I turned off the main street.

In a few moments I found myself passing a neon sign advertising Turkish baths. The thought of all that cleansing was so tempting that I was considering abandoning the shop – until I saw it was Ladies Day.

The telephone was ringing when I unlocked the Cutting Edge. I hurried to answer it. It was Larry.

'Where were you?'

'Having a pee.' It was easier to lie.

'Any sales?'

'Three. Two good, one medium.'

He was pleased and I managed to control my panting.

'Keep it open till six, if you can.'

Of course I would keep it open till six because when it closed I would have to go home to Nell.

'Certainly I will.'

'I can't hear you.' Had I been whispering? My heart was pounding so hard it blocked out my voice.

'A customer needs my attention.' I replaced the receiver abruptly and leaned against the desk.

I wondered whether to lock the shop and hide behind the desk again but in the end I managed to pull myself together. From Larry's point of view it was a good thing I did because from then on there was a stream of customers.

They were all eager to buy, not critical shoppers, if you know what I mean, but every one of them seemed subtly distorted.

Number one was a girl of about thirteen who wanted a present for her mother. That was all right except that firstly, she was enormously fat, particularly inappropriate on a child, the folds of flesh gleaming with perspiration, and secondly, she was determined to buy a knife. There was something upsetting in the way she turned over those knives time and again, fingering the smaller, the bigger, the middle-sized and then going back to the smaller again.

Eventually I burst out, 'Why don't you give your mother flowers?'

16

She looked up at me coldly. 'My mum loves knives.' Her voice was unpleasantly shrill. 'That's why I came here.' However, in the end she left without anything. I expect they were too expensive and I tried my very best to picture her buying a rose from the corner barrow.

Next came a serious young woman with a list. She would have been all right except that she had a dreadful stutter. She found it so painfully difficult to read off her requirements that I began to bound about the shop like an idiot, holding up the objects I guessed she wanted – often wrongly. After ten minutes of this we were both equally hot and bothered.

Suddenly a fierce look replaced what had seemed to me near tearfulness, 'L-l-leave m-mm—'

I guessed what she was going to say before she finished. Not that she was capable of finishing. 'Leave me alone!' I shot back to my desk and then, not feeling far enough out of her way, removed myself to the storeroom at the back where I pretended to rummage among the boxes. While I was still there, I heard the shop door shut and realised she had taken the opportunity to escape.

I re-emerged, breathed out and at once realised she had taken with her one of the blue glazed jugs. Revenge for having such a stutter? Or did she have a stutter at all? Regretting my attempts to help her, I began to check what else she had pinched. But that was all: one blue glazed jug.

I had broken Larry's only rule: never let a customer out of sight, particularly a woman. So when the thieving stutterer was followed by an overlapping visitation of youths, bag ladies and the mentally unstable – by now everybody looked threatening to me – I buzzed about them like a bee. Unsurprisingly, nobody bought anything and when the last alcoholic with red whiskers retreated, I was so exhausted and unnerved that I locked the door firmly and, although I didn't hide, I didn't lift my head when I heard a passer-by stop. One knocked on the door but the blackness into which I'd sunk allowed me to ignore it without difficulty.

Inside myself I felt as if the day's procession of deviants had confirmed something I'd suspected all along: that human beings are corrupt and that their corruption is dangerous.

It was at that moment that I became aware of someone standing the other side of the door to the street. It was a young woman. I was so distressed that I could not see too clearly but I knew she was young and for some reason sensed that she was not like all the others who had paraded through my day. Moreover, when she knocked, a little tentatively, I sensed that she needed me to open the door. She was in need of protection, I thought. So I opened the door.

She came in at once and immediately I could feel the aura of health and purity about her.

You know those Persil ads – perhaps they don't do them any more – when the boy's shirt gives off a special kind of white light? Well, she was like that. Her skin looked as if it had been lightly polished, her eyes were open and clear and her hair was a little damp with that soft curly look after a recent washing.

'Thank you very much,' she said as I opened the door. 'I was recommended your shop and I just happened to be passing.'

I mumbled something agreeable and she started looking about eagerly. 'I'm fitting out a new kitchen!' she explained gaily.

Not wanting to hover, staring at her, making myself ridiculous, I went back to the desk while she wandered around. I sat at the counter and pretended to add up some figures but I kept my eye on her all the time.

Soon she had filled a whole basket with small items and brought it proudly to the counter. She was extraordinarily cheerful.

'This is such fun!' she cried. 'But I promise you I'll be as quick as I can.'

Now she moved on to the large Mexican painted earthenware pots. She seemed to be in love with each one in turn, holding it up, turning it round, lifting the lid on and off, caressing the flower painted on the side. She made comments too, but more to herself than to me.

Eventually she brought one to me, the biggest size, with a blue and yellow flower. But now her brightness was dimmed. 'I really love this one but it's cracked.' She showed me the crack, bending forward so that her hair swung past me and I could smell its sweetness. I had to agree there was a crack.

'You don't have another, do you?' Her anxiety was rising now, as if this one pot held all the happiness of the world for her. She knew there were no more in the shop because when I looked to where the others were, she shook her head fiercely and cried, 'I've been through that lot already. I've looked and looked and looked.'

It began to be terrible. I could feel my hands tremble. In front of my eyes, she was losing that shining light of purity and becoming like all the other monsters of the day.

Intent only on her pot, she dashed back to where she had grouped the other three on the floor and lined them up in front of me on the counter. Although she had no real interest in me, hardly recognised my existence as an individual, she was challenging me to sort out her problem, the only problem, it seemed, she had in the world, since before the crack she had seemed invincible. She looked up at me, appealing. I could find an uncracked pot, her eyes seemed to say, it was just a question of getting myself together and making the effort.

The pressure of her regard was immense and although I didn't do anything as silly as confuse her large dark eyes with Nell's speckled orbs, I did sense that this was a continuation of that terrible feeling I'd had all night, all morning and all day.

In order to escape it and her, I mumbled some excuse about 'looking in the back' and turned away. But before I could even reach the door, she was with me saying, 'Oh, that would be wonderful!' so that I had to pretend I really was looking, although I knew perfectly well there were no pots in the storeroom. I opened the door and mumbled some excuses about not really knowing and being only temporary but she came close after me, insisting about it being 'the big one with a yellow flower and not an orange or a pink one and it must have two handles and not one and, come to think of it, it isn't the very, very biggest . . .'

It was then I began to be angry. It's hard to explain, but I felt that she had come to me on false pretences. I had no need to open the door to her but I had seen her air of purity and calm and let her in. But now she turned out to be like all the others, pushing, demanding, bullying. As we stood on the threshold of that little dark room, I even thought I smelled the odour of woman.

'Why don't you look for yourself?' Again, I was only trying to get rid of her. There was no plan in my mind. My anger was not of an active sort, rather a deep sense of unease. It was nearer physical pain than anything else.

She went in eagerly but almost at once said in a voice that came out ringing loud in that small space, 'It's rather dark.'

That is the last thing I remember. Until afterwards, that is.

CHAPTER
THREE

I HAVE been told that people who wreak acts of extreme violence very seldom remember the exact moment. It is as if nature blots out the memory of what is unacceptable to any rational man. And I thought of myself as a rational man. I did not think I was mad. Not even when I struck at her time after time. I knew I was not in a sensible frame of mind but that is not the same as insanity. I had simply been driven into a corner. It was, in a sense, an act of self-defence. If I hadn't struck out then, I would have gone mad.

This is not a point of view I would expect the victim to understand.

My consciousness returned and I found myself leaning against the door of the storeroom. I was no longer holding the knife which I had dropped onto the floor and my whole body was shaking so vigorously that I could hardly stand. At my feet, the girl lay huddled in a foetal position, her white T-shirt blotched with blood, and blood creeping along the floor from her chest and head.

My first instinct was to ring the police. I came out of the storeroom, walking tentatively like an old man. But when I stretched out my hand to the telephone, I saw my fingers were covered with blood. So I went to the tiny washroom and ran water over my hands and arms and then splashed it on my face. Surprisingly, not that I thought about it at the time, my clothes were not blood-stained at all. Being well educated, I found myself quoting from *Macbeth* as I scrubbed at my hands. 'Will all great Neptune's ocean wash this blood clean from my hand?' But I did not feel the horror of it. It just came to me as an appropriate association. I suppose I was in shock.

After washing, I did not return to the telephone but went back to the storeroom, for it struck me that I had left the door open and that the door to the street was also unlocked. Oddly, this did not inspire in me a sense of panic – perhaps I was past panic – but it made me behave very coldly and deliberately. First I shut the storeroom door and then I locked the shop door. Then I came back to the counter and sat down, for I was still shaking. My body seemed less strong than my mind.

Fleetingly, I again considered ringing the police, but the moment seemed to have passed. Also, with the storeroom door closed and the shop filled with the tranquil sun of the evening, I had some difficulty in believing what had taken place.

Gradually, as my limbs came more under control, I even found I was feeling a kind of calm. I'm not sure how long I sat there but it must have been at least an hour. One thing that never crossed my mind for an instant was that the girl was alive. I knew she was dead. I knew I had murdered her. It was as simple as that. So quite naturally I didn't consider her position as I sat there. She was dead. Out of it. It was myself I had to think about: I who was still around.

It was this sort of thinking that led me to decide to dump her somewhere. I did not directly confront the idea of being arrested by the police, convicted and sent to prison, but I did want to get her out of the way.

Of course, it was all very well feeling that, but a body is

a body, large and unwieldy even when a young woman's and, as I have said, it was a lovely sunny evening. Understanding these facts without consciously considering them, I continued to sit.

It was then that I began to think about Nell; what I thought about was not that now she was married to a murderer but that she would be worried if I was late home. And that if she were worried she would telephone. I began to worry about that more than anything and the shop was so quiet and ordinary that it was fast becoming completely impossible to imagine the terrible thing that had happened in the storeroom.

Eventually, I had the choice of going to reaffirm the nightmare with the evidence of my own eyes. Or I could allow myself to believe that it had never really happened at all.

So that's what I did. I tidied up the shop and went out into the street like any other person. Perhaps being able to behave like that meant I was mentally unbalanced but that's not how it felt.

I walked the same way home as I had come in the morning and in some ways I was a happier person. All the turmoil and anguish I had felt in the morning had died away. I looked at the dirty streets, the overflowing bin liners, the bad-tempered drivers, the tired and sweaty people with a kind of good-humoured sympathy.

No one has ever believed this. They can hardly bear to, I suppose, for they think of it in contrast to the girl, lying bleeding on the floor. It makes me seem a monster of heartlessness which, perhaps, I was. Or perhaps I had too much heart before. Because that frightful action seemed to have put something in balance in my nature.

Nell noticed it at once when I arrived back at the flat. She had bought a bunch of marigolds which flared a brilliant yellow on the table.

'You look better,' she said. 'Did you sell lots?'

As she spoke, fussing a little, straightening the collar of my shirt, I kept looking at the marigolds. Although normally I like flowers in a room, these disturbed me. 'I can't eat with

22

those on the table,' I said, for the supper was already laid, a salad of ham and lettuce.

'I'll put them on the side. I thought they were so cheerful, like sun in a room.'

'Haven't you had enough sun?'

'It was hot today.' She picked up the marigolds and took them to the side-board. 'But pregnant women always suffer from the heat.' She looked away as she spoke and I kept quiet. Yes, she was pregnant. She had been pregnant when we married. That was important. That was tragic.

'Mr Grant was quite sympathetic.' She sat down again at the table and began to tell me in some detail about her interview. Half-way through I went to the fridge for a beer and was surprised once more by my reaction to the marigolds. I harboured really strong feelings against those flowers.

Our meal passed. I did not actually manage to eat anything but that was nothing new in the last few weeks so Nell cleared away our plates and we adjourned to the little sitting room. I had only finished decorating it recently and it still smelled of paint. I didn't mind that, it was a good clean smell.

We watched the news for a bit or, at least, sat in front of it and then Nell tried to stroke my cheek and kiss me. It was horrible. I don't know why she didn't realise. If she had realised, I might have been able to talk to her and if I had been able to talk to her before it happened then it might never have happened. That was the problem, my head, filled to bursting. I rose at once to get another beer and there were the flowers again, blindingly yellow in the dusky light. As I stared, half mesmerised by the distinctiveness of the petals, the roundness of them, I realised where I had seen them before and knew why they upset me so much.

Without giving any explanation to Nell, I rushed out of the flat, downstairs, into the street and picked up a taxi. I was shaking again, so badly that I could hardly pay the taxi. But I was too intent to care what he thought. I know, however, that he waited till he saw me unlock the shop with the proper key because I remember his headlights swirling round as he left. It was almost completely dark.

Inside the timed night light had come on so I could see my way quite easily. I did hesitate before I opened the door, but not for long, because my old plan to remove the body from the shop had taken hold of me with absolute urgency.

I opened the door and, of course, it was like the black hole of Calcutta – I could hardly see a thing. Perhaps that was just as well. At any rate I could see enough to know there was still a huddled shape on the floor. In the back of my mind I remembered seeing an old curtain or tablecloth behind the boxes and that was part of my plan.

I went forward to the girl holding out the square of material, warily like a matador to a bull. Then came my worst moment. A fly flew up into my face, buzzing horribly. It seemed to be enormous and had obviously been feeding on the blood. I was so disgusted that I rushed back to the washroom and was sick, mostly beer.

When I returned the fly was buzzing about erratically, making zig-zag approaches and sounding in my ears as large as a helicopter. Nevertheless, I persevered, spreading the material over the girl and rolling her into it. Once this was complete I could breathe a little more easily. I went and sat behind the counter for a while to compose myself. I even thought to turn off the night light.

Afterwards people asked me why I didn't realise by her warmth that the girl was still alive, but the tiny room was so hot, and I somehow felt that since the blood had congealed she was dead. Essentially, I just knew, without any possibility of a doubt, I had killed her.

By now it was after ten, a good time for people on the streets who have things to hide. The pubs are not yet closing, the cinemas are still running and everyone has an idea where they are going. It was an enormous risk, even so, what I did next, but luck, if that's the right word, was with me.

I unlocked the shop door and propped it open. Then I carried her in my arms out into the street. She felt heavy so I staggered rather. There was no one around at all but even so it was a frightening feeling of exposure. I walked for about

24

ten yards, turned into a little alleyway and then gently laid her down behind some dustbins.

Returning quickly to the shop, I took another little rest before starting what had to be the worst job – cleaning the blood from the little room. First of all, I managed to open the window which gave me some air and enabled me to rid myself of that horrible fly. Then I set to work, removing a heavy pot which had fallen to the floor, using rolls of lavatory paper to mop up the blood. I flushed them away over and over again. All this sounds as if I was covering my tracks as a professional killer might but it didn't feel like that. I did not do it in a spirit of evasion, rather out of a sense of orderliness.

When I had finished I went back to the flat.

CHAPTER

FOUR

A NURSE who had been on duty when I was brought into hospital told me how I had been found. She gave me the barest outlines but my obsessive imaginings gradually built up a picture that has always seemed real to me.

Dawn had not come early behind the dustbins. And this despite the sun which was preparing to unmask itself for another day of long shining. It was warm, even at six, but misty and imprecise. The first people on the streets were unclear to each other. The vast noisy bulk of the garbage lorry moved, slowly and inevitably, like the first tank in the city of an advancing army. Every fifty yards or so it stopped and the team of collectors, spreading out on either side, like soldiers sent out to search and discover, returned with their bags and boxes.

I was found by the oldest man on the shift – he came to visit me later so I know his face. He was always sent to collect the smaller bags and light boxes. He had cursed when he saw what looked like a heavy sack fallen over sideways. 'Jack!' he called. 'Give me a hand.'

Then he uncovered my face. Like my murderer (I thought of him as that when I discovered he left me for dead), the old man, Bill, assumed I was a corpse. There was so much blood and my face was grey. 'Oh, Gawd! Oh, Gawd! That's all I need.'

Then Jack arrived. Jack was a young West Indian, filled with energy – he visited me too and filled in a few more details. 'Give her the kiss of life, Bill.'

'Kiss of life? That's a corpse.'

The other men saw something was up and began to gather round. The foreman arrived. By then Jack had me unrolled and was holding my wrist. 'She's bleeding well alive,' he announced emotionally. 'She didn't even need no kiss of life.'

Now the foreman sprang into action. 'She won't be alive long by the looks of her if she doesn't get to hospital sharpish.' The foreman did not visit me but Jack described the way he said 'sharpish' so intently that they were into a house within moments and dialled 999.

Unconsciousness is a most gracious gift. Yet I was glad to fill in what had happened to me in those lost hours. I thought of them often, during the first few months, the warm night which protected me from death, the subtle dawn, the great noisy tank approaching me slowly with its unlikely knight errants. Bill and Jack. Bill died recently but I still send Jack a Christmas card and now and again he turns up on my door-step. When I was most tortured by the sunburnt face and yellow hair of my murderer, I tried to replace it with Jack's dark skin and shining eyes. One deprived me of my life and the other did his best to give it back to me. Images are the most terrifying of all tortures.

Hospital images are not so particular. Doctors and nurses put on uniforms to depersonalise themselves. My progress from casualty to intensive care threw up no stories. I had become a 'case' for treatment. Not that I forget that it was the doctors and nurses who saved my life – far more truly than Jack – but that they gave me no image. Nothing to counteract the horror of my murder. I had survived murder.

I had joined the ranks of those people who had not just looked death in the face – in these days of road accidents that is almost a common experience – but of those who had looked on the face of death, who had been blasted by an anger so overwhelming that it wanted to destroy life.

I had become a case, even more impersonal because I had no details with me. I had no name or address, only my holed and bloodied body. My handbag, of course, with its pot of cream for the Turkish baths and its one new credit card, was under a box in the shop's storeroom. My body was turned into a kind of play doll without any say in anything that was done to it. I was inspected, swabbed down, filled with saline and blood. I was fed into a machine that threw up pictures of my brain onto a screen because, ironically, it was the heavy pan falling on my head which had caused the worst damage. Swaddled like a pharaoh, I was moved from casualty to intensive care where more tubes were inserted, one through my nose, one through my mouth which, with the original still in my neck because the veins in my arms had collapsed, made me look like a bull after the toreadors had enjoyed a good session. Later, they would stitch up my wounds, try to repair the damage to skin, muscle and tendon.

Yet it was done in the expectation of my death, so the doctor told me afterwards. My head had been cracked right open and a blood clot was pressing against my brain, producing the effects of a stroke. I was unconscious, out of it all.

FIVE

THAT NIGHT Nell left me alone. She rolled to her side of the bed the moment I appeared and never stirred or spoke. I suppose she was angry with me for not telling her where I had been, which was ironic under the circumstances. When I came in she was already in the bedroom and I was able to drink as many cans of beer as there were in the fridge so she probably thought I was drunk too. Even so, she never asked what was wrong, never admitted anything was wrong.

During that sleepless night, by no means the worst I spent, I never once thought about what I had done. I lay awake certainly, but it was as if my life had become a pattern of abstractions. Like a kaleidoscope, they moved continually, but whenever they seemed about to settle into a sensible picture, I managed to get them going again. All night long, I saw and felt and heard triangles and squares and oblongs, sometimes in colour, sometimes in black and white, sometimes with noises and sometimes eerily silent and almost beautiful, like planets circling in a dark firmament. Now and again they became three-dimensional and that was when they slowed down and threatened to form into real images. Very occasionally a voice intruded into the roarings and whirrings and hissings but never for long enough for me to understand what it said.

Whenever I opened my eyes, it disappeared and the dark outlines of the room became very steady and clear. When dawn came I slipped out of the bed and went and sat in the kitchen. The telephone hanging on the wall gave me my first agonising pain because it recalled me to my plan to ring the police. But then I closed my eyes and the abstractions whirled faster than ever.

What I did next gave psychiatrists pause for thought; they returned to it obsessively whenever I gave them a chance. For I dressed, kissed Nell (who pretended to be asleep) and set off for the shop. In other words I behaved, once again, as if nothing had happened.

I walked as I had the day before. The weather and conditions were the same, warm, noisy and dirty, but, instead of being overwhelmed, I felt curiously removed from them. When someone stopped me to ask the time, I was as startled as if I had been invisible. I did not answer him but walked faster. I think he called after me but I am sure I did not act aggressively.

I had begun to shake again when I approached the side-street in which the shop stood. This shaking was a terrifying sensation because it was entirely outside my control. As I walked as briskly as I was able down the street my attention was caught by something flashing. I did not think of it as connected to myself and even wondered about it a little curiously. It was only when I saw that it was the revolving light on the top of a police car parked in the alleyway where I had left the girl's body that I understood. The dustbins were no longer there but an area had been cordoned off with strips of orange plastic. As I passed, a man began to take photographs. He was pointing the camera in my direction and for a moment, I paused. I nearly wrote 'posed'. It was a weird moment.

Then I hurried on, found my keys and, with some difficulty owing to my trembling fingers, unlocked the door. Once inside, my body collapsed entirely. Tears began to pour down my cheeks, my stomach heaved and I could not even get my legs to take me to the toilet. I vomited where I stood, by chance half into a copper saucepan but mostly on the floor. The shop began to smell disgustingly of beery sick. Dropping to my hands and knees, I crawled behind the counter and lay there with my eyes closed.

The patterns began again but much slower, often pausing in mid-dance, as it were, before reconstituting in a new form. There was no sound attached but now my ears, as if highly tuned to a new frequency, were picking up noises from outside the shop, more particularly from the alleyway. First I heard the revolving light, then the clicking as the camera took the photographs. These were soon joined by more voices, distorted as if coming over the radio inside the police car. They were punctuated by buzzings and staccato bleeps.

The voices, although distorted, were very sharp and I thought I was hearing actual words. However, when later I tried to remember what they had been saying, I realised I had understood nothing.

I was told then I could not possibly have heard all that from where I was lying, the whole thing was inside my head. I believe them, for it continued unbroken for several hours.

I was aroused by the telephone. I knew it would be Larry and would have liked to talk to him but could not move. It rang and rang, stopped for a few seconds and then rang again. After a longer break, it rang for a third time. This time I managed to haul myself up by holding onto the stool and then the counter.

'Pat. Pat. Are you there?'

'Yes.' I could not say more.

'What's the matter? What is it?'

I began to cry again, tears falling uncontrollably down my face.

'Are you sick? I rang Nell but she said you'd come to work. Are you ill?'

'Yes.' I managed it once more. As well as crying I was sweating profusely and still shaking.

'I'll come round as soon as I can. But it won't be for a couple of hours. I'll ring Nell.'

'No.'

'Don't be a wombat.' He was so concerned. It was his concern that was making me cry and sweat so hard. But I couldn't let Nell come. Nor did I want her to telephone me so I had the good sense to take the phone receiver off the hook. Then I returned to my corner and in a few minutes the voices and noises returned.

Later, time was documented but, from my point of view, I do not know whether I lay there for minutes or hours or even days. It seemed an endless time during which the pain in my head made me tempted to bang it against the wall. In fact I believe I did a little. It was not exactly a relief but at least a change when there came a monotonous banging on the door. I could not stand but I listened to it and felt some consolation that it was near and real and obviously man-made.

Then it was joined by a woman's voice calling my name. 'Pat! Pat! Pat!' It went on and on until I recognised it. Soon after the calling stopped there were sharp metallic noises and then heavy footsteps came towards me.

Nell's voice was twittering about me being ill but the heavy footsteps did not speak, they just continued their approach. I kept my eyes tight shut, head down, ostrich-like.

'Oh, heavens! Heavens! Pat! What have they done to you?' Her words were addressed to me as an innocent person, almost the last addressed to me as the man I had been before. The policemen were immediately suspicious, I believe, or why else would they have searched the shop?

While Nell tried to make me open my eyes, the policemen poked about around the pots and pans and dishes and cutlery. They made a lot of noise to my over-sensitive ears.

'I thought you seemed odd last night, the last few days, really. Is it your head?'

One of the policemen came over when she said this and examined my head. I could feel his careful fingers moving among my hair. 'He's just banged himself,' he said eventually. 'It's nothing much.'

'Why won't he open his eyes?' Nell's voice was fretful, like a child's. 'We should get him to a doctor.'

'Yes,' said the policeman non-committally.

'You know, we were so worried,' Nell took my hand and held it to her face, 'we thought maybe the same person who attacked the poor girl they found in the alleyway had attacked you.'

At that, I began to cry again, the same soundless watering as before, although now it had to seep out from under my closed lids.

'He's crying!' I felt a coolness as Nell's warm bulk withdrew. 'Oh my God, my God! What's the matter?'

No one could, or at least would, answer her for the policemen were on my track. I heard them first go into the washroom and then into the storeroom. When they went in there I must have half fainted because I knew nothing more until

31

a voice said: 'We want to take you along to the station for a few questions.'

He brought me round by pulling me up because we were face to face when he said that. I could feel his breath on me. I still had my eyes shut.

'No. No,' Nell was saying, somewhere to my right. 'Can't you see he's ill. Look, there's his sick on the floor. He needs a doctor.' But her voice was whining and lacking in confidence.

They took me out to the police car and for a moment the summer's day was warm on my skin. If Nell hadn't been there I might even have opened my eyes but in a second I was bent and bundled forward. She didn't come. At least there was that.

My memory of all these events has a nightmarish quality, in the sense that there is no proper continuity. I was not rational and particularly not after I had decided to keep my eyes closed.

There was nothing they could do about this in the police station, although I could feel their irritation mounting to anger. I wasn't speaking either, of course. This was not a deliberate policy, it was just that my ears seemed to have taken over all my other senses and they wouldn't let my voice speak. At least it was partly that but also that there was so much to listen to that I really didn't have time to speak.

So when they began to question me, 'We would like to know where you were yesterday evening', they were polite to begin with. I listened intently but did not respond. They had sat me down which made it easier to drop my head and keep quiet.

I was on my own because Larry had arrived at the shop just as I was leaving and, realising more about the situation than Nell, had persuaded her to go with him to find a lawyer. It was the sort of thing Larry was good at, finding lawyers, he always had friends where friends were needed. He ignored Nell's protests that I hadn't been arrested, telling her it was better to be safe than sorry. Larry was a careful man which is why he became a good businessman.

I was in the police station for thirty-six hours but it was

the time before I opened my eyes which fixed my image of it. It was dark, hard, empty. My fingers never encountered anything except the surfaces of walls, counters, tables and chairs. It was a blank, filled with voices – a great many voices, a few of them female. They usually spoke kindly and offered me cups of tea which I refused. I was still acting out of a lunatic belief that if I refused to acknowledge what was happening to me, it would all go away.

'We need to find out quite definitely, with corroborating evidence, where you were last night.' They did not know that the terrible thing happened in the early evening. They kept talking about last night. Of course, they were right in the sense that I had moved her body about four hours later. I did not answer.

'It is not helpful to keep silent, you know.' Different voices came to talk to me. Some were rough, some were smooth but in my darkness they all brought the same message: I was a murderer.

After several hours there was a pause in which they allowed me to drop my head on the table. I thought I had been left alone since it had suddenly become very quiet. So my heart jumped sickeningly when I felt a hand on my shoulder and a soft woman's voice say close to my ear, 'It'll be much less painful if you tell me all about it.'

I knew she was right. One small part of me wanted to bury my head in what I imagined as her motherly bosom, but another side was filled with rage. It was always the same with women. By that I mean it had begun with my mother and reached its disastrous climax with my marriage to Nell. The rage was a relief. I threw my arm backwards and obviously made some connection for she gave a yelp and then I began to bang my head on the table. At least it was better than banging her head on the table, as my lawyer said later.

Three men came in then. One was very bad-tempered. 'Stop that!' he shouted. 'Stop that at once. Here, Michael, fetch the cuffs. I've had enough of this bastard for one day!'

In retrospect, I don't blame him. In fact, even then I was almost glad to feel the hard steel clamp my wrists together. I felt safer like that. Strange, really. I also felt like a chicken trussed ready for the oven. My head was full of images like that, perhaps because I had shut off my ordinary visual perceptions. I saw a pair of iron gates often, elaborate gates, ten foot high with ornamental vertical bars and a complicated lock in the middle. Several months later when I'd seen a good deal of iron bars, although a lot less finely wrought, I realised they were the gates at Hampton Court which led from the garden to the fields. I had often admired them as a child.

'Right, Pat,' the tough policeman began at me again. 'I'm going to take you down now and lock you in a cell because you've just committed a very serious crime. You've assaulted a policewoman in the course of her duty.'

I smiled. It seemed such an extraordinary thing to say after the real horror I'd perpetrated. The next thing I felt was a rocking of my chair and I was lying on the floor. I was surprised but unhurt and glad to be on the floor. I crawled further under the table.

The two men, or perhaps there were three, began to confer as if I wasn't in the room.

I think my blind eyes were beginning to make them believe I was deaf too. They certainly thought I was deranged.

'I told you he needed a doctor. He's right off his marbles.'

'I'm not so sure. He might be just faking till his lawyer comes.'

'His lawyer's come. And his wife. And his employer.'

'So where are his parents?' asked the cross policeman, ironically.

'Dead,' said the other policeman. 'In a car crash, six months ago.'

That was true. That was part of the banging in my head. They went on talking and they certainly didn't care about me.

'How do you learn these things?'

'His wife. Wants to tell us everything. She's pregnant. They've only been married a couple of months and he's just finished university. Got a degree too. No marble loss, then.'

'Better let in his lawyer.'

They hauled me up firmly but not meaning to hurt as if my university degree had given me certain rights.

'Your solicitor will be in now.' They spoke to me extra loud and slow. 'You can talk to him.'

But I didn't. Actually she was a woman.

'I'm Ruth Gormley. Larry has retained me as your solicitor. Your wife agrees. I understand you're not talking?'

I couldn't explain myself to her. It was bad luck she was a woman or it seemed to be at the time. I wanted to ask for Larry, but instead I slid under the table. I interrupted her.

'You could nod or shake your head. You don't have to – ' she stopped abruptly and then finished her sentence, 'speak.' I heard her sigh, a brisk unwistful sound and then she sat down in the chair opposite the one I'd just vacated. As neither the room nor the table was big, I could feel her legs and feet settle down close to my back. I wriggled away a little.

'This room isn't bugged or anything. I'm on your side. You realise they will charge you. They are only waiting for a little more evidence, formalities and then there's the girl . . .'

She wanted to shock me into a response and she certainly succeeded. I screamed, 'No! No! No!' I could not listen to her talking about the girl. It was right out of the question so I continued screaming a bit until I could hear definite silence. Soon followed by policemen-type footsteps. Except one of them was a doctor.

He revealed himself at once. 'I'll give him something to calm him down.'

'What sort of thing?' Ruth Gormley's voice was sharp.

'Where do you thing we are, dear? Just a little Valium. Perhaps you'd like some too?'

'Very funny.'

The Valium was a great idea. When they took me down to a cell I huddled up on a bunk and turned my face to the wall. I felt so utterly exhausted that even my hyper-sensitive ears seemed to be going off duty. The world shifted further away and I slept.

For a little while I wasn't a murderer.

35

CHAPTER
SIX

THE BLACK spangles of a changed world hung in front of my eyes. I recovered consciousness, although no one gave me a reason to live.

When I came round, I thought I was lying on the marble slab in the Turkish baths but, instead of sympathetic hands soaping and scrubbing, a man was standing over me with a sharpened stake. I wanted to cry, 'Have mercy!' but my throat was constricted and he raised the stick above me.

'Try to speak. Try and tell us how it happened.'

Unfortunately, the policeman was fair with regular features and a smooth golden skin. As his face approached mine, I felt a strong physical revulsion. I croaked a scream and twisted over violently, wrenching at my tubes and swinging the bottles over my head. I was vaguely aware of a nurse standing on one side of me before passing again into unconsciousness.

CHAPTER
SEVEN

I OPENED my eyes and started speaking again when the policeman read out the charge to me. 'Read it again,' I whispered. It was early morning and they had brought me up to the same room I had been interviewed in the day before. I knew it with my eyes closed; when I opened them it was bigger than I imagined. And my solicitor, Ruth Gormley, was younger and smaller and the policeman's personality did not seem important. I rubbed my eyes which felt sticky and swollen. 'Read it again.' My voice was hoarse and grating, like an old man's or a heavy smoker's.

'You, Patrick William Downes, are charged with the

attempted murder of Lydia Mary Kremachowski on 4 September 1975.'

He read slowly, expressing no interest or surprise that my eyes were now open and that I had spoken. 'I have now to ask you whether you wish to make any statement which, I should warn you, may be taken down and used in evidence against you.'

So many must have listened to these words with misery, anger or self-disgust. But to me they were an expression of joyous hope, of renewed life, of relief so great that, once again, I was crying.

I would have yelled, 'Guilty! Guilty!' if my solicitor had not quickly announced I had nothing to say. For what was I guilty of? Or rather what was I not guilty of? The girl was not dead. I had not killed her. I was not a murderer. Merely an attempted murderer. How had I deserved such an extraordinary reprieve? I remembered the force of my rage, the blows I had dealt her over and over again. How had she lived through them? What strength she must have! I must have looked strange while these wild thoughts rushed through my mind, because Ruth took my arm and tried to calm me. 'Sit down,' she said. 'Now you are talking you can talk to me.' She turned to the policeman. 'I would like a private consultation with my client.'

I sat down and the policeman left. My surging exultation was gradually receding. Ruth said, 'They've found her handbag in the shop. Your case will come up in the magistrates' court tomorrow morning. So the first thing is to decide whether we wish to apply for bail.'

I did not care. I was wondering how I would face Nell. Indeed, would I have to face Nell at all? Perhaps this extraordinary situation I had put myself into would mean I need not see her. 'Where's my – Nell?' I could not pronounce the word wife.

'She's gone home. She'll be back later.'

'I don't wish to see her.'

Ruth's head jerked up. I stared at her for a moment. She had short black hair, tight on her head like a cap and a pale face, wide at the cheekbones with narrow grey eyes. She might have been pretty except for a hard closed mouth and a too-large nose. It was a masculine face.

'I'll see Larry,' I mumbled.

'Oh, yes.' She made a note. 'He'll be back later too.' She looked at me again but this time I turned away. 'I've been here all night, hoping you might speak.'

'I'll speak to Larry.'

She gave that same brisk sigh I had heard the night before and stood up. 'I'm going for some breakfast and a change of clothes. I expect you want something to eat too and a clean-up. I'll see you in a couple of hours.'

She was always direct, Miss Gormley. She was my solicitor but she didn't stand any nonsense. If I wasn't prepared to co-operate then she would let me get on with it.

I was glad to be quietly back in my cell with my eyes open. Some food was brought for me but, despite not having eaten for so long, I knew my stomach could keep nothing down. I did drink half a cup of tea which ran round my veins like heroin. In the next-door cell, a man woke up and began to sing. He was obviously still drunk from the night before. He sang or rather bawled, 'God save our Pope! God save our Pope! God save our Pope! The great the goo-o-o-od . . .' He drew it out on a long low note filled with relish. After he had sung it six or seven times a policeman came down and told him to fucking shut up or he wouldn't get any breakfast. So he was reduced to mumbling another hymn to himself, although now and again, he couldn't resist a little crescendo on the word 'saviour'.

What can I write down about the rest of that day? That I came to a true realisation of what I'd done? It would be nice if I could record that, but a lie. At first my main preoccupation was that Nell should be stopped from seeing me. It was only when I realised that the police had no wish for me to see anyone either – apart from my solicitor whom they could not stop – that I stopped thinking about my poor plump wife.

Even when I thought about her it was not about what she might be going through but rather as a horrible feminine threat. A sort of huge black approaching eiderdown. Right from the beginning I could see Ruth had none of the succubus tendencies notable in women. She was hard, not soft, self-contained, not spreading, resilient rather than porous. If Nell was an eiderdown, Ruth was a trampoline.

She reappeared again at about midday just after I had rejected lunch.

'Why aren't you eating?' she asked at once but not as if she cared.

'I don't want to.'

'You're not ill?'

I didn't answer.

'Of course, you're ill.' She looked down at her note-pad. 'You know the girl might still die.'

I don't know why she said this. Perhaps she hoped by such cruelty to shock some truth out of me, some motive or at least some reaction. For I had, of course, told her nothing. All she knew was that a young cousin of her friend Larry, up to this point in no trouble, had suddenly stabbed a girl nearly to death.

I began to cry again, shivering and burying my face in my hands. I didn't care about her seeing my tears but my head suddenly felt as if it needed holding onto my body.

She listened to my sobs for a bit and then said, 'We must get a psychiatrist's report.'

I didn't care about this either but I was too weak to carry on crying for very long.

Again she let a longish pause elapse before asking, 'You didn't know the girl, did you?'

I would have answered this question but I was still too shaken to speak.

'Your wife and Larry seem to think she was a complete stranger to you. Of course, they're only going by her name. They haven't seen her because she's in hospital, in intensive care.'

It is hard to describe the intonation of her voice, but I knew that the very cool steadiness was daring me to say something, defend myself perhaps, provide an explanation. That would have been something, to provide an explanation. I was angry. I suppose I could have said that, even then, but it would hardly have been much of a defence.

'Not that they would see her anyway. Shall I tell you her name?'

'No, thank you!' I spoke sharply, lifting my head and staring at her.

'So you didn't know her.' She made a note on her pad.

I shut my eyes and leaned back on the chair. 'She smelled like a woman.'

'No, she didn't!' She spoke as sharply as I just had. 'She came to the shop straight from the Turkish baths. She smelled clean, very, very clean.'

I don't know how Ruth had picked up this information so early but it was the end of that particular interview. I turned my chair round and faced the wall. To me, she had smelled like a woman. All the facts in the world wouldn't change my feeling and if Ruth failed to realise that that was the nearest I could give to an explanation then there was no point in our continuing this discussion.

She seemed to understand this because she stood up immediately. 'Your case will come up for committal proceedings tomorrow morning at eleven. I'll see you in the cells at nine thirty. Eventually you will plead guilty but not to attempted murder. Tomorrow you don't have to plead anything. I'll try to get a doctor round to you this afternoon. It would be good to have you assessed in your present state.'

She left then, not attempting to shake my hand or say goodbye. When the policeman came to take me back to my cell, I smacked him across the face. I don't know why. I just felt like letting loose. It was nothing to do with my murderous anger, except perhaps a late continuation of the mood.

The police thought nothing so fanciful. The one I'd hit grabbed my arms and pinioned them so hard behind my back, I thought they had to crack. He called for a colleague who brought handcuffs and fixed me in the same unpleasant position.

From then on their attitude of indifference changed to antipathy. When Ruth returned later in the afternoon she was angry, her nose thinner, her eyes small and mean. 'You'll never get bail now,' she said at once. 'Why did you do it?'

She didn't wait for an answer or even look to see my reaction. I understood she was beginning to lose the sympathy that Larry's friendship with me had given her at the start. All of it was unimportant, anyway, so I began as before to turn my chair on her.

'Don't turn your back on me,' she cried impatiently, waving her pen. 'I've brought a doctor.'

I turned my back more resolutely. For a second when I had heard that 'I've brought . . .' I had imagined it was Nell. It took me a few seconds to recover myself, by which time she had left the room again.

The doctor came in to my turned back. 'I have been asked by your solicitor to make a report,' he said in quiet, tired tones. 'Do you wish to co-operate?'

'I'm not a lunatic,' I said to the wall, adding softly for the benefit of myself, 'Not the way people think of a lunatic.'

'What did you say?' He raised his voice a little but still sounded weary.

I did not answer so he paused a moment and then began to ask me questions. They seemed to be from a prepared list for when I answered briefly, 'Yes' or 'No', he would immediately go on to the next.

'You are Patrick Downes, twenty-one years old?'

'Yes.' I didn't mind his questions.

'You were until recently a student of London University where you gained a second-class degree?'

'Yes.'

'You are now employed by Larry Purley in his shop?'

'Yes.'

'Your parents died six months ago?'

'Yes.'

'You married two months ago?'

'Yes.' It was helpful that he seemed so uninterested.

'Your wife is expecting a baby?'

'Yes.'

'You are accused of attempted murder?'

'Yes.'

The doctor stopped here and stood up. He advanced

towards me, 'Why will you not look at me or talk to me properly?'

There was no point in replying to this, although I felt that since I had told him I was not a lunatic and answered all his questions it was unfair to reproach me.

'Why did you hit the policeman?' I did not answer.

'Have you anything you wish to say to me?'

CHAPTER
EIGHT

LUCKILY I was too ill to realise my world had revolved and set me down on a new plain. When I saw the policeman sitting at my bedside, I did not realise he was the Angel Gabriel of my future. When I think of that time, I think of doctors, nurses and policemen but policemen had more character. To begin with, it was questions.

'Who attacked you?'

I knew in some sort of dim way what he was talking about but I could not frame an answer. That was on his first visit or at least the first time I was conscious of his presence.

The second time he asked the same question but with more urgency. 'Who attacked you?' This time I began to cry and then was sick. It must have been rather depressing for the poor man. The third time he said, 'We know who attacked you now.' And he held up my handbag. 'Your parents will be here soon.'

In fact I saw my elder sister first. Next time I saw the policeman she was sitting beside him. The sight of her looking so terrified made me cry again. But she took my one visible hand and held it tightly. Poor Charmian. She was sure I was dying. She was also afraid I had been raped.

'Tell me how it happened.' The policeman leaned closer to me. They had the suspect safe and sound, charged already with attempted murder but I suppose they wanted to have the story from the horse's mouth.

CHAPTER NINE

In a room under the magistrates' court Ruth asked again if I had anything I wanted to say. This obsession with words startled me. As if anything I could say, or anyone else could say, had any relevance to what I had done. I understood even then that these words they continually tried to elicit from me would be turned into wallpaper and used to cover over my crime.

They thought the opposite, of course. They thought they were looking for an explanation but that was impossible. It was because there was no explanation that I had been forced into action. My silence immediately after the police had found me was the most helpful clue I ever gave them. I resorted to it fairly often afterwards in prison.

At least my appearance in the magistrates' court was short. I stood in the dock but only to affirm that I was indeed Patrick William Downes. Then we were informed of the charge, 'attempted murder', and one of the policemen I had come to know gave the evidence which was 'deemed sufficient'. It was Ruth's turn after that to apply for bail but it was opposed by the police 'by reason of the seriousness of the charge'. I listened to it all negligently, as if it applied to a stranger.

The disagreeable aspect of my court appearance was catching a glimpse of Nell's pink, tear-swollen face. It can't be much fun to be carrying an attempted murderer's baby in your belly. Naturally, I did not acknowledge her presence there and was relieved when I was taken back to the cells again.

We were a stupid bunch down there, no one over thirty,

all goggle-eyed and unable to concentrate. We said silly things too. I mean, apart from the swearing.

Then Ruth came down and looked at me wearily. 'We'll make another application as soon as possible, I promise you.'

I raised my eyes to heaven. 'Alleluia.'

This irritated her and she stopped trying to look sympathetic which didn't suit her anyway. 'There's some doubt over the girl's condition. So I expect that's why you haven't been given bail.'

'Quite right too.' Until then I had not taken in that I was to be held in custody. And even then I did not look ahead to think that what this meant was prison.

'It was a pity about your attack on the policeman,' Ruth said, like a school mistress. 'Although they didn't add it to your charge, it looks bad on your custody sheet.' This was her final message.

When I arrived back with the other men they all seemed pleased to hear I hadn't got bail. They had expected me to get off, I think, because of my 'educated' background. Larry had brought me in a clean shirt for my court appearance and a tie. I did look respectable.

'You're a fucking con, see. That's how it is. You'll get there.' It definitely cheered them up to know I would be off to prison.

'It's the nick for you, of which fact I have no fucking doubt.' The most animated of the group told me this often, but each time with the excited air of imparting new information. We had nearly six hours in each other's company because none of us were taken off until we'd all been sorted out at the end of the day.

Another man began to tell me his life story. 'Fifteen,' he said, 'Fifteen, you wouldn't believe it, would you? Fifteen. Inside at fifteen. Out at sixteen. In again at sixteen and a half. Out at seventeen. In at eighteen. Out at eighteen and three-quarters.' Since he was one of the older ones there, which meant at least another ten years of this, I interrupted him.

'What had you done? I mean, what had you fucking done?'

Even after a few hours, I could see that no sentence was comprehensible without a 'fucking' thrown in.

'Done? Fucking done?' He seemed bemused, stopped in mid-track, his train of thought broken. His face expressed a noble struggle to answer my question but in the end all he could manage was, 'A bit of this and a bit of fucking that', and then he went back to his years, starting however at the beginning. 'Fifteen,' he said. 'Fifteen, you wouldn't fucking believe it . . .'

When we were eating sausages and chips, one of the West Indians came and sat very close to me. I tried to move along a little but he grasped my forearm so hard that I dropped my fork with the sausage on the end.

'That fucking girl. What about that fucking girl?' His very small black eyes managed to make his question absolutely clear.

'No,' I gasped. He continued to hold me, peering even closer. The cell had become intensely silent. It was obviously the question to which everyone wanted the answer.

Sweat began to roll down my body and I could feel my arm becoming slippery under my aggressor's fingers.

'No,' I repeated. 'I didn't. I couldn't. I mean I wouldn't want to do that. That sort of thing.'

'Pervert!' The man dropped my arm, either disbelieving or disapproving. He then astonished us all by producing a head-set which he affixed neatly to his ears.

'How the fuck did you hang on to that?' began someone and then gave up. It was too hot in the cell. We began to talk about that instead.

As a matter of fact, I did not talk but it was a 'we' all the same because I had thrown in my lot with them. I had that good sense left to me at least.

After several hours I asked the time since I had not recaptured my watch. I soon discovered that was a tricky subject with my companions. 'Why do you keep asking the bleeding time, you've got fucking years, haven't you?' He turned to his neighbour. 'What does he want to know the fucking time for?' His voice expressed a personal sense of injury. It was at least half an hour or more before he stopped complaining and appealing for sympathy. 'It's not time he wants. Fucking answers. "What's the time?" ' He imitated my voice. 'If I knew would I fucking tell him? How long does he think I've got?'

At about four or four thirty, the atmosphere changed. Men who had been sitting stood, men who had been chatting became silent. The West Indian took out his earplugs, kissed them and put them in his jeans pocket.

When the policeman came to get us we were ready, near the door. They looked us over, quite disgusted. 'What's this old thing called bail, then? You'd think they'd never heard of it upstairs.'

'We're fucking desperadoes,' said one man, trying to strike up contact. But nobody, least of all the policemen, took any notice. They continued to worry, however, not of course on our behalf, but in case there were not enough police vans. 'No more than sixteen, I've got over here.' He looked at his clipboard with suspicion.

This logistical diversion was welcome. We were escorted out of the building into a car park where two vans waited for us. One of them looked more like a tank with something like a cow catcher on the front and reinforcements round the doors and windows.

'Downes. Get a fucking move on.' I was not consciously lingering, I was merely listening to someone playing the trumpet. I could tell it was live because he stopped once and started again but I could not pick up the tune. It was only when I was squashed into the narrow little cells built inside the van that I realised it was 'An English Country Garden'.

From Marylebone magistrates' court to Her Majesty's prison I heard that trumpet all the way.

We were turned out into a gravelly courtyard. As I stepped down, stumbling a little, I saw an officer dressed in pale blue shirt and dark trousers walking briskly by with a large Alsatian on a leash. That frightened me more than anything and I grabbed the man beside me. 'Why the dog?' Before he could answer I saw the high wall with the wire on top and knew it was a stupid question. He didn't bother to answer anyway.

Inside the building it was dark and very warm. We sat on benches waiting our turn to be processed. After a while one man began to whine that he felt sick. Nobody took any notice and after ten minutes he vomited powerfully, over himself and the floor. This made several men so angry that I was afraid he would be assaulted. The smell was appalling, even after they'd taken him away and dabbed at the floor.

Patrick Downes, twenty-one, ethnic group one. The induction officer took the trouble to tell me there were nine ethnic groups with the white man at the top but I did not feel privileged. I was set to wait for the next stage in a small room with a blue floor and ugly banana-coloured walls and forty or more other men. The heat and smell were even worse than before since there were two open lavatories in a recess. Three large men who seemed to know each other, two white and one black, approached me aggressively.

'What have you got?'

I did not answer, hoping the threat was in my imagination. But the largest took hold of me. 'What have you fucking got?'

I wanted to give him something so I felt in my pockets hopefully. All I could produce was one penny, a handkerchief and a rubber. I held them out eagerly for his inspection, my palm outstretched and flat as one might offer a wild horse sugar lumps.

He dismissed the penny and the rubber cursorily, knocking them to the floor where a shrimpy man dressed in a white boiler suit immediately retrieved them and shoved them deep into his pockets. But the handkerchief seemed to fill him with wonder. It was white and clean, neatly laundered and folded by Nell.

The largest man touched it on my still outstretched palm which was shaking visibly now, reflecting both my exhaustion and my fear.

'Why have you got a fucking serviette, then? You won't need a fucking serviette where you're going.'

This caused merry guffaws in his followers and in some of the others who were nearby. Reassured, I made a stupid mistake. 'It's not a napkin,' I said. 'It's a handkerchief.'

Immediately my aggressor who'd started to turn away to quips about 'nicking napkins for the nick' swivelled round. 'You're telling me what I sees as a fucking serviette is not a fucking serviette?' He waited for an answer.

'No. I mean . . . yes.'

'He said it was a fucking handkerchief,' added one of his henchmen. 'A hankie.' He began to mimic my voice. 'Blow your nose, darling, with your hankie.'

Desperately, I thrust the handkerchief towards my torturer. 'You have it,' I squeaked. 'Whatever it is, it's yours.'

'Who said I wanted it? Who said that? Did I say I fucking wanted it?'

'Then I'll put it away again,' I said, stuffing it back into my pocket, 'and not bother you any more.' I turned to find a corner to hide in but at that moment a group of men, including my tormentors, was fetched by two prison officers. When they came back they had food, Cornish pastie and chips, and no more interest in me. They were just passing the time of day, that was all.

I could not eat. The feeling of solidarity with my fellow prisoners which I'd had in the police cells had gone. When they called me out to continue the process of induction, I went eagerly. I wanted to be among screws not cons.

'Name? Marital status? Drug habits?' I stood in a yellow corridor while he sat behind a desk. He never even looked at me. Then I was pushed through into another small room where once again my handkerchief became the centre of attention.

'This your only possession?'

'Yes.'

'No money? Gold? Silver? Pens? Watches?'

'No.'

'One serviette.'

'It isn't a serviette.'

'Well, if it isn't a fucking serviette then I'm not a fucking screw.'

'It's a handkerchief.'

He stopped then and looked me up and down. He was handsome but fleshy as if he didn't take enough exercise.

Making some deduction or other, he decided not to waste any more words but simply wrote down 'SERVIETTE' in capitals. Thrusting the paper towards me, he pointed to where I should sign.

Unfortunately I then began to cry. It was a moment of desolation which received no attention from the screw.

He indicated a curtained off area. 'Strip.' Still crying, I stripped and let him search me – not very thoroughly for he had obviously recognised me as a pathetic creature incapable of smuggling anything into the prison.

I did not know I had the right as a remand prisoner to hang onto my own clothes but I was pushed through to a corridor in which there was a hatch labelled 'Welcome to Burton's.' Someone said, 'Shower?' I think, but nothing came of it. In a short time I was dressed in chocolate brown shirt and trousers, black second-hand slip-on shoes which did not fit but luckily were too big rather than too small and, clutching a small green towel, I was put into another waiting room.

It may seem that I am noting down the process of becoming a con at too great length. Step by step it cut me off from life outside. I had started the process myself when I attacked the girl, but it was continued for me by the prison system which made it clear at once that the only way to survival was to fit in. As a con (it made no difference that I was officially on remand) I was not only cut off from the outside but also from my crime.

After clothing, there was the doctor. He seemed most concerned about any possible drug habits and made no comment on my swollen, tear-stained face. I had managed to stop crying out of fear of my fellow cons in the waiting room but if he had made one kind comment I certainly would have started again. He did not. He merely wrote down my medical history which was brief.

At this point I began to long for my cell. It must have been seven or eight o'clock and I badly needed to lie down. I was back in the original waiting room which had become even more crowded, airless and smelled of men's bodies, food, cigarette smoke and urine. I began to be worried that I might vomit like the man earlier. Except that I had hardly eaten anything for three days. My head began to throb so that I was frightened it would go into spasm. I imagined the blood vessels in my head pulsing with thick red blood, pumping it round so hard that it was in danger of forming a great lake which would swell the weak skin of its vessel and burst.

For a flash I saw myself as I had been with that knife, but mercifully my head could not stand it and everything became black.

I came to lying on the floor with the doctor and the screw arguing about whether I should go to hospital or not. Clearly this would be an inconvenience to the system so when I opened my eyes and stood up, if shakily, at least without help, they both looked relieved and the screw even gave me a sort of smile.

'That's the ticket. We'll take you next door and give you a cup of tea. You'll be right as rain in a minute.'

The room I was put in was much smaller but less crowded and less smelly. Later, I discovered it was really for Rule 43 prisoners.

'When do I get my cell?' I asked the screw who brought me my cup of tea.

'No one fucking wants to go to his fucking cell,' the screw replied, not unkindly.

CHAPTER
TEN

IT WAS bad luck that the first policeman to interrogate me had resembled my attacker. His replacement was older, thinner and a Scotsman. My parents sat on either side of him but Charmian was no longer there.

'Lydia. Oh, Lydia. You don't have to speak. They know who did it.' My mother began to cry.

But I was feeling fractionally more awake. Perhaps they had reduced my drugs. I wanted to say, 'A kitchen shop,' but the words wouldn't form properly and, besides, my throat seemed stuffed with razors.

'You were in a shop called the Cutting Edge,' prompted the policeman.

Then the actual event began to come back, the blows felling me to the ground, the heat, the disgusting smell of blood, the enormous anger surrounding me like a black swarm of bees.

The policeman must have realised I was about to crack, split open, scream, because he said quickly, 'Was it the assistant, a young fair man?'

I nodded and shut my eyes. Luckily I did not know that this fair young man, once recalled, would be with me for ever.

PART TWO

CHAPTER
ELEVEN

I SHARED a cell in C wing with two other men. There were always two other men but not always the same two since we were all on remand and liable to be convicted or, indeed, freed – not that that was ever an option for me.

The first night no one addressed a word to me, for which I was grateful. I had collected my bedding and my cutlery and plate so there was nothing more to be done. I lay on my bed not expecting to sleep but sleep I did, very well until we were woken at 6.30 a.m. for slop out. My colleagues went out ahead of me, holding a cigarette in one hand and a pail in the other. They were both in their twenties, already showing that doughy pallor which marks the prisoner. They were suspicious of me but not actually aggressive. Their names were Johnny and Ron; Johnny expected to get eighteen months before remission and Ron two years. Ron had pinched a fellow's wallet after stabbing him whereas Johnny had merely got into a fight. 'Provocation, Ron, provocation, see, that's what they've got to take into account.'

They talked apparently to each other but actually in monologues and 'provocation' was Johnny's theme. It was a word, I soon guessed, taken from his solicitor. As his trial came nearer he began to use it every time he spoke so that even Ron who was of placid temper, burst out, 'What is this fucking provocation, then? You broke a bottle, didn't you, and stuck it in the feller's face. He might have been black and bigger than you, I'm not denying your facts there, but where's the fucking provocation in that?'

After Ron took Johnny up on his 'provocation' they didn't speak again until Johnny's trial came up. Instead Johnny addressed bitter comments to me. 'If people don't fucking want to understand, then you're wasting your breath trying to teach them,' or 'Even my mum – and you could put her fucking brains on a button – got the point of what I'm getting at. He's retarded,' he stabbed his roll-up cigarette at Ron who lay on his bunk, 'that's what he is.'

It was a relief when Johnny left. Later we heard via the grapevine that he had got five years. His victim had been so badly cut up that he had nearly died and it was the third time that Johnny had been violent. 'It was fucking drink talking,' commented Ron, who did not bear him a grudge and was beginning to get nervous about his own trial. 'You're not yourself with a drink inside.'

More or less everyone had an excuse for their criminal act which amounted to an obsession. Ron could talk for as long about the dangers of drink and the unfairness of getting a man for what he'd done under the influence as Johnny talked about provocation.

I began to understand why this happened after my first official visit from Ruth. She arrived two days after my arrival. I was taken downstairs into a small room with a table and two chairs, the walls cheered up slightly by a few nondescript obscenities, 'Screw the fucking screws', that sort of thing.

Ruth sat there looking as cross as ever with a pile of papers in front of her. 'I've been waiting here three-quarters of an hour so now I'm in a rush.'

I had nothing to say, nothing. However, I did notice the peculiarity of her speech which contained no 'fucking'.

'I have to go to court.'

This time I nodded, out of politeness not interest.

'So how is it?' This, of course, was answerable but I ignored it and stood up. I was finding the room extremely claustrophobic.

Ruth looked up at me, surprised. 'Why aren't you wearing your own clothing?'

I did answer this. 'They took them.'

'You have a right to them, you know, if they're deemed sufficient.' She made a note.

'I don't mind.' I spoke with a little more feeling. I knew that I did not want her making trouble for me in the prison. I stood out enough already.

'I'm pressing hard for bail,' she said. There was a pause. 'I expect you want news from outside.'

'No, thank you.' I thought she didn't understand anything: not about Nell, not about the prison barriers between us, not about the benefits of that barrier.

She sighed. 'You don't want to know how your wife is?'

'No.' I turned the chair so I could sit with my back to her but she intervened hastily.

'Please, don't do that. We don't have to talk about your wife. I'm your solicitor, not hers. But she wanted to know if she could visit you.'

'No. Is that all?'

'No. No. I'm afraid I've bad news. To be precise, two bits of bad news. The doctor thought you showed distinct signs of mental instability. Now we don't want you to end up in Broadmoor, do we? What we want is "under great stress". Of course, we can and will get other doctors.'

'What's the other bit of bad news?'

Ruth looked at me calmly. I could see her clever grey eyes waiting to assess the impact of what she had to tell me. 'The vi—' she had been going to say 'victim' but thought better of it. 'There's some possibility the girl is brain-damaged. In fact, she is still not out of danger.'

Prison has a way of anaesthetising proper feelings. My only concern was how to survive.

'I only tell you', continued Ruth, 'because it is affecting your chances of bail.'

'I don't want bail.'

'You don't want bail?' At last I had shocked through her professional calm.

'No.' I stood. 'I shall wait for the trial here.'

'If that's the case,' Ruth stood up too and stared at her watch for several seconds as if for inspiration, 'if that's the case, I'll be off.' At the door she turned. 'I'm finding you an excellent barrister. If you want an excellent barrister.' She gave a sharp smile and left.

I sat down again and waited for the screw to collect me. He was good-humoured, glad to have something to talk about. 'Your girl-friend didn't stay long?'

'She's my solicitor.'

'Had to be, in these rooms. Unless she was a peer of the realm. Still learning the fucking ropes, are you?'

'Yes, guv.' I knew enough to call him 'guv'. He talked all the way back, locking and unlocking the doors we met, through corridors and landings until we were back in C Wing. I had no curiosity during this walk to discover the lay-out but at one point he stopped, gave a derisive snort and grabbed my arm. 'That's the fucking magic door which leads to . . .' he paused and then ended with a conjuror's flourish, 'the Muppet House!'

I did not know, or want to know, what he was talking about, but for the rest of the journey back – after two days of twenty-four hours in a cell – it felt a long distance. He gave me his views on this privileged section of the prison where cons played table tennis and only visited their cells when they wanted a kip and spent most of the day talking about how society had let them down. He mimicked educated vowel sounds.

By now we were at my cell door. It was about eleven and the men were beginning to emerge to collect their lunches from the landings. The thought of returning to the herd suddenly seemed intolerable. 'Do you mean it's a psychiatric wing?' I asked my screw.

He looked at me with a shocked expression. After all, he'd been doing the talking. 'No.' He jingled the keys up and down in his hands – many of the screws had that habit. 'It's what I said it was, a fucking Muppet House.'

I went into the cell and lay on my bunk.

'Bad, was it?' Ron and Johnny were curious, if not sympathetic, and when I didn't provide them with any information, they began to grumble. I ignored this except to ask them to pick up my lunch.

'He's an infant, this one,' said Ron.

'We can fucking eat it but we can't fucking collect it,' explained Johnny.

As cell-mates go, they weren't the worst. All they wanted was a simple life, a few friends, a girl, enough money for food and a bit of fun. They didn't want to harm anyone. It was just something that had happened to them. Provocation and booze. They felt innocent emotionally, even on the day they went to court and pleaded guilty.

Five days after my arrival I received a letter from Nell. I was not going to open it until the prison doctor came round.

'You're not eating, are you?' He took me to the third floor so I could look down at the grille which covered the gap to the ground. People used to throw themselves down there before they put the grille up.

'Do you have a stomach problem?'

I found myself nearer smiling than I had been for weeks. Did I have a stomach problem? The first person who showed any concern for me and he's worried about my stomach.

'No. No problem.'

He made a note. 'Then eat.'

After that I went in and read Nell's letter.

Darling Pat,

This terrible thing that has happened to us has not altered my love for you, that is the first thing to say. That's what I wanted to say when you wouldn't let me see you.

Here there were signs of tears. I put down the letter then and found that in the few seconds of reading it, I had grown so tense that I could hardly stand up. Ron and Johnny, playing cards and smoking, affected not to notice. Their heads were bent close together and whirls of smoke floated up from either side of them. I looked at them, my hands began to shake, and in a moment I had clapped their heads together. The crack was resounding, although I don't believe it was very hard.

They both leapt up, side by side, one hand to their heads, the other getting ready for a swing. I stood where I was, looking down, trembling, with a violent desire to be sick.

In the end Ron smacked me across my head but not with much strength. Then Johnny pushed me backwards so I lay on my bed. 'Cunt,' he said contemptuously, 'fucking cunt.' I could see he thought me pathetic and not worth getting into trouble over. Instead they got hold of my letter. They took turns to read it aloud, using a high-pitched girlish voice which in fact was not unlike Nell's. ' "Darling Pat", oooh, aren't we lucky? "This terrible thing that has happened to us", this is classy stuff we're getting here, Ron. This is not your usual "I miss your hands on my . . .".'

I put my fingers in my ears but it didn't stop me hearing. ' "I believe now that the tragedy of your parents", tragedy, just listen to this, probably his mother burnt the Sunday joint, don't you think, Johnny? "affected you much more deeply than I realised. You seemed so calm at the time. You said it had been instan-ta-ne-ous", this is a long word. Here, Ron, see if you can find the sexy bits.'

But Ron had a few more brains than Johnny; he saw that my parents had been killed in a car crash and he scrumpled up the letter and threw it back in my direction. 'It's crap,' he said, collecting the cards which had got scattered on the floor. 'Here, give us a smoke.' So they settled back into their game.

I lay on my bed and thought of my parents. The facts were that they were both fifty-four when they died and they had been married twenty-three years and they had one child who was me and my father worked for an international oil company so they had spent eighteen of the twenty-three years abroad and they had always loved each other and loved me too, when they remembered.

I began to cry.

I did a lot of crying those first days in prison. I did it silently so that it was no real inconvenience to my cell-mates.

Knocking their heads together seemed to have raised my standing in their eyes. I suppose it made me seem more like them. They offered me a smoke now and again and when it was fully established that I never accepted, they explained to me that I should buy the permissible quota of cigarettes and then use them as barter for anything else I might want. In theory, they said, none of this applied to remand prisoners who were allowed to buy goods in the shop and accept presents from their visitors, but in practice it didn't often work that way. Besides, you might as well get into the swing of things for later.

Six days after my arrival, Larry came to visit. We met in

the big gloomy room reserved for such events. He put his hands on me in a part embrace, smiled broadly, said, 'You look great, Pat!' But I could see he was very nervous and his hands felt damp. His face was red and shiny or perhaps I was already reacting to outside skin.

'You've seen the sun,' I remarked, chivvied by his nervousness.

'This is a bum hole.' He looked round despairingly as if hoping the background of cons and their miserable families could be swapped for a sunny watering place. His Australian accent was particularly pronounced as if he was disassociating himself from all this Englishness. Since he had been the one who had always looked after me, I was thrown by his manner. He would move on to questioning me, I felt sure.

'It's inhumane. Unjust.' He pulled himself together a little and sat down.

'No, it's not.'

'Anyway.' He stopped trying to talk and lifted a plastic bag onto the table. He took out three or four books. At once a screw arrived and told him off. No books allowed.

'There's a library here.' I tried to cheer him up, although the truth was I couldn't concentrate enough to read.

'That's all right.' He smiled at the screw who did not respond. 'I want to help you, Pat?' It was a statement with a question mark at the end.

'It's kind of you to visit me.'

His nervousness increased and he pulled out a handkerchief and wiped his face and hands with it. The sight of the neatly folded white square reminded me of my arrival at the prison which now seemed like years ago instead of days and I began to cry.

'Oh, God!' I could hear Larry's muffled groan and then he became angry in a repressed sort of way and thumped the table a few times, saying, 'What a balls-up! What a balls-up!'

The thumping, though undramatic, brought another screw, a more jovial fellow. 'What's this? We don't allow displays of emotion in here, you know.'

'I'm sorry, officer.' Larry reacted like a naughty schoolboy and I stopped crying. The screw looked at his watch and then tapped it for Larry's benefit. 'Five minutes to burn-out, as the match said to the fire-fly.'

Larry became more businesslike and even I sat quietly. 'I have to ask you about Nell.' He put his big brown hands around his face and stared straight at me. 'She is your wife. You chose to marry her. I came to the wedding with Wendy.'

Actually, he had come with another girl-friend called Mary Lou, an American with long thin legs and big breasts.

Knowing I would be rescued in a few minutes I said, 'Nell was pregnant.'

He perked up immediately. Now I had offered him something he could get his teeth into. 'Pregnant. What's pregnant? It's an occupational hazard. You don't marry girls because they're pregnant. If I'd married every girl who was pregnant, the divorce rate would go through the roof. Pregnancy's one thing, Pat, and marriage is another. Come to think of it, I told you that at the time.'

He had told me one evening while we sat drinking beer in his flat and his girl-friend of the moment rustled up a steak in the kitchen. He had used almost the same terms and it had seemed as irrelevant to my life then as it did now.

'You chose, Pat, you can't deny it. You made a choice because you had a choice and that's the way it is.'

I admired Larry more than anyone in the world though in a way he was a bad guide for me because the gap between us was so enormous. He gave advice on the basis of what was possible for him but he might as well have suggested I became a professional ballet dancer.

'Then there's the question of how a stable family background will help you at the trial. You know the sort of thing – loving wife, new baby, waiting loyally — '

'I don't want to hear!' I was screeching.

I looked imploringly at the screw sitting on a dais at the end of the room and, as if in answer to my prayer, he boomed out, 'Time, gentlemen, please.' I was up and away in a flash.

∞   ∞   ∞

THE SECOND week I was inside my hair started to fall out. Ron noticed it before me. 'What's all this fucking Sylko about the place? Have you been sewing up your panties again, Johnny, or is it Patricia here embroidering her initials?'

It was polite of him to put it like this because no young man likes to lose his hair. I had nice fair hair too of which I had been rather proud. In university days I had achieved several decent acting roles because of my blond hair.

The doctor called again when it was clear I'd be bald in a matter of weeks. He took me off to his office which was merely another cell with some shelves and things.

'Have you been eating?'

'Yes.' I had been eating a little more.

'How many cigarettes do you smoke a day?'

'None.'

'What drugs do you use?'

'None.'

'Do your bowels move regularly?'

'Yes.' This was a lie of convenience. And good sense. How could my bowels be in league with my hair?

'Has any member of your family suffered from alopecia?'

'What?'

'Hair loss.'

'No.'

'Thank you. I'll prescribe some vitamins for you.'

A week later Ruth was surprised to see the new me. 'What have they done to you?'

'They didn't need to do anything. It just fell out of its own accord.'

'You look . . .' Words failed her. 'It's your eyebrows too.'

I tried to help her out. 'That's quite usual, I understand.'

'I've only got fifteen minutes.' Ruth was always busy. 'I've got some news for you. The vi—, the girl has recovered a little and is out of intensive care. So I think it's the right moment to reapply for bail.' She paused and gave my head a look in which approval outweighed horror. 'That, er, hair loss could be very helpful.'

'It's called alopecia and I don't want bail.'

Ruth gave me her tight look, a narrowing of the eyes and

a sucking in of the cheeks. If she hadn't put on this disagreeable face, I might have tried to explain a little but instead I pushed back my chair. 'I shall stand trial', I said in what I hoped was a matter-of-fact voice, 'and plead not guilty to attempted murder when you can manage to arrange that.'

'Before we get to that,' Ruth did not like me very much at this stage, 'there's various matters to be discussed and forms to be filled in about financial arrangements for your wife.'

I did not pull back my chair but I signed all the forms she pushed across to me.

'Your trial may not come up for months,' she said as she gathered together the papers, 'during which time you'll have to go to court regularly so that they can continue to hold you here. Months and months and months and months.' The repetition was definitely vindictive.

'Thank you,' I felt my smooth head with my hand as if I were about to crack it open for breakfast.

Everybody was always upset after their solicitor had been. Sometimes one of the trusties would sneak you a cup of tea. More often you curled up on your bunk and tried to sleep.

I slept much of the time and I was asleep when, later in the same week, I was called out again.

'Some people have all the luck,' chorused Ron and Johnny.

'And others have all the hair,' I responded, for recently I had found it possible to treat them amicably, although only in short bursts.

A psychiatrist was waiting to see me with a new list of questions. More words. His questions were a little more frightening.

'Do you have nightmares?'

As a matter of fact I did not have nightmares at that time. That started much later when I was slowly and painfully coming alive again.

'No.'

'Do you have violent headaches?'

'No.' Everybody has headaches.

'Do you suffer from insomnia?'

'No.' Actually I suffered from the reverse.

'Do you often replay in your mind the occasion on which

wanted to hold me. This was odd because she had given up contact with me by the time I was six. It was lying in hospital that made me realise she could only bear physical contact with someone who was completely at her mercy. It explained a lot about her relationship with my father. The Tuesday and Friday evenings when he wasn't visiting me he was visiting his mistress.

But now, I was weaker than a baby. 'When you come out, I'll put you back in your own little bed with your own coverlet I made for you and your own sweet things all round you, and you need never stir. The view's so pretty from the window now.' Our house in Ealing backed onto some tennis courts. 'You'll find the ping, ping of the tennis balls most soothing, I should think. Charmian and I have discussed it round and round and we think you should sell your flat. Of course, Papa does not agree.'

Charmian came on Mondays and Wednesdays straight from the old people's home where she worked. She was an alarming visitor because she talked about God. On and on and on about God. 'He knows about evil, you see. He understands its place in the infinity of our existence. Evil is the single most important proof of the existence of God. Without evil there is no God.'

Charmian had converted to Catholicism a few years earlier, inspired by our father's Polish Catholic ancestry. He did not practise, although he kept a small statue of the Virgin, which had come with him from Cracow, on his chest of drawers. My mother had recently joined Charmian as a Catholic but more, I believed, as a reproach to my father than out of any strong belief.

Up to my attack, Charmian's religion had been quietly romantic and personal but all of a sudden it became part of a fierce public nature. She, too, held my hand. 'You must not feel, because you are suffering, that He has abandoned you for He is the King of suffering and there is nothing you can undergo that He has not undergone a thousand times magnified. In your suffering you will find Him and He will find you. You have the priceless opportunity to be very close to Him . . .'

67

I did not often listen to her, but I was not averse to the sound of her voice, so involved in a world that had nothing whatever to do with me. If I had told her that, although technically alive, I felt dead to all sensations of life, she might have been quite happy.

Nevertheless I was grateful for her care and attention. I could take it for granted, which was harder when friends from university came to visit. They needed to be given something in return. They were most satisfied when they saw the evidence of my catheter or coincided with a visit from the nurse who lifted the cap off the shaven part of my head. Only one of them ever said anything of interest to me. He was a medical student. 'We pay far too much attention to the flesh,' he said, looking under the bedclothes for evidence of my wounds. He placed the sheets carefully back on their cage. 'Actually, everything turns on the bones. Now your bones seem to be in excellent shape.'

I wanted to tell him about my last afternoon and how I was pampering my flesh in the Turkish baths but it was too difficult. Just then one of my doctors came in and listened to his remarks. 'A skeleton is bones.' He signalled to the nurse who followed him to put the thermometer in my mouth. 'Bones are most use for an archaeologist.'

Every nightmare I had, which ran into the thousands once my drug dosage had been lowered enough to release my imagination, became centred around the flesh. At first I relived the moment when the knife had entered through my skin. I dreamed of the blade slicing the juicy flesh beneath. Other thrusts would meet rubbery veins like the tentacles of an octopus. Or sinews and muscle. Or hard subterranean vegetation. Sometimes there was bleeding, the redness swimming across my vision as if I was separated from it by a sheet of glass, but other times the wounds merely gaped empty and open. Occasionally, when the knife was withdrawn, it made a sucking sound but most of the time I dreamt in silence. For those of you who are interested in precision, I should add, however, that the colour was spectacular.

Then, two or three weeks after I had arrived in hospital, the stabbing dreams developed an extension and I was raped by the knife. Since I had been interested in biology at school, I knew what the inside of a woman's vagina looked like and could imagine only too clearly what would happen if a large kitchen knife was plunged into it.

Those dreams woke me up screaming, regardless of the amount of sleeping pills or Valium I had taken. For a while I blamed Charmian as if her earlier conviction that I had been raped had taken root somewhere in my unconscious. But later I realised the rape dream was only a natural extension to my feelings of vulnerability.

Even while I was still in hospital, a psychiatrist came to see me. She was a woman with thick grey hair like a tent on a broad kindly face. 'If you would like to speak,' she had a pleasant low voice, 'I would like to listen. I would be honoured to listen.' I was touched by her but forming words was still difficult and forming thoughts was impossible.

While my body was busily mending itself – quite without my help and rather against my wishes – my nightmares were at their height. I did describe them once to a black night nurse because she moved quietly, but she made no comment. What could she have said, after all? 'But you weren't raped.'

'Not then,' I might have responded, 'but now. Over and over again.'

And what difference does it make, after all?

CHAPTER
THIRTEEN

PRISON WAS the proper place for me. Or so I told myself at the time. The inhuman characteristics which had led me to stick a knife into an unknown and innocent girl suited me for the inhumanity of prison. I did not feel degraded by pouring my excreta into a sink and watching it bubble up and mix with the excreta of other men.

After I had overcome my tearful self-pity in the first couple of weeks of my stay, I was able to live in these conditions without too much hardship, although the daily exercise in the yard remained something of a torture. I found it hard to reconcile the sky above in all its grand unpredictability with the fixed regime under which we lived. I was herded out with the rest and walked round and round with the rest but I was always glad when the doors clanged us back inside again.

It was around this time that the great train robber, Ronald Biggs, made his escape from the same sort of yard in Wandsworth. A helicopter descended and took him back up to the sky. That was a *deus ex machina* beyond my wildest dreams. Afterwards, the authorities stretched lines of wire decorated with orange Bakelite balloons across the centre of the yard. It gave the place a touch of colour. The roses planted in the middle seemed too depressed to flower.

During this period, Ruth was doing her duty as a solicitor. That is, she was preparing my case for trial.

'You'll have to face her, of course.' We sat in our usual little cubicle room, although I noticed someone had enlivened the walls with a new graffiti, 'Old lags never forget'. It was unique in not containing the word 'fucking'.

'She is improving in health, I'm told, although as you know it was touch and go for a bit. In fact, one could argue that her appearance, presuming she doesn't appear too badly crippled – and I gather most of her injuries were to the flesh – will encourage the jury to be lenient. A healthy-looking victim does make them look on the accused with much more sympathy. It's only human nature.'

Ruth talked more than usual on that occasion. She was excited about having acquired a distinguished QC to take my case. 'You may think he looks a little over the hill,' she said, 'when he comes to see you, but don't be deceived. William Burnett-Brown is an advocate with a direct line to the Almighty. Where he pleads, the heavens listen.'

I looked at her with some amazement. There was a flush in her usually pale cheeks and her grey eyes had caught a touch of silver.

'You may wonder why he is not a judge,' she continued,

as if I had asked, 'and the reason is because he does not want to remove himself from the cut and thrust of adversarial debate and he has no interest in hierarchy. As a matter of fact, he is already a knight, by inheritance.' Ruth was definitely blushing now and anyone but the dead lump I was would have picked up some hint of her personal interest.

'There is one other point.' There were several other points but the one that concerned me most was about Nell. 'We need your wife to give evidence about your state of mind, that is, if we are to plead "mitigating circumstances".' She paused and I looked down at my hands. They were as pale and soft as a young girl's. 'She does still write to you, doesn't she?'

'I don't open her letters.'

'It's all very awkward. Not impossible but awkward.' She paused again. 'We could use Larry instead.'

I held up my fingers in front of my face to see if I could see through the flesh. This interview had already been longer than usual and I was hoping to be rescued by a screw. I thought of Arthur, the druggy West Indian who had replaced Johnny in my cell, and his unfocused face seemed preferable to Ruth's inquisitive gaze.

'You see, Nell has given me to understand that she won't give evidence unless you have some contact with her. It's perfectly reasonable from her point of view but, as I tell her, I'm your solicitor. I can't make you do anything. But a good relationship with your wife gives the right sort of impression in court.'

As it happened, that day I had received another letter from Nell which as usual I had not opened but thrown through the bars of my window. Other cons wrapped up their excrement and threw that out of the window but I always threw out Nell's letters. No one seemed to bother. From the exercise yard, I could see all sorts of bits and pieces caught in the rolls of barbed wire around the walls.

'She might be satisfied if you wrote to her,' Ruth persevered. 'A little note. Asking about the baby. Saying how you love her.'

'Shit.'

'I'm sorry?'

'Shit to that.'

'I see.' Ruth was only slightly nonplussed. 'We'll leave that and progress to the matter of your plea. Sir William feels your best chance is to go for not guilty to attempted murder and guilty to grievous bodily harm. He'll have to sound out the opposition — '

'I'm pleading not guilty to attempted murder.' I cut her off, turning away from her irritated face. 'You can go fuck your guilty to grievous bodily harm.' Luckily, at that moment, the screw came in, all in a hurry because he'd been chatting to a friend, and let us have an unlawful ten minutes over time. Despite Ruth's protests, he pushed me out at once so that her voice, almost a wail, followed me down the corridor. 'Think about what I've said, Pat.'

I did not. Thinking was for suckers. Lately a group of con suckers had decided to protest against their landing screw who always called them by their numbers instead of their names. They were all remand prisoners in a line of cells, about two dozen of them. They began to shout, 'Fucking innocent until proved fucking guilty,' in teams of six, over and over again. It drove everybody mad, the cons more than the screws. The protesters refused to slop out or go for exercise or collect their meals. They kept it up for twenty-four hours and eventually the deputy governor deigned to put in an appearance. He was a youngish chap, not without good intentions, and he had one of them out on the landing to talk to him. Anyone within distance listened eagerly. We wanted the racket to stop too.

'We're innocent till proved guilty, right?' The screws had chosen the man to be let out and not for his gifts of communication.

'Are you giving me a lecture or making a complaint?' The deputy governor had his relationship with the screws to consider. On the other hand he didn't want a riot.

'It's like I'm saying — ' The man became too confused to speak.

'We've got fucking names!' came a yell from a nearby cell. 'That's what he's trying to get out of his gob-hole!'

'That's right,' stuttered the con. 'Those fucking bastards call us by numbers like we were animals.'

Now that the deputy governor had got the point he was gone in a flash.

The next day the screws made a special point of calling the protesters by their names but always for some petty indignity or other – untidiness in the cell, smoking after hours, not finishing their food – so that by the end of a week or two, most of them were in solitary because they'd insulted a screw, in hospital because out of sheer frustration they'd got into a fight, or cowed into silence.

So why should I think about this thing called a 'plea'? I was not guilty to attempted murder, that was all there was to it. Nell? Why should I think about Nell? Thinking was a bad habit.

Then Mr and Mrs Burns turned up at the prison. I had signed a visiting order for Larry and apparently they were on it too. Nell's parents had not been a big part of my life, but I recognised them at once even in the gloomy old hall where tables and chairs are laid out as if for a WI tea party and the decoration is a Mickey Mouse poster.

'Table twenty-eight,' the screw told me, looking at his list and I started across, almost cheerfully. Then I saw my charming parents-in-law.

They were rigid with horror at where they were, at what their son-in-law had come to and, I suppose, my new hairless appearance, although I didn't consider that at the time. I considered leaving.

But Larry hadn't been an Australian Schools rugger player for nothing. He had me grasped so tightly that there was no point struggling.

'Mr Burns has taken the day off work,' he said, through his teeth. 'So you behave.'

They sat in a row facing me, one rugger bugger and a pair of mice in a trap. It was difficult to avoid looking at them or them at me but we all did our best.

Then Mrs Burns began to cry. It was the least demonstrative thing going on in the whole room which was filled with people arguing, giggling and feeling each other up. But Mr

Burns was too embarrassed to speak until she'd got herself under control. This was a relief.

'You look well, Pat.' It was left to Larry to make conversation. I've noticed since how often a man feels a compulsion to compliment someone on his good health immediately after thinking he looked a wreck. I knew I looked a wreck. But this was Larry speaking so I really tried to make an effort.

'I'm more used to it,' I said which was a meaningless remark but inspired Mr Burns to say, 'I'm sorry', which sent his wife off into another flurry of tears.

I gave Larry a desperate look. I wasn't so hardened that I couldn't catch the bug.

'Mrs Burns has been talking a great deal to Father Oliver,' he said, 'and she particularly wanted to see you because — '

'I forgive you!' The words came out only just recognisable through her gasps and sobs.

'Yes.' Mr Burns came in quickly, as if it had been agreed and he was afraid of losing his nerve. 'Mary Rose forgives you and, being her husband, I go along with that.'

It was terrible. Worse than terrible. I found I was starting the violent trembling again which made me feel insane.

'Please,' I implored Larry. All this, I should note, was taking place without my once looking at my parents-in-law, particularly not at Mrs Burns from whom Nell had inherited her pink-and-white complexion and her feminine curves.

'You're doing fine,' responded Larry, with a touch of desperation. But he didn't need to take action because now Mrs Burns stood up and mumbling something or other shot across the room, followed closely by her husband. In their haste to escape they knocked into several chairs whose owners cursed them appropriately. It must have felt like an escape from hell.

Larry let go of my arm. 'They're very upset.' I felt like saying that every single person in this room was upset, in this whole prison was upset, but I didn't because I knew what he wanted and I couldn't give it to him.

'I hear Ruth's found you a top lawyer.' He had brought

me newspapers and chocolate which he laid out on the table. 'Haven't any of your friends been to see you?'

'I don't want them. They can't come without a visiting order.'

He looked across at the door where the Burnses still crouched, too scared to leave without him.

He made up his mind to speak but stood up first as if he knew it was an exit line rather than the opening of a discussion. 'I have to admit, Pat, my friend, that I don't understand it, not one bit of it and, as you are obviously not going to enlighten me, I probably never will.'

He was tall and broad-shouldered above me. I knew I should help him. 'That day began badly,' I mumbled, 'and ended worse.'

Larry looked down at me. He was not really taking in my words because he was worried about the Burnses. I don't know why he felt responsible for them. He was my cousin, not theirs.

'It was such a hot day,' I tried again.

Larry gave me a little more attention. 'Now if I could believe you were right off your chump, that would be something.'

'Yes.' I bowed my head. It would be much better if I were right off my chump.

'And in my shop!' He was on his way out but turned suddenly to deliver this, the most passionate of his utterances, the thing he didn't want to say.

'Bloody visitors.' Ron looked up when I got back to my cell. He had a wife and two young children who visited him once a fortnight. He looked forward to it for thirteen days and then it destroyed him.

'Do you think I should see my wife, Ron?'

He looked up from his newspaper, which was more like a comic. 'You have to see them, don't you – till you get the Dear John. That's when you call it a day. My wife's the loyal type, as it happens. I suppose you haven't been married to yours long enough to know.' He shook his head. 'Then again, you may be right, not seeing her, I mean. It's a fucking lottery, that's my conclusion for the day.' He stabbed the paper with his biro. 'Hey, you're an intellectual. What's black and white and red all over?'

Since he had not been much help to me I left him to work that one out.

But later that day, I wrote to Nell.

Dear Nell,

I would like you to start divorce proceedings. I am sure you would too, Pat.

If the censors picked on this letter, it would give them time for a tea break.

Nell wrote back and, for once, I read the letter.

Dear Pat,

Please don't worry about me or the baby. Mother was so glad to see you. It much relieved her feelings. We are all getting ourselves geared up for the trial and, until then, you are right to think of nothing else. Your solicitor is very hopeful that the jury will realise that prison is quite inappropriate in your case. There is no way anyone could think you were a criminal. It is a matter of pleading guilty, they say, and showing penitence. I have been praying a lot lately, sometimes with Mother, and I know I shall understand what you felt soon. Whatever happens, I shall always love you. Love is not conditional. I had a little scare with the baby the other day but now she or he is quite settled again and I could even feel the little feet kicking against my stomach. I wish you could feel it too. It makes it all so real.

Please, Pat, do not give up hope. It will all come right in the end. Sometimes I think of us walking in the sunny fields round Ephesus and I cannot believe all this is happening in the same lifetime.

You are in my thoughts, always.

With all my love, Nell.

So that was the end of the divorce. After reading the letter, I was sick in my slop bucket which went down very badly with my cell-mates. Knowing the ways of the world, I merely grunted, 'Fuck off,' and didn't even try to get permission to empty it.

I could hardly stop Nell appearing at the trial.

FOURTEEN

IT WAS over a month before I was allowed out of hospital. By then the doctors had established that I had not had a stroke but nevertheless the right side of my brain had been dangerously compressed by the blood clot, which explained why I had found it difficult to speak. I had recovered that power now but retained a distinct clumsiness in my left arm and leg. It would improve, up to a point, I was told or, perhaps, if I were very lucky, go away altogether.

When I left hospital, reading from the top, my body looked like this: scar on head surrounded by new prickly growth of hair; random scars on front and side front of my neck, each one not long but crawling across my skin like red malignant caterpillars; running for eight inches down my left shoulder to centre back, a broad and angry scar caused by the first knife wound my murderer inflicted on me. Luckily, I could only see this with a double mirror but, apart from actual pain and seeming to pull on my shoulder, it itched often and its edges tugged at my skin.

My left side, as I have already noted, was in a generally bad way, but my right side gave me little pleasure either since there were small but ugly scars on the back of my hand, which I had used for warding off the knife. I was supposed to be lucky that no tendons or major veins had been severed. The front part of my body was not too bad if you discount a gash, sorry, a scar across my right breast. But my left thigh had been quite severely wounded and gave me a good deal of pain when walking.

'You've made a remarkable recovery,' I was told by different people at different times. But it didn't feel like that to me. I felt like a monster. I make no apologies for going on about this at such length.

A week after I arrived home, my mother announced, with obvious misgivings, that I had an appointment with an analyst. I asked at once whether she was a woman because men were God's first mistake as far as I was concerned. His second was letting me be born. That was my mood. No exaggeration.

Lesley lived in Hampstead and her main claim to be my saviour was that she was happily married with four lovely children. Her husband was supposedly lovely too and there was a hint of a capital 'H' when she spoke of him.

My mother drove me to our first session and I could sense her sitting anxiously in the room outside. Lesley worked from her family home.

'I am more nearly a Jungian than anything else,' she laid down her credentials, 'but I think Melanie Klein has something to teach us women.'

'I'm not a woman any more.' I was scared and in pain that first day, which made me belligerent. 'If I'm anything at all, which I doubt, I'm a victim.'

'Labels are not always helpful.' Lesley was a large pretty lady, with curly dark hair and her glasses on a chain round her neck. She must have been in her late forties. 'We must bear in mind that, even without your traumatic experience, many women of your age have difficulties in coming to terms with their sexuality.'

She was feeling her way for the ground rules, I suppose, because she never talked so much again. 'During my early training I was very interested in behavioural therapy. Eysenck and the Maudsley. The idea is to put the patient through the experience she most dreads.' She looked up at me hopefully, for a response, I suppose, but my leg, in fact most of my body, was aching too much for me to be intelligent. 'Well,' she continued, 'if the patient dreads sticky things you make them sit in an armchair with jam on the arms.'

'I see.' I gave my leg a sharp tap which sometimes helped to ease the pain. 'So in my case you'd get a man with a knife and ask him to stick me full of bloody holes.' I found I had stood up and was shouting quite loudly. I thought of my mother and sat down again hurriedly.

'You've put your finger on a flaw.' Lesley spoke soothingly.

'And even in the case of the jam, there were those who

held that it merely taught the patient to avoid chairs with arms.' She allowed herself a slight smile. 'But, as I said, that was in the old days. All we want is an opportunity for you to chat a little. Twice a week.'

I didn't mind that. It would make a change from physiotherapy. The rubbish she had been talking soothed my fears of a bully or a critic. She seemed motherly in a way my mother was not. Perhaps I could talk to her instead of my mother. 'I'm afraid I'm into therapy on that one, Ma. Here, let me read out bits from the paper while you peel the carrots.'

I was not against my mother, who was doing everything possible to make my life happier and easier, but I did not want intimate conversations with her, even though we agreed about men. Roughly speaking, she thought they were all brutes – with my papa at the top of the pile. It was so long since I'd lived at home in such intimacy that I'd forgotten the tone of their dialogue. It came up very clearly from the kitchen to my bedroom.

'You're back.'

'Usual time.'

'I said you were back. I expect you'd like something to eat.'

'You and Lydia have eaten already?'

'It's better for her, early. Her stomach doesn't play up so much then.'

'I didn't say I minded.'

'Well, then.' There would be a pause as she set down the remains of our supper in front of him. In fact we had probably only eaten half an hour before as he was usually home by seven.

He ate quickly and in silence while my mother clattered pots and pans at the sink. Then he got up and kissed her. I couldn't hear that, of course, but I knew the ritual of old. He kissed her at a time when her hands were in greasy water and her face steamy from the oven. Sometimes she held her hands so that soap suds dripped off the ends of her fingers. It made it easier for them both. Then he left the room, often to see me.

'Have you walked today. Strode out?'

'Yes, Father.'

'So, why aren't you dressed?'

'I was tired. I went to my analyst today.'

'Analysts teach children to hate their parents.'

'You should meet mine. You'd like her.'

'I'd be better off liking a snake.'

'She's supposed to be teaching me to like men.'

'Ha.' He looked a little shifty. He knew I knew about his mistress but she was never spoken of between us. Most things that went wrong in all our lives he blamed on my mother but nevertheless he felt guilty. So he changed the subject.

'I saw your flat today. It looks good. You'll enjoy it. It awaits its owner. Clean. New. Good.'

'Papa.' He knew I was incapacitated. Even if my body was a little stronger, I could never have lived anywhere on my own.

'I know. I know. Not yet. You need your mother. It's natural.' But what he wanted most of all was to separate me from my mother.

When Charmian came home, we had supper all together. Charmian said grace. 'O Lord, who giveth us everything, let us give thee thanks.' I think she made it up herself. I expect she made the old people in her home say grace too.

She and my mother had an intense conversation about their work while Father and I listened. He worked in the local council offices in something to do with educational planning. But he never talked about it. Perhaps he was loquacious with his mistress.

On Friday nights, he didn't come home till late. His mistress was a respectable widow, childless, and I found out about their liaison because she taught at our school. One day when I was a complacent creature of sixteen, she smacked me across my face, shouting, 'That's for being your mother's daughter!' She burst into tears and ran out of the classroom.

I was outraged but even more curious. I had been asking about the child-parent relationship in *A Winter's Tale*. I complained to my best friend of the moment, 'I wasn't being annoying at all. In fact it's the sort of question most teachers long for their pupils to stay behind after class and ask. Teachers beg for such dedication.' I thought I was being witty.

My friend laughed. She was a knowing sort of girl, disapproved of by my mother. 'You know what I think,' she had fat pink cheeks which she sucked in with a little noise so that her lips stuck out, 'you should ask your dad.'

Of course I didn't ask my dad, I asked Charmian who was three years older than me and it turned out that Mother had confided in her one lonely Friday evening.

So that was my family's little secret. I believed then it was not the most important thing in our lives. Before my life met its obstacle I had been cool and ambitious. I was supposed to have started work on a local newspaper in September. And now it was October. At least I had recovered enough to notice the seasons.

When the letter came from my solicitor announcing the date of the trial, I took it to my bedroom. It was a soft morning, a little hazy, and I could hear that a game of tennis was in progress outside my window. I opened it as wide as I could and leaned out. Two girls were playing, wearing proper tennis clothes and giving the whole matter very serious attention. They shouted out the score at each point and ran to collect the balls, bouncing them against the ground or their racquets.

It made me very aware of the gulf that separated me from the rest of the world. I asked myself why that one unreasonable outpouring of hatred should have so changed me that I did not consider myself part of the human race.

Three months had passed. Perhaps my body, at least, was less monstrous. Keeping an objective eye, I stripped off my clothes one by one. Then I opened my wardrobe door and looked at myself in the long mirror that hung there. The immediate effect was worse than on my departure from hospital because I had lost so much weight. My flesh, which had originally retained some of the colour of a warm summer, was now like dough, flaky dough which needed more liquid.

As I watched, shivering a little, goose pimples spread across my arms and breasts in an ugly rash. I was disgusting.

Admittedly, my actual wounds were less conspicuous. The angry red of the scars had dulled to a mellow pink, on their way, presumably, to the promised land of white. I could now lift my left arm fairly freely and use the hand, although without much strength. My left leg was much thinner and flabbier than the right, which seemed misshapen because of the long uneven scar in the thigh.

There was nothing at all womanly about me, no curves, no soft lines. My breasts were almost non-existent and my stomach concave. I had not had a period since the attack which, so the doctor informed me, was due to my refusal to eat properly rather than any psychological trauma. I certainly wasn't going to eat more so that I could bleed once a month.

If I looked like a corpse, it was only appropriate. I thought that when I came to court the judge should ask me to strip. Exhibit A. That should harden the hearts of the jury.

CHAPTER

FIFTEEN

'WHY DO screws think cons are mushrooms?'

'Because they keep them in the dark and feed them full of bull-shit.'

I was sharing a cell under the Old Bailey with a persistent joke teller. I liked it. When Ruth took me off for a final consultation, I began quick as a flash, 'Why do screws think cons are mushrooms?' But she interrupted me sharply.

'Don't give me that old chestnut.' She took my arm eagerly, 'I've seen her. She doesn't look bad at all, not bad at all. Thin, but then lots of girls that age are thin. Limps a little, but she won't be doing much walking for the judge.'

Ruth was not exactly insensitive but tended to see things from one point of view at a time. Luckily my dehumanised brain could not take in the idea of my victim's existence so close to mine.

'If you plead guilty to grievous bodily harm, we'd have a case going for you.'

For two months Ruth had been plugging this one. Sir William was longing to go to the prosecuting counsel or even the judge and do a deal on my behalf. But I wanted a jury to say I was not guilty of attempted murder. That's what I'd been charged with, that's what I wanted cleared.

'Anyway, Sir William hasn't given up all hope of you. He's waiting now.' My barrister was enormous. Like a great silver-haired whale. He hardly fitted into the consultation room. His voice boomed self-confidently and he could not believe I would not see reason. 'You have no defence,' he told me once again. 'You did it. You've told me you did it so why do you want to plead not guilty?'

'I didn't mean to kill her.'

'Well, then, plead guilty to grievous bodily harm.'

It was their language, not mine. I was not going to say 'guilty' however it was dressed up. 'I had no intention of harming her.'

'Oh, God!' Sir William raised his theatrical nose in the air. 'So your instructions remain the same?' I nodded. 'Suicide. That's what it is. Bloody suicide.'

Probably he was right.

∞   ∞   ∞

CHARMIAN CAME to the house the morning of my murderer's trial. She helped me choose what to wear because my mother has a passion for bright colours.

'You must wear a sober suit,' she said, producing one out of a plastic bag. 'You don't want the jury to think you asked for it.'

I felt a little ironical about this since it was patently absurd that a poor creature like myself could look as if she ever asked for anything, let alone sex.

Charmian saw my expression and said primly, 'God knows what you are but they might be prejudiced.'

We took a taxi to the courts, my father and Charmian on the jump seats, Mother and me stiffly side by side, hanging on the straps, and in my case feeling very sick. Mother talked continuously about the time she did jury service. 'It was a terrible case of buggery with intent to murder.'

'Mother!' Charmian protested. There was a pause and Mother squeezed my hand. 'I'm afraid . . . you've got to stop the car!' I cried out and grabbed the door handle. Father tapped urgently on the glass partition. But it was too late. Luckily I had not eaten any breakfast, although this did not cheer up the driver.

'Out!' he shouted. 'Out!' We were in the middle of Oxford Street, nine thirty on a Tuesday morning. My skirt looked and smelled disgusting.

'Stand behind your mother', my father took charge, 'and I'll hail another taxi.'

'She can't go to court like that!' screamed Mother and Charmian was distraught. After all, it was her suit.

'My God!' Father looked at his women and then at his watch. 'There's time to go back.'

So I arrived at the courts dressed in a red woollen suit of my mother's. She was plumper than me but shorter so it nowhere near reached my knees. At the last moment I added a chiffon scarf to cover my scarred neck. Vanity dies hard.

We were back in the third taxi of the day and I was trying not to breathe because everything seemed to hurt. Charmian suddenly burst into tears. 'How can I ever forgive him! I've been trying so hard. I've put him in my prayers, you know. Patrick William Downes. I say it every night. I beg God to forgive him.'

'I'm sure God manages without your help,' interrupted my father who had hardly spoken all morning. He felt for me, I'm sure, and considered this explosion of practical Christianity mistimed.

Patrick William Downes. This was the first time I'd heard his name.

'We all have to approach things our own way, Victor.' My mother gave Charmian a handkerchief and tugged down my skirt.

'It's all right, Mother,' I tried to encourage her.

'How can I be a Christian and not forgive?' wailed Charmian. 'It makes a mockery of everything I believe in.'

'Did you say he was called Patrick William Downes?' I asked. And now it was my mother's turn to burst into tears.

My father took my arm when we eventually arrived at the Old Bailey. I was glad of his solid strength, even though it was masculine.

Lesley, analyst Lesley, met us on the pavement. She was actually smiling. 'There's no hurry. I've checked it out. There are two cases before yours but we might as well go up and wait.'

I had not envisaged this. This long public waiting hall in which witnesses, counsel for both sides, and even the accused mixed hugger-mugger from all the day's cases and all the court rooms.

'At least he won't be out here,' commented my mother with satisfaction. 'He'll be underground in a dungeon.'

They found me a leather-clad bench and I sat down. It felt as if every wound had come alive again.

∞　∞　∞

'WHY DID the screw screw?'

'Because the con-sented.'

It had become boring in the cell. The jokes didn't seem funny any more and I had nothing to do. Ruth reappeared.

'The judge is taking an early lunch. You'll come on afterwards.'

'Why is the judge taking an early lunch?'

'Because it's his court and he can do exactly as he likes. Perhaps he wants a quick one with his girl-friend or perhaps the two first cases were so boring he needed a break. It will run for two days now.'

So it was two o'clock before I was brought up into the dock. Earlier I might have taken a bit of interest in what was going on around me. This was the nearest I had been to the real world for four months. But now I had turned into myself.

85

I looked outwards over the shelf around me but I could hardly make out where the jury sat.

At least my edifice of a counsel was hard to miss.

The prosecution, on the other hand, was a little, weasely man who began giving the details of my case in a whining, high-pitched voice. I tried looking at the jury but they were trying to look at me without seeming to so I quickly turned my gaze onto the wider spaces of the court room. This was a mistake for I immediately found Nell, staring at me with intense, sympathetic eyes. She was by now about seven months' pregnant and wearing the kind of smock which was supposed to hide the bulge and actually made it look much larger.

I bowed my head but nevertheless felt a wave of heat spread over my face and down my body. I began to sweat and tremble violently. Worse was to come. The prosecutor, having outlined the case, turned to the judge and asked permission to produce a witness 'out of turn'. If he'd called her 'the victim' I would have been prepared.

There she was, just as Ruth had described her, a thin girl, wearing a red suit. She had a pale angular face topped by short spiky hair. She was so different from the girl who had come into the shop that my immediate reaction was to think they'd got the wrong girl. This was a passing stranger, brought in to help along the theatre. But then my victim had been a passing stranger who'd happened to be in the wrong place at the wrong time.

In the prison quite a lot of my fellow cons held a real grievance against their victims, even when they were completely innocent. 'What was she doing, forcing her way in after closing time?' That would have been their defence, even working up into real anger. 'If people go barging their nose in, what can they expect?'

As the girl was questioned, first by the prosecuting weasel and then by Sir William, I soon realised that Ruth's picture of her as thin but healthy was untypically optimistic. Her garish suit emphasised her pallor and the skeletal thinness of her limbs. She had a gauzy scarf round her neck which seemed particularly inappropriate, as if she were dressed for a garden party. For one moment I remembered the girl who had come into the shop, strong, healthy, filled with enthusiasm for those Mexican pots. Again, I stopped listening to her evidence and put my head in my hands. Nevertheless, I could not help hearing one of her sentences, 'I did not see him strike the first blow because he struck from behind.'

∞   ∞   ∞

HE WAS dreadful to look at. So white and frail and totally without hair. It was lucky I did not have to identify him because I would never have known he was the same blond, healthy, young man who'd opened the shop to me. Probably he felt the same about me, not that he looked up, beyond the first moment when I came in. We were so close I could have caught his eye. But he was repellent, his skin slug-like as if he had been kept somewhere dark and unwholesome. I knew he had been in prison but I did not then identify it as the unhealthy badge of all men locked up for twenty-three hours of the day. I thought it particular to him. I spoke with my face turned away from him.

'He seemed perfectly friendly, at first. At least I didn't notice that he was unfriendly. He was a shop assistant and I wanted to buy some pots. I had no indication that he was strange in any way. No warning. No instinct for self-preservation.'

My counsel questioned me sympathetically, building up a picture of an ordinary young woman finding herself the victim, that word again, of an unprovoked attack by a man who had been up till then, quite sane. This was a surprise to me. I had assumed he must be a lunatic.

'Would you say there was any possibility of an accident in his attack?'

'I did not see him strike the first blow because he struck from behind.' As I spoke I was aware of a sudden movement from the white slug. Downwards, out of my eye-line.

'Would you please remove your scarf?' my lawyer persevered.

I did so, showing my scars, revealing more of my face.

87

'We also have photographs, your honour, testifying to the deliberation with which the accused attacked my client. This was someone who wished to do murder.'

He was finished with me. But the defence counsel had to have his turn. 'You are obviously someone who has an absorbing interest in your body.'

'Objection, your honour.'

'Yes. Yes. Confine yourself to questions, Mr, er, Burton-Bradstock.'

'Sir William Burnett-Brown,' the very large man who seemed to be my aggressor muttered crossly but then indeed embarked on questions. 'You were coming back from the Turkish baths?'

'Yes.'

'You had been naked there in public for a couple of hours or more?'

'No.'

The judge leaned forward. 'You had not been naked?'

'Not in public.'

'But in front of other people?'

'Yes. Other women.' I could see what he was doing. Trying to suggest to the jury that I had left the Turkish baths all revved up and looking for action. That I had provoked my murderer by my rampant sexuality. The truth was exactly the opposite. I had left the baths as a vestal virgin. 'I went there to get clean,' I added, finding a bit of extra strength. Someone in the public gallery laughed. A woman. It was a cheering sound.

Then suddenly the huge barrister was on his feet and there was a commotion around my murderer.

∞   ∞   ∞

WHEN I bent down, I shut my eyes but far from diminishing the vision her words had conjured up, they increased the violence. I could feel as I had not at the time the sensation of the knife entering her flesh. I saw the iron pot falling, cracking open her skull, my explosion of energy as I attacked her fallen body. Urgently, I knocked my attendant policeman's arm. 'I'm going to be sick.' Too late. Disgusted, he watched as I evacuated my breakfast.

My counsel was summoned. Court adjourned, your honour this and your honour that and I was hustled out in disgrace. Back in my cell, I was only left in peace for a moment before Ruth appeared with the Sir William giant. They began to speak together.

'Please.' I didn't listen. They both went out again. My mind began to feel a little clearer, although the taste in my mouth was vile. I understood that I had been insane to plead not guilty to attempted murder. Of course I had tried to kill her and all women like her.

After about ten minutes, Ruth returned holding a mug of tea. 'Don't ask how I got this.'

'I've changed my mind.' I ignored the tea. 'I want to plead guilty.'

'Now you want to plead guilty?' She seemed more exasperated than pleased.

'I did try to kill her.'

'You want to plead guilty to attempted murder?' Her voice rose to a scandalised croak.

I was beginning to feel tired. 'I did it.'

She took the tea back and began to drink it herself. 'We've always known that. I'll get Sir William.'

While she was away, I rested. The idea of pleading guilty had caused a sense of fateful tranquillity. The little room was warm and, compared to a prison cell, quiet. When Sir William returned I was half asleep. 'Good. Good.' He rubbed his plate-like hands. 'So you'll plead guilty now you see they mean business. I'll be off to see what I can arrange.' He was out again.

In my quiescent state, I had not fully understood. Ruth made it clearer. 'If they agree to a plea of guilty to grievous bodily harm, the judge will dismiss the jury and the whole business will be over, bar the mitigating circumstances.'

'But you don't understand. I was guilty to attempted murder. When I saw the — '

'Don't muddle the issue. Just lie low, that's my advice, lie low.'

I could hardly have been much lower. With no more strength to argue, I did what I was told.

∞　∞　∞

I STUMBLED as I left the court room and two officials leapt forward to help me. But when I came out, I was alone for five minutes because Lesley and my family had to get back from the public gallery. When they stooped to where I sat, they were exhilarated by what they'd seen in court.

'I'm glad he's suffering after what he did to you.' My mother's voice had a triumphant tone.

'Repentance makes it easier to forgive.' Charmian took my hand.

My father put his arm round me. 'He's still pleading not guilty.'

'I want to go home. Please.' They paid attention to me then and soon the message came that I was free to leave.

'I'll stay and see how it turns out,' said my father.

'Me too,' chipped in Charmian as if it were a party outing. I did not blame her for that. The whole event was so outside our experience that none of us knew how to behave.

So my mother and Lesley took me home. They put me to bed and closed the curtains against the glare and gave me an assortment of pills to choose from.

'You'll sleep,' my mother said.

'We'll be near at hand,' said Lesley.

I did sleep soundly for an hour or so but then the nightmares began.

∞　∞　∞

NOTHING HAPPENED for hours, except that a sad little man was put in with me. Then Ruth dashed in. 'Negotiations going well. But we'll finish up in the morning now. Have a good night.'

Prison is the same whether you're in the middle of your trial or not. As usual, I had to go through the whole tedious procedure of entering the prison just as if I had never been there before.

'So you're fucking back!' My newest cell-mate, Abraham, looked at me with extreme displeasure. Against my advice he had placed a bet of sixty cigarettes that I would get off. His reasoning was based on the simple class prejudice that anyone with an accent like mine could not possibly serve more than the four months I'd already been inside.

'It isn't over yet,' I told him, to encourage a quiet night.

'You fucking bet it isn't.' Just for fun he threw a lighted cigarette in my direction. I caught it easily. These things are just a matter of practice.

'Now I'm going to have a fucking jerk off,' he advised, clearly feeling he deserved cheering up. 'So keep your nose out of my way.'

It was great to be home.

CHAPTER
SIXTEEN

THE SECOND day in court was a relief to me because the 'victim' did not appear. I was able to look out from my box as if I had the best seat in the theatre. First the judge called in the jury, then he directed them to find me not guilty of attempted murder but guilty of grievous bodily harm. The simplicity of it won my heart. If I had been on that jury I would have shouted, 'It's a fix!' But they were obedient and like good obedient people were dismissed.

Larry gave me a thumb's-up sign. Perhaps he was giving himself confidence for he was to be questioned when Sir William moved on to 'mitigating circumstances'. It was only the sentence that counted now. The theatre became less exciting as a policeman read out information about me. Boring things – my age, my lack of previous convictions, my job with Larry Purley. There was talk of a social enquiry report, dismissed by the judge who seemed in much more of a hurry this morning.

I began to feel hot and tired and sat back, shutting my eyes, just as Sir William rose to his noble height. Words like 'seriously contrite' and 'under serious stress' roared in salvoes at the judge. Everything had become very serious. Then Larry was called to the stand. He was dressed formally in suit and tie, performing the role of employer. He said I was a totally honest good worker, good person, perhaps a little over-sensitive, always ready to help others. He made me sound like a cross between St Francis of Assisi and the Prince of Wales. He said that he had so much confidence in me that he would make sure there was a job waiting at any time. What he meant was, when I came out. Everybody knew I would get a prison sentence. The only question was, how long.

I could see Nell in the public gallery, flanked by her parents. In the row behind them were a middle-aged man and a youngish woman who had been there the day before and all morning. I suspected they were something to do with the 'victim'. I was careful not to catch a malignant eye.

The judge had a reasonably intelligent sort of face as far as the ridiculous wig allowed it. It seemed fair enough that he should tell me where to spend the next few years. Ruth had said I should expect five or more out of which I would probably serve about three and a half.

'Patrick William Downes, please stand.' The policeman gave me a hand up.

The judge began to speak. Unnervingly, he looked directly at me. I had not been prepared for such a personal sentencing. 'You are pleading guilty to grievous bodily harm. You are a young man who has avoided the worst crime any man can commit only by the merest thread of chance. If your victim had died, life would be the only option. But, despite the near-frenzied nature of your attack, your victim did not die. We saw her here in the court yesterday. Alive, able to stand up and give evidence against you. Now I am given the task of passing sentence on you.'

I listened to this fairly calmly, drawing the conclusion

nevertheless that the emphasis on the near-miss aspect of the case meant that the sentence would top the five years.

'And yet,' he fixed his eyes on my face, 'we have here no villain, no hardened criminal. On the contrary, we have heard that you are a sensitive young man, disturbed by your parents' deaths and suffering from early marital difficulties. Unstable, certainly, but not insane we are told. Already, we have evidence and can see for ourselves what the months you have spent in prison have done for you. I have to ask myself, are you a danger to society? And my answer, after weighing up everything I've heard, is "No". And then I have to ask myself, will prison be a helpful experience towards making you a better citizen? And my answer is, possibly, under certain circumstances – for example, if you are given psychiatric help. And finally, I must decide whether you deserve to be punished. And here there is no doubt. A man, however seriously under stress, cannot go without proper punishment when he has brutally attacked another human being. Nevertheless, taking into account the first two answers to my first two questions, the punishment must not only fit the crime, but also fit the person. Moreover, you have relatives outside prison who are willing to see that your life moves forward on smoother tracks. I was particularly impressed by your cousin, Mr Lawrence Purley, who is willing to put himself *in loco parentis*. Your wife, too, wishes to set up married life with you. There is the prospect of a child. Most important of all, your counsel has impressed upon me that you are seriously contrite for the terrible wrong you have done. Taking all these considerations together, I sentence you, Patrick William Downes, to serve three years in prison. Take him down.'

'Take him down.' A forbidding phrase, evoking an image of a deep dark dungeon in which a man could rot and moulder. As I was led back to my cell, I realised that I was now truly a 'convict' but the term didn't sink in.

Then Ruth appeared, 'bounded' might be the more appropriate term. 'Do you realise, Pat, what this means?' She was so animated it hurt.

'I go back to prison.'

'Yes, yes. But the point is that three years, subtract the one year statutory remission, is two years, of which you've already served four months, and there's always a very good chance of parole after the first year. In fact, what it means is that you may have less than a year to serve. Less than a year to serve, Pat!' She became more and more excited. 'This is a triumph. Sir William is delighted. He sends his congratulations, incidentally, as he had to dash off to a meeting. They'll give you an official EDR but this means you could be out by next summer!'

'What is an EDR?'

'Earliest date of release.' She was impatient in her joy. It was all for me, I knew, but somehow I could not join in with her mood, particularly when she carried on, 'And now you must let Nell come and see you. Bearing in mind what the judge said, I was able to get special permission for her to come down.'

There was no way of stopping her. If Ruth hadn't realised by now that I was the opposite of Sir William's 'young father waiting hopefully to start a new happily married life' (this despite the 'difficulties') then no one else would.

Nell when she came was not, as it turned out, ebullient. 'I'm sorry.' She sat heavily. 'I don't feel too good. Ruth and Larry say it's a great result so I'm glad. I don't know why I kept hoping you'd be let off. I expect I'll feel better about it tomorrow. It's the thought of having the baby on my own. I'm sorry.' She began to cry.

Her defeated tearfulness made her bearable. I managed to touch her hand for a second. 'Where are your parents?'

'They were here yesterday. But Mum didn't feel too good and you know how Dad is about work. He couldn't take another day off. Larry has been wonderful, though.' The thought of Larry's kindness started her off crying again.

'I'm sorry.' I meant it. I truly meant that I wanted her to feel better but I also wanted to get back to my cell and get on with my life.

After a few moments she wiped her eyes and lifted her puffy, stained face so that she was looking directly at me, 'I love you,' she said with remarkable clarity.

Women are so determined to have love and love makes them so determined.

∞   ∞   ∞

My FATHER and Charmian came back from their second day at the courts with tired irritated faces. They would not talk at first, saying they were starving hungry and the tube train back had got stuck in a tunnel for half an hour. So my mother made them sandwiches and I went back up to my bedroom. I wasn't going to beg them to tell me what had happened. I was not sure it was very important anyway. He would be found guilty and go to prison, I knew that for certain. I had not even considered the length of his sentence, assuming merely that it would remove him from my world for some undefined time far into the future.

An hour or two later I went downstairs again. The small front room was cold at this time of year and Father was busy lighting the gas heater. He was bent over with his back to me while Charmian, it seemed, had already left the house.

'He pleaded guilty, you see.' My father held the flaming match steadily in front of his eyes. I sat down in an armchair and looked at my mother. I could see she had been crying. But, then, she cried if the rice pudding burnt.

'Pleaded guilty?' I did not understand. We were in an unpractised area. 'So that means he gets a long sentence?' I waited for them to add more but my father continued fiddling and my mother looked away. 'So. Back in prison again. Excellent.' I thought of my nightmares. Perhaps now that he was thoroughly put away, they would go away too.

'He pleaded guilty to grievous bodily harm!' This was my father exploding round at me and then slamming out of the room.

'It's been a strain for your father, dear.' My mother was gripping the sides of the armchair.

The front door slammed and we both knew he had gone to his mistress.

'He'll tell you more later.' My mother attempted and failed

95

to smile. 'The great thing is that it's all over, now you must pick up your life. Put it behind you.' She faltered to a stop.

'But he was sentenced,' I said. 'He was convicted. He admitted he was guilty, you say. How long did he get?'

My poor mother was still hoping to avoid giving me the precise situation but I was inexorable. He was my murderer. His sentence would do something to recognise and lighten the load of my misery. Now that it was being kept from me, I knew I needed to hear that justice was being done.

'Three years,' whispered my mother, tears starting up in her eyes. 'They say with parole and everything he could be out next year.'

SEVENTEEN

Now I was no longer a remand prisoner I could hope to become a 'trusty' and find an occupation in the kitchen, cleaning or on one of the work programmes. I had not suddenly become a normal human being but my appearance in court, my sentencing, was done. I could settle down.

I had counted without my new cell-mate. As a convicted prisoner I was moved to a different wing, although identical to my previous lovely residence. I was in a two-man cell, locked up most of the day with a man who pissed into his mug for the fun of watching it froth over and then suggested I drank it. That was when he was in a good mood.

The first evening I was brought in – always the worst moment – I was carrying my allowance of writing paper. He snatched it from my hand, even before the screw had gone, knowing he wouldn't interfere. 'Brought your own shit paper, have you?' He tore the paper into confetti and let it flutter across the floor. I ignored him and reminded myself I had no intention of writing a letter.

The point about Charles (such an elegant name) was that

he was high all the time, awake and asleep. He was small, remarkably ugly and mentally non-existent. He had certain responses, all unpleasant, and no kind of rational thought. It was like living with an animal possessed by an evil spirit. I came to think he was, at some unconscious level, aware of his own odiousness and loathed himself even more than he loathed everybody else. That, I decided, was why he made sure he was doped out of his skull.

One of his obsessions was that I was going to steal his dope. I never managed to convince him I didn't use the stuff and after he went I found the wall round his bed riddled with little hidey-holes as if masonry bees had been hard at work. He was also concerned about my hairlessness which he was convinced indicated an infectious disease. In fact all his hostility to me, and everybody else, arose out of defensive fear. He was a cornered rat.

'You leave me alone,' I told him that first evening, 'And I'll leave you alone.' Given that I was six inches taller than him, this made sense even on his terms.

The strange thing was he hadn't actually done anything very bad. Petty theft – from cars, supermarkets – getting into fights, giving his girl-friend a black eye. But, like me, he was serving three years. I suspect judge and jury took one look at him, shuddered and decided the best way to avoid meeting him on a dark night was to lock him away.

After three or four weeks I was taken out of my cell and led along the corridor to the cell which the wing officer screw used as an office. I thought it was in response to a complaint I'd put in about Charles who'd taken to farting in my face when I was asleep.

'I've stuck him for nearly a month,' I said. 'It's someone else's turn. I need a nice con in for a bit of fraud.'

'There's someone to see you.' The landing screw indicated a sturdy man in a short white coat. 'You've got five minutes.'

He started talking at once, assuming I would know who he was. 'We're surprised you haven't applied for the F Wing. I've brought you a form.'

I knew who he was. Everybody knew everything about

97

prison business. He was Dr Renfrew who ran the Muppet House.

'I'm not on Rule Forty-three.'

'That's a common misconception of our work. All prisoners with psychiatric problems can apply. My guess, having looked at your file, is you'd find it very helpful. The sentencing judge suggested psychiatric treatment.'

'No, thank you.'

He picked up his biro and stabbed the form in front of him. 'At least you'll get away from your cell-mate.'

'Do you think I want to swap him for a load of perverts and child molesters?'

'I see.' He got up and left the room. He didn't even ask me to get in touch if I changed my mind. This galled me. I went back to my cell and put my bowl of custard face down on Charles's pillow. This was the sort of thing I did now and again to show I was as beastly as everybody else but this time I was acting out of bad temper. Since he was still out of his cell, it gave me little satisfaction so while I was waiting for his rage, I threw my lasagne at the small barred window. This was better. The mince dribbled down, leaving wodges of pasta and creamy globules like vomit. I would tell the screws I had been sick and let them work out how it had got up there. Then I lay on my bed and went to sleep.

My capacity for sleep remained immense. I suppose it was my substitute for dope. Gradually the absence of dreams began to break down with muffled sensations, no actual dreams with people and events, but sensations of something trying to break into my secure hibernation.

Then Charles found himself in receipt of a pile more of stuff than he was used to. I found him in the morning at slopping-out time, his mouth caked with yellow foam and his eyeballs rolled back. I thought he was dead but I didn't think it was suicide – just an over-enthusiastic attempt to look for the sunny side up.

The doctor, with some relief – suicides don't look good on a prison's record – pronounced him not dead and he was quickly removed to hospital.

Suddenly, for the first time since I went on my honeymoon

with Nell, I had a room on my own. No one who hasn't been in prison can know how that feels. The whole aspect of life completely changes. The air is lighter, sweeter, the space is immense, the quiet, despite the usual clanging noises outside, induces a sense of calm. I had heard of men who broke up their cell a bit to get a spell in solitary and now I understood why. I walked round my little empire on tip-toe, hardly daring to breathe. I knew Charles would be back soon.

But he wasn't. I slept two nights on my own, no snorting, snoring, smelling, pissing from anyone except myself. Until it happened I had no idea of the strain I had been living under. At night I lay on my bed and reached across to the other just to be sure it was empty. The third day I decided Charles had done a better job of reaching for Nirvana than the doctor had thought and I must expect a replacement. I told myself no one could be as bad as Charles. But this was not really true because, although animal-like and disgusting, he was not terrifying. On the corridor I had met men I would be terrified of being locked in with.

I was still peaceful but looking over my shoulder. When would the screw unlock my door and chuck in some new distorted version of humanity?

On the third night I dreamed. When I woke up I knew that it had been about my parents but I could remember no details. There were tears on my face which was the first time I'd cried since the early days of my imprisonment. It was about five in the morning and still dark. I imagined what the sky was like outside, a December sky, perhaps icily black and etched with stars. Over London there was always a cap of dull orange, but I was imagining the sky in the country-side.

My parents had retired early and gone to live in Kent. When they had been killed they'd been driving up to London for an unusual night out. I had bought tickets for *The Taming of the Shrew*. My mother enjoyed Shakespeare more than anything. I had watched the play without them, assuming there had been a misunderstanding – on my side, of course

– and it was only when I returned to my university digs that the police gave me the news.

My mother, who had been in the passenger seat, lived for a few more hours than my father, but never regained consciousness and died before I reached the hospital. It was typical of them to leave this world for the next side by side. I told Nell, who had accompanied me, how glad I was for them. I was glad for them but there was also a bitter snake in my heart which whispered that, yet again, they'd gone off together and left me behind.

If they hadn't died, I would never have become so involved with Nell. She was their inheritance to me. Nell and the house in the country which was now rented. After clearing it up with Nell, I did not wish to see it again.

Nevertheless, it was the sky over their house and garden which I was picturing as I enjoyed the thoughtful benefits of a single cell.

At slop-out time, a not-so-bad con called Davey stopped me. We held our pails a little way away at an angle, like women with shopping baskets. 'They say you're still on your own?'

'That's it.'

'I'm working on it. You know.'

He was not so bad but the thought of him moving into my emptiness filled me with panic. I could already see he had false teeth which probably meant he had bad breath and if he had bad breath his feet were probably smelly and that left out all the nauseating habits that were inseparable from human beings.

'I'm applying for the Muppet House.' It was self-protection.

'You're applying for the Muppet House?' I had given him a nasty shock. No one, except monsters on Rule 43, applied for the Muppet House and this was the man he'd thought would make a good cell-mate.

'Not applying.' I tried to cover my tracks, dangerously rocking my pail in my agitation. 'Judge's orders.' I hurried on, sped in and out of the washroom and back to my cell. I realised that days on my own had cracked my defensive shell. I huddled on my bed, eyes shut, more broken up than I had ever been.

This was not allowed. 'You haven't collected your food.' The screw stood over me, accompanied as usual by the jangle of keys.

I did not try to answer. 'Why are you on your own?' Then he remembered about Charles. Prison movements were often arbitrary and inefficient although, given the overcrowding, it was unusual to have a bed left unfilled. I began to wonder if it was such a bit of good luck. Before, I had found a way of coping, now everything seemed impossible. Did I want to go to the Muppet House? Even that was too difficult to decide.

At lunch time, I was called out to the landing screw's office. I stood facing his Page Three calendar. The woman had the most enormous breasts I'd ever seen. They were entirely circular with pallid little nipples in the middle. They began to seem like two pink eyes, rabbit eyes, magnetising my attention.

The screw was being very friendly. 'Well, Pat, I shall be the first to congratulate you.'

He seemed to wait for a response but I was hypnotised by the rabbit's eyes. 'You're a fucking father! That's your big news for today.'

It was big news because, even with my limited wish to remember, I knew the baby wasn't due for at least a month. 'Yes, you're a first-time fucking father. Isn't that quite something?' He seemed genuinely pleased, probably had loads of his own children back home. I imagined him telling his wife over a cup of tea. 'I informed this young GBH fellow that his wife had given birth and he didn't even smile.' She would tut-tut, feel superior and go, more happily than ever, to help her littlest one off the potty.

'I want to go to the Muppet House,' I muttered.

He was so disgusted by this unnatural reaction that he could only draw one conclusion. The Muppet House was the right place for me. 'I'll pass on the information.' For the first time he noticed where I was looking so fixedly. 'You fucking bastard!' he hissed.

I went out of the office and waited outside to be led back to my cell. I thought: They lock you up because you've done something terrible and you're probably half out of your mind, treat you in a way calculated to turn you into something even less human, and then start calling you names when you don't react in a nice normal way.

'Fucking hell!' I shouted, knocking my head sharply against the wall. 'Can't you see I want someone to talk to?'

EIGHTEEN

MY FATHER took me to my flat a month after the trial. 'You walk. You eat. You talk. You sleep enough. Now you must live again.' He drove me there when my mother was at work. He took the day off and made such an event of it that I hadn't the heart to resist.

'Oh, Papa!' He liked me to call him papa and the whole flat was filled with chrysanthemums, so he deserved something, even if the effect was funereal. I had last seen my base for a future in the sunny summer when it was the newness and whiteness of its surfaces that had filled me with joy. Now they reminded me of hospital. I sat in the kitchen while my father made me tea. He had bought tea bags and a lemon which he took from a bag. He carefully cut very thin slices which he put on a plate and offered to me. 'Still no milk?'

'Still no milk,' I agreed. The greasy bulk of milk made me sick, like most things.

He sat down opposite me. 'You won't grow big and bold.'

'I know.' I could not look at him. Yesterday Lesley had suggested (and she seldom suggested anything) that my father could be helpful to me. I said to her, 'It is not my poor father who has made me beware of men. He is beware of women, owing to my mother, and has to sneak away in secret to his real woman. All this has been going on for years and it is not as important to any of us as you might think.' I saw by her meditative calm that she was not convinced so I tried again. 'My murder — '

Here she interrupted me as she always did. 'He was not, is not your murderer because you are alive.' She told me that because she knew I thought the opposite.

I started again, 'My father cannot alter my feelings towards men. He is separate.'

I must have repeated these words aloud in my little flat for I suddenly became aware of my father's face across the table, staring at me oddly. I smiled and sipped my tea. The sharp lemony flavour traced its way down my body, giving little tweaks and twinges.

'You look better,' said my father, approvingly. 'I understand you won't sleep here now, but I shall bring you back again. Again and again.' I walked around. Apart from the kitchen, there was only a bed-sitting room and a bathroom the size of a cupboard. There was no place for anyone to share it with me and I could never sleep here alone. I sat down on the bed.

'You won't always be tired,' said my father, 'but now you must push yourself a little further each day.'

'Thank you. I might come here and write.' It was odd to hear myself say that. I tried not to see my father's excitement. For a moment I saw reflected in his eyes the clever daughter I had been, head girl of my school, editor of the student magazine, conscientious member of the university. He was determined I should not lose touch with the ambitious, successful young woman I had been.

'I can bring you here any day. It will be good for you to be alone.'

We left then, locked together, for the flat was up three flights of stairs and the weakness down my left side made them arduous work. It was part of a large house near Portobello Road and when we came out onto the pavement I was amazed by the noise and the icy coldness of the air. Opposite there was a row of three shops, one garlanded with Christmas lights and the other selling Christmas trees. Seeing where I was looking, my father led me over.

'Just a small one.' He smiled at me as if I were a child.

'Where are you going to put it?' We both knew my mother always found a tree and decorated it lavishly on Christmas Eve.

He looked hurt. 'It's for you. For your flat. Next time we come, I'll bring lights and decorations.'

'No. No.' In a moment he would be suggesting a crib with little Lord Jesus. But then his expression was so wrinkled and downcast that I added, 'The tree on its own would be lovely.'

So he chose a tree in a pot and I sat in the car while he struggled to get it back up to the flat. The obstinacy of my father is immense. As I waited in the car for what extended itself to a long half-hour, I began to have some sympathy with my mother. She had married a bully.

He returned gleaming with the satisfaction of a job well done. 'That's what was needed. Something growing.' He understood I was tired but he did not know or refused to know I was in mourning.

'Lunch time.' He started the car.

'I'm tired. I want to go home.'

'Of course, you're tired. Of course you want to go home. It's natural. But first we will pay a visit.'

He had kidnapped me, knowing I was too weak for a proper fight. I decided to sulk, twiddling the knobs in front of me to make the car hotter. He was never cold, indeed suffered from the heat so it would serve him right if I caused him a touch of discomfort.

He wound down the window, imperviously cheerful. 'It will take twenty minutes, if the traffic's not too bad.'

'I'm cold.'

'It's because you are inside too much.' He wound up the window fractionally.

I did not speculate on where we were going but shut my eyes and tried to slip into a kind of low-level sleep which I found useful to pass the time. 'Here we are.' The car stopped with a jerk outside a heavy built block of mansion flats. My father leapt out and opened my door.

'I'll wait here for you.'

He was agitated, his face red, his hand on the door shaking slightly. 'I want you to come. Please, little Lydia.'

How could I resist his pleading? He helped me, with great gentleness, up the wide stone staircase and then left me standing as he went to the row of doorbells. My self-absorption still precluded any idea of our destination. It was only after we had left the lift, a shaken, old-fashioned affair, and stood outside a black front door that I began to wonder. But then we were inside.

'This is very difficult. Very difficult.' Because she had been my teacher, I recognised Miss Mottram (she had always been known as 'Miss' at school) at once, although her face was much pinker than before and her hair greyer. She had also put on weight. She looked like an ordinary middle-aged housewife. 'Your father insisted. I did not wish it.' She was very nervous.

'Sit down, both of you!' my father commanded. 'This is a good thing. I will pour some sherry.'

Miss Mottram sat down obediently and I sat down because I was tired. Her nervousness made her talkative, which is not how I'd remembered her from school. 'I woke up with a horrible cold, a fever, so I thought it wise not to take it to the children, although very probably I caught it from one of them in the first place. I do hope I don't give it to you. That would be unforgivable. Keep your distance, I'd say, keep your distance.'

I had every intention of keeping my distance. 'No sherry for me,' I told my father, hoping to express my extreme displeasure by my clipped tones.

But he was determined on a course of action. He stood in the middle of the room and raised his glass. 'To the two women I love most in the world!' His theatricality was ridiculous but perhaps it helped us for we became audience, passively watching.

'You may think it odd', he continued, as if delivering a speech, 'that I should bring you together like this after the years that have passed,' he paused here, giving me time perhaps to consider the years. He wanted me, I think, to look at his poor old mistress and see that she deserved sympathy or, at very least, recognition. But I was selfish, bound up in my own unhappiness. Her unattractiveness, the tasteless lack of style about her shiny tables and bright chintz and dried flowers, made me more heartless, not less. The pile of exercise books, further proof that she was no fancy woman, made me close my eyes and wish myself almost anywhere else.

'Barbara and I have known each other ten years,' continued my father, 'ten years in which she has been the good angel in my life.'

I opened my eyes and looked at Miss Mottram, maliciously expecting a smug acceptance of my father's compliment. But her face was more anxious than ever, deep frown lines crossing her forehead and her eyes moving nervously from her lover to me. I could hardly avoid realising she was as unhappy with this speech as I was. It reminded me of her conscientiousness as a teacher, her care for and attention to all our petty faults. I was reminded of what I had forgotten from the time I had discovered her relationship to my father to this moment, that I had liked her as a teacher.

Now she stood up, interrupting my father who was still speaking although neither of us listened. 'I'll make some sandwiches. Lydia is so pale.' Before she hurried from the room, I saw tears of pity for me in her eyes. I saw so few people that I had forgotten the effect of my appearance, particularly on anyone who had known me before.

My father glanced at me and poured himself another sherry. At home he never drank sherry. 'It was time for this.' His voice was levelling off from its declamatory heights. He examined his face in a gilt-framed mirror, pushed back his thick grey-black hair. 'I am old.'

'Have you brought Charmian here?' I asked.

My father smiled. His teeth were good, although decorated by gold caps of which he was obscurely proud. 'Charmian took fright. Hardly had we crossed the threshold.'

'Perhaps she felt sorry for Mother,' I suggested primly.

'That is not relevant.' He was grand.

'I don't see why,' I began but was stopped by the image of Miss Mottram chopping sandwiches in the kitchen.

'Charmian takes a religious view,' said my father. 'She has a right to it. I do not argue.'

We both became silent and I even took a little sip of sherry which I regretted at once, however, since it felt as if a live electric wire had been thrust down my body. 'Oh, Papa!' I wanted to be cuddled against his barrel chest but his mistress came in with the sandwiches.

'They're Marmite and salmon paste.' She offered me the plate. 'I hope that suits.' They both sat down.

'It is unusual that both Barbara and myself should be off work on the same day,' announced my father.

I bit into a Marmite sandwich, hoping for strength and comfort.

'I am so terribly sorry about your accident,' began Miss Mottram, all in a rush. She stood up in her agitation, making a shiny table rock.

'It wasn't an accident.' I put down my sandwich. That had been a mistake too. 'It was a deliberate act of wilful murder.'

'Oh, yes, of course.'

'I'm afraid I'm going to faint.' She led me to a bedroom which had pink curtains and pink frills on the lampshade. Trembling and sweaty, I allowed myself to be laid out on her bed.

'You shouldn't have brought her here,' I heard Miss Mottram whisper fiercely to my father, 'she's too weak.'

'It is good and right.' He didn't care if I heard. 'She is hiding herself.'

After that, I fell asleep.

My father sang as he drove me home. It was an old Polish marching song that he often hummed, but I'd never heard any words before. He sang the same words over and over again:

> *'Ulani, Ulani, malowane dzieci*
> *Nie jedna panienka za wami poleci.'*

'What does it mean?' I asked him.

'It means I am happy.'

'But what do the words mean?'

'I have forgotten. Perhaps it is a lullaby. A mother soothes her child.'

'It's far too rousing. Martial, in my view.'

'Martial, in your view.' My father took a hand from the steering wheel to pat mine. 'You are my soldier.'

'I need sleep.'

'No. No. You need to live!'

This cast me into silent irritation for several minutes, broken eventually by my father shouting above the noise of the traffic – we were circling Shepherd's Bush Green – 'After your birth, your mother was no longer welcoming.'

'What?' A lorry had passed on either side of us.

'She did not want me in her bed.'

This was a lie since they still shared a double bed but his message was clear. 'Oh, Papa.' Did I have to know such details about my parents' lives?

My father's good humour continued through our arrival at home. My mother was still at work so between us we prepared supper.

She arrived cold and tired, the underground had broken down so she had walked the last stop. When she saw our efforts, she stopped complaining and went upstairs to her bedroom. After a while I followed her up because the house is small and I could hear her muffled sobbing. Perhaps she meant me to.

'How did you know where we'd been?' I asked her.

'He always looks like that when he comes back. Happy.'

'And what about me?'

'You were close. Doing things together.' There was not much more to be said because it was true. Our visit had drawn me closer to my father and changed the balance in the household.

The next day I explained all this to Lesley. It produced a magnificent silence. She had explained to me early on in our meetings that she did not believe in the Freudian approach of non-participating analyst and indeed, towards the end of an hour, we were often in a friendly dialogue. But not that day. 'It was all right,' I said, hoping for approbation. 'It was true I nearly fainted but then I lay down on her bed, on the bed where they must make love and it was not disgusting.'

Lesley shifted in her chair. She was a heavy woman and when she moved, the chair creaked. But that was all the reaction she gave me.

When I came out of her room, my mother, who drove me to my sessions whenever possible, gave me an ironic smile which told me she knew what I had been talking about. I was filled with impatience and anger. Why should I spend my time trying to understand the mess my parents had made of their life together? I had been recommended to Lesley because I had been all but murdered and only by chance not raped.

I brushed past my mother and went to the car. We drove home in silence. I knew she imagined that my silence was loaded with her experiences with Father. It was not. It was about myself.

It was snowing the following morning. Usually I stayed in bed till lunch time but on this occasion I waited for my parents to go to work and then dressed. My clothes depressed me. I had bought no new ones and those that I had from last winter were far too big. I piled on two of my mother's sweaters and left the house.

The sensation of being outside without an attendant gave me an attack of vertigo. The snow swirling about, lightly but continuously, increased my sense of disorientation. I stood still, undecided whether to return, defeated, or persevere. My attention was distracted by a robin sitting watching me from the top of our front railings. The snow was hardly settling but even so he would have made an excellent illustration for a Christmas card. He seemed unafraid of me, putting his head first on one side and then another with a quizzical expression. I expect he wanted crumbs or bacon rind but he had given me the courage not to return to the house so I walked past him and out on to the pavement.

There were not many people about. Our small street led into a noisy main road with about ten minutes' walk to an underground station. But it was after rush hour and there was no sense of urgency in the women shopping with push-chairs and small children or the assorted collection of unoccupied persons found in any big capital.

I was one of them now, strolling along by the shop windows, my purpose personal and unaccountable. I passed a small shop, not the sort I used to visit but showing a long quilted coat in the window. It was a dark cherry colour, warming even to see. I went in at once and made them take if off the model.

'It costs eighty pounds,' said the assistant in a surprised voice. They had not expected to sell such an expensive item from a shop which mainly dealt with cheap sweaters and grey Terylene trousers. 'It was really for show,' she explained. But I bought it all the same. It would be protection for me, armour against the world.

By the time I reached the underground, I knew I was heading, in a dream-like way, for my flat. It was only when I arrived that I realised I had no key to the door, neither outer nor inner. I stood on the outside steps feeling tired and foolish.

'Press the top bell. She's always in.' A strange man's voice in my ear caused me to cower in fright by the wall.

'I'm sorry, I gave you a start.' I reminded myself of my red suit of armour and told my heart to slow down. 'Your dad bought the Christmas tree from me.' He had seen me from the shop across the way.

I found my voice. 'I didn't hear you come.'

'Press the top bell,' he repeated, presumably wondering what sort of maniac I was since I was still hanging on to the wall. 'I'll ring for you, then I must pop back.'

An American voice answered the bell and somehow I was inside and going up the stairs, very slowly, a step at a time. She was waiting for me outside my flat, and explained she kept a spare of keys for all the flats because she was a writer and around most of the time. 'It's great to be able to welcome you!' she exclaimed, so that I did my best to smile and look pleased to be welcomed, although I still felt shaken. When I did not invite her into the flat, she invited me to hers. 'Come afterwards for a drink.'

Her extreme friendliness made me suspect she knew my

history until I recalled that many Americans were kindly in this way. Since the attack I had deliberately cut myself off from old friends, not that I had ever been very sociable, all my real contacts coming from editing the student newspaper. It was hard to believe in those days.

I sat in my flat beside my father's Christmas tree and watched my breath blow white on the cold air. The street noises were loud and alien. After a while I could separate the buses stopping a little way down the road, the cars and general traffic taking turns at a busy crossroads, the vans delivering or collecting at shops further along.

It reminded me of my digs in my last year at university. That had been in London too but further east, part of what some students grandly called Bloomsbury. There had been a boy, called Paul, who thought of nothing but Virginia Woolf and Vanessa Bell and Lytton Strachey. He was pallid and thin and wore little pince-nez and after a while I realised he was trying to look like Stratchey. He cultivated me because I was editor of the newspaper and one day he took me to the National Portrait Gallery to see Henry Lamb's painting of Strachey. The likeness between them was striking. 'Are you related?' I asked.

'Not yet,' answered Paul. He was that sort of person. After I had printed several of his less obscure articles, he revealed that he planned to be editor of the *Times Literary Supplement*.

'You're just a literary snob,' I told him. 'There's no meaning in that sort of élitism. It's a snake eating its tail, perpetuating myths.'

He was hurt. Clearly I should not have treated his dream so roughly. 'So what do you expect to find out from the national newspapers?' he asked me. 'Myths are perpetuated there too but they're bigger and more dangerous.'

'I shall tell the truth.' My hauteur had silenced him. Besides, he believed me. I was well known for my directness and determination. That was how people would have described me then, direct and determined, ambitious, not very interested in making friends.

'I knocked but you were somewhere far away.' The American woman stood in front of me, holding a cup of coffee in either hand. 'It's so cold in here. I knew you'd need this.'

'I don't drink coffee.'

'It's tea.'

'I'm sorry.' I took the cup and she sat on the edge of the table.

She said, 'I've been hoping to see you. I know about what happened to you. I hope you don't mind.' She did not wait to hear if I minded or not. 'Any attack by a man on a woman must be borne by all women everywhere. I expect your shrink tells you things like that?'

She stopped and to my surprise, I found myself responding, 'My shrink wants to make me believe all men are good and kind and I was just unlucky.'

Her bright little eyes stared disbelievingly. 'But that's criminal. Even by British standards. Doesn't she know how a woman feels?'

'I don't think she believes my feelings are important. Or at least she knows they're counter-productive. The main thing is for me to get over it. Forget it. Wipe it out.'

'But you can't do that.' The American's voice became more impassioned. 'You're not the same person you were before. You'll never be the same.'

'Lesley, that's my analyst, shrink, sees it all in terms of me, my problems from before.'

'She's laying it on you?'

'No. Yes.' I tried to think. This conversation was so extraordinary. Lesley certainly told me that my future health was entirely my responsibility, that I must put myself right. 'She does make me feel guilty.' I looked up at the American hunched forward from the table. 'Because I don't try hard enough.'

'But that's terrible! Terrible! He's the only guilty one. Your attacker. You are a victim. He's made you a victim. But that doesn't make you guilty.' She paused suddenly. 'Hey, drink up your tea.'

I drank up my tea. It felt good. Something had turned round inside me, was flowing the right way. I became aware of the American's intense stare. I looked up. She was quite small, I saw now, with short reddish hair and broad thin shoulders. Her eyes were a dark brown.

'I wasn't raped, you see.' It was confusing because I felt like smiling.

'Of course you were. We're not talking about technicalities here. If a man sticks a knife in a woman, he sure as hell rapes her. Don't you know anything?'

I realised I didn't know anything. 'What's your name?'

'Maureen Kenneally.' She seemed uninterested in her name. I expect she wanted to talk more about rape. I thought of Charmian and felt like laughing. This was what it was about. For the first time in months I felt warm. I undid some of the clasps on my coat.

'That's a beautiful coat.' She was sitting on the table swinging her legs, drinking her tea. Beyond her I could see the snow straggling down the window.

'I just bought it.'

'That's good. You bought a coat. That's terrific!'

She seemed to understand everything. Tears began to run down my cheeks. Blinking them away, I saw her blithe look change to anxiety. 'I'm happy,' I managed to say. That was an exaggeration. A corner had lifted.

She slid off the table, pulling down the wrinkles in her jeans. 'Tea break over. Back to my desk.' Although I was still crying, she collected my cup with cheerful energy and made for the door. 'Give me a call when you're planning to stay the night.'

When I stood up, my bad leg buckled, my back ached and my hands shook. There were no mirrors in the room but I could imagine what I looked like. So why did I feel cheerful?

NINETEEN

'So why did you fucking do it?'

This was the first time anyone had asked me this question and it was now six months since I'd dug a knife into an innocent, unknown and defenceless girl.

Perhaps if I'd had parents living, they would have asked, but I doubt it. No one dares face the questions behind the answer, that is if there is an answer at all. The man who dared ask was an Irish psychopath who'd murdered his wife and his mother-in-law and done a half-hearted job on himself. What I'd done held no fears for him.

There were usually five of us in the group therapy session. With such a small group, there was time to put each other on the spot. I could see Dr Renfrew looking a little more interested than usual. 'Because I was angry,' I said. 'Because I was so fucking angry I had to kill something.'

This admission produced a sympathetic response. The group knew about anger. Well, perhaps not the addicts or child molesters so much, but it made them feel happily superior. At least they did not lose their temper. We were a weird bunch of people in that little room. To gain admittance we had to pass the hospital annex's criteria:

1. Have at least nine months of our sentence left to serve.
2. Willing to consider forgoing parole, or a portion of it, if necessary.
3. To be prepared to mix with all categories of inmates, i.e. Rule 43.
4. Not mentally ill.
5. Not receiving medication such as anxiolytics, anti-depressants or hypnotics.
6. No recent history of suicide attempts/gestures.
7. To be at least average IQ and literate.
8. Preferably under forty years old (negotiable).
9. To be prepared to accept the prison's containment conditions.

Even if you got through on all these, you were only put on a trial period initially. We were thirty-six in my day and under continual threat of closure. Dr Renfrew talked about his problems nearly as much as mine. He was a bit of an old woman but I liked him all the same. He was the first person within the prison system to remind me I was a human being not an outcast. It sounds corny now but it is what I felt then. The next step, he enjoyed telling me, was to recognise that I had not been cast out but had cast myself out.

'Fucking anger. Yeah. That's it. That surely is IT.' As if unable to contain his thoughts in words, Gerry jumped to his feet. His chair fell backwards with a bang. He was drawing attention to himself when I was supposed to be centre stage. In my view, there was nothing wrong with Gerry that a large dose of lithium wouldn't cure.

I looked round the rest of the group. There was Harry who looked sixty, a wizened little man, but was actually still in his thirties. He wanted to make little girls happy but then when he got close to them, something seemed to go wrong, not his fault, and he made them very unhappy instead. He sat next to Carey, a handsome young bully who couldn't keep his sexual largesse to himself. He insisted it was the boys who made the running, although a couple of sessions ago, he had made a bit of a breakthrough and admitted that now and again he came across one who rejected his advances and then he just had to persuade him. Carey cried a lot, noisily, filled with self-pity. He was a big baby and his mother's darling. She was a regular doting visitor. I didn't see much hope for Carey. He was too stupid to learn.

Dr Renfrew told me often, 'You're clever. You can sort yourself out if you want to.' He reminded me of Larry.

The other group member that day was called Gary, a West Indian, very anxious, who had hardly seen the outside of prison since he was a child. At first I couldn't understand why he was allowed into the unit. He seemed a real no-hoper but then I got to know him a bit.

It was Gary who picked up the chair after Gerry had

knocked it backwards. The point was Gary really liked people. He was only in his middle twenties, a nice person, his anxiety stemming from this niceness because he was worried all the time that the atmosphere was going to turn nasty and someone was going to get unhappy. He was too sensitive. Had been all his life. From the age of ten or eleven he'd found things felt much easier when he was on drugs. So that was his problem. Drugs. Everyone used them in his area, he liked to tell us, finding excuses as we all did. 'And you've got to do a shop or something to get the fucking dosh.' I liked Gary. He was an innocent.

He put the chair straight and said to me, 'What gets me, friend, is you don't have no need to stick that girl.' He was trying to help.

'It felt like I did,' I began. I was a little diverted by Gerry who was wandering round looking as if he might take a swing at someone.

'Sit down, Gerry,' Dr Renfrew said sharply. And he did. We all relaxed. The doctor turned to me with a kind of earnestness which was part of his professional bag of tricks but encouraging for all that. 'Go on, Pat. Take us through your feelings on that evening.'

I couldn't do that. It was far too much to ask. He knew that but he put the question down as a signpost to the future.

'I told you. I was filled with anger.'

'But you had no worries, man. You weren't lacking,' Gary persevered. We shared a cell. He knew me well and it didn't make any sense to him.

I ran my hands over my head. It was an unconscious habit, inevitable fascination with the smoothness. But this time my fingers felt something more than skin. I circled round the spot, making absolutely sure. 'Hey, there's something growing here!'

They all came crowding round. Nobody liked my hairlessness. Fingers pressed on my skull enthusiastically. 'Get off!' shouted Gary. 'Let me see.' They were quiet as he peered closely.

'Hair!' he pronounced eventually, as proud as if he'd created it himself. 'That's hair poking through your skin.'

Now Dr Renfrew, who'd remained aloof, came over and bent down. I was still sitting. 'A definite five-o'clock shadow.' He smiled at me. 'Congratulations.'

I had been three weeks in the Muppet House and I'd started growing hair again. Something must be going right.

We weren't in therapy sessions that often. Actually it was called 'Psychology' sub-headed 'Anger Control', 'Social Skills', 'Relationship Skills'. When we weren't doing that, we were at craft workshop or French class or drama therapy which was where we acted out our hang-ups. But most of the time we played table tennis. I got very good at table tennis. During my fourth week I organised a tournament.

Dr Renfrew appeared half-way through and watched me shouting at poor old Harry. 'Come on, you old bugger, imagine Carey's a little kiddo and give him what for!' Prison vulgarises the most sensitive.

The doctor, his white coat flapping open to reveal T-shirt and jeans – he liked to make us feel at home – called me over. 'I'm sorry to interrupt, Pat, but I wonder if you could spare a moment.' He was always very polite, in that way unlike us. The tournament would probably fall apart if I left it because all the contestants preferred arguing to table tennis but I didn't mind too much. You learnt not to mind anything too much in prison.

A woman was sitting in Dr Renfrew's office which actually was an office, unlike the usual converted cells. 'This is Liz Miller.' The doctor introduced us and we shook hands. 'She's writing an article on prison conditions and wondered if you'd talk to her?'

I didn't mind that either. If she had been my solicitor, my cousin Larry, my wife, now a mother, or my parents-in-law I would have declined the offer. Dr Renfrew had agreed that while I was in a kind of therapy, however gentle, I should not have to face them. But speaking to a stranger was OK. I could cope with that. Besides, I knew this unit was under constant threat of closure so perhaps I could help by singing its praises.

'I'll leave you together.' It was good to be left alone with the woman. She was about forty, attractive, business-like.

She immediately produced a notebook. That made me feel secure.

She questioned me simply at first. Name. Age. Sentence. History of criminality. When I answered 'none' to this, she seemed surprised but made no comment. She hardly looked up at me at all, perhaps feeling it would be intrusive or perhaps just nervous of being in close proximity to a man who was inside for GBH. I didn't tell her exactly what I had done and she didn't ask me.

Soon I was going to town on the Muppet House. 'It's changing all our lives,' I burbled, only pausing when a screw brought us in cups of tea. I realised I was enjoying myself, holding forth to an intelligent woman.

But the tea gave Ms Miller a chance to interrupt me. Suddenly she was asking different questions. 'Who did you attack?' 'A woman?' 'How badly hurt was she?'

'Look, you're supposed to be asking about prison conditions.' I felt myself flushing, my voice changing.

'I'm so sorry.' She was very apologetic and, of course, I didn't want to seem a hysterical neurotic. I had been proving how unlike I was to some of the people in there. I had been aligning myself with her. So I took control of myself and said, 'I don't know anything about my victim. That's not the way things work.'

'I see,' she nodded and scribbled on her notebook. I tried not to seem too relieved. 'I didn't ask you if you were married?'

I put my tea cup down which I had been holding in self-defence. 'Yes.'

'And does your wife visit you?' Since I didn't answer, she added, 'I mean, does she support you still? So many prisoners seem to have little or no outside contact.'

She was thinking of her article, I could see that. Visiting hours, family rooms. In a moment she would be enquiring whether I favoured conjugal visits as allowed in some foreign gaols. I had been too successful in convincing her that I was as sane as everybody else. I looked to the door, hoping to see a white coat.

'You are still married?' she persisted.

'Yes.' I stood up. In a moment she would ask me about my hair. I was proud of its courageous development, the fluffy down like a chick's feathers, but I didn't want her comments. 'I should go,' I said, still fighting to keep my voice flat. 'I'm organising a table tennis tournament.'

'That's terrific.' She made a note. I was beginning to hate her clever face. 'Just one last question. What did you do for Christmas?'

'Christmas?' At least she'd nearly made me laugh. What did she think I'd done for Christmas, a day that had passed a couple of weeks ago with a lack of staff and an excess of food. 'Eat,' I said, moving to the door.

'And the others?' For the sake of the image of the Muppet House I should have answered, 'Sang "Silent Night, Holy Night",' but the truth popped out of my mouth. 'Wanked off,' I shouted and then, carried away by her astonishment I decided to enlarge. 'Most feel it appropriate to relieve their frustration once or twice a day but on Christmas Day there's no holding them. It's squeeze cocks till they burst. All hands to the tiller.'

After that she left in a hurry and I went to my cell. Outside I could hear the tournament degenerating into shouts and obscenities as predicted. It took the strain off my feelings a little and I didn't go to interfere. Instead I lay on my bed and gently held my cock.

Dr Renfrew and his assistant Dr Cook were just beginning to approach the question of sex with me. I refused to talk about it at all in group therapy. What could I learn from homosexuals, child abusers and black addicts? That's what I thought, anyway. I could actually count the number of times I'd made love in my life. Nell was always the recipient.

I first met Nell when I was drawing up the schedule for the university film club. She appeared in my room saying she wanted to help, be a dogsbody. It was flattering to have a pretty girl as a dogsbody. Besides, she was very efficient, dealing with the printers and even defending me when other members of the committee questioned my choices.

We started going to films together once or even twice a week. We both preferred classics rather than contemporary trash. After we had watched *Wuthering Heights* together, she looked at me wonderingly, 'You never shed a tear, do you, however sad the film?'

I looked at her red-rimmed eyes. 'I'm more the critical type,' I joked. 'Analysis and appreciation before emotion.'

'I'm afraid I'm hopelessly romantic,' she confessed to me humbly. I should have been warned. She looked very feminine with her fairish tumbling hair and appealing speckled eyes. Normally, I would have steered clear but our working relationship gave me a sense of security.

We knew each other in this way for about a year and then my parents were killed. It was just before the start of my last term. I was already working very hard, conscious that I had a great deal to catch up with. I was reading English, which I loved, but had not pinned myself down securely enough. I had to carry on working hard if I wanted a decent degree, I told myself, not without reason. There was no time to mourn for my parents. There was a cremation service near the village of their retirement and then they were gone, had gone. For good, this time. I felt absolutely alone.

I returned to my room and tried to settle down. There was no reason to see Nell.

One evening she came round. I had not invited her to my parents' funeral but she knew of their death. She brought me a pot of flowers – that was a typical kind of Nell action – and kissed me on my cheek (we never did more than that). 'This is for you to look at when you're sad,' she explained. 'Personally, I find growing things most cheering.' Suddenly I was reminded of my mother who, since my father's retirement, had spent hours each day in the garden. To my horror, I burst into tears.

She came forward and gently took me in her arms. We lay down on the carpet together. It was an animal skin brought back from Africa by my parents. She stroked my forehead and temples as a much older woman might have done, a mother, perhaps, but not mine. Never, never mine. Not quite true. Oh, forget that. If Nell had told me at once that she loved me, I would have taken fright but she didn't speak at all, was merely a consoling presence.

Gradually her fingers became not only soothing but arousing. I could feel her breasts pressing softly, not threatening at all. But still it was she who showed me what to do, who undid my clothes for me, held me till I was fully aroused and then carefully slid me inside her. It was a tremendous relief. But not loving. Not on my side. When we lay quietly together I thought of nothing, that was the joy of it.

'I love you,' she did say it finally. I felt grateful to her, pleased with what had happened – to be a virgin at twenty may not be extraordinary but it is certainly unusual. When she said, 'I love you', I assumed it was all part of the experience, not something that would take over my life. She did not ask me if I loved her but left soon afterwards.

I went to bed and at first slept in airy fields. Then the dreams began, a distorted and very physical replay of my recent union with Nell. It was frightening because everything that had been quiet and comforting had turned into violence. The colours, red, purple, yellow, were ugly. Even Nell's nice round face looked older, witch-like. I knew why that was. My room was cold but my body boiled, thrown into a fever by my experience.

However, by five or six, I had cooled down, this terrible reaction to love worn itself out. I slept again, waking finally at nine with peace restored.

When I next saw Nell I said, 'Hi.' We were in a coffee shop. And she said, 'Hi,' too, blushing deeply, but I was determined not to make too much of it. That seemed very important so I sat at her table where she was drinking hot chocolate with a girl-friend and made general conversation. Then I left. This made it possible, I felt, for further contact without high sexual expectations. As you can see, her point of view was not in the forefront of my thinking. She was unlucky to meet me.

After my insulting performance with the woman journalist, Dr Renfrew cottoned on to the idea that my problem might have something to do with my relationship with the opposite sex. He made me describe my first sexual experience. When I had finished the story I have just told, he asked, 'Did you take no responsibility for what had happened?'

Since we were sitting together in unusual privacy, I had time to think of a proper answer. In fact I took so long to think that he went out to deal with a hysterical display in a next-door cell and returned five minutes later, looking rather squeezed in the face. Dr Renfrew took a lot of insults from us all. 'Well, have you thought?' I could see he had lost track of our conversation but I did have something to say.

'It seems to me that my instinctive sense of not wanting to get into a deep emotional and sexual relationship with Nell', it was something to be able to pronounce her name, 'showed a serious, if unconscious, responsibility for her welfare. She would have been much better off without me.'

We both knew this was a cop-out but it was also true. He couldn't argue, although he might have tried if he had more time or energy. But a screw was beckoning him from the door. Trouble. I smiled sympathetically and went back to my cell.

In the Muppet House, we loonies were encouraged to note down our thoughts so here is what I wrote on that day: 'Is there a moment when a life goes wrong or is there a linked chain of moments?' I laid down clues but no one had the time to pick them up.

CHAPTER
TWENTY

MY MOTHER drove me and my suitcase to my flat grumbling all the way. 'After what you've been through and what you still go through, it's not right you should be on your own. It's your father who's persuaded you. For selfish reasons of his own.'

Ever since the afternoon when my father had kidnapped me and taken me to his mistress, my mother had been more openly critical of him. She was driving with a fixed face of irritation. I wanted her to understand. 'You know I've been going there several weeks now?'

'You don't know what it's like to be alone in a place before you've slept there.'

'I've told you. There's the American girl above. Or I could ring you.'

This softened her a little. 'You can telephone me anytime, night or day. Sleep is boring, dear. My little dear. I like being woken up.' This was more her normal self. By the time we had arrived, she was parodying her concern. ' "Cluck, cluck," goes the mother hen. "Cluck, cluck, cluck." '

I could lean on her shoulder and make a joke of the two of us staggering up the stairs. 'I'll still need you to drive me to Lesley.' I teased her when we'd lugged my case up to the flat and were recovering on my two kitchen chairs.

'Oh, Lesley!' My mother pretended to disapprove of my analyst but only for form's sake. She had begun to believe that the big motherly woman dared to say all the complicated things about the dangers of the big bad world.

In fact Lesley's chorus, more like my father's, was, 'Confront what you fear and the imagined terrors will go away.'

It was Saturday, that day I re-entered life with my mother, nearly a month since my father brought me. The Christmas tree still stood there, although its needles had dropped in wavy patterns on the carpet. 'Dad brought me that.'

'I'll sweep up the mess and then your silly father will have to carry it downstairs.'

'To throw away?'

'If you planted that it would be like a fish-bone in no time.'

I remembered how my father had explained it as a symbol of life and smiled. I watched my mother find my new dustpan and brush and sweep up the needles energetically. Crawling about on her hands and knees in her angora sweater, she was like a furry animal. I was reminded of what my father had told me about her 'unwelcoming' aspect in bed. It seemed strange that his mistress, Miss Mottram, who had seemed as unyielding as one of her heavier shiny tables, should be more receptive to the touch.

I caught my mother's eye as she reared upright from the door and blushed. It was ridiculous that I, who, according to Lesley, was suffering from a dangerous aversion to men,

123

particularly in any sexual aspect, should be speculating about my parents' sex life.

I had explained it to Lesley. 'I was never very keen on boy-friends. I haven't changed as much as you think. I just jump away when men come near me now, especially if they have fair hair and are reasonably young. I feel safer with women. So what's wrong with that?'

She listened to me because that's what she was paid for but I sensed her disapproval. She had a curious habit of winding a greyish curl round the cord from which her spectacles were suspended when she disapproved of what I was saying. She was too knowing to be my mother. My mother was not knowing at all. She was emotional and stupid and at some point she had gone cold on my father.

'It's icy in here, dear.' She had come back to sit with me.

'You should go back and make Dad's supper.' It was strange to me that they still had this domestic unity but I accepted it as the left-overs on the table of love. Nor did I view my father's mistress with complete seriousness. After all, she had marked my excellent English essays with green ink. 'Content good, form incomplete'. Perhaps her mind had been on my father at the time. She had seemed surprised when I'd been accepted by a university.

'I will leave you, then.' My mother covered her angora with a coat and a scarf which she tied carefully round her neck. It was painful to sit watching her slowly preparing to go and leave me on my own.

I went to the window, peered through my optimistic striped curtains. With an increased sense of panic, I wondered why we had come at tea-time when night would come so quickly. Perhaps she hoped to make it impossible. She did not want me to suffer. Or was she afraid of being alone with my father?

'Remember it's Sunday tomorrow and both Charmian and I are available all day.'

Her voice sharpened me a little. I focused on the street outside, the brightly lit shops opposite and the people passing on the pavement. 'You mean Charmian is available when she's not in church.' My voice came out squeaky as if in criticism.

My mother hastened to respond. Criticism was her favoured emotion. 'Charmian has her own problems and her own solutions.'

'Yes. Yes. Sorry.' Now I needed to push her through the door. I did not disapprove of Charmian's religious conviction, although I did not see what exactly it solved. I knew she was coming to see me the following afternoon and I was pleased. 'Mother. I wish you'd go.'

She did go then, just a little hurt. She understood me quite well. 'I'll ring at nine o'clock. If you hear the phone ringing at nine, that will be me.'

'Thank you, Mother.'

At the door she stopped once more. 'Are you sure you don't want me to unpack?'

'No. No. No.' I pushed her, gently, through the door.

I was alone. Each time I'd come to the flat this sense of being alone had given me more pleasure. It was as if the damage in my mind and body could only heal when I was entirely alone.

I walked to the centre of my room and just stood. Echoing my father's idea, I thought of trees, how they grow out of the ground, straight and strong. I felt my body, so twisted and distorted, right itself a little. Then I went to the kitchen and poured myself a drop of whisky. I knew that the price I had to pay for solitude was the terrors of the night. But I had an hour or two still. Just time enough.

I went to my case and took a hard-backed writing book out of it. I opened it at the kitchen table and placed a pen ready near it. This is what I wrote:

3 January 1980
My life has suffered an interruption of seven months but now I shall make it start again. Resolutions: 1. Do exercises daily. 2. Make contact with other human beings wherever possible. 3. Think up journalistic ideas with a view to taking up a job in a couple of months. 4. Write this diary regularly. 5. Abandon self-pity. 6. Be honest

with Lesley. 7. Be nice to my mother and father. 8. Be patient with Charmian. 9. Read three newspapers daily. 10. Read from a serious work of fiction and of non-fiction daily. 11. Try to understand.

Looking back now, it seems extraordinarily hopeful, particularly in view of the arid weeks of struggle that followed. It was an effort even to get out of bed, let alone carry out grandiose plans. My main occupation – talking to Maureen from upstairs – did not even make it into my schedule.

Maureen Kenneally was writing a novel which gave her plenty of time for chat. She also supported herself by doing a bit of feature journalism for American magazines with names like the *Seattle Seeker* or the *Air-Line*. She had a private income and lived well, wearing expensive clothes and buying good wine and delicacies like gravadlax. When I picture her it is with a plate of gravadlax accompanied by a pot of dill sauce. 'I am thin because I am thin,' she used to say, 'not because I don't eat.'

I discovered later that this was only a partial truth. For years she had employed a mild form of bulimia to keep her legs sliding into an acceptably narrow pair of jeans. When she thought she'd overeaten she made herself sick by prodding her gullet with her finger. I came at just the right time for Maureen. Without me, she might have had to admit she was a talker not a writer, but with me to hand, she could pretend to be writing her novel while spending most of her time in my flat drinking endless cups of tea. Besides, I needed help.

'You are inconceivable. Unconceived. You are virgin territory.'

'I am also a virgin.' Sometimes I could startle Maureen more than she startled me.

'You mean that really? You really mean that!' I had to pay for impressing Maureen by listening to lectures about the role of women. Soon I realised her attitudes were contradictory. She told me that women were far superior to men in every way and that they could lead successful independent lives without men and yet she was shocked to discover I was a virgin and never became more animated than when discussing the men in her life.

Men came, rather nervously, up the stairs past my flat and into hers above. I would hear them moving above my head and Maureen's special kind of laughter she saved for these visits. 'They are slaves,' she would tell me, if she sensed my surprise, 'slaves to my sexual needs. I am queen to their bee.'

This would have been more convincing if the men were at her beck and call. But gradually I realised that she found men easy to attract but hard to hold on to. Her energy level threatened peace of mind. It was this high energy which stimulated my own lassitude. She would appear about ten in the morning, 'I have planned your life perfectly!' I would be sitting in bed or at my kitchen table, a pall of inaction hanging over me. 'From ten to eleven you will write your diary. Then tea-break, when I appear. You will then make calls, prepare a healthy lunch. Afterwards you will rest for an hour. You will then take a walk, possibly with me, although we must take into account my heavy work schedule.' At the time she spoke she was deeply into writing an article entitled, if I remember it accurately, 'Ants: The Housemaker's Agony'. All her subjects were most unlikely and needed much research.

I was grateful for my schedule. After my walk, which included shopping and did not exist when I had my physiotherapy or analyst's couch, I was supposed to come back and work for three or four hours.

'I have studied your biorhythms,' Maureen assured me. 'They're on an upward chart from three o'clock. You are at your peak between six or seven in the evening.'

I thought that it was then that Patrick William Downes had struck. His biorhythms must have been surging too. Since knowing his name, I had thought about him more personally. I knew he was in prison, although not which one, and my other feelings of hatred enjoyed the image of him suffering in an unhygienic and overcrowded cell. I read newspaper articles about such conditions with vengeful pleasure.

Lesley disapproved of this, saying that I must come to terms with my problems, without recourse to useless thoughts about my aggressor. Of course, she knew that when he was released I would have to learn to live in a world that contained both of us, but she never spoke of that.

Maureen, typically, longed for me to describe to her every ghastly moment of the attack. She encouraged me, not subtly. 'It is extraordinary to think you actually know the feeling of a knife slicing through skin and flesh and muscle.'

'I don't.' She looked so disappointed that I relented a little. 'At first it felt like a blow and then the Le Creuset pot fell on my head and I don't remember much more.' I had no intention of sharing my nightmares with her. She was supposed to show me a world outside them.

One Sunday afternoon, my sister Charmian came to visit. Maureen had just arrived and clearly had no intention of leaving, so despite misgivings I made them both cups of tea.

Charmian was happy on Sundays. 'You're Lydia's American friend. I'm so glad she has someone to watch over her.'

'Her experience is not unique.' Maureen fixed her small bright eyes on Charmian who leant towards her spilling some of her tea into her lap. 'It is the lot of women to be abused and men to abuse.'

Charmian reeled back but only to *mieux sauter*. 'You cannot judge the sinner by the sinned against!'

'Victim,' corrected Maureen. They were on the same wavelength. I left for the bathroom and they didn't even notice.

Actually, I didn't mind them discussing my situation as if I didn't exist. It seemed quite sensible that they should try out their theories on each other rather than me. Charmian wanted me to forgive and turn to God for support and comfort. Maureen wanted me to accept my role as a representative of suffering women and hate all men, except when I was entertaining them in my bedroom.

Everyone had theories about my situation. My father thought I should forget all about it, and plunge into my planned career as a journalist. My mother thought I should give up and weep on her bosom. And Lesley thought I should imitate her and middle-class English women everywhere and make the best of a bad job.

Nobody understood what I felt like. My life was a question of existing day by day, minute by minute.

'But you can't believe in God!' Maureen's cry from next door showed that they'd moved on from me as a subject for conversation.

I took up my notebook. 'The indignation of the unbeliever suggests a sense of failure. Believing is more successful than not believing. Charmian's certainties are likely to cause Maureen much agonising. She likes to be the one to lay down the law.'

'But over hundreds of years it's done more harm than good!' Maureen's voice again.

Charmian's was indistinct but now and again I caught words, 'forgiveness' often, 'understanding', 'unselfishness'.

I wrote it in my diary. 'The Christian notion of selflessness is quite alien to Maureen's outlook and, if we were to take it seriously, to most people's lives in England at the moment. We are all consumed by the desire to make sense of our own lives, to find the Nirvana of self-fulfilment and happiness. We start from ourselves and never progress much further. When Patrick William Downes tried to murder me, he destroyed my central self. In order to create it again, I have to be selfish so Maureen suits me better than Charmian.'

When I went back into the room, Charmian was pinker than usual and turned to me guiltily. 'But how are you, Lydia?'

'Good.'

'Papa has a message for you. He is such a coward, our father.'

'No, Charmian. Papa is brave.'

Maureen looked from one to the other of us. Her expression told me we talked differently between ourselves. But then sisters, unless they become true friends with views in common, walk across a minefield.

'He is having, I'm afraid, a financial crisis. It's your flat.' Charmian twitched her cardigan together. It was black, with brightly coloured flowers knitted into the neckline. Her cheeks had become the same colour as the flowers. Probably she was blushing at the consciousness of pleasure at my problems.

'But the flat's lease was bought with the money from my godfather,' I said.

'Papa pays the rates, electricity and telephone bills and also gives you money.'

'I must meet your papa.' Maureen couldn't resist interrupting.

'He's not your type at all,' I answered tartly, at the same time as Charmian moved closer to me.

'He says you must start making moves towards earning money. He can't keep you for many more weeks.'

I was insulted. I felt like screaming, throwing things. After all I had been through! My self-pity pictured my father as a little tin-pot despot, exerting power over the weak and innocent. I thought of him as a man again and to his masculine ego added Miss Mottram. 'If he wasn't a bigamist, there'd be no problem!'

The room stood still. Charmian was horrified and Maureen hardly believing her luck. 'Your beautiful papa a bigamist?'

'She's joking,' said Charmian stiffly and rose to her feet. 'It's time I went.' At the door, coat and scarves recalled her Christian duty. She also remembered I was a disturbed person. 'I'll be back next Sunday.'

I stared after her, still angry. I felt our sisterhood a threat. She had the right to say things I didn't want to hear. 'No wonder you live in a foreign country,' I said bitterly to Maureen who was still basking in the drama.

'I'm going, I'm going.' Even she saw I was best left to work out my own rage.

Throughout that night I wrestled with the idea of turning back into a human being, of talking to people who talked to me in a rational way, of being given assignments, of drinking tea in an office, of using a typewriter, of being available. I did not even sleep enough to have nightmares. At about six, as the traffic was increasing once more in the street, I realised that I had become proud of myself as someone suffering and distinct. I did not want to give up this role. It saved me from the real horrors of what had happened, the squalid pointlessness of it all, the dreary physical downgrading of my body.

My heart pumped too fast and I became so hot that I threw off my duvet. This was at the centre of what I must accept, that my case was small and uninteresting. It had never been more than a few lines in the newspaper. Even to my own family, it would not be the most important thing for ever.

Then I did doze a little and immediately the two faces of Patrick William Downes, the blond avenger and the guilty hairless gaolbird, appeared in front of me. I awoke trembling and thought that *he* was the key to my future. I would always be important to him. He would never forget me. He would carry the guilt for as long as he lived. He was the other side of the see-saw. Once more unable to sleep, I picked up a book from my bedside. It dated from my childhood. In the morning I found I had copied out this verse:

> *One, two! One, two! And through and through*
> *The vorpal blade went snicker-snack!*
> *He left it dead, and with its head*
> *He went galumphing back.*

CHAPTER
TWENTY-ONE

As THE months passed Dr Renfrew made things tougher for me in the Muppet House. He said, during therapy so all the perverts heard, 'You're a father, isn't that correct? A father who won't even see his only child, *isn't that correct?*'

It was hard to remember we had once liked each other, Dr Renfrew and I. He resented the way I organised my fellow idiots, as if I knew I was better than them. He thought I was becoming arrogant instead of coming to terms with my weaknesses. He tried to bring me down in front of the others but it seldom worked because I was tougher than him. I'd survived prison as a prisoner for seven months. He just went in and out. That's a doddle. I despised him for thinking he could teach us anything.

When he started the father business, I shut my eyes and groaned. He was so exasperated he left the room. He quite often left the room in the middle of a session. I thought he was madder than us. He came back in a few minutes and, feeling I'd won my point, I said, 'I didn't choose to be a father. It happened.'

The others guffawed and felt in their trousers obscenely but I was immune to that sort of behaviour.

'You were married to her.' Dr Renfrew shut his eyes, showing this conversation was duty not pleasure.

'Only because she was pregnant. I was mixed up.'

'He was mixed up, the poor wee fellow,' Harry or Gerry or Carey mimicked me. I was a popular chap now. I had back a medium head of hair and I organised things for them. I was King of the Rule 43s. I suppose Dr Renfrew was right. I had become arrogant.

'Your son exists.' The doctor's voice hit a new low of weariness.

I should have been warned by his perseverance. The following day Larry came to visit me. He came regularly, once a fortnight, bringing a whiff of the world outside. I didn't give him such a hard time as I had at first. Now he was planning for the future, talking about parole and jobs. Nell was off the menu, of course, I told him that at the beginning. 'If you talk about her, I won't talk at all.'

But all along he had hopes, because that Tuesday he said at once, 'She's outside, boyo.'

'Who's outside?'

'You signed the order. You know who's outside. And Bruno too.'

I must have signed it in my sleep. I knew the baby was called Bruno because Nell wrote me letters and now and again I weakened enough to read one. Larry sat opposite looking guilty and hopeful. His hair was darker during the winter but his skin kept a good colour and I could tell by the taut breadth of his shoulders he was still working out. It was a wonder he bothered with me at all. 'How are the girl-friends?' I asked him.

'Your son is waiting outside.'

'Oh, bring fucking Bruno in!' I shouted. 'He's not worth all the bother.'

Larry began to have his doubts. He gave me a false smile. Perhaps it crossed his mind that a man who had stuck a knife in a girl might, equally well, dash his baby's brains to the floor. On the other hand he was determined to see me in a rosy light. The baby arrived. It was big and ugly and seemed to be giving Nell a hard time, waving its fists in her face. She looked pasty and swollen and terrified, not at all the girl I'd first met.

She sat down next to me and I patted the baby on its round skull. 'He looks healthy.'

'He's like you, everyone says.' She made this ridiculous pronouncement without looking at me but I could see her sad, speckled eyes filling with tears. At the other side of the table Larry frowned warningly. He needn't have worried. I had no intention of being cruel to her. I just didn't want her to be in my life. It continued to amaze me how no one could give me the credit for understanding my own needs. But once you're in prison, everyone thinks they know better.

'He's two months today,' whispered Nell.

'That's good.' I gave his dome another friendly tap. It reminded me of my own when the hair was just starting to grow back.

'Nell's living with her parents.' Larry tried a smile.

Nell opened her mouth, glanced at me and then closed it again. I guessed she was going to make the point that this was a temporary measure till I came out. Instead she said, 'He's very good at night. Mum says that's because he's such a size. It's surprising he is, considering he was premature.'

I could think of nothing to say to this. I was struck by an awareness that I had spent so little time with Nell and knew her much less than any of the perverts and drug abusers and child molesters I was locked up with. Perhaps this was why I could sit with her and not suffocate. She was becoming less important.

'That's right. Daddy's smiling at you.' I may have smiled so I let it pass. Nell's face perceptibly lifted and she began to hoist up her bag from the floor at her side. This was difficult with the baby on her lap and she gave me a longing sideways look. Larry turned away as if dissociating himself from her plea.

I took the baby on my lap. It was much more solid than I'd expected, a fat bundle of responsibility. No wonder Nell looked so exhausted. Its skin when seen close at hand was reddened in parts and scaly but its eyeballs were clear and glistening. It stared at me and then began to dribble. The milky spittle ran down sideways into its blue cardigan.

'He's happy with you.' Nell looked up from her bag. She took out a packet of photographs which she held in front of my face one by one. Burdened as I was, there was no way I could avoid seeing the hospital bed and the naked baby and the huge flaccid body of Nell.

'Mum took them. Since you couldn't be at the birth, she thought some photographs would make you feel more part of it.'

At this point Larry, more sensitive to my feelings than the lump I'd married, stood up and yelled, 'What we need is a cup of tea!' The abrupt noise made the baby cry, providing an excuse for the photo show to end and the baby to be returned to its doting mother.

As if recognising its time was up, it bleated pretty continuously from then, requiring constant loving attention. I tried to catch Larry's eye. Had I not done more than my duty? Did he not understand the torture?

When they had left, I sought out Dr Renfrew in his office, a privilege occasionally accorded the disturbed. 'Do you honestly feel it best if I return to my wife when I leave this place?'

As I have said, he was out of sympathy with me and avoided my eyes as he spoke. 'If a prisoner is to be released on parole, he must give evidence of a stable home.'

'Shit to that!'

He gave a weary sigh and half covered his face with his hands.

'I have a home. My parents left me a whole house.'

He did not bother to argue. His expression told me his opinion of that piece of bravado. Probably, he didn't own a house himself. I was not surprised when he told me he was busy.

I went back to my cell and, ordering my cell-mate to fuck off, began to pace up and down. I told myself I harboured no sentimental feelings for the baby. A baby was about as remote from my life as a space alien. My sense that others would consider this an inhuman attitude increased my irritation. The baby was big and strong, I told myself, capable of looking after itself. If it needed anything, it needed a mother and it had that. Fucking lucky Bruno.

I had forgotten my feelings of relief in escaping from the main prison into the Muppet House. The additional freedom had made me restless. Sleep, my previous solace, came in short bursts and then often disrupted by complicated dreams. I no longer shrugged off the implications of being among mainly Rule 43 prisoners. When we were led out for our exercise and received the usual abuse from any prisoner who happened to be out on the corridors, I became angry instead of keeping my head down.

'No-hope bastards!' I yelled, or 'Iron-headed pot-holes!' Pathetically, I tried to signify I knew something they did not. They were jealous of our special privileges, I did know that.

One day I got into a fight. It was with my old cell-mate, Charles, who had not achieved a self-croak after all. He was sweeping down a corridor, an unlikely sort of trusty. I passed one corridor below and out towards the exercise yard. His voice came from above stopping my line, who enjoyed abuse as long as it was not directed at them. 'Piss-pots piss into the same pot, buggers bugger into the same hole, finger artists squeeze the same tube . . .' It went on like that, sexual filth directed at me as I waited in line, trapped and vulnerable.

I got up to him quite easily. A Rule 43 prisoner in the Muppet House is not expected to break ranks, race up a flight of iron stairs and jump on a fellow prisoner. Rule 43s are the victims, not the aggressors. I don't know why he was still there when I reached him, probably just enjoying the drama. He had a broom and I only had bare hands.

I came round in the isolation cell. I didn't feel too bad, although the floor had given me a crick in my neck and various parts of my body were sore. Charles must have really laid into me with that broom. On the whole I experienced a sense of relief which made me feel more relaxed than I had for several weeks.

The bad news came later. At five o'clock a screw fetching me in a last meal and a blanket smirked, 'Worth it, was it?' I would have answered, 'Yes' but he wasn't interested. 'So, you've earned yourself a change of scene.'

I thought he meant solitary. The next morning, at 6.30 a.m., I discovered the truth. 'Bad boys have bad times.' The screw who collected me and took me back to one of the main prison wings was even more cheerful. He knew the likely treatment for a con who was perceived as Rule 43. There's no point in pretending I was not frightened. I was terrified. But I was no longer intent on avoiding trouble as I had been for my early months. Now I knew the game. My fight with Charles hadn't been long enough. I was not going to put up with the verbal harassment and psychological warfare I'd seen directed towards other men suspected of being secret Rule 43.

'On fucking Dr Renfrew's orders, guv?'

'Fucking Dr Renfrew,' jeered the screw. 'They'll send along your stuff.'

'Who am I in with?' That mattered.

'Two lifers who don't like no trouble.' His breath, so early in the morning, still smelt of beer from the night before. He was not a pretty sight but then neither was I.

'Don't I get to see a doctor?'

'What? Something wrong with you?' He stopped and surveyed me with mock concern.

'Nothing, guv.'

'You want to take a piss?' That was gracious of him, although the pleasure was diminished by a sharp pain somewhere in my stomach area.

The two lifers were sullen but not aggressive when I came

in. They indicated my bunk without speaking. Perhaps it was too early for them or perhaps the prison grapevine was operating a bit more slowly than usual. I waited tensely for the call to collect breakfast. My head banged like a hammer and my hands shook when I stretched them out.

They unlocked our door but I still didn't have my plate or cutlery. 'Get on out.' The screw was fed up with excuses. So I went down this new corridor, as wary as a beast in the jungle, and joined the queue. Immediately the men moved away on either side of me. So they knew.

'You're wrong,' I said. 'I'm not on the Rule.' But they knew what I knew and, besides, I was different, educated – and the breakfast was shit.

The space was the best of it. When I reached the top of the queue, the man in front turned sharp close to me and shoved his plate hard into my midriff. Winded, I ducked over, giving the man behind me the chance to deliver a few good kicks to my shins.

The screw looked away. No help there and I couldn't take on the whole queue. That would be seen as provoking a fight. Without attempting to get any food, I turned back for my cell. I couldn't have eaten anyway.

A few hours later, the landing screw arrived. 'Aren't you going to make a fucking complaint?'

I lifted my head off the bed, 'What about?'

'What about? You ask me?'

'No complaint.'

'Don't say I didn't ask.'

'You asked. I said "No".' He went then and I shut my eyes again.

The lifers were smoking dope. They had no interest in me. The dope filled the room with a heavy sweetness which I soon felt in my own lungs. At exercise time, I couldn't move. The screw gave me a shove, not unkindly, and then commented, 'One day, you'll float right off your heads.' I felt too ill to explain I wasn't smoking. The other two went off and left me.

The pain in my stomach was now worse than the pain in my head. When they came back I was groaning. It annoyed them since they were trying to concentrate on a game of cards, played for cigarettes. 'Stuff that noise, can't you?' They were not unfriendly either.

The day passed very slowly. The lifers went in and out. One of them seemed to be doing some course, I could hear them chatting about it. He was improving himself, he told his mate whom he seemed to be encouraging to join him. 'You've got to improve yourself,' he repeated over and over again, 'or you go the other way.'

I thought, dazedly, that I was 'going the other way' pretty fast now. By evening I was unconscious.

It turned out that my spleen had been ruptured by the broom handle with a bit of help from the plate. They told me that in hospital. Not about the broom or the plate. They also told me I'd never get my parole now and I would probably lose some remission too. If you're in for grievous bodily harm, getting involved in fights isn't a good idea. I didn't care. I was happy in the hospital. They were generous with pain-killers and repairing a ruptured spleen isn't a very big deal these days. Meanwhile I was out of the system, out of all systems, as a matter of fact.

It was too good to last. Larry came in to visit me one day when I could no longer even pretend I was suffering. 'You're going up north, I hear.'

'I applied to go to Grendon,' I said. 'What's happened about that?'

'I expect they don't think you're a fit subject for psychiatric treatment.' He looked at me coldly. No one liked me much at the moment. Larry and Ruth and Nell had always worked on the theory that my attack on the girl had been a ghastly aberration, an out-of-character isolated incident. When I got into trouble in prison, this theory tottered. They didn't take into account the growing up I was doing inside gaol. They clung on tenaciously to the immature boy I had been, an English graduate, sweet, clever, wound up so tight I had to burst.

'I was getting on well in the Muppet House.'

'That's not what the doctor said.'

'He doesn't like me.'

'He said you were disruptive, a bad influence. The others followed you because you were cleverer.'

'Thanks.'

'That wasn't a compliment.' We stared at each other with dislike. Finally, Larry stood up. He had an Australian sort of temper, quiet till aroused. 'You're a rotten sort of sod, aren't you?'

I didn't need him ticking me off, fucking Aussie cousin. I thought I'd try smoking dope. Those lifers had been remarkably easy-going.

CHAPTER

TWENTY-TWO

I WAS not very popular on my local newspaper. My extreme thinness, my nervousness, my physical deformities – they were not really as bad as that but felt like it to me – were off-putting. Originally, I'd seen my stay there as no more than a small stepping stone to a real newspaper. A couple of months, I'd thought, a summer job. But now summer had long passed and I was a different person, constrained, ugly and morbidly sensitive. No wonder I was not very popular.

The office was small, one floor of a modern building divided into squares for the editor and managing editor, leaving one larger room for us reporters and another for the two secretaries. It managed to be both cold and stuffy and the main light source was a broad neon strip running down the middle of the ceiling. At the end of the first day I felt so ill that the editor, Mr Harvey, a sad-looking man, became worried. 'Perhaps you should start by working part time?'

'Just send me out on a job. I'll be all right then.'

My first assignment was to report on an old people's home which was threatened with closure after cockroaches were found in the food stores. The matron met me, heavily on the defensive. She was too old, too fat, too stupid, I could see that at once. Life had given me a lot of experience with matrons. 'I'll show you the kitchens whenever you want,' she wheezed. 'No one's ashamed of the kitchens. The inspector had a grudge, that's what we all think.' She had frizzy grey hair and little watery blue eyes which looked at me pleadingly.

'A grudge?' I probed, getting out my notebook.

At that she took fright and I learnt my first lesson in journalism, don't ask the interesting question first. So we went round the home and half-way round I learnt my second lesson, the reporter is representation of her paper, not another human being. Miss Broadley's watery little eyes looked at me without seeing me, Lydia Kremachowski. That was when I knew I could be a journalist.

'It's very nice, your home,' I told Miss Broadley for I had the power of Solomon and was impressed by the smiling, comfortable old ladies. 'I've never understood why people make such a fuss about cockroaches.'

She looked at me doubtfully. Was I trying to trick her into admitting the state of her flour bins?

'Don't worry,' I laid my hand on her arm, 'I'm on your side. I think the inspector had a grudge.' I had my story, 'Old People's Home in Danger: Unfair Accusation'. I took quotes from the comfortable old ladies and a photograph of a pretty one who still had her teeth in. I enjoyed an aura of Joan of Arc.

I was lucky. My piece was printed and started a bit of a campaign to save the home. I wrote other pieces and saw a paragraph quoted in a national newspaper. My analyst and my feminist friend were impressed. Even my mother was pleased for me and Charmian commented, 'It's nice to see you're planning to do good in the world, even if that old people's home doesn't sound as if it's worth saving.'

Quite consciously, I decided to try to follow up stories where there seemed to be an injustice. Soon my arrival was greeted in the office by, 'Here's one for you, Lydia. A boy squatter just rang to say he's burned all over from a banger shoved through the letter-box.'

I went off to meet these people with an interest that for a

year I'd reserved for myself. I was not undiscerning, priding myself on distinguishing the fraud from the truly put-upon. My physical stamina, so low when I started, increased steadily.

Gradually, visits to the office became less of a strain. There were four other journalists, besides myself and the editor, and of them, I was only interested in two. Both young, like me, Herbie and Sue, hoped to use the paper as a springboard for more exciting things.

Sue was exceptionally pretty, with perfect skin, neat features, very long chestnut hair and a stunning figure. She could have been a model but she wanted to be a journalist. She told me that between the ages of fifteen and twenty-one she'd had so many men in love with her that she'd simply become bored with the whole idea. Her last boy-friend had been a journalist who retaliated when kicked out of her bed with the bitter imprecation, 'You're just a body, a glossy, terrific, meaningless fuck!'

Three years later she had reached our little newspaper. Her ambition was to be a personal columnist on the *Daily Express* and tell people 'the way things really are for a girl'. I admired Sue when I stopped being frightened of her good looks.

Herbie was tall and ungainly, with too-long legs and neck. He had very black eyes and dark straight hair which made him look Italian or French. He was twenty-seven but he looked younger and spoke jerkily as if he were struggling for words. I thought he lacked confidence which, as I discovered later, was not altogether true.

Sue and Herbie liked each other and worked well together so it was a relief when they began to like me a little. I'd been working there two months and the winter weather had just started to soften at the edges when Herbie took me out for coffee. It was the first time I hadn't gone straight home from work.

'I've guessed why you want to be a journalist,' he said. 'Hiding your own story by telling others.' He said I tried to camouflage myself by wearing clothes which were more my mother's generation than my own. 'You don't want to draw attention to yourself,' he said, 'but the effect is exactly the opposite.'

'So why do you want to be a journalist?' I was only a little offended.

'People. Anyone. I keep files on people I've met. I've done it for years. I've boxes and boxes. Physical characteristics, mental attitudes, religious views, politics, sex, love.'

'Have you done me already?'

'You're difficult.' I felt pleased by this and subdued a smile.

'Let it come,' said Herbie. 'You hardly ever smile.'

'You don't smile much either.' Nevertheless, his was a benign presence in my life. Although he was a grown male, he did not feel like a man to me, not as my father did, or Patrick William Downes who still came to me in my dreams. If Herbie touched my arm, I hardly withdrew.

After another couple of months, I even took him back to my flat. It was a warm late-April day and I had the windows open and daffodils on the table. I had hardly found the cork-screw to open the wine Herbie had bought before Maureen came tapping at the door.

'I thought you were celebrating,' she announced with satis-faction. We were not celebrating. 'Hi. I'm Maureen. You must be Herbie?' As far as I knew I had not mentioned Herbie's existence to her. I was beginning to appreciate her loneliness.

'Get out three glasses,' I said cheerfully. Not so long ago she was the only person I could talk to.

Now she settled down to find out everything about Herbie. But after a while the tables had turned and she was telling him about a clever little rich girl who felt out of place with her bridge-playing, martini-drinking mother. While they talked, I sipped at my glass of wine and felt a breeze from the window lift my hair. I was letting it grow as long as it would. I pictured the scar under it but, without as much loathing as usual.

'You are lucky,' Maureen commented the moment Herbie had left.

'What do you mean?' I knew exactly what she meant.

'He's so sympathetic.'

'Don't start imagining. You know my feelings about the masculine. Herbie's not like that.'

Maureen began to smile and then changed her mind. I should have been warned. The next time Herbie dropped in – we were covering a story together and needed a lunchtime sandwich – Maureen was upon him at once. Above her usual skin-tight jeans she was wearing a T-shirt which stopped round her midriff. She posed all over my flat in a way I thought utterly ridiculous.

On the way out I turned to Herbie. 'Sorry about Maureen.'

He looked surprised. 'What's wrong with Maureen?'

Feeling foolish, I changed the subject quickly. I was now seeing Lesley just once a fortnight, although she assured me I was free to call any time I felt desperate. But as the only time I felt really desperate now was in the night, I spared her that. Lesley was very pleased with me.

However, I was keen to hide Herbie's existence from her, knowing that, like Maureen, she would draw the wrong conclusion. But one evening, at the end of my session when I was gathering my papers together – sometimes she allowed me to talk about my work – I just came out with it. 'Herbie says I dress so badly because I'm trying to look as unattractive as my mother.'

'Herbie?' She pulled her grey curl towards her spectacles with an intensity which belied her fake casual voice.

Since it was the end of my session I was able to get up and leave without expansion. Walking to the bus stop afterwards, I was struck by the importance that sex or, at least, a relationship with the opposite sex, seemed to play in everyone's thinking about me. It was particularly odd, I told myself almost with a feeling of complacency, because it was not at all important to me. I hadn't been very interested before the advent of Patrick William Downes and now I was totally turned off. However, that did not impair my functioning as a human being. Just look how well I was getting on with my job!

In this unusually self-congratulatory mood, I pushed my poor thin legs to run for a bus, which they did, and caught it.

A few days later, I left the office at about nine o'clock with Herbie. 'Let's have a drink,' he suggested. We walked in companionable silence. It was just dark, the pavements still busy and I had a cheerful sense of being one of a mass of young people. I had stayed late to finish a piece about illegal abortions on fifteen-year-olds which would run this week. I felt pretty good.

We walked for about ten minutes, not anywhere in particular, I thought. Then Herbie said, 'Want to come in?' We had arrived at his flat. I knew he shared it with a changing cast of four or five but I had never been there before, nor realised it was so close to the office. It surprised me, although I went up quickly and curiously.

'I don't believe it.' Herbie surveyed the big untidy room. 'There's no one else here.'

'I've scared them away,' I joked.

'It's a miracle.' Herbie disappeared and I settled into one of the many faded armchairs. The only other furniture was a low table and two large cushions fast losing their stuffing.

'It's a mess.' Herbie returned with two cans of lager. 'We're all men at the moment and we're all working.'

I laughed. 'Unacceptable implications there. Why should women clear up?'

'Don't pretend to be Maureen.'

So I didn't. But there had been something about the way he said Maureen's name.

We sat together, drinking our lager, chatting a little, tired. Then Herbie came over to me. I thought he was going past to switch on the television, but instead he stopped and sat on the arm of my chair. He put his hand onto my shoulder and then ran it along the back of my neck and under my hair.

It was frightful. Only by an enormous effort of will did I stop myself screaming. My body became so rigid that it hurt and his finger-tips as they touched my scars seemed to be red hot.

'Please. Don't.' I eventually managed to whisper. Then I began to shake.

Poor Herbie. He was the other side of the room in a flash. 'Sorry. I didn't know you were that bad.'

'I am.' The words came out through chattering teeth.

'That's terrible.'

144

I tried to remember why it was not terrible, not even important, but my frozen brain couldn't argue against the absolute conviction in his voice.

Herbie sat down and was silent for a while, letting me recover, I suppose. But after a bit he couldn't resist starting again. 'Doesn't your analyst help?' Since I didn't answer, he continued, 'I mean, I know what you went through but that was nearly a year ago.'

'Herbie, I . . .' What was I to say? That I didn't think he was that sort of man? It seemed ludicrous now. He liked people, he liked women. Being thin and ungainly and comfortable to be with made no difference at all. I had been fooling myself. He was normal. I was not.

'Don't cry.' Herbie stood up and then sat down nervously. How do you comfort someone you can't touch? I could see him thinking.

Then he made things worse. 'I thought Maureen was exaggerating.'

I thought about this and then felt, given the shivering idiotic wreck I was, that it might be as well to know the worst. 'You screwed her, did you?'

Herbie seemed taken aback. 'Maureen?' There was another pause. 'Look, I told you how I feel about people. I like all kinds. I like having sex. It doesn't mean so much to me. I hope it will one day. But it doesn't at the moment.'

'I suppose you screw Sue too?'

'Oh, yes, twice a day in the ladies' toilet!' Herbie felt he had taken enough. He came and stood in front of me looking very red and angry. I cowered, although not altogether honestly. I felt better now he was being emotional too. 'You're determined to be tragic, aren't you? I know what happened to you. We all know that. It's in the air around you. You won't let anyone forget, least of all yourself.'

'You're unfair,' I said, but too quietly to pierce his sound and fury. He was unfair because he didn't know the effort it had taken to step into the office the first day. No one, I thought, crying again from self-pity, could possibly understand. It wasn't in Herbie's nature to shout for long, so he stopped quite soon and sat on the floor. 'Anyway,' he said, looking at his shoes, 'everybody has dark secrets. One day I'll tell you what happened to me as a child.'

This competitive problem-mongering seemed to strike him as funny for he suddenly began to smile. 'What the hell! I just wanted to touch you a little, stroke you a little. You looked pretty in that big ugly armchair. It's not worth all this.'

'No. I'm sorry.' My voice was as stiff as a rod but inside I was quivering.

'I'll tell you what, I'll walk you home. Will you scream if I pull you up?'

I held out my hand and let him give me an energetic tug. I couldn't go on apologising.

So we walked back together. It was cold and dark and not very nice but walking was a good idea. By the time we got back to my flat I was so tired I couldn't think at all. We parted almost silently but not on unfriendly terms. Just before I fell asleep that night I realised that someone had wanted to touch me lovingly, deformities and all.

In the weeks that followed Herbie made no reference to our evening in his flat and showed his usual interest in my work. The difference in his behaviour was that he kept a good space between myself and him. It was quite conscious, I'm sure, a tease to remind me of my desire to set myself apart.

Meanwhile summer was coming along, growing out of a warm spring into a windy wildness which was most unlike last year. I dreaded the anniversary of the attack in a way which Lesley explained was quite to be expected and Maureen designated 'a neurotic display of wish fulfilment'. It was she who told me my real problems were masochistic but we hadn't got on so well since I'd indicated I knew about and had been upset by her fling with Herbie.

I hated the summer exposure of skin. The scars round my neck and shoulders were still red and puckered while my left leg was discernibly thinner than the right. I mourned my strong pure body as it had been at the Turkish baths on that hot summer evening. Patrick William Downes, whose presence in my life had been squeezed out by my reporting activities, by the poor old ladies, misunderstood squatters and unfairly discriminated against women, now returned at full strength. I woke often at night, crying out or in tears.

My family were particularly sympathetic at this time. I often went home on Sundays and allowed my mother to pamper me. She had forgiven me for knowing about Miss Mottram and even made ironic reference to the situation. 'Your father is out exercising his animal nature,' she would say. 'Men are so ridiculous.'

Charmian was gentle and admiring of my new career. We shopped together because I didn't mind her seeing my body and she nobly restrained herself from mentioning God more than was bearable. I rewarded her one evening by going to mass with her. She seemed to be the only person there who did any praying, rather than reciting or singing. I found that touching but when I commented she looked embarrassed. 'I expect they're holier than me.'

'Are God and the Church the most important things in your life?' I asked her.

'Yes,' she answered simply.

'Then why don't you become a nun?'

'I haven't had the call.' She was serious and had to be taken seriously. 'And, anyway, I'm frightened.' She looked at me and I looked at her and I thought what a lot of frightened women there were in our family.

My fourth month at work was celebrated by a mysterious meeting called by the editor for all the staff. He was normally a nervous, short-sentence man but on that morning he wove phrases in what seemed to be a prepared speech. 'The paper is losing money which is not good but not irreversible either for, contrary to expectations, our circulation has increased which shows a marketing potential, despite an economic deficiency.' It was not clear to any of us what he was driving at.

'The question that is being asked – ' continued Mr Harvey, anxiety visibly rising, 'asked by our owner – is whether we are property targeted, whether we are, to put it baldly, the right kind of paper. That being so, I thought it right to call you in for a meeting and let you know there might be changes.'

So that was it. Changes. Sue commented bracingly that the only change which interested her was when she moved off to a better newspaper. But I was unsettled. 'What does it mean?' I worried at Herbie. Eventually, I trapped him in a wine bar – sitting at the usual distance, of course. 'Please, Herbie. I won't pass it on.'

'Some Australian wants to buy the paper and make it free. You know, rely on ads to bring in the money.'

'But they'd still have reports, stories?'

'I guess so. He's young, I've heard. Nil experience in newspapers. Perhaps he'll need us more than we need him.'

CHAPTER
TWENTY-THREE

It was May when they took me up north, along the M1 in a van. There was only one other con in there, an old man who snuffled and snored like pug dog. In the end I gave him a belt and then he was quiet. Unfortunately, my poetic sense was not stirred by the spring green country on either side of the motorway, so I settled down with a newspaper instead. It was a rotten newspaper because I'd got it off a screw but at least it passed the time.

I'd more or less existed day by day, no past, no future, but in the week I'd waited to be transferred, time had become a little too prominent. All cons get that way, they say, seeing time as a worse enemy than the parole board, or at least in league one with the other. And now I'd joined the club.

Remembering that the old pug man had volunteered that he came from Coventry and had been in and out of prison most of his life, I gave him a shove. 'What's laid on for us in Stafford, you old fucker?' If my treatment of an old man, who had done me no harm, shocks or surprises, then see it as an indication of how I had changed during my months under Her Majesty's Prison Service.

His watery old eyes rolled. 'What d'ya mean?'

It had been a stupid question. He had obviously done nothing, inside or out, except a little light burglary, for years. I was tempted to belt him again but desisted. If it was seen by the chaps in front, it would do me no good. As well as a more proper appreciation of time, I was also starting to see the causal effect of my actions. It was May. Before my fight I could have been paroled to come out at the end of July. Sitting in that stuffy van, I faced the realisation that I would at some point come out of prison. It was a devastating idea. Up till that moment I had despised the cons' obsession with the time of their release. Some of them literally thought of nothing else, planning over and over again what they would do, how many million fucks, what food, what smokes, what glories of sensual fulfilment liberty would bring them.

Liberty to me had meant Nell and a terrible fear of what I had done. I had no sensual delights to look forward to. Liberty was unimaginable and best left that way. So it had been for all those months, by the time I found myself sitting in that van. And, very gradually, something had changed. It was a hardening, as I see it now, a dulling of my sensitivities. It certainly was not any better understanding of myself or the causes of my crime. I was not repentant. I had not matured. I was just tougher, more capable of taking on the world.

I kicked my travelling companion, not out of malice but merely as the means of communication he understood best. 'Give me a smoke, you sodding shit.'

He did, quickly. It was in this positive spirit of adventure that I arrived at my new home.

The first morning, having shaped up my cell-mate with a bit of tough talking, I banged long enough on my door to make even the most dilatory screw take a bit of notice. 'Are you having a fucking heart attack or something?'

'I want to put my fucking name down for all the fucking educational courses this fucking establishment lays claim to.'

'What the fuck's that to do with me?'

149

'Because you're my fucking friend. And you're going to sort out those forms so I don't wait fucking months.'

He wasn't a bad screw, that particular one. He did all I asked him and even got me taken to the library that very first day. I'd hardly read at all since I'd been inside, which was perverse (but then I had been perverse) because I'd had access to an excellent library with a proper librarian and things coming in from outside. My cell-mate who had dread-locks to his waist and a fearsome squint, saw me reappear with a pile of books and emitted inhuman squawks of dis-tress. I suppose it was as threatening to him as it would have been for me if he'd come in with a caseful of knives.

'Relax,' I told him, kindly. 'This is for my side of the room. You can carry on with tits and arse.' These delectable portions of the female anatomy were pinned up over every inch of wall above his bed. Interestingly, they were almost all of the white-skinned variety. I assumed this a bit of wishful thinking till I saw his girl-friends at visiting times. All white, all pretty, all apparently devoted. Sometimes they even came in pairs. It was several weeks before I discovered he was in for pimping.

It was strange having something to do in the day. Not that my classes were often, three times a week in the afternoon, but I managed to join a gym class too and now I was no longer tarred with the Rule 43 brush, I could go out for exercise without worrying and linger around the corridors at slop-out time and volunteer a bit of help if it were wanted. I had decided to make the system work for me.

Three or four weeks of this new me and I was called into the deputy governor's office. No one likes these sort of meetings. The screw who escorts the con is disapproving of the very existence of a deputy governor. He takes it slowly in an effort to miss the appointment and, if he can't escape, looks at his watch meaningfully throughout the interview. The con assumes that any contact with authority is bad news, although an unadmitted fantasy that he is about to be released, pardoned or cleared of his crimes makes him at heart a weakling. The deputy governor often looks uncomfortable too – at least, the good sort with a touch of better feeling do. The bad sort just enjoy throwing their weight about.

My man was the good sort. He told me at once to sit down, a hopeful indication, and even got my names right. He was younger than usual, wearing a red V-necked pullover with a shiny well-washed face and expression to match. 'You were at university,' he said in a mixture of accusation and commendation.

'Yes, sir.'

'What was your subject?'

'English, sir.'

'That's what I heard. How would you feel about starting a paper here?'

This needed more than 'Yes, sir'. 'I'm not a journalist, sir. Not even a writer. What sort of paper, sir?'

'Prison news. Anything you like. To be frank, it's mostly to give our printing workers something to print.'

Of course he didn't expect me to say no. 'I might get parole.'

'So we hope.' He looked a little bit edgy. Perhaps it was the smell of lunch beginning to seep under the door. 'You'd have time to get it under way. One issue.'

'Yes, sir.' He was disappointed in me, I could see, but I could not quickly slip into the role of poacher turned game-keeper. It wasn't the fantasy release but something much more complicated he was offering me. It called on me to work towards my future. I went back to the cell as anxious as any screw could wish.

Since it was five thirty I had, in theory, missed my last meal, so I had nothing more to look forward to than a long evening with my private pimp. Lately he had taken to enter-taining me with stories about his business life; these shocked me at first but soon had a dulling effect on my brain. They were exceedingly repetitious and usually ended up as a kind of refrain, 'And then I cut her up.' Sometimes he expanded. 'Not badly, see, but to show her who's boss. They like to know that, tarts, it makes them feel safe, see. So I cut her up, not badly. The sodding blue swine had no reason to pick me up. It was a misunderstanding, see. She visited me

151

regular from the first day I was in. But you can't tell these fuckers anything.'

He was misunderstood, perhaps, but so boring that on the spur of the moment and with a view to shutting him up I said, 'I'll print it if you like, in my paper I'm editing.' He was immediately suspicious and did shut up but it made me think. Why not? All I needed was a tape recorder and a good strong editing pencil. Case histories from the inside, that's what it would be.

So the next morning I banged on my door and the not unfriendly landing screw came along in no hurry and said, 'Mr Editor, is it now? Don't come asking things from us. You'll have to fill in all the forms in the fucking world from this day on.'

'Pardon, guv,' I replied, making fun but warily because I wanted him on my side. 'I might turn the spotlight on you lot, too, you know.' This struck him as even less appealing but he got the tape recorder for me. Or, rather, got the endless permissions through. Larry brought the actual machine. I wrote to him and asked. It was a slice of humble pie after our disagreeable parting.

'This is triffic, Pat, triffic news. A triffic preparation for the big world!'

The visiting room was pretty oppressive, a huge barn of a place which even in summer had the chill of death. At intervals a fan set high up above the dais where the screws preside roared and bellowed but I never felt any hot air. Larry was undaunted, his permanently bronzed face gleaming, his hair snappily sun-bleached. The contrast between us cousins must have looked quite something.

To restore the balance a little, I started joking around with my cell-mate, the dreadlocked pimp, who happened to be at the next-door table. He had three visitors today, all with outstanding physical attributes. One had beautiful yellow dreadlocks to her waist and was entirely clad in black leather and chains. 'I hope you've got a padlock for this one and then you can give me the key.'

Larry let me go on in this vein for a while and then grabbed my arm. He was and is a strong man. 'You haven't changed that much, Pat.' Patronising bastard was what I thought. How did he know how much I'd changed? How did anyone in the world, except me, know or care? However, I came to heel all right, because I wanted my tape recorder.

'Strange coincidence you going into journalism, Pat.'

'Hardly that. What's the coincidence?'

'I own a newspaper now. Just a local rag, losing money like there was no tomorrow, but I plan to turn it into a free paper, get the money side sorted out and then move on from there.'

'All advertisements, you mean?'

'I'm not buying a newspaper to avoid the news.'

I waited for him to talk about me. It's impossible not to be self-centred when you've been in prison for a year. 'So what's in it for me?'

'Journalism. Always a possibility.' Larry patted the tape recorder. But I could see his attention was wandering. At the table behind me, a couple were having a fierce row in whispers while their two small children littered the floor with potato crisps. The man was getting angrier by the minute, the woman more beseeching and tearful. It looked almost certain to end with a spot of violence. Everybody whose own conversation had reached a desultory stage was turned into a voyeur.

Larry said, 'Why don't they stop him?'

'He hasn't done anything.'

'Not yet.'

'They'll stop him then.'

But the woman, really she was just a girl, hardly more than eighteen and pathetically thin, suddenly grabbed her children, push-chair and all, and shot off across the room towards the exit. The man stood up, took two or three furious paces and then returned to the table and put his head in his hands.

'You see. He's in prison,' I said. The voyeurs turned away in sympathy. After all, it had been the woman who had the upper hand all along because she could run away.

'So what are you going to put in your paper?' Larry asked me.

'I might ask that man', I indicated the head in hands, 'why they were arguing.'

'He won't tell you.'

'Oh, fuck off.'

It sometimes seemed impossible to speak to someone from the outside. Larry went off and bought us both cups of tea. He wanted to get the hell out – for which I couldn't blame him. We drank our tea in silence – if you call silence being surrounded by thirty or forty visiting couples or groups. Then Larry reached into his close-fitting back jeans pocket and produced an envelope. 'It's photos of your son,' he explained.

'I saw a photo.'

'He was a baby then.'

'He can't be much different now.'

Larry smiled. 'Do me a favour and just take a quick peek.'

I did him a favour and Bruno, the bear, had got bigger, I could see that, even though he was covered all over in stretch towelling.

'He looks a real bruiser,' encouraged Larry.

I debated whether to give him my lecture about how Nell was nothing to do with my life now, but he was beginning to look restive and I didn't want to drive him away. Handing him back the photos gave him enough of a clue. He had probably imagined I'd stick them up on my wall – facing my friendly pimp's tits and arse.

'Any more help I can give you, apart from the machine?'

'I'm just waiting for another chance to get before the parole board.'

Larry looked surprised, so I enlarged. 'It could be before Christmas.'

'Oh, yeah. Yeah.' Perhaps he was beginning to like prison visits. At any rate, he suddenly seemed less than thrilled at the prospect of my release.

'Isn't that why you were telling me about this paper you're buying? Planning to give me a job?'

'Yeah. Nothing's fixed.'

Nothing's fixed. I wanted to burst into tears. Blub like a big baby. Did nobody understand? 'I've got to go.' And now he had to go. I stood up so that I could make the break. It's better that way.

'Don't forget the machine.'

'I won't. Thanks.' I took the recorder to the screw and then started the long walk back to the cells. It was summer, I reminded myself. Larry would drive down the M1 in whatever flash car he was sporting, I should have asked him that. Why hadn't I asked him about his car? He might even have a girl waiting outside in jeans as tight as his. The evening would be light for hours. They might stop at a riverside pub and sit under a weeping willow with glasses of beer and wine. I pictured it like a commercial with no real dialogue because I had no idea what they would say to each other. At some point, I supposed, they would find a bed somewhere and then they would make passionate but easy love. It was near enough the longest day so perhaps there would be a sinking sunset coming through the window and illuminating their limbs in a rosy glow. With these fantasies, I lay on my bunk and waited for the call for supper.

I called my prison newspaper *Insiders*. It was a mucky little thing because no one with any talent contributed. Half of them couldn't construct a sentence at all without using 'fucking'. That was my only creative act as editor. I banned 'fuck', 'fucking' and all other derivatives. It gave the 'True Confession' section a weirdly unconvincing feel but I didn't care. I wanted to be able to show my little runt to the outside world. It was going to be my passport to the world of journalism, I told myself. No need of whiz-kid cousin Larry at all. I began to make big plans for myself and used all my letter allowance by writing off to local newspapers in Newcastle, Coventry, Oxford, and about six or more other towns. I did not receive one reply.

So then I started on smaller publications and finally I received a proper letter from the editor of a Dorset magazine based in Dorchester, who said I could call on him when I was out. Now I had something, entirely unrelated to my past, on which to build my future hopes. Now I could picture myself in a little room in the old part of a pretty little town, watching the seagulls flying over the roof tops while I composed a clever little piece on Thomas Hardy. I might even wander out to the neolithic earthworks of Maiden Castle, which I knew was nearby, and gaze confidently round me, king of all I could see.

These dreams floated in a vacuum, far from Nell and Bruno, from the ownership of my parents' house, from Larry and his newspaper. I was planning a delightfully uncluttered rebirth for myself.

About this time, I made my only friend inside. He was an accountant, serving a year for fraud. He was very shocked when he discovered I wouldn't do much more for nearly murdering a girl. I didn't tell him that – it was not a bit of news I bandied about, no True Confession for me. But you can't keep much secret in gaol.

He appeared just as I was becoming overwhelmed by the newspaper and sorted things out. He was clear-minded and since he'd been out on bail he had not yet fallen prey to prison lassitude. Unlike most others, he actually finished every word he spoke and even every sentence.

'Why did you do it, Jock?' I asked him, inevitably. It seemed so peculiar that a man like him should risk losing everything.

'Greed,' he said smiling. He could even give proper smiles. 'A good old deadly sin.'

'Did you need the money so much?' It had been seventy thousand pounds, not enough to change his life. 'You must have been earning pretty well.'

'I was tempted and I fell. It looked so easy. I never thought anyone would miss it. It was a company that dealt in millions. In fact it wasn't missed. But I'd underestimated the difficulty of hiding it from the tax man. I normally made forty thousand a year.'

Forty thousand seemed such a fortune to me that I understood him less and less. Our friendship was not based on any particular sympathy for each other – I have no doubt he considered me out of my mind – but on a shared ability to read and write and think logically. He joined my English classes and wrote an essay, I remember, entitled 'The Morality of Thieving' which argued that society needs thieves to

156

take up the slack money, inefficiently accounted for. It ended, 'The thief is the watchdog of our society.'

One afternoon when we'd been allowed out of our cells to put together the newspaper he said to me from under his very thick black eyebrows, 'Of course, mine was a victimless crime.' I understood he was probing me but said nothing.

'When I get out,' he continued, 'I'm a villain to nobody, unless you count a nationalised industry and the Inland Revenue, which everyone hates anyway. But you've got someone out there who hates you. Weird.'

I felt myself turning very hot and red. I saw, too, that my hands, sorting the pages of the newspaper into piles, were beginning to shake. Two different instincts battled. One to burst into tears and crawl under the table, the other to pick up the stapler from the table and smash his enquiring face with it. Since the former would have involved a too-great loss of self-respect, I did the latter.

CHAPTER

TWENTY-FOUR

THE AUSTRALIAN was called Lawrence Purley. He pinpointed the office one hot August morning and we were all introduced. Larry, as he told us to call him, had that year-round tan, hard-body look, as if he'd be more comfortable out of his clothes than in. He stood in our editor's grubby little room like a man from outer space. Dust, highlighted by the sun, danced like particles of energy round his head.

'I want you all to be involved in this!' he exhorted. But I don't think he saw any of us, particularly me who stood at the back behind lanky Herbie. It was the sort of occasion that still made me nervous. 'I may own the newspaper but I don't own you, by which I mean to say that you're the people truly in control. Without you, the paper doesn't exist.' It was stirring stuff which none of us quite trusted. He did become a little more specific with the news that we were moving to different 'better value' printers but that was swallowed up by bottles of champagne popped open in celebration.

He had already noticed Sue's charms and insisted on pouring her champagne himself and touching their glasses together.

When he left, I teased her, 'At least your job looks safe.'

She turned on me angrily. 'Don't be so childish. Flirting with a girl is one thing, giving her a job quite another.'

Since the Herbie incident, my own feminine qualities, previously growing a little, had gone into reverse. I was thinner again, limped more ostentatiously and tended to wear baggy cotton trousers which made me look like a scarecrow. I favoured black hooded T-shirts because I was still self-conscious about my scars and the hood dropped in a cowl round my neck.

Lesley commented, 'If you're not careful you'll find yourself with dieting obsessions and then we'll have a whole new set of problems.' She was spread into her chair like a couple of cushions, so I didn't take her seriously. Large women always want thin women to be fatter.

I told her, 'I don't dream so badly. I understand about the relationship between my mother and my father and how it affected me. I'm confident in my work. Perhaps now is the time we should part company.'

She became huffy. 'Of course, if you honestly believe that you can go forward without any help at all then I would be the last person to stop you. My list of clients is always too long. But I have to tell you that I consider your mental health in a very delicate balance indeed and, speaking as your psychoanalyst and friend, I cannot advise you to leave.'

Thanks, Lesley. 'In a very delicate balance indeed.' I hated her at that moment but I was too scared to leave. My routine of flat, office and interview was based on a precarious self-confidence.

When Maureen eyed me appreciatively in the flat one evening and said she was glad I was not playing the sexist game of trying to make the best of my appearance, I burst into tears.

That night I dreamed of Patrick William Downes again, reliving the terror of the attack in the detailed way that Lesley had explained to me was compensating for not remembering anything much of it beyond the first stab. The anniversary had actually passed several weeks ago without any strong emotion on my part, which made it odder to find myself, once again, trapped and writhing.

I could not get up next morning but, since it was Sunday, I rang my father. It was still only seven o'clock. He said, 'I'll tell you what. We'll go to the sea.' He rang off before I could protest. I got out of bed shakily and looked out of the window where I'd already heard the vans and stall holders setting up for the weekly Portobello Road thrash. 'It's going to be a glorious day,' a voice said inside my head, although I certainly did not feel it.

The day was destined to be like that all along, an inner voice who told me how things were – the scenery beautiful, the people kind, and the experience enjoyable – and myself who was impervious.

'I knew you wouldn't mind Barbara coming,' said my father, opening the car door to reveal his mistress. He was dressed for the sea in nautical T-shirt and shorts under which his legs were startlingly hairy. Miss Mottram looked more normal in a cotton dress.

'Hello, Lydia.' She was nervous. 'Would you like to map-read?'

We drove about a hundred and twenty miles to a piece of the Dorset coast my father insisted was the most beautiful in the world. It took us a very long time because Miss Mottram was 'having trouble with my water works' as she put it and we had to stop every hour or so. In one small town we bought a huge picnic, including a litre of wine. 'I like to get drunk to the sound of waves,' my father said and Miss Mottram giggled.

'I'm sorry to break into your party, like this,' I said irritably. 'It can't be often you get a chance to go off together.'

'It's your party!' replied Miss Mottram. I had replaced her in the back seat so she swivelled round to make her point.

It was impossible to misread the unselfish generosity shining from her face.

When we arrived at the beach she continued to be charming, buying a windbreak from a stall because she said the wind was too brisk for someone delicate like me.

'Nonsense,' said my papa. 'Lydia has always been as tough as an old turnip.'

But she insisted. Since it was such a glorious sunny Sunday, there was a crowd of people near the lane leading to the beach. But we walked away, heads down, and soon we were on our own with sand and pebbles and shells leading down to a deep green sea and behind us whirling heights of yellow cliffs. If I had been feeling more gracious, I would have admitted it was a perfect spot.

My father never needed praise. He watched approvingly as his mistress began the lengthy process of putting on her bathing suit. Then he turned to me. 'Aren't you going to swim?'

'I didn't bring a bathing suit.' I should have known this would bring out his bullying nature.

'What about your pants and T-shirt?' In order to avoid an argument, I took off my jeans and then ran down to the sea very quickly so no one would see more than a white flash of my body. The water was cold but not as cold as I'd expected. I found I could float quite comfortably while the hood of my T-shirt swayed below me. Now and again I caught sight of the mistress, her hair encased in a flowery bath hat, or my father splashing at speed for not very far.

They were still out there when I returned and opened the bottle of wine. I even took off my T-shirt and, protected by the windbreak, let the sun dry my body. It would be too much to describe me as 'full of physical well-being' as my inner voice commented, but I certainly experienced an unaccustomed sense of ease and security.

My father stood over me with a look of horror, 'Emaciated and scarred.'

'I'm starving,' I said to cheer him up and grabbed a roll.

'I wish I could eat so heartily.' Miss Mottram patted dry her ample thighs.

'You will,' commented my father ungallantly. After a while he stopped eyeing me side-long.

It was, in fact, a real day out with almost no drawbacks until the end. We had reached outer London and I was in the front seat again. 'So, which of you two ladies shall I drop back first?' asked my father.

Miss Mottram opened her mouth to defer politely, but before she could speak, my inner voice came out into the open, except now all the sugar had turned to vinegar. 'It depends if you want to screw,' I said aggressively. So I have to admit that did rather spoil the day.

My father stopped the car and shouted at me angrily, 'What did you say?'

I might have repeated it but Miss Mottram was quicker now. 'She's just a disturbed child, Victor. Don't take so much notice.'

The teacher speaks. That put me in my place all right. So I kept quiet and my father drove on grimly without comment. In the half-hour it took to reach my flat, I tried out the idea that my outburst had been a defence of my mother but it didn't even convince me. So when I got out of the car, I bent towards his window. 'I'm sorry. It was a wonderful day.' Through his grimness, he allowed a tiny smile.

The Monday after that voyage out of town, Larry called me into the editor's office and tried to give me the sack. It was yet another hot day, the second hot summer running. I was wearing my usual T-shirt but also conscious that my face was unattractively red after the day by the sea. The editor was nowhere to be seen and Larry had taken over his desk. He was frowning over a list when I came in. 'You're Lydia Kirk?'

'That's me.' Kirk was my new journalistic name.

He frowned some more and tapped a vulgarly gold biro on the desk.

Despite the sinking pit feeling that my first job was about to end prematurely, I decided to put up as bold a front as possible. 'Are you editor now? Giving assignments?'

'No. No.' He was still distracted but, strangely, hardly glanced at me. It was as if the name alone interested him.

Looking back, it seems to me he was exceptionally slow recognising who I was. But then victims are not supposed to reappear and here I was in a very different context. Perhaps I even looked different. Certainly I had grown my hair long and could, when I wished to, walk without limping and did not wear little suits with gauzy scarves. Or perhaps he was one of those men who only look at women when they're attractive.

At any rate, he proceeded with giving me the sack. 'It seems, Lydia,' he was always familiar, 'that you were the last to come so you must be the first to go.'

'I thought we were "the people really in control",' I quoted him as tartly as possible. I knew that my only hope of retaining any dignity was to attack.

'Yeah. Yes. You're right to remind me. There will, of course, be compensation.'

'Mr Purley,' I began and then stopped because I had stood up to make my point but the strength of my emotion had made me dizzy and now I needed to sit down very quickly indeed. I bowed my head for a second until I could overcome the weakness. As I looked up our eyes met and it was his turn to look faint.

'You're the girl, the girl who . . . Your name isn't Kirk.'

I managed to stand up again before he finished. I knew that line of old. 'My private life has nothing whatsoever to do with my work on this newspaper, even if it is your newspaper.'

'No. I . . . It's not that . . .' Poor Larry. He later told me that in all his loyal campaigning for his orphan cousin he had absolutely never considered the existence of the victim. She had been a stranger, a name, not a real person at all. And here she was standing in front of him, trying to make him feel uncomfortable for giving her the sack.

For once he could think of absolutely nothing to say. 'So when do you want me to leave?' I asked, retreating to the door.

'Uh. Oh. I've got to . . . think.'

So I backed out and the next day I received a letter.

Dear Lydia Kremachowski,

There is something I would like to discuss with you which is best done out of the office. Would you care to join me for lunch next Tuesday, 22 July? If you are in agreement, I suggest we meet at the Kensington Hilton at twelve forty-five.

With best wishes,

Larry Purley.

The formality of this letter surprised me as much as its contents. It was particularly strange since Larry was still round and about the office. I decided to show it to Herbie but he hardly reacted. 'One thing, I know he doesn't fancy me.' I tried to get his attention. 'And I can't believe he feels that guilty.'

'He's got a lot on his mind.' Herbie, who had been turning pages of the daily newspapers in our never-ending search for local stories, made up his mind and turned to me, fully. 'Actually, he's made me editor.'

I could see why my news was not so important after all. 'But that's tremendous!'

I talked to Maureen about the lunch. 'Men are often peculiar,' she said disdainfully, 'particularly Australians.'

In the end I diverted myself from speculations about the reason for the lunch by fixating on the clothes necessary for such a grand location. It was Charmian who eventually chose me an elegant cotton suit and insisted I wore shoes with heels, something I had not done since the accident. 'It's absurd,' I protested in the shoe shop as I tried to accommodate my protesting left foot. 'I just hope Mr Lawrence Purley appreciates all the trouble I've gone to.'

'Lawrence Purley?' Charmian stopped, shoe in hand.

'Australian. I told you.'

Charmian said nothing more, but bent down to help me with the shoe.

The Kensington Hilton was not so smart after all and I had to make my way through compact crowds of tourists to reach the dining room. Eventually I found Larry at his table, most of the way through a large whisky. He sprang up as I approached and I saw he was sweating and ill at ease. That made me feel less nervous, although more curious. He ordered me a glass of wine and then became silent.

'I'm so glad you've made Herbie editor,' I said politely.

'Yeah. A talented guy, I'd say.' He was silent again.

'We've such a small set up, it's important we get on.' This was a lead into my sacking or not sacking – but he didn't pick it up.

'Yeah. It's the same with all small businesses.' Silence.

'I gather you have quite a few of those?' No answer. 'Businesses, I mean.'

'Look here, Lydia . . .' At last he was making up his mind. But my wine came and he sank back again. Now I was becoming nervous and could no longer keep up my chatter. After a long silence, he began quietly.

'I must tell you. I'm Pat Downes's first cousin.'

I felt myself engulfed in a wave of scarlet. It was a mixture of all kinds of emotions including anger which, I am proud to say, came out on top – at least temporarily. 'How can you sit there and tell me that? Do you know what you're saying? Do you know what that man did to me? Aren't you ashamed to be sitting there talking about this to me? How dare you even mention him to me? How dare you?' I was shaking so much I had to stop and I was terrified of bursting into tears.

'I didn't know what to do.' He seemed to be grinding his teeth. 'I don't know what to do. But I felt I should tell you. That seemed right. I felt we should talk about it.'

'Talk about it! You and me?' I found another burst of energy. 'Oh, yes. I can see you'd like to talk. Find out I'm all right, forgiving, forgotten all about it, perhaps. Well, I haven't forgotten. And I never will. And I'm not all right. And I never will be. And you should understand something, that I don't ever want to talk to you about it. And I don't have to stay here.'

I stood up just as the waiter came along with the menus and partly because he was blocking me in and partly because I realised I did not have the strength to walk away, particularly in Charmian's silly shoes, I plonked back down in my chair.

Larry, after managing with some difficulty to rid us of the waiter, sighed heavily. 'We should have met somewhere else.'

I did not have enough energy left to say we should not have met at all, so there we were, facing each other across a small table.

'Do you want to know what I think?' His voice, not usually very Australian, suddenly took on antipodean contortions.

He was gloomy and I was sullen. Exhausted. So far I had only reacted out of automatic emotion. I hadn't thought at all. Naturally, he was a bit more in control.

'My thinking is this. Take it or leave it. You were done a terrible damage by my orphaned cousin, Pat.'

I didn't want to know he was orphaned. He was a man, too big to be an orphan. But I didn't say anything.

'He did you irreparable damage. As you've pointed out. I accept that. Irreparable. Then what happens?' He was really trying to think it through. An observer would have given him credit for that. 'Then what happens is he's put into prison. Quite right too.'

'I'm in prison!' I found myself crying out, something I'd never said before.

'Oh. Is that so?' He was surprised. 'You are in a kind of prison.' He thought more. But it didn't really make sense to him, I could see that, even though he believed I deserved humouring.

'He put himself in prison and he put me in prison,' I muttered. 'I tell you, he doesn't deserve talking about.'

'I'm sorry.' He paused. 'I'm so sorry. I should have said that at the beginning.' He straightened his bowed shoulders and looked round the room. 'You couldn't eat something, could you? I'm starving and they'll throw us out if we don't order soon.'

I could have walked out by now. I was physically capable of it but instead I let him order me some pasta. I even drank some wine. Then he tried to start again. 'You want to forget all about it, don't you?'

'I can't ever forget all about it.'

'I see. So what do you think about it?'

'Oh, God. I think Patrick William Downes, your cousin, ruined my life.'

'I see.'

'You don't see. You weren't there. You don't know what it feels like to be murdered.' I was too excited again. My voice screeched and my legs shook. I shut my mouth and determined not to react again.

'I could just leave you alone but then I've still got to decide whether or not to give you the big E. You see, what I'm trying to say is you exist in my life. I in yours. We've had no choice in the matter but we do have a choice now.'

'Your cousin is a monster, an inhuman beast.' I was back in my refuge of quiet sullenness.

Larry became reflective. 'I don't know. I haven't treated him as if that's true. But perhaps it is. Recently, he bashed a fellow convict with a heavy stapler. He made quite a dent.'

'How can you say that? How can you say that?' I couldn't stop myself getting worked up. 'How can you talk like that?'

'I don't know how to talk. That's my point. I'm trying to find a way through.'

Our food came. He had a huge steak but no chips, only salad. 'I'm interested in health,' he told the waiter who felt convinced he wanted chips.

'I've done my best with Pat,' he began again, after carving off a lump of raw meat. 'I've tried to help him.'

'I don't want to hear this.' I twirled the pasta round and round the plate.

'No. No. I see that. You make that clear. Well. It's a chance in a million. But there you are. Perhaps it's not so odd, after all?'

'What do you mean?' I was wary now. I could see he was building up to some new bombshell.

'Before this stapler business I was sort of thinking I might put him on the paper.'

'He's in prison,' I whispered.

'Yeah. Longer now, I suspect.'

'I work for the newspaper.'

'You're probably right. That's what I was thinking. How

can I give the big E to the girl Pat stuck a knife in? Ever read a Greek tragedy? I haven't. But I guess they're a bit like this.'

Greek tragedy? I stared at his face warily but he was not making fun. We looked at each other for the first time. After a moment or two I began to eat my pasta.

'I've been thinking all kinds of things in the week since I saw you.' He smiled at me now in a kindly, paternal way as if he too was conscious of a new calmness. 'But you haven't had that week. It isn't fair on you. At any rate, I've made up my mind, you won't be getting the sack. That's for one hundred per cent.'

After that we both more or less called it a day. He drank coffee and we toppled out into the foyer where the tourist trade was still booming. I realised I couldn't go back to the office with him.

'You go home,' he said, without prompting. 'I'll tell Herbie you'll be in in the morning.'

We were both shell-shocked. I was aware of not hearing or seeing properly and when I had struggled my way back to the flat I immediately got into bed and fell into a deep sleep. Mysteriously, I dreamt of a fat lady in trousers and anorak, who, when I woke up, I identified as one of the pushing tourists in the foyer of the Kensington Hilton.

CHAPTER

TWENTY-FIVE

'Why DID you do it? Why did you do it?' Suddenly it was the question of the moment. Psychiatrists popping out of the woodwork, a special place being made for me in Grendon, if I was prepared to co-operate. But was I prepared to co-operate? The deputy governor, still with his nice kindly face, above his school teacher's sweater was deeply disappointed in me. I was summoned to his office.

'Why did you do it?' He was genuinely mystified. 'You're

a clever chap. Everything was going so well. The newspaper about to come out. You with more freedom than anyone in the whole prison. I just don't understand.' He was so concerned I felt sorry for him, even though he hadn't stopped all the petty penalties of breaking prison codes coming down on me.

'He only needed a stitch or two.' I refused to meet his eye. I did not feel like being frank. Actually, I didn't know what frankness meant, but I could see a desire for it shining in his face. 'It's more serious than you think. Not the wound. But the effect on your future. You were given a short sentence because it was believed that you were not fundamentally a violent and dangerous man. The judge and jury decided your violent action was isolated and out of character. You'd spent four months in prison on remand as quiet as a dodo. But now what? Now what are the authorities supposed to make of you?'

'I've changed.'

He sighed. 'You're your own worst enemy.'

'What a cliché,' I said. 'If I'd picked up a stapler and hit a friend with it outside prison, no one would have complained.'

I was surprised he bothered to answer me. 'Firstly, that's not true. And secondly, it's not relevant. You are in prison.'

'And likely to be here longer than expected,' I added for him. I could see he was not going to waste any more time or thought on me. He'd tried. I'd failed him and now I could go back and join the degenerate herd from whence he'd plucked me. This interview was just to salve his conscience.

The newspaper came out. Jock, plaster across forehead, took the credit. By mutual arrangement we kept far from each other. He'd accused me of being a violent villain and I'd proved him right; that's how it seemed to him and that's how, perhaps, it was. It certainly set back my dreams of a little room in a Dorset country town. Since one of my punishments was to be barred from my classes, I had more time on my hands than ever. It also made me slightly more popular with my fellow cons and my gaolers. They had thought me a bit intellectual, stuck up, but now I was nicely down to their level. The next time I was offered a joint, I put my hand out. I said I was not prepared to co-operate at Grendon. No community therapy for me. I would see out my time like any regular con.

TWENTY-SIX

LARRY AND I began to develop a strange friendship – which is probably the wrong word. I told no one in the office of his identity. I did not tell my family about him, or Maureen, or Lesley. They began to suspect, with happy excitement, that I was conducting a secret love affair. Once Larry drove me up to Hampstead for a session with Lesley and she happened to be looking out of the window.

She restrained her curiosity till I was about to leave. 'He hasn't waited for you, then?'

'Who?' I knew perfectly well.

'The dashing blond in the Porsche who dropped you here?'

It was true. Larry and I were about as likely a couple as a gerbil and a golden crested eagle. A string of girl-friends passed through his life in the months when I saw most of him. The most striking thing about them was their variety in terms of race and colour. I asked him once, after I'd got to know him well, 'Why do you never have English girl-friends?'

'It's a colonial hang-up. They make me feel inferior.'

I laughed. But later I realised it was this feeling of being an outsider, still raw at that time, which made him such a good cousin to Patrick William Downes.

The second time we met, a week after the first, it was a blustery day with warm rain spattering ineffectually across the pavements. Nevertheless Larry suggested we walked in Hyde Park. I pointed out that I wasn't much of a walker for reasons he knew.

He gave me a cursory glance. 'I'll drive us to the middle.'

'I don't know why I've come.' I said. But the roar of the Porsche drowned out such feebleness.

In the end we sat in a glass restaurant on the edge of the Serpentine. 'Someone told me this was designed by the same person who designed the elephant house,' he said.

'It doesn't look substantial enough to keep elephants in,' I said. It was hard to start our conversation again. We ordered sandwiches and beer. The rain became stronger, battering noisily against the glass.

'The grass could do with a bit of rain,' he said.

'Yes,' I agreed. 'It's nearly white.'

'Have you been thinking more?' he shouted suddenly above the uproar. A streak of lightning flashed above the trees.

'Yes. But I haven't come to any conclusions.' Thunder rolled across the water. 'Actually, I don't know how to think.'

'Same here.' This was cheering. It made the chasm between us a little less uncrossable. It had grown dark now and since no one had bothered to switch on lights – or perhaps there were no lights – we could hardly see each other's faces.

'I'm famished!' His expression was heartfelt.

I began to laugh. The whole situation suddenly seemed absurd, us sitting incapable of speech in the middle of a glass box on the edge of a lake. 'We're sure to be struck by lightning,' I cried.

Larry began to laugh too. When we'd sobered up, he took my hand across the table and said, 'You look different when you laugh.'

This brought me back to earth pretty quickly and the brief storm was already subsiding round us. 'I used to be a good-looking girl,' I said. 'I liked my face and my body. I was comfortable with them. They did what I wanted efficiently. I didn't have to worry. When I went into that horrible shop,' I didn't know then Larry actually owned the shop, 'I was coming from the Turkish baths. I loved the feeling of purity it gave me.'

Larry listened. He was a good listener for once, very concentrated.

'Now I'm a different person. Disfigured and frightened.' I wanted him to make some comment. Perhaps disagree with me, I don't know. We were interrupted by our food arriving and he said nothing. I continued. 'Your cousin had attacked me. Except that I never considered he could be anyone's cousin. He was all badness, completely evil, inhuman. It felt better thinking that way. I knew other people could feel differently. In my family, for example, my sister made a point of saying how she could forgive him. But she's a strong Catholic, for which I respect her. But it makes her different, doesn't it? She's following rules. She has to forgive or she isn't a Catholic. Anyway, it didn't happen to her.' I paused. I thought jealously of Charmian who hadn't been attacked and had all kinds of certainties.

'Why don't you say anything?' I said, rather irritably. When I paused Larry had begun to eat his sandwich hungrily. He swallowed his mouthful and put the rest down reluctantly.

'I wanted to hear how it felt from your point of view. I'm truly interested. I don't think you're ready to hear my side of things.'

'You mean Patrick William Downes's side of things?' I began to be angry. 'I certainly don't want to hear how he's liable to chesty colds and one of his feet is a good half size bigger than the other!'

Larry eyed his sandwich with absent-minded longing. He was not at all put out by my rage; he almost seemed to be smiling.

'I'm not joking!' I shouted.

'I know. It's so difficult,' he muttered and then turned his head to look all the way round at the view from our glass box. The rain had already reduced to a patter and there were indications of a break in the clouds beyond the leafy fringe of the park. While he stared round as if trying to think of something to say, I began to nibble at my sandwich. I felt happier now I'd shouted a bit.

'Do you still see an analyst?' He leaned towards me, concentrated again.

'Yes. She wants to make me feel normal, like other women, keen on men and babies.' I paused. 'As a matter of fact, I don't think I was ever particularly like that, even before.' I stopped abruptly, stunned by what I'd said. I'd never admitted such a thing before, never for a moment suggested that all my problems could not be laid at the feet of Patrick William Downes. I took a sneaky look at Larry, trying to gauge if he'd gathered the importance of what I'd said, but once I'd stopped speaking he'd returned to a contemplation of his sandwich.

'Oh, please eat it!'

'You remind me of someone. But I shan't tell you who.'

CHAPTER

TWENTY-SEVEN

DESCENDING INTO a pit of sloth and iniquity – that is, becoming one of the large band of dope smokers – changed my life for the better. Since I didn't smoke cigarettes I could barter with that ration, which was an agreeable occupation for my superior wits. Dope brought me into mainstream prison life, gave me a daily occupation and something to look forward to. Now and again the prison had a bit of a crack-down but mostly marijuana was seen as another kind of Valium. Harder drugs had to be much more carefully concealed but I was never into that.

Meanwhile, life went on outside. Larry, my most faithful visitor, let a couple of months pass by at this time. He wrote, however.

The newspaper is settled down now, advertising coming in not quite as fast as I hoped but building all the time. I've retained most of the staff except for the editor who had a tinge of death. They're an interesting mix, almost all young and there's one girl I would like you to meet. She reminds me of you.

Nell continued to send me photographs of the ever-fattening Bruno. After my interlude with the stapler, a reproachful tone dimmed her usual cheerfulness. 'Bruno and I were so hoping you'd be home for Christmas . . . my parents too . . .' She was living with her parents who, I am sure, would have absolutely dreaded having me home for Christmas. I did answer that letter.

Dear Nell,
You should face it. Something nasty happened. Your young husband nearly murdered a girl and now he's in prison where he belongs. There his main occupation is dope (marijuana) and making the days slide along easily. The only good thing, from your point of view, is that he doesn't want to have anything more to do with you. So why don't you just thank your fucking stars and start a new life without him!

I put in the 'fucking' to scare her off. No such luck.

Dear Pat,
We all realise the strain you are under or at least realise we are in no position to understand what you are going through. I have this dream you'll be out on New Year's Day. Bruno might even be walking by then.

She was an optimist about everything.

In August it was very hot in our cells, even though we stripped down to our underpants. The grass in the exercise yard was burnt as pale and dry as hay and the air smelled of the excrement thrown from cell windows. Once I picked up a lump because it was wrapped up in a piece of comic and I felt like reading a comic. The cons round me thought that pretty funny so at least someone got a laugh.

I was very low, very demoralised, no dreams of Dorset country towns now. I was told no one could help me while I was using dope. That was surprising, that someone was showing interest. One evening my cell-mate came over and began stroking my cock. He was young, good-looking, not obviously homosexual. I was sleepy, a bit stoned and found it altogether an agreeable sensation. So we lay together and he stroked my cock and I stroked his and after we both came, we fell asleep. It was quite peaceful, really, quite uneventful.

In the night, after he'd gone back to his bed, I woke up and began to worry. 'I'm not gay,' I said. I used that term so as not to hurt his feelings.

'Nor am I.' He was awake too.

'Just thought I should say.'

'Oh, fuck off.'

He was called Billy and I suppose we did have what you'd call a homosexual relationship. It grew, of course, because we had so little else to do but we were never in love.

'I'm married,' I told him on another occasion.

'Oh, fuck off.' He was a nice man, inside for seven burglaries. He showed me a picture of his girl-friend. She was dressed in black leather from head to toe and sitting astride a motor-cycle.

'That's the public version,' he said. 'Someday I might show you the private. She's a model, you see, much sought after. It's for her I pinched the gold.' The gold had been his seventh burglary from a jewellery shop.

'Want to see the private version?' he asked me one evening. It was Scheherezade, as he assured me she had been christened, astride the same bike but with no top on and her leather trousers fast unzipping. I found it very exciting which Billy noticed at once. He propped it up at the end of the bed so we could both see it when we lay down together.

'There is an even more private version,' he said, 'but this will do for now.'

Afterwards, I commented, 'I guess that photo proves we're not poofs.' As usual, he told me to fuck off. When Billy was released at the end of September, I said, 'I don't know who I'll miss more, you or Scheherezade.' So he gave me the photograph. I used it for a while to keep my hand in, as you might say, but after a bit I lost interest.

I did have other offers from those who thought they knew

the way it was with Billy and me. But I never took them up and no one ever forced me. Luckily, I still had my reputation as a man who likes a bit of violence. Billy remained a happy memory, however, and I was truly sorry when I heard he'd got into trouble roughing up his girl-friend. I hoped it wasn't the beautiful Scheherezade.

Summer seemed very long but at last some leaves blew over the prison wall into our exercise yard. I could see the tops of three tall trees if I bothered to look up and they were varying shades of golden and brown. Everybody became more energetic with the cooler weather. My probation officer told me there was still a place for me in Grendon if only I'd leave off the drugs. I answered that didn't she know I was too near the end of my sentence for Grendon? I was expecting an appointment with the parole board any day.

A new deputy governor who had seen my first issue of the newspaper summoned me to ask if I'd produce a second. 'Just don't throw anything.' He frowned at my record sheet.

I was feeling more energetic so I took on the newspaper. It was impossible to avoid all hope when I might have only three months left to serve.

Larry came. He had asked for a visitor's order for a friend but he came alone. We sat in the hall of despair with the giant blower doing its worst and Larry began to apologise for deserting me. 'It's been a busy time, setting up the newspaper.'

'You wrote to me about it.'

'That's right.' He seemed uneasy.

'So you decided not to bring your friend?'

'She was busy.' Again I was struck by something evasive in his manner.

'Good friend, is she?'

'No. That is . . .' He looked down at his big hands as if for help.

I thought to myself, So some girl's finally snapped her jaws shut round that handsome blond head. The thought made me smile but I didn't press him any more. I wasn't that interested.

'I'm working on a job for you in Manchester.'

'What's wrong with London?'

'Nothing's wrong with London. But a mate of mine might have something for you in Manchester.'

'I liked the idea of the south.' I watched his face, again quite flustered. 'I thought you more or less bought this local paper to give me a career.' This was supposed to be a joke. I still wasn't taking the idea of release seriously enough to care as much as he thought I did.

'I can't just chuck people out to make room for you.'

He seemed about to get angry so I cooled things a bit. 'I've nothing against the north. I just don't know it.'

After he had left, I was struck by the happy thought that if I was working in Manchester, I could not be living with Nell. I wrote to Larry and told him that, all things considered, I thought it very likely I was destined to be a happy Mancunian. I had always preferred the accent to Liverpudlian, I told him to show I knew what I was talking about. Meanwhile I had my date with the parole board.

Working on the second edition of the newspaper made time important again. Nor could I smoke so much if I wanted to think straight.

'I want this paper out for Christmas,' the new deputy governor told me. He was different from the other, had no interest in me personally, but felt himself in competition with his predecessor. 'That first edition was OK if you like to be depressed but I like my prison to be a cheerful place, particularly at Christmas. Get some holly berries in, pretty girls, a splash of colour.

'It's printed in black and white,' I said.

'That's enough fucking crap from you, Downes.'

Still, he did leave me alone and by the middle of December the second issue of *Insiders*, mark two, was doing the cell rounds.

It had its quota of moans and groans, sob stories about broken relationships, which were absolutely never the fault of the con, but it also had a few funny anecdotes and sub-Larkin poetry and even real solid news from outside. I wrote a good piece on drug abuse which not so subtly hinted that if the cons had something interesting with which to fill their days they wouldn't want to disappear in a waft of magic smoke.

Two weeks before Christmas the parole board had pronounced me perfectly ready to take my place back in society. My visitor, coming earlier, a booted lady with red hair and an American accent, did question me closely about my place of abode but apparently Nell convinced them, in the end, that I would be with her; there was no point in disturbing that idea. 'You know you'll have to report to the police weekly,' my redhead told me. Yes, I knew. She talked to me and I wrote down all this stuff as to why I should be let out. But the real point was that I was a clever young man from a good home who had been unlucky. I guessed the parole board would be impressed by the newspaper.

So I was due out on 31 December. Larry knew and had said I could sleep for a while in his flat. Nell knew and I did not face what she expected.

On the day before Christmas Eve, I was holding one end of a paper chain made of a row of Father Christmases – the other end was being held by a very bad-tempered lifer – when my name was called.

I dropped the chain and was conscious of a row of nice old red-coated gentlemen swishing to the floor. It was a charmingly inappropriate beginning to my last twenty-four hours in prison, although the cursing from the lifer up the ladder gave it a bit of an edge.

'Eight o'clock, the morning of 24 December. You're fucking unlucky, Downes,' the escorting screw told me. 'You'll miss the chef's famous turkey with two veg, roast potatoes, bread sauce, cranberry jelly — '

'And piss gravy,' I finished for him. 'I had the benefit of it last year.'

I lay awake all that night. I had spent eighteen months in prison. So now it was time to go. Go where? I was no nearer knowing.

PART THREE

TWENTY-EIGHT

IT WAS extremely cold on the pavement outside the prison. I had been given back the clothes in which I had arrived, apparently unwashed. Since I had committed my foul deed in the middle of an exceptionally hot summer, they were, to say the fucking least (but I must drop the swearing now I'm outside), inadequate for Christmas Eve. Thoughts of the cold and how to combat it dominated any sense of elation or fear.

Three other men had been released at the same time as me but one had been picked up by a car driven by a woman. The second had set off with a purposeful stride, probably in the direction of the railway station. The third, just in front of me, a skinny boy who hardly looked old enough for prison, was immediately pounced on by a couple of police and whisked off to face further charges. I thought that a kind of cheating.

It was neither raining nor snowing but the ground seemed slippery beneath my feet and the air drizzled. I looked up at the high brick walls with the little Alice in Wonderland door now firmly closed and wondered if it had been sensible to inform no one of my earlier date of release.

Eventually I realised I must move while I was still capable. I started slowly, body shaking, feet numb. It was getting on for nine o'clock by now and as I neared the centre of town, people appeared around me, all hurrying on, all well wrapped up. I entered an area where there were shops, modern, with sharp angles, decorated for Christmas. There was no sign of the station so I found a café and went inside to warm myself up.

'They're not open.' A woman was cleaning the floor.

'I'm sorry,' I said, sitting down on a chair.

She advanced on me with what I assumed to be a look of

hatred but nothing like enough aggression to budge me. 'Why are you dressed like that?' She was a plain woman, overweight, wearing trousers and a shabby cardigan. I did not answer her question but concentrated on enjoying the warmth moving along my limbs.

'You've come out of prison. Your skin's as white as paper.' To my surprise, she came over and sat at my table. 'What you need is a brandy.' A moment earlier I had half expected her to call a policeman and now here she was telling me I needed a brandy.

'Just sit there a second.' The large brandy she brought me had a deciding effect. I went to the station and bought a ticket for London. To whom should I give the benefit of my first day? Should I strike sense into Nell once and for all?

The tight walls of the train compartment were reassuring. Part of my coldness, I realised, had been from the agoraphobia of standing unprotected under the sky. On the other hand, the train moved at a terrifying speed. Being out of practice, I had sat in a smoking carriage without thinking. Soon, I began to feel like a puff of the old weed. Everybody had been at great pains to tell me where I could get it in London; the far end of Ladbroke Grove seemed the most accessible location, but I had nothing now and a long train journey. Nor did I have anything to read.

'It is smoking, you know.' A man smoking opposite me suddenly barked. Had I been staring, talking to myself? I stood up and moved down the train. Settling for a moment in front of a woman with a small child, I wondered how Nell was getting on with her parents. I smiled at the child who immediately let out a piercing shriek so I moved on again.

By the time we arrived in London the calming effect of the brandy had long passed. The crowds on the station made me decide to travel on at once to Mr and Mrs Burns. That's where I was supposed to go, anyway. A loudspeaker played 'Good King Wenceslas' and a straggly youth dressed as Father Christmas rang a dinner bell. It would be bad luck if the Burnses thought I had come to celebrate the birth of the Saviour with them. Although the station was under cover, I was beginning to feel cold again and very tired. It seemed a long time since I'd left prison. I was used to a more gradual way of life.

The train for Sunningdale was still steamed up, fetid and dirty from the thousands of commuters it had delivered earlier. Hardly anyone was going my way, making me feel an outsider, almost a ghost. Pressing my face into the dampness of the window, I drifted into a half sleep.

At Sunningdale, it was raining properly. I managed to walk through the station to the exit but then lost my nerve and stood still, staring dismally outwards.

'Want a taxi, do you?' He was a large, florid-faced man, wearing a dark suit. I was about to agree when I realised I could not remember the Burnses' address. 'You won't find many taxis outside rush hour. But I just happen to have a car handy.' He laughed. 'If you can call it a car.'

It seemed easier to follow him – even when I saw he was driving a hearse. 'See what I mean?' He laughed again. I got in quickly to escape the rain. 'Left? Right?' I indicated left hopefully and we rolled away.

'I had to deliver some ashes, you see, to the twelve fifteen. That's why I was at the station.' I stared out of the window as he talked. I was closer to events than I had been inside the train but still enclosed. I looked avidly, pressing my face close to the glass. The rain was making everyone hurry. As we followed a line of traffic, people, heads down, shoulders hunched, were overtaking us. They were mostly women because we were opposite a row of shops. They carried shopping bags or swung them on push-chairs. One hooded figure caught my attention. I was sure I had seen her before.

I was studying her intently when she looked up. The car – the hearse – was stationary at a traffic light and she was very close to the edge of the pavement.

'Pat!' she mouthed and I fell back in my seat. But I had come to see her. I leaped out just as we started to move again. I flung myself out of the door which was rather high and, catching my foot on the kerb, fell forward heavily. Unfortunately, Nell's push-chair was directly in front of me and I landed more or less on top of it. The baby inside began to scream and I lay winded on the pavement. There was an excruciating pain in my left ankle.

'What's up?' The driver of the hearse, ignoring the hooting of the traffic barricaded behind him, parked decisively and came to join the fun.

'He's my husband,' volunteered Nell bravely.

'Trying to get away without paying,' commented the driver who turned out to be a cynic. He hauled me to my feet, not unkindly.

'Ow!' I exclaimed hopping.

'It's his ankle,' suggested the driver but Nell was diverted by the baby who was screaming even louder.

'I can pay you,' I offered gloomily. Even through the pain and confusion, I could see this was not the way to approach an unemotional hello-and-goodbye-for ever-Nell. The hearse had been a mistake.

'Just fuck off,' I told the driver, handing him a fiver. 'I'm sorry,' I said to Nell who had quietened the baby – a much larger baby, I noticed – by rocking him in her arms.

'Yes. Yes,' she said, either to him or to me and began walking slowly, steering the push-chair with her free hand. But the bags on the handle were heavy and it kept tipping backwards.

'Take the bags off,' Nell commanded me irritably. I didn't blame her. It was raining steadily and I was shaking (mostly with cold) and hopping at her side.

'I'm sorry,' I repeated. At least the hearse had driven off, releasing from behind it a stream of frustrated drivers.

'What were you doing in that thing?' she said.

'I don't know. It was just chance.' She looked as if she would cry so I advised firmly, 'Don't talk now.'

But she couldn't resist. 'I didn't even know you were out. It's such a shock.' The tears began to roll down her face. I thought, She's going to get a worse shock when we get to her house.

'Stop here a moment.' We were passing an off-licence so I went in and bought a bottle of champagne.

Thus we arrived back at the Burnses' house, a family reunited, wet but intimate and *en fête*. It was no wonder my intentions were misunderstood. Nell's parents were thrilled. It was lunch time and, although they were only having a snack of bread and cheese, we would open the champagne at once.

As I had earlier suspected, they did not miss the significance of the date. 'It is all I have ever dreamed.' Mrs Burns looked proudly round the lunch table. However I noticed Nell ducked down her head in embarrassment so I did not despair.

Bruno was better than I had expected. He sat in a high chair and ate consistently without throwing too much food around. He had fair hair, blue eyes and scaly red cheeks but at least he did not dominate. After lunch he went for a sleep. Soon afterwards Mr and Mrs Burns disappeared for a walk. Nell and I were alone together. She settled herself in a chair, one plump leg hooked under the other. 'Now we can talk,' she murmured, blushing.

My voice felt a very long way from my mouth which may have been due to exhaustion so I let her begin. 'It has been so long.' This was an undeniable truth. 'And we hardly know each other.'

Perhaps she did not want me, after all. I was certainly no catch.

'Bruno doesn't know you.' She sighed. 'I'm working, in a solicitor's office nearby and, until Larry finds you a job, we can live here in Sunningdale.'

Now it was necessary to speak. I looked at Nell and, in that deceitful way of memory, remembered how soft and comfortable she'd been in the consoling days of our early relationship – those that had begot Bruno. I forced myself to face her, noting that her chestnut hair had darkened and her previously pink complexion grown pale. 'I came here to talk to you.' I stopped.

'Yes. Yes.' Her nervousness was increasing. 'I knew you wouldn't be able to write to me from', she gulped, 'prison. I understood why you didn't answer my letters. I . . .' she gulped again and stopped.

'I am not going to live with you!' I cried shrilly. 'It would be a farce. A travesty.' Her face was dissolving in front of me, a product of my hysteria and her misery. 'I have to go away. Be on my own. I would go mad if I stayed here. It's nothing personal. Not now, I mean, against you. I hardly know you. As you said. But it was when we were together that I fucking well nearly killed a girl!' I stopped, panting.

Nell was crying. The tears flowed silently down her face without her making any attempt to stop them. I tried not to think of all the dreams I was smashing. Why do women dream? How could she still think she loved me?

When I had finished – I produced more despair and anger and even good common sense – I didn't look at her but went into the kitchen and made a pot of tea. I thought it was the first time I'd taken such a simple action for over a year and a half. As I carried a tray back to the living room, my ankle began to hurt again. I tried hard not to limp, frightened of arousing Nell's maternal instincts.

'I'll go before your parents get back,' I announced. This was optimistic. I had almost no money and could hardly walk so I sat down again. She went out and reappeared with the baby. Now I knew I was leaving I felt better disposed towards him. 'He looks well.'

Nell put him on the floor and we both watched as he tried to pull himself up to a standing position by holding onto a chair. 'He's strong,' I commented encouragingly. The moment my foot stopped hurting, I'd borrow some money and be off to London, to Larry.

Nell still wouldn't speak to me. But the baby forced her to become more capable. She had to take him away to change his nappy and when she brought him back, make sure he didn't pull things off the table. Her catatonic misery had passed.

'Your parents will be soaked.'

She looked vaguely out of the window and then turned to me with a sharper expression. 'You blame me for what happened, don't you?'

She didn't need an answer because we both knew it was true. Now I really had to go. I stood up shakily. 'I need to borrow some money.'

She went to her bag and took out a ten-pound note and a five-pound note. 'That's all I've got.'

'Thank you.' She picked up the baby and we both went to the front door. When she opened it, I must have begun to shiver because she suddenly thrust the baby at me, saying, 'I'll get one of Dad's sweaters for you. Your clothes are packed in a case. Do you want them?'

The baby in my arms looked at me with round wondering eyes. Then he began to smile, clearly not a child sensitive to atmosphere. Nell came back carrying the sweater and a case. She took the baby from me without comment, he was chuckling as if in a happiest-baby competition. I put on the sweater.

'Goodbye,' she whispered when my head was inside the sweater.

'Goodbye,' I replied when I'd popped out again.

A few yards down the street, I spotted Mr and Mrs Burns coming my way. They were walking arm in arm, hopeful and happy. I quickly crossed to the other side of the street.

CHAPTER
TWENTY-NINE

FOR THE rest of the year I saw Larry at least every fortnight, privately, that is. We met in strange places, as if we were secret lovers. He never came to my flat and I didn't even know where his was. That was where he took his girl-friends.

Herbie noticed or thought he noticed what was going on. He was reproachful. 'I thought you were my friend, but you don't trust me at all.'

'Larry and I are trying to work something out.' Herbie looked unconvinced. He came to my flat and looked unconvinced lying on my floor. His dark eyes stared up at me. 'We don't have a sexual relationship,' I added pompously.

He laughed, not as nicely as a friend should. 'That I can believe.'

One lunch time, Larry stood me up. We were supposed to be meeting in a modern hotel along the Cromwell Road. I left the table which had been correctly booked in his name and stamped about the foyer, wondering why Larry liked these sort of vulgar anonymous places. Of course that's exactly why he did like them.

Then I telephoned Herbie. 'Want to have lunch on Larry?'

He came, looking delightfully out of place, and we settled down either side of a table with a bottle of wine. 'So what's it all about?'

'We talk,' I said, disposed to be open, on whim or out of pique, 'about my would-be murderer.'

'Why should Larry be more interested than me?' His tone was rather rude.

I smiled. I had wanted to tell him for some time. 'Because Patrick William Downes is Larry Purley's first cousin.'

Herbie was impressed. 'It's very odd', I continued, 'to consider that a man has ruined your life and to hate him so much that you want him dead and then to discover that he's being looked after, given life and hope for the future by someone who you rather like. It takes quite a lot of discussing.'

'He knows him, then,' said Herbie.

'He's like a father to him.' At that moment I saw Larry coming across the dining room. When he spotted Herbie he began to be angry, and then changed his mind.

'Hi boss,' Herbie greeted him.

We all had lunch. 'I have news,' announced Larry, guessing at once that I had told Herbie. It was me, after all, who was secretive, not him. 'Pat will be out by New Year.'

I expect he was glad Herbie was there too because they began to gabble to each other while I decided whether to throw a bottle, storm out or sink back in my chair. Naturally, I did the latter.

'Well, there you are.' Larry turned back to me.

'I suppose this is one of the things you've discussed.' Herbie still sounded a touch cruel.

We had discussed the eventuality of his release but never the certainty.

'I don't think he should ever be allowed out.' I discovered some wine in my glass and drank it quickly. 'That's my position and I'm not changing it.'

'That's your rightful position,' Herbie agreed sycophantically.

'As a matter of fact,' I added, 'that's not my position. My true position is that I want him dead.'

'How extraordinary!' Herbie swayed forward as if magnetised by me. It was an exaggerated posture and made me suspect he was making fun. 'I always thought you were against capital punishment.'

Meanwhile Larry was looking shocked. He was good at looking shocked. His eyes turned into round balls and his nose wrinkled shorter than ever. He took me seriously.

'This is such a horrible place.' I addressed Larry teasingly. 'Why ever do you like it?'

'I don't like it at the moment.' His food hadn't come and I expect he had an important meeting in five minutes. Little minnows like Herbie and me should have reminded ourselves constantly that he was the man to call the tunes.

'I apologise, Larry,' I turned to him graciously, 'for both Herbie who shouldn't be here and myself who is ungrateful.'

'Yes,' agreed Larry briskly. 'The point is I came here with a challenge for you, Lydia. I suppose you might say it's been my plan all along. Now that Pat will soon be out, I'd like you to accustom yourself to the idea of meeting him.'

My gracious smile did the vanishing trick.

'No hope, by the looks of her,' commented Herbie, cheerfully. I like to think he said it in my defence.

THIRTY

I PICKED up a Christmas present for Larry on the station. It was a Father Christmas in a glass dome. When you shook it, snow swirled around. While I was buying it, I put down the suitcase and didn't feel like taking it up again. I had very little money left but I felt better with my snowy scene to indicate seasonal goodwill. I held it carefully for I was trying to negotiate London in rush hour on a Friday which was also Christmas Eve. Even getting out of the station took a lot of nerve. When I reached the pavements, I couldn't seem to keep up the same speed as everyone else. The result was I kept getting knocked and bumped. In fact the pavements seemed to be moving along themselves, like escalators, so when I saw an empty taxi I threw myself at it with passionate relief.

The driver was disposed to talk. 'You're the first person I've picked up today without shopping bags.'

'I haven't any money.'

'Ha, ha.' He laughed as if I'd made a bad joke.

Larry lived in one of those grand Thameside conversions miles away from anywhere. I realised I should have fore-warned him after I'd rung his bell four times without an answer. It was nearly seven o'clock, very cold indeed, and the towering brick wall above my head reminded me of the walls of prison. The taxi had gone, taking my last money with it, so my options were limited. I tried the bell once more.

'Who's there?' It was Larry's voice, bad-tempered and distorted.

'It's Pat.'

'Pat who?' This was depressing.

'Cousin Pat, the gaolbird.'

'Oh, God.' At least he buzzed me in.

When he opened the flat door, waves of heat lapped outwards. It needed to be hot because he was wearing only a towel around his waist. As usual he was a golden brown and his hair was wet and tousled as if he'd just had a shower. We made our usual contrast. In one of his large leather armchairs a girl, also wrapped in a towel, sat looking at us, presumably thinking just that.

'Sorry to disturb you,' said the visitor from Outer Space.

'We've finished.' Larry looked at the girl who smiled a little uncomfortably.

'It's hot in here.' I made my way to the other chair.

'You're a week early.' Larry made an effort to smile too. 'I'm really glad, you're out, Pat. We'll have a celebration. This is Helen, Helen this is Pat, who you know all about.'

'Congratulations, Pat.' Helen looked as if she meant it so I began to relax.

'Why are you limping?' Larry came after me, hovered sympathetically. I felt tears starting in my eyes.

'I twisted my ankle.' I tried to make a story of it. 'I was jumping out of a hearse to catch Nell.'

'So you've seen Nell already.' He looked so pleased that I didn't have the courage to tell him why.

'What he needs is a bath.' Helen was lovely, as smoothly delectable as posters on cell walls. I felt myself stirring and thought lounging in hot soapy water sounded like a good idea.

When I came out, having put on my dirty clothes once more with some reluctance, they were dressed too, sleek and ready and waiting for a jolly night on the town. I had rediscovered my Father Christmas in a snowstorm which I now presented to Larry. 'Happy Christmas,' I said.

'Thanks, Pat.' He peered closely as if he'd never seen such a thing before. 'He looks just like you!' Helen laughed and Larry shook it up so that the snow swirled and whirled. He set it in the middle of a table and started for the door but I couldn't help noticing they had been drinking something which had not been offered to me. It is hard to behave well when you're dead beat, your ankle throbs and you're at the mercy of your vulgar rich Australian cousin.

'Don't I get a drink?'

'Oh. Did you want one?'

Did I fucking want one? What did he think?

Larry put his arm around my shoulder. 'I'm glad you saw Nell and the baby.' His weight pressed on my ankle. I began to limp more obviously. It was becoming clear to me that Helen was a bit of a new passion with Larry and that he was having to make an immense effort to incorporate me into his evening. Not giving me a drink was a small release of anger. We took the lift down to the bottom of the building.

'My ankle hurts. Why don't I stay behind? It's way past my bedtime.' But they wouldn't hear of it. Maybe Larry's heart sank at the thought that my bedtime would take place on his sofa.

'Come on now, we'll take your weight.' They took an arm on either side and put me into Larry's Porsche. Helen was stuffed in behind us, leaning forward so that her soft hair tickled my neck and her sweetish scent floated around my nostrils. I closed my eyes and told myself it was bliss. At the restaurant, there was a small problem because I wasn't wearing a jacket. It was quite a grand restaurant but Larry knew the owner who looked Chinese and spoke English with a French accent.

'He's my cousin.' Larry had his arm round my shoulders again, 'He's the black sheep of the family. Even got thrown out of the Foreign Legion. That was yesterday.'

I tried not to look like a black sheep but it hardly mattered. We were in, anyway. I think I slept through most of that meal – at least, although I tried to do justice to the endless progression of food and drink, I cannot remember speaking a word. Nor can I remember anything they said either.

By the time I staggered back into the flat, I was blind and deaf and dumb and felt as if I were wrapped in candy floss. It was then that Larry, excited, I suppose, by the wine and company, sent Helen off to his room and decided to have a serious talk with me.

I don't believe he consciously meant to be cruel, however much he regretted what he was missing in the bedroom. He sat opposite me in the other big armchair and said, his honest blue eyes piercing the candy floss, 'So you saw Nell?' The question mark was gigantic, endless.

'That's right.'

'And was she well?'

'Tip-top.' I was drunk, flaked out, didn't he know that? 'Can't this wait for the morning?' The point was that I knew he, like everybody else, thought the very best thing I could do was go to live with Nell. It was neat and nice and it was on my parole sheet.

Larry poured himself a whisky but again didn't offer me one. Not that I minded. Not in the least. He sat opposite me again, trying to look concerned but not quite disguising his irritation.

I looked at the Father Christmas sitting on a bed of snow in the middle of the table. 'Happy Christmas, Larry.' It must have been hours past Christmas already but neither of us had thought. 'This is a great place to be sitting for my first Christmas of freedom.'

He did raise his glass but not with much cheer. I was seeing the tenacity which made him a good businessman. 'We must talk this through, Pat. It has to be done.'

'Now? Does it have to be now?' My pink candy floss was beginning to shred. I thought that I'd been awake getting on for thirty-six hours.

'You have to make plans, Pat.'

I think he must have been drunk to be quite so insistent. 'Why don't you go to bed, Larry? Helen's waiting.' It came out insulting, although I hadn't meant it that way. Larry's face set more fixedly in my direction. He was like a limpet mine, determined to make me explode.

'When are you going back to Nell?' He was shouting, I think.

'Oh, fuck it, Larry. You know. *You know.*' I began to yell. 'You know I'm not ever going back to Nell. Why are you saying this? What's the point? You're drunk. You know what I think of Nell and her baby. You're supposed to be protecting me, not sending me back where it all started.'

'What do you mean? What do you mean where it all started?' He was screaming now, standing up and stamping. 'It all started when you stood in my shop and took up one of my kitchen knives and stuck it in one of my customers. How do you think that made me feel? Do you think that's the way I like to conduct business? Selling knives with blood dripping off them? I expect you thought it would make a nice advertisement, "the Cutting Edge, the kitchen shop for murderers. Knives that cut through anything, skin, gristle, bone, no organ out of range . . ." ' He went on longer but at this point I knew I was going to vomit. So I made a zigzagging dash for the bathroom where I missed the lavatory but made the bath. I hung there, shaking.

Some time later, Helen came to get me. She led me back into the lounge which was empty and put me gently into the sofa. 'He's drunk,' she said.

I nodded.

'I'll clear up the bathroom and then you can get ready for bed.' She was so kind, she made me sit in the chair and held my hand till the shaking quietened a little.

While she was in the bathroom, I tried to calm myself by going through all the times Larry had helped me. He had to be allowed one outburst or he would be a saint. He wasn't a saint.

'You can go in now and I'll make up a bed for you on the sofa.' Helen was a saint. I washed carefully and found she had laid out a pair of Larry's pyjamas for me.

The lounge was empty when I returned, one lamp lit, a welcome quietness except for voices from the bedroom. I tried not to listen.

Helen reappeared and held my hand again. 'Larry's drunk too much,' she repeated. 'But it's not that. He's put himself in an awkward position. Larry doesn't react well in awkward positions.'

I began to drift away from her voice which was far too soothing to convey any threat.

'You see, he's got to know the girl.' I heard her pause requesting a question.

'What girl?' My voice sounded drugged, doped, half asleep.

'Oh, God. You know, the girl you . . . the victim.' She stopped, embarrassed but still having failed to convey her message.

I gave up and closed my eyes. A moment or two later

Larry was in the room again, storming around, shouting at me, dressed only in boxer shorts decorated with red lips. The red lips mouthed and pouched and pursed. Helen hung in somewhere behind for a bit and then gave up and sat in a chair. Half-way through the tirade I buried my head under the blanket but that didn't stop the words coming through. You have to imagine them delivered at an increasing level of antipodean emphasis.

'You're a bastard, a selfish bastard! Though I insult the memory of my dead aunt. You're a cunt too, although that insults all the great race of women. You're a mean-spirited, self-centred twerp, a twerpess, a weedy pillock, a pip-squeak, a lemon, a teeny turd, a wanker, a twinky and twanky wanker! You make me sick and that makes me sicker because you're my cousin, my clever English cousin, and I want to be proud of you and hold you dear like you were someone special, like you were someone I loved. When your parents were killed, I was filled with sorrow. I was amazed at the sorrow I felt and I told myself I should look after you. That's what I knew was right. I felt good about that. Huh!' Here he gave a satirical bellow. 'And what did I land up with? A murderer, a fucking murderer!' For a moment he seemed to have run out of steam but it was only that his mood had shifted from straight anger to disconsolate anger. He stopped shouting.

'For example, have you for one moment, one little shitty moment, thought what it was like for her? No. I can answer for you. Not for one shitty moment. It just happened. That's how you view it. A fucking tragedy – for you, that is. Your view doesn't extend any further.'

He became so gloomy that he sat down. I risked popping my eyeballs and nose over the top of the blanket. At least he wasn't going to hit me now and I needed to breathe. Helen stood with her back against the bedroom door frowning miserably. I wondered whether it was worth defending myself.

'All this because I won't go back to Nell – not that I was ever really with her.'

Larry lifted his successful golden head and looked at me

wearily. 'No. Not just because of that. Although you may have problems with the police. It's just that I've seen a little bit of the damage you've caused and it's made me look at things differently.'

A faint notion of what Helen had been trying to tell me began to penetrate.

'It doesn't matter.' Larry looked at his naked splayed feet. 'I've got a headache and God knows what time it is in the morning.'

'You're my only friend, Larry.' I tried not to whine.

'Yeah. Yeah. But just tell me one thing, Pat.' He didn't seem to be angry any more. 'After what you did, how can you live with yourself?'

Out of the corner of my eye, Helen made a little move towards me and then stopped. I thought hard. I thought of all that time I'd spent in prison during which survival was the top priority. I thought of the discussions I'd had in therapy groups, in private with psychiatrists. I considered the endless conversations with other cons about what they'd done and how it had affected them. What did Larry want of me that was more than that?

'I've done my time,' I said.

He didn't even answer this so I repeated it to Helen. 'I've done my time. I've taken my punishment. I've admitted my guilt. What does he want me to do? Beat my breast night and day? Or perhaps he'd rather I shot myself. That would be simpler, wouldn't it? No problems for anyone then. I can see it's uncomfortable having a murderer – nearly – sleeping in your sitting room, particularly when it's Christmas and everything should be jolly good fun!' I was beginning to work myself up now. My eye was caught by the Father Christmas. I got out of my bed and picked it up. It was hard and smooth and round in my hand, like a champion ball, good and weighty too. I passed it from hand to hand, feeling the surging temptation of anger. Larry and Helen were both looking at me, both suddenly wide awake, eyes staring.

I was so powerful with that glass dome in my hand, Larry in his silly shorts, so vulnerable.

Helen said something – 'Don't', I suppose – but that had

196

no effect on me. I was filled with exultation and rage, on the point of entering that black loss of consciousness where violence becomes possible. I could smash Larry's nose, his face, his balls. I could smash up all that patronage and superiority which turned me into a weak pathetic creature, a twinky wanker and all those other twerps and turds he called me.

And yet I would not have done anything if Larry had stood his ground, facing me four-square, my big Aussie cousin. It was when he turned his back that I couldn't bear it any more. It was a gesture of disgust and derision, as if he was giving me up as a bad job. Screaming I can't remember what, I flung the glass dome at him with all my strength. I meant it to hit him all right but he did an easy sidestep and glass, water, snowflakes and Father Christmas smashed into the wall.

I sank to the floor and burst into tears. When I next looked up, I saw Helen carefully picking up the pieces. She had Father Christmas's head in one hand. I registered with a mixture of resentment and awe how women always remained practical, whatever the situation.

Larry stood over me. I sensed he was no longer angry, not even drunk, but he said nothing. Soon he went over to Helen. I could hear him trying to make up with her, being charming and apologetic. He was lucky.

'It'll be light in an hour or so.' Larry went to the curtains. His flat had a spectacular view over London but I wasn't too interested in that. Then Helen came over with a box of tissues. She blew my nose, made me get up off the floor and tucked me back into the sofa.

'We'll talk in the morning,' she said. I guess we were all glad to leave it at that.

THIRTY-ONE

I WENT home for Christmas. I took Maureen with me, whose contradictions between attitude and behaviour I was now inclined to attribute to loneliness. The house was decorated from top to toe. 'It was your mother's idea.' My father had a gleam in his eye.

Maureen became over-excited at being part of a real English family Christmas. She was particularly pleased with the crib which Charmian had set up in the corner of the dining room. 'It's not just decoration to her,' she told me seriously.

We went and sat in the living room. My father was already there, reading a newspaper with some difficulty since the nearest lamp was wound about with red tinsel. The ceiling was criss-crossed with cut-out lanterns, the mantelpiece was strung with Christmas cards and Charmian was just finishing hanging silver and gold balls on an enormous tree. 'You've left out the lavatory, Mum. I'm disappointed,' I shouted.

'Your mother is cooking us a magnificent supper.' My father gave up trying to read and took off his glasses.

I leaned back in my chair and closed my eyes. What had happened to this house in the couple of months since I'd last been here? It wasn't just the absurd gaiety of paper chains and baubles. It was in my father's voice when he talked about my mother, in my mother's movements as she caressed the saucepans.

'You look cheerful, Papa.' I said.

'And why shouldn't I be cheerful on Christmas Eve? If Christmas Eve is not for cheer, then tell me when?'

I tried to remember last Christmas Eve but it was part of that dark and cloudy time when my misery and self-pity stood between me and the rest of the world. He had bought me a tree, I remembered, as a symbol of new life but I took no care of it and all the needles dropped off. Besides, it was about then that I met his lady love.

Leaving Maureen addressing my father on 'woman as the heroine of American Mid-West literature', I went to the kitchen. I could tell by my mother's back that she was singing inside. I had never known my mother to be happy.

Without turning round, she announced, her voice round and full, 'She's gone, if you're wondering. Gone. Scarpered. Vanished to her sister in Canada. She wants to start a new life before it's too late. It's a miracle . . .'

'Mother. Do turn round. What are you talking about?' I don't know why I was so slow.

She had been basting a large bird and when she turned round, she held up the spoon like a fairy's wand. 'Her,' she trilled, eyes shining. 'She's realised I'll never clear off and Papa will never clear off from me so she's cleared off herself. Finally, she has behaved like a sensible woman.'

I did not respond appropriately. 'Oh, poor Papa!'

'Poor Papa!' She was not even angry but made as if to rap my knuckles with her greasy wand. 'Your papa is a survivor, dear. And besides, she was growing old.'

I still did not respond appropriately. 'Oh, poor Miss Mottram.' I thought of her on the beach, so game, and in her ugly flat, surrounded by tables.

'You're too young to understand.' My mother was still unoffended. 'It's undignified to be a mistress when you're middle-aged. Everyone's happier now. Look at it this way,' my mother began to giggle, 'Canada's gained a first-rate English teacher.'

'Well, then. I'm pleased for you.' At last I rose to the occasion, hugging her quickly before she could resist. But she didn't resist, even returned a touch of pressure. When she resumed her attentions to the fowl, it was with a more meditative air. She tapped its golden breast. 'You are well, dear. That, too, is part of my celebration.'

I drew away. This passion everybody had for making me well. 'Well'. What did they mean? Of course my physical injuries had healed. Of course I could walk better now, do my exercises without much pain, swim if I felt like it. But what about the scars engraved in my leg, running along my neck, shoulder, breast, on the back of my hand where I saw them every day? Did they know that I remember what happened to me every single day? And at night in my dreams. They all made the same mistake, even my warm-hearted analyst. They were all trying to make me 'well' like other people are well who haven't had a knife stuck in them by a perfect stranger.

I pulled further away from my mother and sat at the kitchen table. I wondered if she knew that Patrick William Downes was due out into the world, our world, my world, in a week's time. I thought she didn't.

'I am well,' I said. 'But not in the way you think. I am not recovered. I am not the same.'

'Of course not, dear.' My mother seemed flustered. Perhaps she did know his release date. 'You must not assume I'm stupid because I'm your mother. I meant you function well. You hold down a good job. You are alive and interested in things around you. I admire you.' She looked at me, smiling, and I saw she did admire me. All this because Miss Mottram had pushed off to Canada.

I still had not told her about Larry and the extraordinary thing that he wanted to happen. I looked up at her. She was crouched down, putting the roast back into the oven. A sudden warmth of sentiment made me want to crouch down beside her and stroke her woolly back. I must have been six or seven since I'd last felt the urge for that. Her fault?

'You were always so independent.'

And here, she was, echoing my thoughts. 'Daddy's girl,' I agreed.

'So clever.' That was true. I had been the first one in our family ever to go to university. Encouraged by my father, discouraged by my mother. 'You had Charmian.'

'Oh, yes.' This conversation was remarkable. It was an honest dialogue without rancour. I began to feel restless, afraid it would break, keen that it should break. Again, I was glad I had not told her about Larry. She would not have been able to deal with that. That was my problem, my secret. To avoid temptation, I left her and went back into the sitting room.

'The feminine gut is not only longer than the male but also thicker and stronger.' Maureen was nervous or she would not be talking such rubbish. And yet my father did not look

200

as if he was harassing her and Charmian was sitting under the Christmas tree in a blissful lump.

'Why are you talking such rot?' I interrupted her.

'It's a game,' said my father. He still had that gleam.

'I thought you hated games.'

'Not a bit of it. We each have a minute to talk about a given subject. I gave Maureen "gut".'

'She was brilliant,' contributed Charmian who I now saw was holding a stop-watch. It was perfectly ridiculous but there we were, sitting round on Christmas Eve playing games. Laughing. Even my mother joined us and delivered one minute on 'gravy'. That set off Maureen on the subject of a woman's role not being in the kitchen. But no one took much notice, least of all my mother.

'Demarcation lines are for work,' my father eventually roused himself slightly, 'not for home and especially not for Christmas.'

That night I opened my eyes after a nightmare and saw silver tendrils wavering round my dressing-table mirror. I decided they were magic water plants and watched them for a long time until I fell peacefully asleep. In the morning I saw that my mother had decorated my mirror with tinsel.

After breakfast, we all went to mass and when we arrived back the telephone was ringing. I reached it first.

'Hello.'

'Lydia?' It was Larry, his voice distinctive.

'Yes. Happy Christmas!'

'Oh. Uh. Happy Christmas.' He seemed unconvinced. It was odd for me to be the positive one. 'I'm calling with a bit of news.' There was a pause and I thought I heard a woman's voice whispering urgently.

'What news, Larry?' I asked gaily enough but it was my voice carrying on as before. We only had one bit of news in common.

'He's out.'

I became aware that everyone had gathered round me. If they were not to become part of this nightmare on Christmas Day in the morning, then I must dissimulate, smile, disarm their anxiety. 'Hold on a minute, Larry.' I turned to the anxious faces. 'It's Herbie, something about work. Confidential. You make coffee.' It was an Oscar performance. Even Maureen left.

'Larry?'

'Present. Look, Lydia, wouldn't you like to get it over with?'

'What do you mean, Larry? What are you talking about?' I tried desperately not to shriek. Had he gone mad? 'This is Christmas morning. I'm with my family . . .'

'That's what I thought. Christmas.'

He was mad. 'I never said I wanted to see him. I don't want to see him. He's mad.' Everybody was mad. 'He's dangerous. You told me, he's been attacking other people in prison.' I realised my voice was rising. 'Where is he, for God's sake, Larry?' I had to ask. I needed to know he was somewhere stable, not walking down the pavement towards me, this minute, banging on the door. I was panicking. It was rising inside me, stopping the breath reaching my lungs, turning my limbs to bits of rag.

'He's in my flat.'

'He's in your flat!' I sat down. He wasn't coming along the pavement but he was in Larry's flat.

'You knew he'd come to my flat. He's my cousin. I help him. It's my fucking duty to help the bastard!'

I registered that he sounded in nearly as an emotional state as me. It was weird. 'I can't take it in.'

'What do you mean? He's here. We've discussed it. Don't go hysterical on me now. I've got enough hysterical people to cope with without you.'

Definitely this was not the usual Larry. 'I won't be bullied, Larry. I don't have to be bullied.'

'Bullied!' It was an explosion.

I held the receiver away, considered putting it down but was drawn back by a woman's voice.

'My name's Helen. I'm sorry to intrude but I'm afraid Larry's in a bit of a state. He hasn't slept all night. He's upset. He wasn't expecting his cousin, you see, for another week.'

'I know.' A girl-friend apologising for him. The trembling was starting now and the hot and cold sweats.

'I didn't think he should shout at you like that. He's not being very rational.' She had a nice soothing voice. 'I just wanted to explain to you. He won't speak to you again. I've persuaded him. Next week, perhaps.'

'Where is he?'

She knew who I meant. 'In the flat. Here. Asleep. Next door.'

'Thank you. Goodbye.' The receiver was wet, glistening. They came in after I'd put it down. So I told my father, my mother, everybody. It was still Christmas morning when I'd finished but near enough midday to pour drinks all round.

'You're very quiet,' I said because no one seemed to have a view, not even Maureen. My father came over and held me.

'The point is,' I said from within his arms, 'despite all my meetings with Larry, despite all our discussions about me and my attitude and about the changes wrought by time and the need for forgiveness for a whole future and the role of the law as moral arbiter, I never really thought he would come out. Not really.'

CHAPTER
THIRTY-TWO

I SLEPT better than Larry. I could see that on his face when I woke. He was sitting near me, staring at the table. He wasn't used to difficulties and drama, of course. He was used to things going well, within his control. I had come and upset his order and it was hard not to be a little smug about it. Why should I be the only one to suffer?

I watched him for quite a few minutes while he still thought I was asleep and after a while I began to feel sorry for him. It wasn't his fault he was part of the bright ordinary world outside. I was glad I hadn't hit him with Father Christmas. I stretched my arms off the end of the sofa and pronounced cheerily, 'Freedom.'

He jumped and then glared. This was worse than I'd expected. 'Yeah. Freedom.' His tone was mean and ironic.

Despite enjoying the clean pyjamas, the softness of the sofa, the space and warmth of the room, so different from a prison cell, I saw that my welcome was limited.

'I'll be off,' I said. I wasn't afraid of facing the truth. Of course, he'd liked me better when I was locked up two hundred miles north. 'But I'll need money.'

'Sure, you'll need money.' He was sullen. He probably had a blistering hangover.

'Where's Helen?' I tried to look at the golden watch on his golden wrist. It seemed to be one o'clock. Time for Christmas lunch. I thought better of suggesting that. There's no one worse-tempered than a good man conscious of behaving badly.

I lay back until my stomach announced a need for coffee and at the same time I remembered about the girl. The so-called victim. Hadn't that been the lovely Helen's explanation for his behaviour . . . ?

'I'm in too deep,' he mumbled as I got out to search the kitchen. 'I've lost my cool. I've lost my sense of proportion.'

Perhaps he was asking for help. Deciding discretion was the better part of valour, I headed for the kitchen anyway. I found my clothes there, clean and dry and folded. How could I fail to be cheerful with service like that? Prison gives you that, at least, an appreciation of small comforts.

Larry came and stood over me while I was smacking my lips over a cup of really good coffee. 'Last night went wrong,' he said.

'My fault', I smiled up at him warmingly, 'for coming out a week early.'

He sat down opposite me. 'What were you like as a little boy?' His seriousness was hurtful to my good humour.

'Like other little boys. Cars. Football.'

'But you were cleverer than that. How old were you when

I first came over? Sixteen? Seventeen? You were very thin. I thought you worked too hard. Or something.'

'My parents loved each other more than they loved me, if that's what you're trying to say.'

He looked surprised. This was old ground to me. If he was trying to trace the roots of a psychopath, he need look no further. Deprived of affection from an early age. So then where are we?

'You didn't seem angry.'

I had no comment. What could he be thinking? Did he want to hear how I'd regularly beaten up my mother? But I loved my mother. I longed for her. Forget that one. My father wasn't so bad either. 'One of the first things I want to do is look at the house my parents left me.'

He looked at me wanly, almost blankly, so I carried on extemporising. 'Perhaps I'll get the tenants out, live in the country. Or perhaps I'll get the tenants out and sell the house and travel round the world.' It seemed a good idea to point out that I was a man of resources when I could get my hands on them.

The businessman was galvanised for a moment. 'The rental barely covers the mortgage but I kept it going as an investment for the future.' He sank back again. 'You're not even going to give Nell a chance?'

'I'm doing her a favour.' He was so down, he didn't even argue with that. 'I'm a mess. I've been retarded by two years in prison. I'm a jumble. I'm not fit to be a husband. Bruno the Bear will be happier without me.' I could see my frivolous manner was beginning to grate but I was set on my tracks now. 'I'm hungry. Starved. Famished.'

'Yeah.' He looked round the kitchen. 'Helen's gone for some food.'

'Great! That's great!' Shops open on Christmas Day – that was something. I bounced upright. Shadow boxing, that was what I was doing, ducking and weaving. Even in his reduced state, he could have felled me with a chosen word or two. 'I'll clear up my bed.'

I was used to tidiness. I liked things to be tidy. He followed me back again, still lugubrious. 'When I heard what you'd done, I never hesitated. You were my flesh and blood. I never condemned you. Never. Not to anyone. Not in my dreams. Something terrible had happened to you and you needed me. It had happened to you, that's what I thought. I never blamed you. I didn't even try to understand. I made a few excuses, talked of your parents' car crash, but that was the limit of my understanding. Now I think I was afraid of not being able to feel sorry for you.' He stopped here. It was quite enough.

'You were very good to me,' I said.

He gave me a fleeting, sideways sort of look. Not nice. Then he sighed, half smiled. 'I thought I could play God.'

This was beyond me. If it was God I wanted to talk about I could have let myself be caught by all those chaplains who chased about the prison system.

'You haven't changed in two years, have you?' He was so full of wisdom, it was unbearable. Stupid, too. Of course I had changed. I was tougher, braver, more of a man. I knew things he didn't. I could see he didn't want that sort of answer.

Luckily, Helen came in. She was even prettier in daylight, pink-cheeked above a huge box of groceries. I jumped up at once and took it from her. She smiled and thanked me. I could become her favourite person. If I stayed around long enough.

'Can I help you cook? I haven't cooked for nearly two years.'

'You like cooking?' She was delighted. As her cold morning glow subsided, I saw she looked exhausted.

'Amazing place, London,' I continued chattily as we unloaded the stuff. 'Shops open on Christmas Day. Amazing.'

'We were going to eat out.' Larry came in behind me, still depressed.

I wondered whether to get angry but I actually felt pleased and grateful to them both. The idea of facing the world on my own after yesterday's experiences was not appealing. I applied myself eagerly to peeling potatoes.

Larry drank coffee behind my back. This seemed to cheer

him up or perhaps it was the smoked salmon Helen was laying out lovingly, strip by strip. At any rate, he left us to put on some good heavy beat music. Things were looking up. Another few minutes and he'd opened a bottle of champagne.

'I thought I'd never want another drink,' he said as he poured me a glass. 'And never want to see you again. But here I am pouring us both a glass of bubbly.'

'Life's like that,' I ventured, 'unpredictable.'

'It isn't the unpredictability. It's the inevitability.'

'Ah,' I said, not understanding. Besides, I had the lettuce to wash.

'We are inevitably locked together. Same family. There it is.'

'That's nice,' I said.

'But I have to tell you, Pat, that I'm not on your side any more. Now I've stopped to think about it I realise I don't like what you did and I don't like you and I don't forgive you.'

'You don't have to forgive me,' I mumbled. I turned round and caught Helen's eye. She attempted an encouraging smile.

'You're right there. I don't have to. And I don't. I'm not sorry for you. You don't care. The bitch of it is I like the girl you did it to. That's it.' He became more animated, his dead-pan gloom lifting like the flap of a curtain. 'I had this plan, you see, to bring you together, make everything OK for you both. Forgive and forget. Stupid. A very stupid idea. You're not capable of even understanding what I'm talking about. I'd be doing her the worst favour in her life introducing you to her.' He suddenly banged one mutton hand into the other.

'I'll hand you over to Ruth, that's what I'll do. She'll look after you.'

'Who's Ruth?' He had still not recovered his calm after last night, I saw.

'Ruth's your solicitor. You know Ruth.' His eyes were brighter.

'I'm not a parcel.'

'Ruth can sort out your house for you. Your job. That Manchester job I've been working on. Ruth loves helping young men.'

After this unilateral decision, we had an agreeable lunch with Larry making polite conversation and Helen serving this terrific food that we were still eating when it became dark. Helen was an angel, an angelic woman with none of the velvet-covered claws of Nell. I even showed her my prison newspaper and she said all the right things. 'That's real,' she said. 'Real life, real people speaking.'

I looked at Larry but he was lying back in his chair, replete. 'You must show it to Ruth.' He stretched out both his muscular legs and then his arms. He glanced at Helen and then beyond her to the bedroom door. I got the message.

'I need a walk. A constitutional.' I did not and I was not happy either at the thought of Helen lying under that heavy body but he was my host and I needed a bed for another couple of nights.

It was very dark and cold outside. No one walks along that part of the river at seven o'clock on Christmas Day. I hugged Larry's coat round me – it reached well below my knees – and pictured, for the first time what the old cons would be doing inside. Nothing, of course. Smoking. Wanking. Playing cards. It isn't even cosy in prison, I reminded myself.

After about half an hour, I felt ready to return but, even assuming that Larry had an energetic get-up-and-run-with-the-ball attitude, that did not seem a long enough absence. My hands deep in Larry's pocket I found my fingers curling round a car key. That was the answer. I could sit in the Porsche, turn on the heater and radio, make myself comfortable. I had never passed my driving test so there was no question of driving, just somewhere to be warm and comfortable while I waited for the screwing – no, I must not insult Helen – the love-making to stop.

Larry hadn't bothered to put the car away. There it stood, all on its own, under a lamp-post. I hurried forward and was cosily installed in a trice. Now the new hard-angled blocks of flats, the partly constructed climbing-frames of scaffolding and the still underdeveloped ragged spaces were quite acceptable surroundings. Warmed up and relaxed, I soon fell asleep.

'Excuse me, sir.' It was like one of those B movies, the twisted face peering in at the window. 'Can I see your licence?' He'd obviously been mouthing at the window for some time. I woke up enough to wind it down.

'I'm not driving anywhere.' He was a young policeman, impatient, on duty over Christmas and not paid quite enough to put him in a good humour.

'Your driving licence and the car's papers.'

'Look, officer. I'm sitting in this car, not driving it. It belongs to my cousin who I'm staying with.'

'So where's he?'

'In his flat.'

'So why are you down here?' I sighed an exasperated sigh which annoyed him further. 'A lot of cars go missing in this area. This is an expensive car.' He realised he'd overlooked a bit of the procedure. 'Would you mind stepping out of the car, sir.'

I stepped out. It was not a B movie, it was a bad dream. In a moment he'd breathalyse me and find me positive. 'What are you worried about, officer?'

'Suspicious circumstances.' He had a bullish, stupid face. I began to realise I had to find the energy to take him more seriously. I was out of prison on parole.

'Why don't we ring my cousin's doorbell? It's only a few yards away. He'll explain.'

'We can ring him from the station.'

He was determined to take me in, give everyone on duty something to do, make their night worthwhile. If I looked up I could actually see the light from Larry's apartment. But it might as well have been on the moon. We walked together, side by side. I wondered how long it would take them to discover I'd come out of prison yesterday. Not long. Sod's law. My prison training began to take over. You're in their hands, let them run the show.

Larry was not pleased to get a call from the police station. At least they put me on the line. I explained what had happened. My captor had become much less aggressive once we reached the station and I realised I had been his passport to light and company. He sat beside me, quite cheerful, as my story was proved true. He even apologised to Larry. 'It's a funny area where you live. Sometimes we get a bit too careful.'

He then began nodding and giving me sidelong looks which I interpreted rightly as a reaction to Larry explaining why he might have thought I looked suspicious. He put down the receiver and turned to me with a self-satisfied expression on his stupid face.

'Out yesterday, eh?'

'You'll have to drive me back,' I said. Was it only yesterday?

We hardly talked, Larry and I, when I was delivered back. No hope of sympathy there. The escorting policeman gave him the car key, as if I were a naughty boy, not to be trusted. My bed was already made, with a sandwich set beside it. From the bedroom I could hear the sound of the television, but Helen did not appear.

'We've retired.' Larry wouldn't look me in the face.

'Fine then. See you in the morning.' If he could he would have put me in solitary but instead he left me comfortable and cared for. That's what I told myself as I switched off the light. What I couldn't do was go to sleep. Even when I closed my eyes I seemed to see the shapes in the room, the bulk of the furniture, the vacuum of corners, the glint of pictures and glass table, the long folds of the curtains. I was not used to so much in a room. I opened my eyes and switched on the light. The silence was absolute, not a peep from the room next door. I realised I had no idea what time it was and I also saw the telephone, still a remarkable sight for me.

The speaking clock told me it was eleven twenty-two, still Christmas Day. I tried to think who else to telephone and then I began to wonder what had happened to my watch, which I had left behind on that jolly summer's day.

Even directory enquiries was an excitement for me. Soon I had the Burnses' residence number and I was ringing into what must have been a sad and sleeping house. I didn't even have the excuse of being drunk. It was Nell who answered. 'Happy Christmas,' I said. I imagined her lumpy, night-smelling, standing dazedly in her nightdress. 'What did you do with my watch? It was my father's, you know.' To do her justice, she put the phone down without so much as an audible gulp.

CHAPTER
THIRTY-THREE

THAT CHRISTMAS was enough to make you believe in God. I have never been treated with such care and kindness. Whenever I seemed quiet, someone would be there to suggest we play cards, put on a tape, have a drink or go for a walk in Richmond Park. The walk was in the afternoon.

'If only we could borrow a dog, we'd look like a real family party.' My father drove us, we three girls squashed into the back, complaining cheerfully about the size of each other's bones. We drove right into the middle of the park so London receded to tower blocks on the horizon. Not far from where we parked a herd of deer scattering under the black leafless trees made me feel we were entering a landscape painting. It was a good, diminishing feeling.

'We're all in London too much,' I told Charmian and Maureen who walked on either side of me. Of course, Maureen could not leave the unspoken subject for long.

'Surely, you can't help but be curious about him?' Her words caught up in Charmian's who started at the same time to compliment me on my brisk stride.

I chose to answer my sister. 'I still go to a physiotherapist once a week but that's more for my shoulder than my leg. Even my left hand is nearly back to normal.'

Charmian, so spiritual, so uninterested in the flesh, liked playing hospitals, so she gave me all kinds of anecdotes and advice while I breathed deeply and, of course, considered whether I was curious to see Patrick William Downes. Are you curious to see someone you've thought of every day for 578 days? Who you hate? It was not a question I could answer, except to say, as I had to Larry, I didn't want to see him, I was frightened of him, he was my nightmare, my black hole. Perhaps I was curious too but, if so, it was not strong enough to overcome my fear. What I wanted was to see him wiped off the face of the earth. Besides, I had seen him twice. Admittedly, they seemed like two different people, the healthy sun-gold young man who had attacked me when my back was turned and the pallid, hairless slug who had faced me in court. But that could mean he had now become a third person, strong again, violent, hair grown in any shade at all.

'No. I am not curious to see him.' I stopped to confront Maureen.

Charmian took my hand. 'That's decided, Lydia.' My parents joined us and they gathered around me again as they had in the house, a protective circle.

'You've faced enough,' said my mother.

'You've got your job to consider.' My father smiled encouragingly.

I managed to begin walking again. While we were standing there, we had all seemed so enormous, huge swollen bodies of emotion. He had seemed large, too, hovering over us in a wicked genie-like presence. I had lost any sense of where we were, of the deer and trees and sky. But now I could feel the leaves crackling under my feet and once more I became aware of being part of a landscape and our sizes reducing into proper proportion.

I addressed my mother who had taken Maureen's place. 'Sometimes I feel so enormous I blot out the rest of the world.'

'Madness is total absorption in the self,' commented my mother.

'The only true happiness lies in living for others,' added Charmian.

'Do you remember how you kept saying you forgave him?' I did not need to look at Charmian to know she would understand immediately.

Serious conversations were unusual in our family. 'It was very hard.' She was unsure. 'I couldn't bear the emotions he made me feel. I hated him not just for what he'd done but the situation into which he'd placed us. He seemed to have done something to you that was unforgivable. But I couldn't live like that. You can say my forgiving him was weakness, if you like.' Charmian always made out the worst case for herself.

'I can't forgive him.' My mother was fierce, her wintry grey face suddenly taking on colour.

'Dear. Dear.' I behaved as if it was not my concern. I was calmer, it seemed, more light-hearted than them. 'I thought forgiveness was the basis for Christianity.'

'Then I'm not a good Christian.' My mother, I suspected, was not just thinking about Patrick William Downes.

THIRTY-FOUR

I woke up in the morning with a burning sensation in my ankle. This was my 'conscience' getting its own back for my telephone call to Nell. It was leaping out of the hearse to see her which had twisted it in the first place. I hobbled off my couch and into the kitchen where I found Helen making breakfast like a good wife. She looked guilty when she saw me and immediately cut a slice of bread and put it in the toaster.

'I'm sorry about last night. The police, I mean.' She was thinner and paler than I remembered as if something was draining away her pink-cheeked vitality. A combination of Larry and me, I suppose.

'It was hardly your fault.'

'But I should have been around when you arrived back.'

This was touching. I took my toast and sat opposite her. If Nell had expressed as much sympathy I would have hated her for it. What was happening here? 'Well, thank you for thinking that anyway. I'm afraid I took it out on . . .' I refused to say 'my wife' but I was not sure if 'Nell' would mean anything to her. I paused.

'I heard you telephone.'

'Oh.' She had me stumped. 'Did Larry hear?'

'No.' She smiled briefly. 'Luckily.'

'Quite.' We sat in silence. It was now two whole days since I had left prison and my head was just beginning to clear. 'Larry's very angry with me, isn't he?'

'Yes.'

'For not going back to Nell?'

'Yes.'

'What do you think?'

She looked at me so long I thought she was sure to say, 'But I hardly know you,' but instead she pushed her hair from one side of her head to the other and said so quietly I had to lean forward, 'I don't think you're fit to live near a baby, particularly when it's your baby.'

I saw she was blushing with embarrassment but it wasn't that which made me feel a dark redness start from inside me and well up into my face. It was pain and humiliation. Here was a kind, objective woman telling me, face to face, that I was a danger to my own child. If anyone had spoken to me as she had done in prison I'd certainly have socked him one. And I'd been in prison a long time.

I sat there, rigid, hoping she wouldn't say any more. And she didn't, except, 'I'm sorry', on her way out of the room.

After a while I became a little more relaxed. I cleared up the kitchen, even taking pleasure in the washing and the drying and the wiping of surfaces. Then I thought I might return to my sofa-bed but when I entered the sitting room again, a transformation had taken place. The room was extremely bright, lit not only by sharp winter sun but by lamps ejecting white triangles onto the ceiling. As I hovered at the doorway, a roar of sound, as if African jungle music had been crossed with the 'Hallelujah Chorus', rolled towards me. In the middle of it all, stood Larry, god-like, with arms folded.

I determined to keep the tone light, 'The Day of Judgment, I presume?' It's extraordinary how people worsen under pressure. Now that I was not turning out to be the character Larry had planned, pleased and amenable, ready to start a new life along the lines he proposed, he turned out to be childishly domineering.

'I am not judging you, Pat. That is not my right.' The glare of the room was exhausting. I headed for a chair and collapsed there as comfortably as possible. Larry swivelled round so that he could still fix an implacable gaze upon me, a gaze, incidentally, which contradicted the apparent meaning of his words. Of course he was judging me.

'I'll take this Manchester job, if it's still going.' We were both shouting above the music.

'Yes. Yes,' roared Larry. 'You should do that. Get digs there. Get working.'

It struck me that there were a lot more hours to the day and I couldn't carry on at this level. 'I'm off to see my parents' house if you can lend me a few pounds.'

'It's Boxing Day,' said Larry more quietly since we were in a quieter patch of the music and, at last, he sat down.

'I'm going anyway.' I stood. One up and one down, it was absurd how much we disliked each other at that moment.

'Stealing my car, perhaps?' That was a pleasure to me, seeing him behave so badly. 'I need a drink. What time is it?'

'I haven't got a watch.'

'You haven't got anything.' He was certainly letting it all hang out. In a moment he'd be back to saying I didn't deserve to live. Fuck him.

'Bye. Bye.' I was out of the door and running down the stairs before he'd had time to do more than stare bemusedly at his large bare feet. 'It is not that I want to go but that I can't bear to stay,' echoed in my head as I hopped down four flights of stairs (ankle hurting) and hit the street.

Larry stood there waiting for me. Trust him to take the lift. 'Don't be ridiculous,' he said wearily.

'I want to go to my house.' I was the sullen little boy, thwarted in his desire.

'Your house? Your house?' He seemed genuinely bewildered. I stood on the pavement where a faint smell of the river added a spice of salt and filth to our conversation – it must have been low tide.

'My house which was my home. I told you yesterday. I want to see it. Catching up with the past, that sort of thing.'

'But it's Boxing Day. Why should the tenants want to see you on Boxing Day?'

'Perhaps they won't be there.' Prison teaches you a few useful lessons, like not taking too much notice of Boxing Day. After all, I was supposed to be free now.

Then Larry had a selfish inspiration. 'I'll drop you there. But you'll have to make your own way back.' Clearly he envisaged the joy of a few hours without me.

It was midday, the sun gleaming off the Porsche, London not quite as empty as I'd expected, but soon we were dashing along the motorway, heading west to the little village of Silverhill. He dropped me at the gateway. It was one of those largish houses which make up for its position on the main road by a truncated driveway ending in a swirl of gravel. I walked over the gravel, gloomily shaded by rhododendrons and laurel, until I stood in front of the house. No curtains were drawn and the sun, coming from behind me, turned the closed window panes into black pools. It was a regular retirement home, pitched roof, mock-Tudor frames, pretentious door set in the middle like a child's drawing. There were no cars to be seen.

I thought it looked expensive and wished mortgages did not exist. I was fifteen when my parents bought the house, a skinny, immature sixteen when they started living in it and I spent my first holidays there. I went to the side of the house, found the gate locked to the main garden and climbed over it, past the dustbins in their usual place and onto the lawn, well mowed, the pond in the middle, the apple trees and vegetable patch beyond. It was a big garden but dull.

I had been very bored indeed in that garden. It was best on hot days when I could take my Eliot and Larkin with a rug and lie flat on the green grass under the blue sky. The grass was wet now so I went over and sat on the stone coping round the pond. There were some dark leaves, set on prickly stems with orange berries that I remembered from other winters. 'Cotoneaster', my mother had told me they were called; the prickles discouraged the birds from eating the berries. Correction: I had been very unhappy indeed in that garden.

My mother had become keen on 'Nature'. She said there was so much more of it in England than in the dried-out places they'd been posted to in the last years. She joined a ramblers' society and reacted crossly when I suggested that if she liked that sort of thing, she should live in the real countryside and not in a suburban imitation. 'But your father likes to be in easy reach of the City,' she had replied. She had not added that it might be useful for me, too, who had just left my boarding-school for a tutor's in London. She talked about berries, birds, the sky and my father. But never about me. Never at the time, never later.

The stone coping was cold on my bottom and, despite the sun, I was beginning to feel cold all over. The house, I remembered, was always very warm. Both my parents had become thin-skinned over the years. I, who only joined them from my English school in the country for one holiday in three had a more energetic bloodstream.

I spent a lot of time throwing off sweaters and opening windows. I could hardly sit through a meal with them, the dining room was so hot, and in the evening I could never talk to them for more than a few minutes because they stayed so close to the fire. I told my mother she would be fine if she wore sweaters instead of silly blouses and dresses but she wanted to look feminine. She liked looking pretty and she liked my father complimenting her. 'I don't like being all muffled up,' she told me when I complained of the heat. 'I want my body to breathe.'

But now I was cold and looked at the house with a certain longing. Telling myself it belonged to me, I headed for the window to the downstairs lavatory which had never properly locked. It was over two years since I had been in the house, not long perhaps but in that time my parents had died, I had married, nearly killed a girl, been to prison, become a father and come out of prison again. I should have felt a different person.

The window was unchanged. I pushed through it, used the lavatory since I was there, noticing as I did so that the wallpaper was also unchanged, and then entered the main body of the house. Or at least tried to but the door was locked. Without hesitation, I put my shoulder to the thin wood and waited for the sound of splintering. Then I was inside.

After the noise of my breaking and entering had subsided, it felt very quiet. Wandering from room to room, I might have been the ghost instead of my parents. The house was still warm but some rooms had been rearranged considerably. I reached my parents' bedroom. Double beds look much the same. This one was covered with some white lacy material. I sat on it picturing the way my mother, who retained always a fairness of skin and face, had looked to my father. She was his princess to the last.

I always thought of him as older than her. I was the beloved son of their loving loins, except that it wasn't like that. When my mother looked at me it was with anxiety. Why was I not eating? In bed? Out playing? Working? Meeting friends? Her instinctive reaction when she saw me was to worry that I was not employed, preferably out of her sight. She took more pleasure in a cotoneaster than me.

She would not have recognised herself in this description. She thought she was a loving mother, doing everything for my own good. She counted her anxiety as love. But it didn't feel like that to me. It felt as if she was easier and happier when I was somewhere else, which I had been most of the time anyway because of their postings abroad. They had learnt to live without me. My father never kissed me at all, and when my mother kissed me it brought tears to my eyes because her skin was so soft and smelled so sweet and was removed from me so quickly. I should have got used to it but I never did. It was pathetic. Worse, it was perverted. I loved my mother too much.

Kicking off my shoes, well, it was the least I could do, I lay down on the white coverlet and shut my eyes.

It was an accident, how it happened. Pure accident. They were away, for once not together. She had gone to a friend's, he to some college reunion. I was alone in the house. That hot, hot house. I took off my clothes and got into their bed. It was a nice comfortable bed, like this one, perhaps this very one. I fell asleep. She came home. It was just a muddle. So simple. She thought I was my father.

I was asleep. I was naked, that's true, in their bed, but I wasn't expecting her back. That's true. I think that's true. It wasn't my fault. She undressed. She got into bed. Of course everyone has always said how like my father I looked. Perhaps she'd had a drink or two. I don't know. We never talked.

She began to fondle me. I woke up and I knew it was her. I looked up at her. She was naked, her breasts enormous above me. Her eyes brilliant, even in the dark. I thought she knew it was me. I really thought that. I was aroused. My God. So simple.

She screamed. She smacked and cracked her hands about my face and head. She pulled my hair. She drove me out of the room. I went out into the garden. It was surprisingly light and very cold. I sat out there all night.

In the morning I heard my father's car come back and went over the garden wall. I didn't come back for two days. I don't know what she told my father. About my absence, I mean. She would never have told him about the other thing.

When I came back, it had gone, vanished, never been. Nothing was different. Nothing. Truly. But I wish she hadn't died like that. With him. It didn't give me much of a chance.

I went to sleep on that white coverlet. I was like Goldilocks, a wicked interloper. An outcast.

Like Goldilocks, I was woken up some immeasurable time later, by angry shouting, 'Who's been sleeping in my bed?' or something very like it. I did not leap up and jump out of the window, partly because I would have broken my leg and partly because the shouting receded again and I was left alone.

Tentatively, very tentatively – I would have real problems if the bears had rung the police – I carried my shoes and crept downstairs. Talking was coming from the sitting room. It was beginning to grow dark and through the half-open door I could see a lamp covered with a patterned material which I didn't remember. Sitting beside it was a youngish dark-haired woman, sleek as a seal, and standing by her side what must have been her husband, tall, with a confident, vulgar voice. He was haranguing someone else out of my vision.

'I don't care if he does own the house. I'm the tenant. If he breaks down a door, as of now, it's my door. If he sleeps on the bed, it's my bed.'

'You're quite right.' A woman's voice answered him, a vaguely familiar voice. 'Legally you're quite right. Absolutely right. What I am pleading is mitigating circumstances. I am appealing for you to act charitably . . .'

It was my solicitor, Ruth. Half smiling, I sat down on the bottom stair. Let her get me out of this one. And she did, without even letting them know I had just come out of prison. 'A little disturbed' was how she described me.

'Get him out of here, then,' my tenant said eventually, 'and prepare yourself for a whacking big bill.' This idea seemed to mollify him.

Ruth came out, precise and cool as ever, and found me on the stairs putting on my shoes. 'Come along.' Perhaps she was afraid I might attack my tenants but I didn't care about them and felt more sleepy than anything else. Ruth took my arm and, under the tenants' mistrustful gaze, led me from my parents' house. Naughty boy, Pat, I thought to myself. Smack, smack.

Ruth's car, not interesting like a Porsche, stood in the driveway. 'Larry phoned me,' she explained briefly. I looked back at the house where the well-groomed couple stood in the door not quite shaking their fists.

'Lucky I came.' Ruth saw where I was looking.

Then my heart did lurch unpleasantly. 'You mean I could have been back inside?' She didn't answer. 'Thanks,' I said.

'Yes. I'm taking you to my flat where you can stay till tomorrow.'

'Cheers.'

So that is how I took up with my solicitor.

THIRTY-FIVE

My BODY grew sleeker. The thicker coating of flesh cushioned the effect of the scars so that they were no longer the most noticeable feature about me. I was not so desperate to hide. Instead of physiotherapy, I joined an exercise class. It was held in a grim basement room, not at all grand and no one seemed to notice how I struggled and sagged. For me, even that much was a triumph.

After Christmas Larry had made a public announcement. 'The paper is not doing as well as I expected,' he informed us in his heroic Australian style. 'And since I'm not in the charity business, I must make changes.'

I thought at the time that his delivery of 'not in the charity business' was unusually fierce but could hardly guess at my involvement in the decision. 'A free newspaper is a good concept and by that I mean a money-making concept,' he went on to tell us, 'but not if it looks like a rag. Nobody reads a free rag. They throw it in the garbage bin. A free paper needs to look fifty times more appealing than a paper that costs.'

It turned out that he was telling us that we were now to become a glossy magazine, with articles about food and clothes and an emphasis on the famous. ' "Photo-gossip" is hot,' he informed us. It seemed that the photographic editor would be the most important person on the paper. I could hardly see a place for my kind of journalism. Herbie, initially swinging his legs on the desk, had become so rigid that it was easy to tell he hadn't been warned of this new development. After we left, he stayed behind with Larry.

Sue and I (Sue not as glaringly pretty as when I'd first met her) chatted hysterically. 'I'm certainly leaving,' Sue cried. 'It was bad enough admitting you worked for a freebie without being forced to write stupid pieces about vulgar bores.'

'And who will want to read about the mentally unstable cast out into a cold world?' I added. This was the piece I was presently writing.

'We'll both leave,' said Sue.

But at the end of the day Larry descended on me, and soon we were sipping champagne in a dark red room with a bar at one end and groups of little tables festooned with olives and sophisticated nuts and crisps.

'I don't know what I'm doing here,' I protested weakly. 'You're just another greedy businessman.'

'Oh, I know you're all angry but there's something I have to say to you.' Here he stopped totally and gulped at his glass as if it held water. I refused to speak. 'Yeah. Well.' He began again. 'I've tried to help you, Lydia. When I discovered who you were, I thought it my duty to try to help you. And you've impressed me.'

'Thank you, Larry.'

'No. Not that.' Absent-mindedly, I presumed, he started on my champagne. 'So I thought it was in your interest to get to grips, if you know what I mean, with my cousin. So I rang you on Christmas morning. I shouldn't have but I did. It was all part of the same belief, that you and Pat were both human beings.' Since he paused here I put on my most satirical expression, although I expect it was lost in the gloom.

'That was too simple, I guess.'

'Yes,' I agreed.

'So that's what I wanted to tell you. I was wrong. You should have nothing more to do with him. You're OK. You're doing great, girl, so stay that way.'

Gradually, it dawned on me that he was speaking under the pressure of deep emotion. Because this particular subject still took me over like a bad dream, I tended not to be very sensitive to what was going on round me. But now I saw he was sweating, his voice even unsure, trembling. I was not sympathetic but I was curious. What had happened to make him lose command in this way? As if he guessed what I was thinking, he began again, hesitatingly.

'I had him staying with me. My little cousin. My orphan cousin.'

I decided I didn't want to hear this line again so I stood up.

'No. Don't go. Please?' He was appealing to me. I looked down on his yellow crinkly hair, his blue eyes, his suede-covered shoulders. He needed me, which made a change. I sat down again.

'He came on Christmas Eve. He'd left prison that morning. He was limping, strange, not properly dressed for winter. He'd been to see his wife and baby.'

'I need another glass of champagne,' I said. After all, he'd finished mine.

He ordered and carried on talking. 'I was surprised. Helen was there.' I didn't interrupt to ask whether Helen was his latest girl-friend. 'The truth is, I didn't want him in my flat. He was interrupting my Christmas. But we rallied round, Helen and I. Helen's a good girl. She's kind. We went out for a celebration dinner. I drank too much. And then I realised I hated him. Deeply. Probably always had. Slimy. Cold. Twisted. Selfish. Unhealthy. Vermin. I wished he was back in prison. That was the good part. He is all those things. Now I can believe he meant to kill you. He's turned into the man who could do that. He isn't a whimpering boy any more, pitiable. He's a nasty vicious man. He hated me too. He wanted to smash my face in.'

'What with?' I didn't want an answer. I just wanted to stop him for a moment.

'What with?' He looked bewildered. I had managed to break his chain of recall. 'A heavy glass object.' He made more of an effort. 'It had a Father Christmas in it. He'd brought it for me as a present.'

'And then he wanted to smash your face in with it?'

'Yes. That's the point. He didn't manage it because I side-stepped. But he wanted to. What was I going to say? I was telling you . . .' He faltered unhappily.

'Was Helen there?' I felt powerful asking these questions. Now I wanted to know the answer. He hadn't attacked me with a glass Father Christmas.

'Yes. That's it. Helen didn't see him as I did. She saw a pathetic creature, abused by the system. She saw a victim.'

'I don't know,' I said since he had stopped again, although

still seeming in profound thought. 'That's just words.' I spoke airily as if it had nothing to do with me.

'Oh, yes. Words.' He was becoming bitter now. 'But Helen had to go further than words. We got rid of him so that Helen and I could have a bit of what she was there for. He went quite happily. And the next thing I know, there's a policeman on the line saying he was caught stealing my car. Bad enough, you'd think, but Helen blamed me. "That's it!" she said, in a quite unnatural tone. "No more screwing till you give him the attention he deserves." So the next morning when he insisted he had to see his parents' house, I drove him there. On Boxing Day. Crazy. I hated him.'

I was beginning to feel dizzy. The champagne, the darkness, his passion.

'I left him there and went back to Helen. "Let's enjoy ourselves," I said to her. But she was unresponsive. Unresponsive, that's an understatement. I couldn't even touch her. "What about Pat?" That's what concerned her. "How will he get back?" "What the hell do I care how he gets back?" In the end I rang Ruth. She was his solicitor. She went out to him. So I told Helen, "You can relax, he's taken care of." He was taken care of, as I thought. But then I get another phone call, a few hours' later. At least, it's not from the police. It's from Ruth.'

'Why are you telling me all this, Larry?' I interrupted him. I wanted to go home. I wanted to talk to Herbie. I thought of his diffidence, his lanky body with longing. 'I don't want to hear any more. It has nothing to do with me.'

'No.' He gave me a half glance, the first time he'd looked my way for some time. 'I've nearly finished. The point is that Helen's gone off. Just because of him. Fucking bastard.'

I stood up. 'You're not telling me, Larry, anything I don't know. In fact, I might say, I told you so.'

'If Ruth hadn't been there, he'd have been done for breaking and entering. And Helen blamed me for taking him there.'

'Goodbye, Larry. I don't want to hear about Patrick William Downes ever again.' He didn't seem surprised. Of course now he felt just the same.

THIRTY-SIX

RUTH WAS terrific at the beginning. She knew prison. She left me alone, asked no questions, told me I could use the spare room in her flat until I went up north or any time at all.

I had met her first in police cells, then in court cells, then in court and afterwards in the little green rooms, more like cells, reserved for solicitors visiting their clients. Or peers of the realm, visiting whoever – their friends, I suppose. I had always liked that touch.

'Laughable, isn't it?' I said, making conversation on that first drive back from my parents' house. 'The way we're dropped dead once we're out of Her Majesty's care.'

'You've got a probation officer, haven't you?' She was snappy. Being terrific did not mean she was particularly sympathetic. She knew too much about ex-prisoners for any encouragement in self-pity. Besides, she did not have a gentle nature. She had a hard greyish face, narrow eyes and cropped hair. Her voice was strong, her figure spare and straight. She was short on any of the obviously feminine characteristics.

We had supper, or, at least, bread and cheese, on a table that she only partially cleared of her papers. She was so unlike Larry's Helen you wouldn't believe she was of the same species. But I felt comfortable with her.

'Have you done this before?' I asked her some time in the first few days.

'Yes,' she answered briefly, not looking at me. She seldom looked at me, as if my appearance, too, was part of my right to privacy. Or perhaps I just looked so unpleasant.

I had a cold and my pale prison face was decorated by a red swollen nose, chapped lips and the little running eyes. I still had no proper clothes since I had never recovered my case from the station. I didn't mind any of this particularly. Together with my still aching ankle it gave me an excuse to stay in bed, which I did for my first five days in Ruth's flat.

My little room, functional and soon fuggy, was not unlike a cell.

In the early evening of the tenth day Ruth came in, opened a window and addressed me straight. 'I'm expecting a visitor. I want you out. I'll glow you money for the cinema and a pizza. I don't want you back till eleven forty-five.' Her precision made it easier for me, although I wondered if she had invented the visitor because she seemed to have no friends. In the flat there was no sign of any life outside work.

The film was badly made, badly written, a thriller in which violence took place at immense speed. This was ridiculous. Although in my own case, I had suffered a kind of black-out during which violence had been done, in all my conversations with violent criminals it had been the slowness of the whole experience which had impressed itself on their memory. 'He wouldn't talk.' 'She wouldn't give way.' They told it as if it happened in slow motion, frustrating them so that they must try harder and harder.

These thoughts spoiled any slight pleasure I might have had from a crummy film, so I left early and proceeded, obediently, to the Pizza House. By the time I'd finished the pizza and two lagers I was already feeling tired but a waiter assured me it was still only ten fifteen. 'Coffee, sir?' It was good being called 'sir'.

'No. Another lager.' After the fourth lager it was ten forty-five and I felt too cheerful to bother any more about Ruth's instructions. For the first time since leaving prison, nearly two weeks ago, I felt free. I was no longer dominated by anxiety, exhaustion, cold and ankle. I skipped along the pavement singing a little refrain,

> 'I care for nobody
> And nobody cares for me . . .'

There was no problem getting into Ruth's flat. She had given me a key on the first day, although she had probably forgotten since I'd never used it. I went through the small hallway into the sitting room. There I stopped and looked round. The lampshades were draped in squares of pink material casting a rosy glow. The sofa, decorated by a tasselled silk shawl, was pulled up to the low table which, instead of being piled with books, bore the remains of a meal, smoked salmon, rolls, pâté and an empty champagne bottle.

I sat down there and checked that the bottle really was empty by tipping it upside down. It was hard to avoid the evidence, so absurdly out of character, that Ruth was entertaining a friend.

I should then have gone discreetly to my room, but I felt too comfortable and comfort was my main preoccupation at that time. So instead I put up my feet along the sofa and waited, humming a little.

He came out of Ruth's bedroom backwards, heaving and spluttering like a whale out of water. He was still putting on his jacket, smoothing his hair. He was tall and wide, a quite remarkable presence in that little flat.

When he turned and saw me, I put up my hands in deprecation and defence. 'Don't mind me,' I said. 'I'm nobody, not important at all.'

But he did mind me, and as he exploded, I realised who he was. I could not remember his name but I knew he was the towering QC who had defended my case so ably in court.

'What the hell do you think you're doing here? I can tell you if you're a burglar, you've come to the wrong address.' At this he pulled out a small gun from his pocket which he pointed at me. 'And if you're one of those pathetic creatures who blame me for landing them where they belong in gaol, then you'd better make a move before I make sure you're thrown right back in again!'

I began to giggle because he was just so far off the mark. Ruth appeared from behind him then, looking pale and thin and exactly as usual, not at all as you would expect a woman full of bubbly and the glories of a sexual orgy. I needed to keep laughing about that.

'Go to your room, Pat.' Her voice was not raised, but the gun was still pointing my way, so I made haste. Even so, I could hear their dialogue.

'I'm sorry. But he's not what you think.'

'Clearly. Obviously. Precisely. If you send him to his room.

Perhaps he's worse than I think.' The man's anger needed a moment or two to roll downwards.

'I felt sorry for him.'

'Ah. One of your lame ducks.'

I shut the door after that and got into bed. My cheerful feelings had evaporated. Shortly afterwards Ruth appeared.

'I blame myself, not you,' she said in her clipped voice. 'I should have realised you were incapable of self-discipline.'

'I can't think how you can want sex with a disgusting old man like that!' I retaliated from under the bedclothes. Indeed the thought did make me feel sick. Or maybe it was the lagers.

'He has a brilliant mind,' she began before I leapt out, pushed past her and dashed for the bathroom. There I saw the remains of a lasciviously green bubble bath before vomiting my whole supper into the lavatory.

That evening was certainly the low point of my relationship with Ruth. The next morning, she shook me awake early and told me that today I was to sign on for my dole money and that if I hadn't done so by the time she returned from work, she would kick me out.

I looked at her blearily. In the night the name of her lover, Sir William Burnett-Brown, had come back to me. I decided, however, seeing her tense impatient expression, not to mention it.

The next few days were tricky. Having forced me to sign on, checked when my probation officer would be assigned and given me various cleaning tasks round the flat, she then turned her attention to the job that was supposed to be waiting for me in Manchester. Why Manchester? I never did discover. Probably Larry had met someone who owed him a favour. It turned out the job was hardly journalistic, just some sort of dogsbody position on a philately magazine. In vain, I protested my total ignorance, even dislike, of stamps.

'You're spoiled.' Ruth gave me a glinty stare. 'I've found you a bed and breakfast for Monday to Thursday and then you can come back down here. The travel will take a huge chunk off your wages but come if you like.' Given I was still on parole, she probably thought I was lucky to be allowed to move around at all.

Ruth reckoned rightly on my lack of independence. I arrived in Manchester on a grim and grey afternoon. Too cowardly to study a map or work out the bus system, I took a taxi to the address Ruth had written down for me. It was a large run-down house, far from the centre of Manchester. Immediately I entered it, I was reminded of prison: the smell, the drabness, the atmosphere of too many people in too small a place. I had imagined a house, a home, cosily cared for by a motherly northern woman.

'This is a welfare hostel, isn't it?' I asked a young man lounging in what was a kind of untidy office.

'Kind of.' He took my name, quite friendly. Behind him a girl, lounging in the same sort of casual yet watchful way, picked up a piece of paper.

'You've got a job, haven't you?'

'I wouldn't be here otherwise.'

'No. Of course not.' She smiled but it was a professional smile, a social worker's smile, designed to take down my aggression.

'This is an ex-cons' place, isn't it?' I said.

The man answered, 'No. Some are. But it's not specific.'

'Do you report on me?'

'We're just here to keep an eye.'

'You report on me.' I watched the two of them exchange a glance. Then the girl took a step or two towards me. They're trained in that, body language, when to advance or retreat. 'You don't have to stay here. In fact, we're pretty short of rooms. We don't usually take people out of our catchment area.'

Now I smiled. At least this was more honest. 'I've no choice, have I? You know I'm on parole. I'll stay. For the time being, anyway.'

The girl showed me my room on the basis that, 'The dining room's open for breakfast and for snacks any time.' I knew she thought I was ungrateful for what was a cheap, protected pad but I had seen the squalid little room, facing a wall. I had to live there.

My working conditions turned out to be only slightly better. The office I shared with the editor and his secretary also looked onto a wall, although the wall had a window in it, looking into another office remarkably like our own.

The editor was a nervous middle-aged man who knew a lot about stamps but almost nothing about editing a magazine. I discovered this at once because I joined them during the week when the magazine was due to go to the printers. Since it was published bi-annually, this was a rare and terrifying event and threw him into a hysteria bordering on madness.

His brain had scrambled so badly that the orders and suggestions he tossed out one after the other to me and his young fat secretary made no sense at all. Luckily the secretary, who was called Marion, had a phlegmatic nature and only carried out those commands which made any sense.

We went out to lunch together. 'He's always like this at printing time. The trouble is, he gets in so much stuff over the six months and he can't bear to throw any out – particularly when it's to make room for advertising.

'But doesn't someone else lay it out?'

'Oh, yes. He'll be in tomorrow. But he gets a bit over-excited too.'

She was nice, Marion, friendly but not over-friendly and even rather pretty if you overlooked her obesity. That was quite difficult, actually, as she must have weighed twenty stone.

The next day Fred joined us in the office. He was about ninety, extremely deaf and so frail on his pins that whenever he stood up Marion waddled over to give him a supporting arm. He was also, as she had indicated, over-excited. It seemed a miracle the magazine ever came out at all. But there were stacks of it along the walls, down the corridor outside, proving its continued existence in the world for at least as long as me.

There was no time for lunch that day. Or the next. 'We'll be calm as a flat sea', Marion told me consolingly and showing a touch of poetry, 'once it's off to the printers.'

'What about proofs?'

'Oh, we don't bother with those. We pay the printers enough, after all.'

It struck me that night as I lay on my nasty little bed from which a pervasive smell of unwashed men could not be erased, that in the hopeless disorganisation of *The Philatelist* I was presented with a challenge. If a challenge was what I wanted. I returned to my novel of contemporary England with which I was trying to fill the prison gap in my knowledge. I fell asleep after two pages.

I went back to Ruth's that first weekend although I had to borrow the money for the train. She was welcoming, in her undemonstrative way, meaning that she had a can of beer for me and some bread and cheese.

'So, how was it?'

'A mess. OK. Who owns it?'

'Larry tried to buy it or at least the present owner tried to sell it to him.'

'But he didn't.'

'No. As you say, it's a mess.'

'I thought that's what businessmen did, bought little messes and turned them into big successes.'

'I think Larry thought it could only ever be a little success.'

'But the owner's still hoping?'

'Right.'

So that's why I was there. 'I'll give it a chance, anyway,' I told Ruth.

'That's big of you.'

Ruth was pleased with me, despite her sarcasm. I think she'd half suspected I'd come back and stay back. Perhaps a lot of her lame ducks did that to her – ruining her love life. But I disappeared very early Monday morning and after a week or two, I didn't even come back every weekend.

The editor, I discovered from Marion, was also the owner. He had inherited the magazine from a fellow philatelist who had received passionate letters from him over twenty or thirty years and thought he was the right man to take it over. At the back of my mind, a little plan was forming.

All this sounds as if I was being very positive and organised for a man who had just come out of prison with 'severe personality problems'. A plan may have been forming, but my day to day life was so circumscribed as to be almost stagnant. That way I could just about cope.

In the morning I had my breakfast with whatever dull and hopeless cases happened to achieve entry to the dining room. Then I took two long buses round the outskirts of Manchester to the office. There I stayed till six, having nowhere else to go, usually having lunch with Marion.

Marion's company suited me very well. Like me, she had her problems. I seldom saw her without a slimming magazine in one hand and a bag of sweets in the other. Under her influence, I grew to like chocolate and sweets myself. It was cheaper than smoking.

In the evenings I lay on my bed, reading, listening to the radio, sucking, sleeping. With no money and no friends, there was not much inducement to go out into the dark, cold streets, although occasionally I did go to the cinema. However I found that the contemporary movie fired me as little as the contemporary novel. In three months, I never saw central Manchester at all. In the weekends, if I did not travel down to London, I spent almost the whole time sleeping or watching television in a little smoke-filled room.

CHAPTER
THIRTY-SEVEN

How CAN I write down what happened between Herbie and me? It will seem as if it came out of the blue but it didn't, not really. It was just that I had been gradually changing and then one day I was ready. One evening, actually, the evening that Larry had told me Patrick William Downes truly was beyond the pale and I should have nothing more to do with him. For some reason this news left me feeling energetic and I went round to Herbie's flat to talk about it. He was writing something, alone. He sat at the table and I lay on the floor and I told him that Larry had come round to my way of thinking.

'So now he's an accredited monster, does that make things better or worse?' He came over and sat cross-legged beside me.

'He was always a monster to me.'

'But you sounded relieved as you told me. You look happy.'

'Larry wanted me to believe he was something else. He tried to make him human for me. He wanted me to forgive him. Now I don't have to. It is a relief.' Eventually, as I mused about my feelings, he lay down too. We were like two stone effigies in a church lying side by side on our backs.

Herbie got up. He went over and put on some Bach. Then he came back and stretched out once more. We were about a foot apart from each other, the music playing, the light dim, the floor hard beneath us. I was surprised to find I wanted to make contact with him. I reached out to find his hand. The warmth was comforting.

'Lydia?'

'Yes.'

'If I kiss you, will you scream and faint?'

I found I was smiling. 'I'll tell you what, why don't I try it instead?' So I crouched over him and kissed his lips. 'There.' I sat back on my heels. 'Stage one accomplished.' I lay down again.

'Well,' said Herbie, rolling over so his face was against my hair, 'what's happened to all the *noli me tangere*?'

'I've forgotten my Latin.'

Herbie was always talkative. The introduction of sex did not turn him into someone else which had always been one of my terrors.

When he kissed me, he asked, 'Can I put my hand under your hair?'

And I replied, 'Please, Herbie,' because I wanted his hand stroking my skin. He took off my shirt and talked his way down my body. 'You have soft skin, Lydia, and the white markings on it', a polite way of describing my scars, 'are

233

distinguished, not ugly. Like a kind of tattooing or a white on pink zebra. Some might pay to obtain the same effect.'

Even though he made me smile, I was still ashamed of the scar on my breast. He touched it delicately with his fingertips. Keeping one finger on the spot as a sort of marker, he looked up at me. 'I didn't know you were scarred there.'

'How could you?' Bending his head again, he licked along the tender stripe, tickling a little but soothing too. Then his mouth moved to my nipple.

He looked up again. 'I hereby solemnly promise that I will not kiss your nipple without paying proper attention to your scar. Remind me if I forget.'

This speech with its promise of a future made me happy. 'I don't love you, Herbie.' But he was not listening, too busy wriggling my jeans off my hips.

'You have to help a bit,' he admonished me.

So I lifted myself up while he tugged at my ankles. I didn't love him but I loved what he was doing to me. He stroked my hips and then pulled down my legs so that they were aligned side by side. Then he sat back on his haunches and contemplated the two together.

'You're like one of my doctors.' I was embarrassed by his concentration.

'One is thinner than the other.' His voice was not sympathetic but informational.

'I know.' He ran his hands up and down my thighs, feeling the sensitivity of the scar tissue which made me pull away and then moving to separate my legs. Herbie was perfect for me. Instinctively, he had found the only way I could bear to be handled. He combined physiotherapist, analyst and lover. In fact he became so interested in the first two roles, rolling me over so that he could judge the distortion to my left shoulder that I began to be slightly worried that the lover had slipped away.

But that was good too for I was the one to remind him, who suggested that he, too, might as well remove his jeans.

'I'm in no hurry,' he told me. And, determined to prove his point, got up to put on some more music.

While he was gone, I looked down at my body and could

hardly believe that it was the same which had caused me so much pain and humiliation. I welcomed Herbie with wide open arms. Perhaps I would fall in love with him.

Looking back to those weeks of physical awakening, of healing, it seems strange that I kept a part of myself back. Even when I was at my happiest and most satisfied, making love any time we had a spare hour or two, I knew there could be even more. Perhaps it was because we were friends first, lovers second. He cared more for his career, himself as an editor, and I cared more for the self that I was nurturing so carefully. Despite all my disclaimers, Patrick William Downes was still the most important man in my life. He was behind everything I struggled to do, his action towards me was the question mark which dominated my whole life. When I interviewed an old bag lady, a young boy who'd run away from home, a pop star who believed sex was the best religion, I was trying, unconsciously, to answer that question. If it wasn't all so painful and difficult, you could even have said he did me a favour. But it was agonisingly difficult still, even after I had Herbie.

But 'having' Herbie is hardly an accurate description. For however loving he was to me, however sympathetic and understanding, however much I satisfied him, I knew he 'had' other girls, women. That was what he needed. He never talked about them to me but nor did he take particular pains to hide signs of their presence if they had been in his flat, or his absence if he'd spent a night away. Perhaps that was another reason why I was not 'in love' with him.

My virginity held a particular fascination for him. He liked to question me after we'd made love. Yet I was embarrassed even with him, to explain. To say 'I preferred a Turkish bath' to making love sounded odd, cranky, and I didn't want to be that any more. 'I just didn't find the right person,' I told him eventually. Let him take the credit. But he wanted more. So I told him that I had been a clear-eyed swot through school and university who was too nervous of self-exposure to make intimate friends. That pleased him.

'You take to it all like a duck to water.' Herbie beat a tune on my stomach. I liked the way he treated my body without too much fuss. I liked his businesslike approach, too, checking on each occasion that I wasn't planning 'to make him an unmarried father'.

'I do not want to be a mother, Herbie.' I'd told him more than once, but he still asked.

'Few young ambitious women think they want to be mothers. Of course they don't want to be mothers. They've only just shaken off their own. But they still get pregnant.'

'You must know very odd young women.'

I was so pleased with myself I couldn't resist telling Lesley about my new life. 'Herbie is my friend and lover,' I told her. 'Friend first, lover – easy and affable lover – second.'

'I never thought you were so modern.' She twisted her grey curl. 'Now you really don't need me any more.'

I did and I didn't. In the night when I was on my own, the dreams still came. My body, instead of being grateful at all the loving attention it was getting, turned itself back into ghastly forms. Wounds gaped, poured blood. If they healed, they pulled the skin and sometimes even the limbs into frightening contortions. As always, I woke up sweating and trembling and thinking of Patrick William Downes.

At least I was braver now. I would get out of bed, make myself a cup of tea and, if it was impossible to throw off the threads of fear, I would read or work on whatever I was trying to write – usually, these days, an interview with a property developer's wife. On my very worst nights I had an arrangement to bang on my bedroom ceiling which was Maureen's bedroom floor. But she took so much pleasure in this that I only did it as a last resort.

Recently I had read Maureen's novel. It began, 'Leonora Lemon Cake flew to the top of the tallest chestnut tree in her garden and there she squatted, skirt bunched neatly under her, throwing conkers at her children.' I thought this very funny and told Maureen that I'd always loved nonsense.

'It's in the genre of fantasy,' she told me furiously. 'Not nonsense, not even funny. It's a way of saying things about women in our society without being locked into any particular structural definition.'

'I like it,' I said. 'Did Leonora shell the conkers first? And were the little Cakes collecting conkers at the time?'

I never could resist teasing Maureen. I myself have a straightforward approach to life. Everything I do or write is based on the possibility of improvement or, at least, explanation. Perhaps that was why my dreams continued so violent, in external revolt against my rational daytime self. Perhaps that was why Patrick William Downes haunted me still.

Even Maureen had her moments of clarity. 'I didn't know you were so keen on Herbie. If I'd known I'd have stayed clear.'

'Thank you, Maureen.' I did not want to discuss Herbie with her. She would have been perfectly prepared, I was sure, to compare his sexual performance with the two of us. I was far too fragile for that.

'Of course if it upsets you . . .' said Maureen.

At the office, the atmosphere of a newspaper producing, on however humble a scale, news once a week, with all that entailed in deadlines, on-the-street stories and general tension, gradually changed to the sluggish beat of a limited circulation glossy being dropped through the best people's letter-boxes once a month. Unfortunately, it was an immense success. The advertising, mostly for houses costing half a million, doubled with each issue. Worse still, after the fourth issue Larry increased all our salaries by so much that it would have been a crime to leave.

'We have been corrupted,' Herbie commented gloomily. We were talking after making love. He ran his fingers down the scar on my leg.

'Speak for yourself.' I twitched my leg away from his fingers. 'I'm merely saving enough money until I can make the move to a proper newspaper.'

'Oh, you'll never move.' He was smiling, I think. 'Far too vulnerable.'

I think he meant neurotic.

THIRTY-EIGHT

It was early spring before I felt strong enough to move ahead with my plan for buying *The Philatelist*. I told Ruth at once.

'I never thought you'd stick it out,' she muttered.

'I want to sell my house, buy the magazine. Can't you hear me?'

She was lying out on the sofa, which was unusual, and her eyes appeared to be closed. 'I told you. The house is far too mortgaged to be worth selling.' But she sounded uninterested as to whether I believed her.

It was Saturday lunch time and I was a little more awake than usual. 'You look terrible,' I said, in the dispassionate tones we favoured in our conversations to each other. 'What's the matter?'

In answer, she began to cry, fairly silently but with spectacularly large tears. This was not her role at all. I was unable to respond properly, particularly as she gave me no explanation but continued for some time. I began to feel pretty sad too. Life's a pretty sad place when your protector is sobbing her heart out.

'Please, Ruth.'

At last she sat up and wiped her face. 'I hadn't cried before. I'm sorry. Such an old cliché I'm ashamed to tell you. But I expect it's all part of the cure. I've finished with William.'

I resisted saying, 'That's good.' Sir William Burnett-Brown's path had not crossed mine again, I was happy to say, but that was only because he visited Ruth during the week and joined his wife in the country over the weekend. I thought she still saw him regularly.

'It's a good thing, of course.' She looked even sadder than before.

There was nothing I could say so I went and sat by her. I picked up her hand which was pale and fragile. Again, this gave me a pang.

'I finished it.' She looked down at her hand. 'That should

give me strength. I wanted it to end. I didn't love him any more. It was just habit.' She pulled herself up a little. 'Actually I was beginning to find him physically revolting.'

This was better. I gave her hand an encouraging squeeze.

'But ten years is a long time.' She sank down again. 'And now I won't see him any more, except in court, I'm afraid I might fall in love with him again. He's so exciting in court.' She sighed in a desolate way and collapsed as far back as she could with her eyes closed.

'I think you've done the right thing!' I was stout, a probation officer, counsellor, full of superficial conviction.

'What do you do about sex?' she murmured, keeping her eyes closed.

'Rather little,' I answered mechanically, although shocked by the question.

'I've wondered.' Her eyes were closed like a child pretending she wasn't there. 'Is that what went wrong with your marriage?'

'I'm not gay.' I thought of my prison experiences.

'So what do you do about sex?'

'I told you, not much.' I dropped her hand to indicate my irritation. She might be in confessional mood but that did not mean I had to match it.

Her eyelids flickered. 'I suppose there'll not be much sex for me now.'

'I think sex is optional and overrated.' I stood up. 'That's why love was invented to make sex bearable. If you're not in love there's not much point.'

She sighed dismally. 'Ten years is a long time.'

'Ten years!' How could she possibly have been in love with that fat old man for ten years?

'We've been lovers for five years and nine months but I've been in love with him for exactly ten years.'

'I'm flabbergasted.' I sat down opposite.

'Oh, really.' At last she sat up properly and opened her eyes. 'I would have thought you'd have learnt much more flabbergasting things in prison.'

'The main point about prison is repetition, not surprise. In a way that's the only flabbergasting thing about it, that

239

everything happens over and over and over again. It was a relief, not a surprise, when order broke down. And I was inside less than two years.'

Ruth was much recovered now. She stood up and headed for the kitchen, saying over her shoulder, 'I shall consider that I am recovering from a ten-year gaol sentence.'

I followed her. Now that the crying fit had passed I was beginning to enjoy this new talkative Ruth. We sat down at the table and drank tea. 'Since I'm sorting out my life,' she said, her narrow eyes sharply on mine, 'I'd like to know your intentions.'

I laughed, without getting even a smile in response. 'Do you want to kick me out too?'

'Possibly. But I don't mean just towards me. To yourself. To your wife. To your child.'

Ruth was never fair, never less than brutally direct. My nice sympathy to her woes did not soften her in my favour. 'Nothing.' I bent low over my tea.

'Your wife is going to take you to court for upkeep for the child. She doesn't care about herself. You're lucky.'

I could have said I had no money. Instead, I poured the half cup of tea remaining over the table. It spread quickly, satisfactorily.

Ruth sprang up, enraged. 'You're such a baby! Such a baby! Pathetic!' She found a cloth and ran it round the edge of the table, catching the drips. 'Now you finish it off.' She flung the cloth down on the table and slammed out of the room.

I decided to break a few things. I opened the cupboard and quite calmly began dropping plates and bowls onto the floor. Since it was lino-covered, they didn't make much noise and only a few broke so then I began throwing them at the wall.

Ruth returned in a rage. She snatched a plate from my hand, then picked up the tea-sodden cloth and threw it at my face. 'I can't believe it!' She hissed, not screamed. 'You'll pay for every one. You'll pay double.'

This time I slammed out of the room. I rushed to my bedroom and got into bed but she followed me at once. 'Just because I mention a few of your duties and responsibilities to you, you think you can go round smashing up my flat. But I can tell you I happen to be your solicitor and it is my duty and responsibility to see you behave like a decent citizen and human being, too, if possible. So, if you don't like it, you can leave this instant – this instant. I told you I'm sorting out my life so I might just as well take the occasion to sort you out too!'

She went on in this vein for what seemed to me, huddled under the blanket, for hours. However after a while I realised two things, firstly that I was not in the trembling emotional state in which I expected to find myself and secondly, that if I didn't calm her down I would be doomed to Manchester *ad aeternum*. But to calm her down, I knew I must communicate. Definitely her rage was escalating over my hibernation. I stuck my head out.

'Sorry.' I was not accustomed to honest and voluntary communication. 'Sorry.' I shouted since she didn't seem to hear. 'I'm sorry, sorry, sorry!'

'You are?' She sat on my bed. There was peace.

'That's not good enough,' she said. 'What about your son?'

'I have no money.' I could hear my sulky voice.

'You earn a wage.'

'A tiny wage.'

'Then give a tiny sum.'

I knew what she was talking about. She was talking about a principle, the same principle that every psychiatrist, social worker, friend, probation officer thought about whenever they saw me.

'No.' I whispered. Then the whisper rose into a scream. 'No! No! No!'

'Oh, be quiet.' Ruth turned her back on me but did not go. 'I suppose you resented her pregnancy. I suppose you hated the idea. I suppose you don't see why you should pay for a baby who ruined your life. Come to think of it, you only married her because she was pregnant, isn't that it?' Her voice was cool. The old Ruth, the solicitor, setting out the facts dispassionately. I stared at her intently and she looked back at me with understanding but no sympathy.

241

'I'm afraid it's not reason enough,' she said eventually. 'Not unless you really are insane. Perhaps you are. But, personally, I think it's a pretence. Even when you break up my kitchen. But it still makes you dangerous. You nearly killed a girl.'

Her face was marble white, considering, giving me judgement. 'You're a dangerous mess,' she said. 'Inside. But you're not doing so badly outside. I'm a mess, too, inside, but I'm a very good solicitor. But then I don't want to hurt anyone or anything. Why do you want to do that?'

She was so cold that I almost felt as if I could give her an answer. I wanted to please her. I didn't want to be thrown out of the flat. 'I don't know,' I said in a voice that tried to be accomodating. 'I was unhappy. There was a terrible pain in my head. It had built up all that day. I was filled with hatred and terror.' I stopped, couldn't start again. An image of my mother's face, pinkish, silver-gold-framed, pansy eyes staring not at me but at a point beyond my head, took the place of Ruth.

'You'll still have to pay something for your son.' Ruth was inexorable.

'What's the point?' I murmured, still seeing my mother's face. 'What's the point if I'm not going to see him? If I'm not going to love him. It's a lie. That's all it is. A falsification. Why should Nell want that?'

'You're his father. You don't dispute that, I presume?'

I didn't answer. She hadn't understood again. 'I was sent away to school when I was seven.'

'Your parents worked abroad, if I remember rightly.' She was just about patient but not enough for me.

'I'm sorry. I won't pay money. But I will go and see them.' I don't know why I said that.

She looked surprised and I felt surprised. I even smiled out of a kind of hysteria. 'You can come too. As my solicitor.'

It is mysterious the way things happen. I had not been in contact with Nell since Christmas Day, despite three or four pleading letters and now here I was planning a visit as if it were an expedition, a trip, a jaunt.

'In that case, we'll go tomorrow,' said Ruth. 'I'll call my

ex-client lame-duck mini-cab driver. And now you can clear up the kitchen.'

The next morning, Ruth was taciturn. I suspected she had seen my problems as a diversion from her own without imagining the reality of the experience.

However, with her usual efficiency, she told me to buy presentation chocolates when I picked up the newspaper and was already chatting to her tame mini-cab driver when I returned.

'You didn't sleep, did you?' I said trying to instil a human element into the operation.

She looked surprised. 'What's sleep got to do with anything?'

I decided not to explain how much time I spent sleeping and we went out to the car in a fairly grim silence. She carried the chocolates and I carried the paper and a packet of cigarettes I had also bought. It had struck me that what I had been missing recently was a good drag on a good fag but, on the other hand, it may have been merely to irritate Nell and her parents, who were dedicated anti-smokers.

We could hear the baby's crying from the street. It gave me a horrid feeling in my stomach, as if someone had hit me there very hard and left an open hole.

'Don't forget we've come to talk about the appropriate level of support for the child.' I rang the doorbell. 'Your child,' she added, a bitter look passing over her face.

The door was opened right away by Mrs Burns. 'We've just come back from church,' she said. I had forgotten this aspect of Sunday and found myself blushing but perhaps that was because the small house was very warm. 'We've all had colds,' she added, leading us into the living room.

'I'm sorry.' Ruth took off her coat. 'Sunday is a bad day but Pat works in Manchester during the week.'

'Of course.' Mrs Burns looked at me for the first time and I thought how much she must hate me but her face merely expressed nervous agitation. 'I'm glad you've come.' She even tried to smile. Oh, God. It certainly was Sunday.

'Will Mrs Downes be coming down?' Ruth showed a professional grip of the situation.

'Yes. She's just setting Bruno to rights. Mr Burns has had to go out.'

Once Bruno, the unwanted bear, came in, the atmosphere changed. Now Ruth was disturbed and Mrs Burns calm. The child walked straight across to her – first time I'd seen him do that – and said, 'Sweetie, Gran,' with a charming lisp. Nell, coming in behind him, shook Ruth's hand and then sat modestly on a chair. There was a distinct feeling abroad that the star of the proceedings had entered the room.

If he hadn't been my child, I would have described him as handsome, curly fair hair, big blue eyes, a stalwart healthy-looking body, and if his nose was dripping rather, he had the excuse of a cold. Having received his sweetie, he stood between his granny's legs staring out at us with unblinking, curious gaze.

Ruth began to ask questions about finance and future plans. Nell, who was smaller than I remembered, said she had already started a part-time teaching job and would eventually hope to go full time but she didn't like to rely so much on her mother for baby-sitting. There was a feeling of good sense in the room, only marred slightly when it suddenly dawned on Ruth that Mr and Mrs Patrick Downes were still legally unseparated.

'I just wanted something on a friendly basis,' said Nell, looking at me for the first time. Again I noted how much she had shrunk from the heaving porpoise who had made life in bed so unattractively full of noise and movements during our ill-fated coupling.

'My daughter is very loyal,' said Mrs Burns suddenly. I was shuddering at the time.

'I do not ask for loyalty,' I said in clear tones. 'I do not require it. Loyalty is misplaced.'

Ruth sighed and cast a nervous glance at the child. 'He does not deny fatherhood.'

Nell sucked in her breath just at the same time as her mother did. Then one of their tummies rumbled. I could not tell which. 'I expect you want your lunch?' I suggested.

Nell turned big eyes on me. I knew she wanted me to chuck little Bruno under the chin, bounce him on my knee, put him through his paces. 'He's a real little stunner,' I said. 'He does you proud.' Tears filled Nell's eyes.

'He doesn't know who I am.' My voice had a bit more grit in it.

'That's true, anyway.' Mrs Burns answered me grit for grit. I thought the effect of holy mass was beginning to wear off.

'I can't be his father,' I appealed to Nell. 'Except on paper.'

'That's clear, then.' She looked down at her knees.

'We should be going.' Ruth put down her coffee cup. I have failed to mention that Mrs Burns had coffee and biscuits waiting in the living room.

I stood up. Bruno made a dash for a biscuit. His hurtling body collided with my legs. Tottering, he grabbed for support, found the table edge and gripped. Unfortunately, it was not the table edge but the tray on which our coffee cups had been neatly replaced. Down they all came on his head, dripping dregs, pouring sugar from the bowl, showering biscuits. It was an apocalypse.

Nell began to cry in earnest, Bruno howled, I stood helpless, Ruth murmured, 'I'm so sorry,' as if it had been her fault.

'Doomed,' I commented.

'Get out of the way, do, you big lump.' Mrs Burns took control. I warmed to her a little. I felt like a big lump.

'We're in the way,' murmured Ruth, with untypical lack of decision.

'It just can't work out,' I announced to the room, at the same moment as Mr Burns returned.

'Oh, God!' I believe he raised his eyes to heaven.

'We are going,' I announced again. I looked round. Bruno was sitting on his grandmother's knee, composed once more and sucking a biscuit. Nell had stopped crying and was crawling about the floor picking up bits of china.

'Not much is broken,' I said consolingly. To my surprise she suddenly sat up on her haunches with a fierce squirrel-like expression. 'I'd like a quick word next door,' she said.

It was either bravery or cowardice. But I found myself in the kitchen with her alone. 'You have black streaks on your face.'

'It's from the mascara when I cried.' She produced something that looked like a nappy and began scrubbing at her face. 'I wanted to look pretty for you.' She blinked less gloomily than I would have expected. 'I was giving you a last chance, you see.'

She had that look on her usually blank face that makes one grab for a chair. I grabbed for a chair.

'I have met this doctor . . .'

'There's nothing wrong with you,' I interrupted her. But she put up her hand. It was annoying the way she put up her hand, like a policeman directing traffic. You go right, you go left, you stop and if you're exactly obedient, you may be allowed to go straight on. Perhaps it was this quality, sensed under the romantic prettiness, that had attracted me at the beginning of our relationship.

'He's in a general practice round the corner, that's how I met him. When Bruno was ill. He has a child exactly the same age. A little girl called Elsa and a little boy too, but his wife was killed in a car crash last year.'

I could see where all this was leading to. 'How neat,' I said. 'He needs a wife and I don't.'

'Dad thinks we might be able to get our marriage annulled.'

I began to feel very, very sad, partly because I was used to her wanting me; my position was based on my rejection of her need. The other part was more complicated. It was to do with my childhood, the thing I don't talk about, my parents' death, my whole delightful history.

'You must do what you like.' I understood now why she had been crying in the living room. It was her youth she was saying goodbye to as well as mine. I must have looked near tears myself for she came over and hugged me. I let her, feeling the warmth of her woman's body through her thin sweater. Last chance, going, going . . .

'You never liked me touching you.'

'Not your fault.' I was ironical and sad. I had actually enjoyed the feel of her body.

'Perhaps you prefer men,' she said with the same requiem expression. It is extraordinary how a certain parting frees you to say what you think. Only now were we skirting the idea that it was our unblissful nights that had caused so much damage. In a minute, I thought, she would tell me how inexperienced we had both been. She might even add that the doctor, even if so recently and tragically bereaved, had been able to show her a thing or two. But we were past all that now. 'It doesn't matter to you whether I like men or donkeys.'

She blushed and moved away. 'I'm sorry. I didn't mean to pry.'

So I said sorry too. I even went over and pecked her on the cheek and wished her all good luck for the future with a better man than me.

Gone.

When I came out into the hallway, Ruth was standing there with the door open. 'Our driver's becoming restive.' She gave me an aggressive frown.

'That's it, then.' They all gathered to see us off. My other family, I thought. Already, their faces were closed to me, even the little boy; Bruno was uninterested, playing with a door knob, turning it backwards and forwards, forwards and backwards.

It had stopped raining outside and a thin wash of acid yellow was colouring the cloudy sky. I bent into the mini-cab quickly and Ruth followed. She felt something on the seat between us. 'You forgot to give them the chocolates.'

'It's Lent. Mrs Burns would never eat chocolate in Lent.'

Ruth turned away from me and looked out of the window. She seemed disturbed by the visit, as if meeting my other, unwanted life had not been quite what she expected.

It was still Sunday, sunny, spring doing its best to crack open the buds on the trees. On impulse, I asked the driver, 'What's the nearest big park?'

'Richmond. I'll take you to Richmond Park because then I can eat my Sunday dinner and pick you up after.'

Ruth wasn't taking this seriously. 'I've work to do.'

I took no notice. 'We both need some fresh air.'

I held the box of chocolates as we walked, and ate them one after the other. I offered them to Ruth but she always declined in an irritable manner.

247

'Do you know how old I am?' she asked as we stood staring at a wide black pond. It glistened a bit from the sharp light but not enough to take out the blackness. I imagined lying at the bottom of it with the water like black silk sheets above me.

'In your thirties,' I said. 'Old.' I smiled at the water, hoping to see a reflection. I popped a chocolate in my mouth to see if the movement helped but it caused not a ripple.

'More than ten years older than you. A mature woman. Another ten years and I'll be middle-aged.'

'It's breaking up with your dirty old man that makes you feel like that,' I suggested. 'You'll soon get used to it.'

'Oh, you're so stupid!' She turned her back on me and walked away. I was hurt. Surely I had been talked down to enough by women for one day? As a gesture of defiance, I threw the empty chocolate box into the water but it looked so flaccid and ugly that guilt overcame me and I turned to find a stick to fish it out. Ruth was standing a few paces away, watching. She came back and held onto me as I leaned over the water with my stick.

'If I let go of you, you'd fall right into the muddy water.'

'It's not muddy. Anyway, I don't care.' I had the box well prodded now and was drawing it towards me.

'The point I was trying to make', resumed Ruth as I became vertical, 'is that, although you are years and years younger than me, a mere child indeed, you are, indisputably, a father. It's very muddling.'

'You can't be jealous of that.' We began to walk again, me holding the dripping box of chocolates until we found a refuse bin.

'The reason I finished with William was my growing sense of sterility.'

'I thought it was because he was old, arrogant and hideously ugly.' I was trying to cheer her up more than being merely aggravating and she took it that way. She even creased her face a little into something approaching a smile.

'You've given birth,' she persevered.

'Men don't give birth.'

She stopped under a very large oak tree and turned her

face as far back as it would go. 'I used to feel really safe under big trees until I was told about lightning.'

'You are in an odd mood.' I turned up my face too and admired the black cat's-cradle of branches silhouetted against the sky.

'It's you,' she said. 'You coming and him going. It's made me think. Usually I just work. I expect I'll settle back to that soon. But I don't have many friends to talk to about this sort of thing. They don't expect it from me and I don't like to shock people.'

I tried to think of what she'd said that was shocking. 'Is that why you have waifs and strays like me?' I asked. 'Instead of proper friends.'

'I suppose so.' She went up to the damp, greenish trunk and laid her hands on it. Then she turned round to me. 'When we get home, I'd like to make love to you, quietly, gently, in a friendly manner.'

I gaped, felt myself blushing.

'Is that so dreadful?' She was a little defensive but she didn't take it back or laugh it away.

We continued to walk and I said nothing because I was too embarrassed. Soon we were approaching the gates where the mini-cab waited. I began to be very nervous and the palms of my hands were clammy. By the time we arrived back at the flat, I was actually shaking with anxiety. But Ruth was calm enough, peeling off notes to pay off the driver while advising him how to take hold of his life.

Once we were inside, she went to the kitchen and put on the kettle. I followed her, like a prisoner awaiting sentence. 'You look so terrified,' she said. 'I meant what I said under the tree. I would like to make love quietly, gently, with you but, on the other hand, I've got a massive pile of work waiting. You're handsome now, you know, and young and you made that beautiful little boy. Personally, I never want to have a child but he made you seem potent, desirable.'

I began to blush again. I couldn't help noticing her legs in her tight trousers and her shoulders in her sweater and even her hips, half hidden by a wide belt. She was a thin, plain woman but she didn't seem like that then.

'The other thing, of course,' Ruth turned off the kettle, 'is your wife. I can't come between you and a happy reconciliation.'

'She's found a doctor,' I gasped.

'The extraordinary thing is – quite extraordinary,' Ruth stared at the kettle, ignoring or not noticing my remark about the doctor, 'I seem to have become absurdly obsessed with you.'

'Ruth.' I thought of all those months lying on beds in prison, on beds in my hostel in Manchester, all so lonely. 'Let's go to bed together.'

'But it's so absurd.'

'You've said that once already.' I went over and took her hands. We had hardly ever touched each other. I thought to myself that her attraction to me was undoubtedly a reaction to the demise of Sir William Burnett-Brown QC but I didn't really care. Besides, I liked the feeling that now I seemed to be persuading her.

So we went to her room and took off our clothes and, miraculously, it was all right. Not spectacular like in books but all right. At the end she mumbled something to me I couldn't hear.

'What? What did you say?' I leaned across her. It was nice to be familiar with her naked body.

'Optional and overrated, that's what you said.'

'Oh, I don't take that back.' It was like that with her, friendly, not so unlike lying down with Billy in prison. There were no big commitments on either side, no trumpets screeching love.

CHAPTER
THIRTY-NINE

I HAD TO leave that silly magazine. It wasn't just because
Larry reminded me of things I'd rather forget. (I couldn't
forget, of course, but I'd rather.) It wasn't even that Herbie
was becoming less satisfactory – no progression would be
the right way to describe our affair. But, most important, I
wanted to be a real journalist. I began to write up stuff on
my own, send it to newspapers and magazines all over the
place. Maureen said my flat looked like a post office.

She came downstairs and sat dismally among my piles
of articles, out-going envelopes, returning envelopes, letters,
newspapers. I was organised and brisk and she was dismal.
Maureen had breast cancer. She was at the stage when everybody told her how lucky she was it had been discovered so
early and how good the prognosis for recovery is these days.

'I think sympathy is out of fashion,' she told me. 'Now
that people have learnt to pronounce the word "cancer"
without fainting they've forgotten just how frightening it is.'

I considered this. Had I received more sympathy because
what had happened to me was not appropriate for respectable conversation?

'I feel extremely sorry for you,' I said, licking an envelope.

'You've no choice. I'm here, sitting on your table, moaning.
You know about my short op and my long treatment, about
how and when I feel sick and how and when I am sick and
my worry about the scarring tissue, given its place on my
lovely tits, and my obsession with hair loss, not yet occurred,
and my total, absolute inability to think about anything or
anyone except ME!' I did know all this, she told it me daily,
which I accepted as her right. Partly because I did feel sorry
for her, partly because I didn't love her enough to suffer
deeply on her behalf and partly because her illness made me
continually aware that I was, at least, in working order.

'I might go home.' She sighed.

'Home?' This was a surprising concept. Ever since I had
known her, I had received the strong impression that 'home',

as it represents mother and father and childhood and growing up had never been part of her life. 'You mean "home"
as in the US of A?' I asked her.

'Home as in misunderstanding and misery.'

'But what about the life you've made here? The friends.
The contacts. Your writing.'

'Oh, that. That, my dear enthusiastic Lydia, is that.'

Still, I did not give up. I had a personal investment in
her energy, her feminism, her bossiness, her nosyness, her
stupidity, her kindness. 'It must mean something to you.
You've been here ten years. You have a flat. You can't throw
it all away just because you're — '

She interrupted me with a derisory guffaw. I was glad to
have made her laugh. 'Go on. Say it. Just because I've got
cancer and with such a good prognosis too!' She lifted her
legs, longer and thinner than ever, off the table. 'You're the
same as everybody else. You think I should pretend it's not
too bad, that I'm not shit scared, that I don't feel fucking
dreadful. You want me to be strong and cheerful. Well, I'm
telling you now, it's not in my nature.'

She did not say this with malice so I went over and put
my arm round her hunched shoulders. 'I'll miss you,' I said,
only realising it was true as the words came out. Whose life
would be carried on above me now?

'You can visit me in America when your success makes
you restless.' Now her voice had an edge of spite. She could
not bring herself to approve of my ambition.

Over the last months she had become more my sister
Charmian's friend than mine. Charmian had fallen in love.
Charmian was going to get married. Her future husband
worked for a Catholic magazine. At first I had found myself
patronising him. After all, here was I fighting my way into
the big world of national journalism and there was he, a big
strong man, content to stay in a little backwater – for life, I
expected.

Charmian said, 'Joseph does exactly what he wants. That's
why he's so happy.' But I did not really believe her. I thought
her obvious respect for his talent and strength of character
was a symptom of true love not a reflection of the reality.

When she brought Joseph to the flat I saw a tubby man with a beard who might have been middle-aged although Charmian assured me he was only thirty. 'I never thought I'd marry,' he told me. 'Then I met your sister.' They held hands on my new sofa and I passed the wine around.

Maureen came down and kissed Charmian several times and congratulated Joseph with tears in her eyes. 'It makes me feel so good!' she cried, several times. 'It gives me faith in the future!'

She and Charmian went off shopping for the wedding and she planned her date of departure especially so that she would not miss the day. I noted all this but was too selfishly absorbed in my own struggles with my career to be intimately involved.

Then Charmian fell ill. It was only flu but we were supposed to be choosing her wedding present and, since I felt myself incredibly busy all the time, I was irritated at having to change my schedule. 'Joseph will come instead,' Charmian suggested and, bored, ill or irritated herself, put down the telephone.

So Joseph and I spent an hour in the kitchen floor of a large department store choosing bits and pieces for their new flat. He was absorbed, explaining that his whole mood could be changed by the shape of a mug.

I was impatient, decided he was joking but soon realised he was merely being honest. 'This handle is curved at the edges,' he said. 'The bottom of this saucepan is far too thin,' he said. 'That colour red wouldn't suit a boiled egg first thing in the morning.' We walked among rows of equipment while he looked for the one meant for him.

I asked him, 'Don't you leave anything to chance?'

'There is so much chance in life,' he turned to me with a wise look on his round face, 'that my little exercises of choice are like drops against a deluge. But I make them all the same.'

'But what about Charmian?' I asked. 'She might not agree with your drops.'

He laughed but did not answer me and we continued our parade round wastepaper baskets, doormats, mixers and mixing bowls. Gradually, my slightly hostile curiosity slid into boredom but then that too changed and I found myself oddly short of breath, hesitating, wanting to lean and find supports. I said nothing to Joseph because the room was a basement, warm and airless, so, I assumed that was the problem. Besides, I thought we must be finished soon for he had a whole basket of carefully chosen items.

'Now,' announced Joseph, 'we come to the all-important matter of knives!'

It was idiotic, absurd, thoroughly laughable, but I knew then why I had been feeling so strange. It was that awful sense of repetition building up stealthily to this moment. To faint, crumple up, fall onto the lino-clad floor was the easiest thing in the world.

When I came round I was sitting on a chair in an office with my head between my knees. Joseph stood over me with a sweet look of anxiety and a shop assistant held a glass of water.

'I'm so sorry,' I murmured. I smiled. I thought of reasons why I might have fainted because the truth would be too uncomfortable for us all but they did not ask me. 'I'd like some air.'

So Joseph escorted me out of the shop and after we'd walked for a bit I remembered his basket of items. 'Oh, Joseph! Everything you chose. You've left them behind.'

He smiled, squeezed my arm. 'Perfect example of chance in operation.'

I thought, But it wasn't chance. I smiled.

'Care for a quick bite to eat?' We found a coffee bar nearby. It was nearly two o'clock so we had it almost to ourselves, although it was clearly still recovering from a massive influx of bodies. When the table had been cleaned and wiped and we had ordered open rolls, Joseph looked me in the eye. 'Of course I've guessed why you took the happy course of passing out of this difficult life. I should apologise. I'm afraid Charmian had led me to believe, your past was, in effect . . .'

He paused, apparently searching for the right word. 'Past,' I suggested.

'Well, yes.'

He was very shy. I liked him so much then. 'I'm glad Charmian's marrying you.'

'Oh yes.' I could see he was not going to let the subject of my past disappear. 'You seem in command of your life to a much greater extent than most people.'

I thought. 'I like working out other people's stories,' I suggested. 'And I want the stories to be printed.'

'And you don't care who the people are? They don't have to have any relevance to your life?'

'I like talking to people who have horrible problems. But they have to be the sort of problems people will enjoy reading about. Like prostitutes,' I added, having recovered enough energy for a touch of defiance.

Recently, I had spent several evenings hanging around King's Cross and talking to the girls who worked the patch. Most of them were perfectly free with their experiences so that I was sure I'd manage to sell a piece.

'There's nothing wrong with trying to be successful.' Joseph's round face blinked at me. His eyes were close together, shiny buttons sewn lovingly in place. 'But have you ever tried applying your own views and experience?'

'I'm a journalist.' I was huffy. Huff, puff and I'll blow your question away.

'Yes. Yes.' He became soothing at once. Yet still could not resist one further prod from the depths of his Catholic magazine soul. 'You have been a victim,' he said. 'You could share so much.'

'I deal with victims all the time.' My voice was raised in ugly self-defence. 'What do you think prostitutes are? They're victims, aren't they? And old people evicted from their homes? And young mothers with no homes. And young boys on the run from homes. And wives who get more than a black eye. I'm doing a postgrad on victims. Victims are my speciality. If someone says "victims", someone else will say Lydia Kremachowski – except I've changed it to Kirk. L. L. Kirk.' I stopped. Why was I rattling out my victim credentials?

'That's good. Excellent.' Our rolls had arrived and he bit hungrily into his. The boy who served us looked at me curiously. I suppose I had been shouting. I tried to eat but could not swallow the hard bread.

'I just want to get on with things,' I said quietly, trying not to sound sullen. I still liked him.

'Good. Good.' He didn't want to provoke me further but I knew he was disappointed. I could see as he chewed and chomped energetically that all my shouting had not answered his question.

∞   ∞   ∞

I TOOK Herbie to the wedding and Maureen, three days after her course of radiation had finished, came too. The links between all three of us were stretching thinner. Herbie came to the flat to pick us up. He was wearing a beautiful cream linen suit which made his black hair and black eyes blacker and his pale face elegantly wan. It changed the shape of his body, disguising the limp flop and turning it into a fashion model's stoop.

'That suit must have cost a bomb.'

He looked at me defensively. 'I need it to impress.'

'You're that sort of journalist now, are you?' We had not made any sort of love for weeks and I did not feel any reason to hold back.

'I'm an editor.'

'Aren't you writing any more, then?'

He shrugged. It transformed him, that well-cut suit. I believe it was made of pure linen. 'I hardly see you, Lydia. I miss you.'

'I've been working on a piece about bullying in schools. A commissioned piece, I'm glad to say.'

'Good for you.' He was wistful, the suit not quite so dominant.

'I bet you meet beautiful girls, Herb?'

Now he sat down, stretched out his legs, looked at his shoes which I noticed were at odds with the rest of him, being scuffed, dirty and down at heel. I warmed to him a little and sat down not too far away.

'Beautiful girls like young editors of glossy magazines and I like beautiful girls.'

'That's great,' I said going off him again. Had he always been conceited?

'On the other hand, I'm very fond of you.'

'Even though I'm not beautiful?'

'The way you were using the term did not suggest you wanted to be included in their company. The beautiful girls you envisage enjoying my company are brainless, floozies and empty-headed chicks.'

'Oh, Herbie!' He shut his eyes. 'You've always liked women too much.'

'Too much for you.'

'I'm not that keen on you.' I stood up again. 'I'll go and see where Maureen is.'

When I came back he was going through all my piles of articles and ideas. 'You are working hard.'

'It suits me. Maureen will be down in a moment. She's feeling pretty grotty, incidentally.'

'Oh, God. Cancer.' He sat down again. 'I'm surprised you haven't written about that.'

I changed the subject. 'It's going to be a very Catholic wedding.'

'I love religion.'

I looked at him with exasperation. He took my point without me making it.

'What I mean is that I find deeply felt views interesting. I am not suggesting I am close to the Church myself. Incidentally, shouldn't you be with the bride?'

'She didn't want me. I think she's having a sort of mini-retreat in preparation. At least, she said she wanted to be alone.'

'She is wearing white, isn't she?' Herbie smoothed his exquisite trouser legs with sudden disquiet.

'You won't be over-dressed. My mother's wearing a pink and white flowered dress decorated with silver.'

At this point Maureen sidled in, looking distinctly green. 'Herbie and I are talking about clothes,' I said to try to divert

257

his horrified gaze. He had not seen her since her operation and treatment.

'Clothes! How disgusting!' Maureen pulled at her own beige suit which hung on her like a potato sack. Then she noticed Herbie's suit. 'Oh, darling, you do look a swell!' I was impressed by her generosity. 'I'll go and find myself a hat.' She disappeared again.

I looked at my watch. 'We should go in a moment.'

'You're so busy, so organised, so efficient.'

I didn't mind Herbie making fun of me but when we were all sitting in the taxi, Maureen's hatted head out of the window because she felt queer, I realised it spelled out the end of our affair. We were in retreat from each other now.

It was a long ride to the church because it was a hot September Saturday morning and London was blocked with tourists and coaches and cars.

'I always thought the English married in the country,' commented Maureen wistfully.

'You're thinking of America,' I told her bracingly. I knew more about the 'home' she was going to and how. She had described the Vermont woods and the clapboard house and the stoop and verandah round it.

'Larry asks about you often.' Herbie grabbed my arm just as we reached the church. 'He says that when he buys a proper newspaper he's going to make you features editor.'

'Why not editor?' I was peering at the church through the window, the little crowd gathering outside, the statue of the Madonna above the door, the intention of a marriage clear for all to see. This was my sister who had never met a man before Joseph.

We stood outside and I looked at the spire, grey and gritty from dirt but making its point all the same, silhouetted against the heavy blue sky. Inside it was dark, only daisies flaring white along the pews and on the altar.

'Oh, the hopefulness,' mumbled Maureen. I left Herbie and her then to take my place in the front pew. My mother was already there, turning round, mouthing, patting the seat beside her. The moment I sat down she moved close to me, clutching onto my arm.

'It seems so sudden,' she whispered.

Change always seems sudden, I thought to myself. I would miss Herbie.

PART FOUR

FORTY

I FINALLY persuaded Ruth to sell my parents' house. She grumbled all the way. 'You'll just blow the money – not that there'll be very much – you'll just blow it on something idiotic and then it's gone for ever.'

This was nearly nine months after I had begun working for *The Philatelist*. She should have known that if I could stick that for so long, I was capable of taking a little change in my stride. I had moved out of the hostel after the first couple of months, finding myself a small room in a run-down hotel near the centre of town. In the weekends, when I went down to London, they let it by the hour. Ruth thought that was disgusting. 'How can you bear to sleep in the bed?' she exclaimed, as if truly horrified. But I didn't care. It meant my rent was very low.

The house had been remortgaged to pay off my parents' debts so I wasn't expecting much when it was sold.

One Saturday evening in September, Ruth presented me with a cheque.

'It's a fortune!' I could hardly believe it: thirty-five thousand pounds. Less than a year ago, I had stood outside the prison, feeling as if I had nothing. It was impossible not to feel expansive.

'I'll tell you what,' I said, 'I'll take you out for a slap-up meal. Larry too. I owe him something. Don't I owe him something?'

Ruth gave her pursed-up solicitor's look. She liked to be my patron and she hoped Larry did not know about our affair. 'You take him.'

'But that's not the point.' There was certainly no point in becoming exasperated with Ruth. 'I'll take him to lunch some other time.'

It was a stupid idea to want Larry back in my life again. Not yet anyway. I needed quite a few more steps along the road to success. I kissed Ruth. 'You are the cutest solicitor I've ever fucked.'

She did not like this sort of talk. Her life was so serious. When we got into bed, I could feel her clients' problems rattling round inside her head. It took ages for her mind to leave them behind and join up with her body. It was quicker if we'd had a few drinks. We'd had more than a few that evening.

'Ruth?' I came back from the bathroom, my head refreshed and clear. I was always like that after our sex. 'I shall go ahead with buying the magazine as soon as possible.' I sat on the edge of the bed, looking down at her.

She rolled over to me. 'Get an accountant to check it over first.'

'I have. At the moment it just about breaks even. If I double its price, bring it out monthly, up the ads by a third and improve circulation by half again, I'll make a whacking profit by the end of the year.'

'Fine.' She put her legs out of bed. 'That's fine by me. Soon you'll be a regular businessman.'

I knew she thought I was proving something to Larry. I watched her white angular back as she stumbled along to the bathroom. I had never felt the sun burst with Ruth and I counted on the fact that she hadn't with me.

It was so simple turning that magazine round. Anyone could have done it if luck, or in my case, bad luck had thrown them its way. It's hard to believe just how crazy for information stamp fanciers are. My masterstroke was realising that philatelists are an international bunch. A national newspaper was a waste of paper. By the end of my year as owner I was selling as many to Canada and the United States as I was to the UK. Success made a few changes in the office. The editor went at the beginning, of course, but lovely fat Marion who I'd shared lunch with on my arrival amazed me by turning into a different person. She stopped eating sweets or anything else much and suddenly was the person to be most relied on. 'I'm an obsessive, didn't you realise?' She seemed disappointed by my surprise at her change. She had always had a pretty face but as the pounds and stones fell away, she was revealed to have a pretty shape too.

One day, a hot late-August day, I took her out to lunch and, over lemon sole, felt interested enough to ask her, 'But why didn't you do this before?'

'Eating was my only excitement. I felt passionate about chocolate chip cookies and liquorice all-sorts and mango ice-cream and pork spare-ribs in a spicy sauce and very very dark chocolate.'

'Put that way I see what you mean.'

'But now I am passionate about the magazine. Incidentally, I think we should change its name.'

She was like that, now, prepared to take over my responsibility. I was beginning to enjoy her company more than Ruth's. Ruth had become a bit of a bore lately. Far from being made happy by my visits, by our sex between work, she was more critical than ever, hardly smiled and told me I was becoming the sort of tough-skinned entrepreneurial man she detested. I didn't take too much notice, except to wonder what she had against success. Perhaps she preferred it when I needed her to hold me together. I began to spend more weekends in the north.

One steaming Saturday afternoon I was walking through Piccadilly, Manchester, passing the smart hotels and wondering if I longed to stay there, when a man came rushing down the steps, couldn't stop at the bottom and literally knocked me to the ground.

Apologising energetically but as if his eye was still on the clock, he hauled me to my feet and was about to depart when we looked, momentarily, into each other's faces. I could even put a name to him. He was Wilson, the deputy governor of Stafford Prison who'd first set me to writing the prison newspaper. Of course, to him I was one con among many. 'Stafford gaol. Two, three years ago.' I helped his memory. 'I started a paper.'

'Oh. Ah.' He smiled and took hold of my arm with what I felt was rather too enthusiastic a reaction. After all, the affair had hardly ended well. I prepared to leave but he was gazing at me still. 'I'm at Strangeways now,' he said. 'Late. On my way to do a press interview. What I mean to say is you should come along too.'

I protested I was on the way to work. I pointed out that I was dressed inappropriately in jeans and a T-shirt. I said I was not going with him. But in a few seconds I was hurrying along at his side. 'All you've got to do is say how prisons should be improved.' We were almost at a run now.

'But I don't want people to know I've been in prison.'

'Use another name, then. I can't remember your name. Call yourself Elvis Presley.'

'I don't care about improvements for prisoners.'

'Then that's very selfish of you.'

By now we'd reached the newspaper's offices and as I hadn't escaped yet, I realised I must be too curious to leave, so I went up with him.

The interview was hostile, which is why Mr Wilson had spotted me as a godsend. 'This is Miles Gordon,' he introduced me suavely, 'who came into my care during the long-forgotten follies of his youth. Out of the goodness of his present respectable citizen's heart, he is prepared to look back, substantiate or deny', here, he smiled at me, 'some of my thoughts.'

The interviewer who wore a beard, sneakers and a short leather or plastic jacket turned his pad in my direction. 'What were you in for?'

I stood up. 'I am not here to answer personal questions.'

'My readers will want to know how bad you once were. If you were very bad, they'll believe you more than if you were a little bad.'

'Your readers can go fuck themselves.'

'I see.'

I sat down again, rather pleased with myself. I smiled at Wilson who frowned. It was very hot in the office and I noticed our interviewer had started to sweat under his jacket and beard. I leaned back thinking that my newspaper experience, although limited to prisons and stamps, had taught me that you don't have to answer questions.

'Miles started up a newspaper for me in prison,' volunteered Wilson, soothingly. So after I'd looked round for this character called Miles, I told him all about that. And one thing led to another and soon I'd told him every fucking thing wrong with the prison system and he was taking notes so fast his beard was dripping and Wilson kept quiet, nodding in the corner. An hour passed in a flash.

Wilson held up his hand. 'I have to go. But I want you to know I endorse everything Miles has said.' Now that he was no longer my boss I could see he was quite young, in his thirties. 'I hope you manage to print some of it.' He looked in a space above my head and quoted: ' "Her Majesty's Prison Service serves the public by keeping in custody those committed by the courts. Our duty is to look after them with humanity and to help them lead law-abiding and useful lives in custody and after release." '

After he'd gone, Steve (the journalist) and I (Miles Gordon, ex-con) had coffee in the newspaper's canteen. It turned out he was passionate about stamps. I managed to disguise my own lack of interest and offered him the chance of writing as many articles as he liked for the magazine. 'What I would like is an introduction to your editor.'

'No problem. The editor's indulging in a touch of social conscience at the moment. He can't get enough on prisons.'

I showed enthusiasm. I had never very seriously thought of journalism as a career but chance and other people seemed to be pushing me in that direction. Not that I would want to write about prisons for too long.

That weekend I went back to Ruth and told her first about the interview. Just as with my decision to buy *The Philatelist*, I only gave her the news when I had already made up my mind. When it came to what was most important in my life, I left her out.

It was still hot in London. The flat smelled of the pizza she'd warmed up for us both, some wax furniture polish the cleaner used on Fridays and even a whiff of underclothes drying in the bathroom. Ruth always washed them just before I came as if to establish the flat was hers to use as she liked.

It was late, after eleven, when I told her. 'I thought you wanted to forget about your time in prison,' she commented dourly.

'I do.' Except when we made love, we sat apart from each other, respecting each other's separateness.

'But if it's a way of getting an opening to a newspaper, you'll change your mind?'

'Quite.' I was not ashamed. It was my life, to use as I liked. Ruth sighed. Almost groaned. 'Come on. It's not that bad.' I could hear my voice, sharp with something like dislike. Did I dislike Ruth now? 'You never approved of me becoming a businessman either.'

'I think it's time you found yourself a flat. You have the money.'

That night I stayed in my own bed. In the morning I woke early and took Ruth a cup of tea. Her pinched face (this was nothing special, she always looked pinched) surfaced above the bedclothes. 'How nice.' She took the mug with real pleasure.

Sitting on the bed with her, I felt a surge of affection which surprised me after the sense of dislike the night before.

'You don't want sex with me any more, do you?' Her clever eyes looked at me over the rim of the mug. They were encircled by fine layers of wrinkles which puffed up a little underneath. But it wasn't because she was ten years older than me that I preferred sitting on her bed drinking a cup of tea rather than getting into it.

'I don't mind,' she continued as I found nothing to say. 'You don't have to feel embarrassed. My work's always been the most important thing in my life. You were part of it. You're not any more.'

It suited me to believe her. But she had let me get too close. You don't make love to someone and not know how they feel. She would miss me more than I would miss her. 'I won't stay here any more,' I said.

'Oh, you can still visit.' For a second the thin line of her mouth wavered. I thought that she was unlucky with her lovers. They did come from her work. Perhaps she should look outside.

'Miles Gordon might interview you.' I tried a smile. 'It would make a good piece. The solicitor's point of view. "Locked into a cell with a murderer".'

'You won't get any secrets out of me.' She sat up straight, revealing the T-shirt she was wearing on which was written 'Grow up before you grow old'. She would be all right. Besides, only an idiot could find me lovable.

After that weekend, I spent several months without returning to London. I rented myself a decent flat at the top of a large old house. It had just been painted white and gave me a feeling of starting afresh. Miles Gordon was very energetic, at first writing about prisons but soon covering trials, and stories which touched the editor's conscience. My conscience remained unstirred. But, then, I was trying to do a job. For the first few months I wrote ten stories to every one I got printed. It was from my patron, the editor, that I first heard L. L. Kirk's name. 'You want to learn to write like her, Miles,' he advised me.

'How do you know it's a her?' I asked. We were sitting in his office which always gave me a terrific sense of importance.

'A knowledge of human nature. She writes like a woman. Close to her subject yet cool. Individual. You should read her stuff.'

So I did. It was OK, I thought. A bit stark. Silly name, too. More like a thriller writer than a journalist.

Meanwhile I had a wedding invitation. From Nell. My wife. My ex-wife. The divorce had gone through without making much impression on me, ably handled by Ruth. There was even an annulment on the way. But now Nell was going to get married. I pictured that little round Bruno as a page. I asked Marion if she'd care to come out to supper.

Although I was still nominally editor of *The Global Philatelist* (new title), Marion did just about all the work. She imagined I'd asked her out to discuss our plans for the next quarter and arrived at the Chinese restaurant of my choice carrying a bulging folder. It struck me that she didn't even know I had been married. Perhaps I should have saved it for my next visit to London and Ruth, even though we were no longer close. 'This isn't a working meal,' I made Marion check her folder away with her coat. It was the first time I'd wanted to take a look into the past. This was an occasion.

We drank pale, cool beer and I sat across from Marion, wondering if there was any trace left of the fat sweet-eater. It seemed a possible way of raising the subject of Nell. But, on the other hand, I had no wish to talk about her psyche. We were here to answer my need.

'Did I ever tell you I was married?'

This was not the bombshell I'd anticipated. 'No longer, I presume?' She looked into her beer.

'No. No. It hardly lasted beyond the honeymoon. My wife was a pain. She made me want to scream and bang my head against the wall. I hated the fact we were man and wife. I hated the fact we were man and woman. I was very young.'

She let me get this far without interruption and then she gave me an absurdly benign smile that made me lose my train of thought. 'I was married young too,' she said. 'I was madly in love with a man. Not your story at all. Madly in love. He was much older than me, divorced with two children. He was only interested in my youth. When that became boring he disappeared out of my life. He lives in Canada now with a third wife.'

Was she really old enough for all this history? We both looked at each other assessingly. I had not even got beyond preparing the ground for what I really wanted to say but now I saw that she was determined to match my reminiscences with hers, my enthusiasm was somewhat dulled. We ordered delicate portions of food and I started on another beer. I knew it was childish to be competitive about such things but it struck me that she had not had a child, she had not attacked an innocent stranger. She had not been to prison.

'We had a child,' I began, 'by the ridiculous name of Bruno. I didn't want him, of course, because that's why we got married and I didn't want to be married.'

'You're very clear about your feelings.' Marion still wore the complacent expression of a happy nun. 'I don't know whether I hated or loved my husband but when I found I was pregnant, I didn't want to have an abortion as he suggested. But I lost the baby anyway.'

'I'm sorry.'

'It was for the best.'

This was ridiculous. 'You know I was in prison?'

'We were told when you first came to the magazine. I used to think about it often.'

So I did exist in her imagination. 'What did you think?'

'I thought that you can be imprisoned in all sorts of different ways. I was imprisoned in the huge body I'd created after my husband ran off. I ate sweets and biscuits constantly to keep myself there.' She looked up hesitatingly.

I had given in and was grinning hysterically. We were twins, Marion and I. Nothing had happened to me that hadn't happened to her. If she didn't have a blue-eyed Bruno lurking reproachfully in her past, she had a baby who had never been born. Our food came, diverting us from murky clouds of grievance to decorative dishes of not too much sustenance.

'I don't look back much now,' commented Marion after we'd settled down again. 'I find it too confusing.'

'But Nell is getting married.' I attempted a light-hearted smile. 'Next week.'

'It depends whether you've got a guilty conscience or not.'

Was conscience the darkness that gathered round me late at night? 'I don't believe in the conscience.' I spoke bravely. 'It does no good.'

'As you say.' She speared a mushroom and shook the juice off it with great care. I was reminded that she was an obsessive, unbalanced. She still could not eat a mushroom in a normal way for fear it might set her off on the bags of liquorice comforts again.

'What do you mean, "As you say"?' I gave my tone a good dose of aggression. We needed some hard edges to this conversation, I thought.

She shrugged. 'I suppose I was talking about myself. All sorts of things went wrong in my life and I always blamed myself. Then one day I thought this is not my fault. It was a great relief.'

I felt myself flushing. Her simplicity, her confidence was stupid and offensive. In the last months I'd spent enough time with men and women convicted of all sorts of things to know everyone's guilty, no one's guilty. I gave her a punchy lecture on this, emphasising the role of society as nurturer, judge and healer.

She listened politely and when I'd finished nodded. 'I agree with all that. But that's not what I was talking about.'

I became sulky. I knew far more than her about this sort of thing. I knew it from inside and outside. 'There's no other way to talk about it,' I grumbled.

She began to eat a shred of cabbage with as much energy as if it were a hunk of bread. I watched her pretty mouth chewing away, making a meal of it. She's only a jumped-up secretary, I thought, who has a gift for organisation. It had been ridiculous to think she would be helpful over the subtleties of Nell's wedding. I ate too, over-stuffing my mouth in reaction to her and ordering a third beer without even offering her one.

She finished her plateful, wiped her mouth with her napkin and put it on the table. 'I'm sorry I've made you cross.'

I poured some gluey stuff on my plate. I felt childish and ready to cry. The restaurant was large with a black ceiling and Chinese masks decorated with red ribbons hanging in each corner. It was dreary and forbidding and my head was beginning to buzz.

'I don't expect you wanted to hear all that about myself. I'm sorry.' The first apology had touched me. The second I decided was self-indulgent and irritating. 'I'd like some coffee,' she said. 'And then I'll be off.'

I tried to pull myself together. It would be a real disaster if by my rudeness I drove her away from *The Philatelist*. Sorry, *The Global Philatelist*. She was essential for my future. 'I'm sorry too.' I frowned, staring at my plate. 'This wedding's got to me.'

'Yes. It will be better when it's over.' She managed a smile. I was grateful. My tears receded. We looked at each other again and all should have been well except that she felt compelled to explain herself.

'What I was trying to say was that the individual has to feel happy with himself. He has to forgive himself. He has to like himself. And if he feels guilty, he has to sort out that too. I thought that maybe you're still blaming yourself. But now I see from what you've said about society and everything that you're not. So I'm sorry.' She had become confused. She lowered her eyes and I saw that she was thinking of something that made everything she had said seem untrue and ridiculous.

'Nell's marriage has no link in my mind with the attack on the girl!' My voice was too loud.

'I'd really like a coffee.' She looked acutely embarrassed. I could see she thought I was drunk and, despite more than two years' working together, did not trust me.

'Perhaps you think I'm going to pick up my chopstick and stab you,' I said.

Her eyes swivelled away desperately. 'I'm sorry I've upset you—'

'I know what all your silly psychiatric jargon was leading up to. It's the same with everyone. There's a victim in my life. That's what you think. That puts me beyond the pale. I don't show enough remorse, any remorse. You don't think I have a right to sympathy. You think Nell's lucky to have escaped from me and made a new life. You think sweet little Bruno's life would have been ruined. You think that somewhere around there is a woman whose life has been ruined by me. You think I should make fucking reparation for the rest of my life.' She didn't think any of these things, I knew that even then. But it was a relief to say them out loud. They were the buzzings in my head. As I spoke her eyes grew wider and wider until, suddenly, I was reminded of the young Nell. I stopped abruptly, got up and went to the lavatory. I thought she would be gone when I returned. I stayed away some time, sluicing my face with cold water till the heat and beery fumes began to give place to more accurate wavy lines.

273

She was waiting, hands in lap, when I returned. She looked Buddha-like, tranquil and expectant at the same time.

'I'll walk you home.' I knew she lived somewhere nearby and there had been enough verbal apologies.

The air was cold and dank, clinging unpleasantly to our faces and distorting the light coming from the old-fashioned street lamps. I thought of the last court case I'd covered. The accused had been a boy of sixteen who'd been caught knocking down an old lady and stealing her handbag. It contained a postal order from her son in Australia worth fifteen pounds. The boy had been caught trying to cash it. He had been in youth custody for three months since. In that time he had tried, once by cutting himself, once by hanging himself and once by banging his head on the wall, to commit suicide. Who was worse off, I wondered, the old lady, who as a result of the mugging had gone off to live with her son, or this boy?

'I live here,' Marion pointed to a doorway with six well-lit bells.

I could have invited myself up, put my arms round her soft neck, pressed my hard cheek against her face. It was nicely lit for me by the bells. But I had some sense left and her eyes had looked like Nell's.

'We need a long meeting,' I indicated the folders, 'by the size of that pile.'

She had not painted her lips since eating and her mouth looked pale. I kissed it briefly, just enough for an apology. Or to keep my options open.

CHAPTER
FORTY-ONE

Two YEARS after I left Larry's glossy, I entered a young journalist's award. The prize was a job with the national paper that sponsored it. It was open to anyone under thirty who had never been on the pay-roll of a national paper and was writing in the social services field. It was a conscience-of-the-wicked-press prize. There was a winner and five runners-up with the presentation taking place in the boardroom of the paper. The judges were all very important journalists and editors. I thought it was the sort of occasion that could change L. L. Kirk's life.

L. L. Kirk was absolutely me by now, an energetic young woman who wore tight jeans and a leather jacket and covered the kind of stories that took more time to research than most other journalists could be bothered with. I got near to people. The piece I sent in to the competition was called 'Hot life in a cold climate' and described the difficulties of prostitutes in Finland. I travelled now too.

A career changed my attitude to time and that changed my attitude to everything. When I woke with a nightmare now, it was immediately supplanted by my complicated itinerary for the next day. When I opened an envelope one bright July morning, telling me I had won the award, I stuffed it into my pocket and rushed to catch the underground to the City where I was talking to a stockbroker who did most of his work from a remote Scottish island because he wanted to feed money through to the islanders.

In the evening I looked at the letter again. I had already taken off my shoes because it had been hot all day and my flat never airs itself well. But now I took off my clothes too and lay naked on my bed. I did not pay much attention to my body any more. I seldom saw Herbie, who mixed with the rich and stylish. I had not needed physiotherapy for over a year and, although I tried going to a gym for a few months, the full and irregular pattern of my life, soon made me decide it was just too difficult.

Now L. L. Kirk had won an award and she took a moment out of her busy schedule to look at her body. It was pale, slim and still young. It was a perfectly ordinary body, except for the scars and the continuing difference in size of one thigh from the other. Even the shoulders, which had seemed so tight as to be deformed moved with reasonable fluidity. I stretched, touched myself, and then returned to my thoughts.

I was a success. I had made myself a success. My scars might have been caused by a car accident. If I wanted a man again, I told myself, this is what I would tell him. There was nothing degrading in a car accident. It was an impersonal sort of accident that might happen to anyone. Perhaps, if I tried hard enough, I could convince even myself of the accident line and then I would no longer feel picked out, except for success.

L. L. Kirk had new friends. They started calling me L. L. and then that became Lily. So I was Lily Kirk as well as L. L. Kirk and Lydia Kremachowski. The light was going from outside my window but it was still very hot. I could hear the man who had taken over Maureen's flat moving about overhead. He was an estate agent and clumped about in heavy fashionable shoes which gave me a headache. He read Herbie's free glossy and told me he had written in suggesting they gave an Estate Agent of the Year Award. Apparently, he received a letter back from Herbie saying it was a terrific idea and, by the way, did his firm advertise in the magazine?

Maureen wrote to me from America. She was ill and depressed and after a bit she sent only postcards and, at the time I won the award, I hadn't heard from her for months.

Charmian, on the other hand, was exceptionally happy with her Joseph and they were soon joined by a little baby called Theresa, after the saint of Avila, not the Little Flower. Every few weeks I went to see them and, although the distance between our present lives, should have been unbridgeable, we managed rather well. Charmian was my link with the past. She and my mother, who had stopped working and exchanged the house in London for a prettier house in the country, were the only people who still thought about me with special sympathy. My father had always thought special sympathy a bad idea. Quite often he came and stayed in my flat when he didn't want to make the journey to the country. So he said.

The real reason was that he had found a new girl-friend.

She was twenty years younger than him and he was ashamed of his weakness. 'Please, don't tell your mother,' he begged me. 'It's just a last fling. Nothing more. Male vanity. It would kill your mother if she found out.'

'She won't find out from me,' I said. But I despised him for it all the same and refused to meet the girl. If I could do without sex, so could he.

At the awards ceremony, the editor pressed my hand and looked into my eyes. 'I've admired your writing for some time. We must make sure you have a regular spot.' I took him seriously. I desperately wanted to have a regular spot. 'Your nearest rival isn't half so pretty.' He looked round the room.

'Which one?' I asked.

'Miles something.'

'Miles Gordon.' I knew the names of all the runners-up. 'He didn't turn up so you can't know whether he's pretty or not.' I left him then, deciding one of us had drunk too much to be serious. This was the first time I spoke out loud the name of Miles Gordon.

After the awards I took a taxi to the Turkish baths. I had been meaning to go back there for some time and this struck me as the perfect opportunity. I was strong, I was drunk and I had the time. Moreover, it just happened to be ladies' afternoon.

Foolishly, I had expected it to be exactly the same. I had looked forward, if with trepidation, to the cubicles like old-fashioned railway sleepers, with their wood-panelling, little beds, tulip-shaped glass over-lamps, red wool curtains. But instead I found the upper room filled by white plastic deck chairs with green and white striped seats. My clothes had to be put into a locker. Downstairs it was better, the kidney-shaped cold dip, elegantly lined with marble was still there and the same or similar potted plant.

Further underground, the sauna was in the same place and beyond it the hot and cold rooms, still painted gold, still ornamented with coloured tiles. I began the process, telling myself that if I no longer had the perfection of hard virginity, I had a real place in the world. Most of the other women were still the ladies I remembered from before, scraping off their skin, oiling their hair, shaving their pubic hair.

How had the hard virgin reacted to that? I couldn't really remember. By the time I reached the marble slab I had begun to see that this was not to be a walk down Memory Lane after all.

The body shampooer recoiled from the scars on my body. She wore a workmanlike black bathing suit and her hair was tightly screwed away from her face. In the old days she had been a resting actress now she looked more like a resting teacher. 'I don't want to hurt you.'

'Go ahead.' My face was pressed against the cool marble. 'You won't hurt me.'

Someone else did that, I said to myself, feeling the soapy bristles spreading over my skin. But that's in the past.

CHAPTER
FORTY-TWO

LIFE MOVES faster when you have a career. No time for lying in bed wondering how you feel. Marion had been right. Once Nell was married, I hardly thought about it any more. I was still free-lance but working almost full time for the Manchester paper. Of course I wanted to get back to London. I entered an award for young journalists writing in the social services field. I actually made it to a very long list of runners-up which seemed clever until I discovered there had only been fifty entries. When I read that the pseudo thriller writer, L. L. Kirk, had won, I told my editor it had been given to a woman for reasons of positive discrimination. I still couldn't quite believe in myself as a real journalist.

Nevertheless, I continued writing, trying to branch out from the courts and prisons to more general reporting.

I began to sleep with Marion. Although physically unlike Ruth, her independence made her similarly unthreatening.

278

Here was a woman fully engaged in a busy working life who had suffered from too great an emotional involvement in the past and didn't plan to make the same mistake again. We worked together, we discussed together, we had sex together. But we never spent a night together and we never talked about a future together and the word 'love' would have knocked us down with a feather. Or so I assumed.

On one occasion when she asked me about my mother – it was only an idle question – I left her flat hurriedly, even though I had only just undressed. The following morning she said she did not wish to pry. I always knew that when I did leave Manchester for London I would leave Marion too. I supposed she knew this but I certainly didn't let it worry me.

Once we went on a trip to London together. Now the magazine was successful, other backers had become interested and I was toying with the idea of selling. At the back of my mind, I imagined Larry coming begging with an open cheque book. This potential backer was scared off by my high demands and since we had time to spare, I took Marion to have a drink with Ruth.

She had just arrived back from court and looked very businesslike in her dark suit. She looked old, too, and tired. Already, it seemed unlikely that she had been my lover. Her flat, too, had lost the few traces it had ever had of me. Ruth had returned to being my solicitor and wonderful old friend. That was how I introduced her to Marion.

'Ruth, a truly wonderful old friend.' I suppose she had stopped caring too much for me by then because she accepted this as if it were exactly what she wanted to hear. Perhaps she had another needy lover. We didn't talk about things like this.

She did tell me that Larry had finally married Helen – the girl he'd been with when I came out of prison. 'Everybody's getting married,' I commented fatuously.

'I'm not.' Ruth did not smile.

When Marion added her bit, 'I'm not either,' I thought it necessary to contribute cheerily, 'And nor am I. So that makes three of us.'

We needed big drinks after that. The idea of marriage makes everyone tense, even those who have no interest in the institution for themselves. I began talking about how much I needed to be in London, gulping my vodka, looking from one woman to the other. I felt pretty good.

Later, on the train back up to Manchester, Marion put down her book suddenly. 'It's different for men, I think?' I could see the threat in that. The question mark thundered. I had been trying to work out the figures for suicide in English prisons in relation to suicide throughout European prisons. But it was never wise to duck that sort of approaching storm.

'Men are different, there's no doubt. But in what particular way were you imagining?' This was brave, even foolhardy. The light was dim in the carriage but even so I could not miss her intensity.

'No woman, for instance, could behave as you have done.'

'You are thinking personally.'

She sighed. Her hair was greenish, shadowing her usually rose face into something murkier. 'I keep thinking of that girl you stabbed. I can't get her out of mind. She's coming into my dreams.'

'Sounds more like nightmares,' I commented, jovially.

'I'm not frightened of you. Not physically.'

'I am glad.'

She ignored my irony.

'But there's a closed area in you, where that girl lives.'

'Rubbish!' I stood up. I shouted. The carriage was fairly empty but those that were there turned their faces expectantly. I sat down again. We were both silent. I began to massage my thighs which I'd banged against the table when I'd stood up. The train slowed down and stopped at Crewe. It started up again. I tried to look out through the grimy windows but the darkness reflected back my own face, draining it of colour, turning it into a skull.

'I served my time,' I muttered.

'That's not the point.' Since she was not giving an inch, I stopped talking.

We never did finish the conversation because a few days

later, the deputy editor of the paper whose award for young journalists I had not won, wrote to me, offering me a trial job. He said he had particularly liked my entry and had a space on the diary pages while one of the editors went off to have a baby. He said he knew it wasn't my sort of thing but it might be a start, that is, assuming I wanted to get onto a national newspaper.

I said, yes. Yes. Yes!

FORTY-THREE

I KNEW a man called Miles Gordon had come to join the paper but I didn't meet him. Then his writing began to appear. He was only working on the diary so they should have been trivial, gossipy snippets but his always stood out from the others. In his first month, he covered a strike among rubber-goods workers which no one else had noticed, a visit by an unknown Peruvian who turned out to be the next Polish presidential candidate, the murder of six dogs by their walker, a prison riot over salmonella, also unnoticed by anyone else and a bar-mitzvah party which ended with the parents and six guests in court for affray. Each item only took a few lines.

People said how energetic he was. Although I had never met him, I gave him a physical shape. I made him small, dark, febrile, Miles Gordon a bland cover for something more secret and scavenging. Then I overheard one of the secretaries describe him as blond and dishy so I was forced to revise my image, although I felt certain the bony, dark person lurked inside him. Large, dishy blonds are not usual among journalists.

I read his stuff and I had no reason to be jealous because I was the one who was writing the long, in-depth pieces. I was becoming a bit of a youthful star on the paper. Each day I sifted through invitations to launchings, interviews, conferences, as well as the feature writing I wanted to do on my own account.

I had accepted an invitation to a day's sixth-form conference organised by a charity who helped prisoners re-enter into the world, because one of the speakers was a feminist activist who had also spent two years in prison for killing her husband. I planned to hear what she had to say and then ask for an interview.

That morning, 27 October, a Thursday, I woke so early that the lamps were still on in the street outside. I got out of bed and stood behind the curtains watching the night thin as if ink was diluted by water. Gradually the blueness disappeared altogether leaving the street a pale silvery grey. It began to rain slightly. I had watched so long that I was in danger of being late. I was also very cold, my feet almost numb, as I dashed to get a cup of tea.

∞   ∞   ∞

I SHARED a flat in London with two thrusting young men, a bookie and a salesman for a firm of toymakers. It was in Ealing, very small, but we were never there all together so it hardly mattered. On the morning of 27 October, a Thursday, I woke early. There was no heating in my dingy little room but I didn't mind that either. Lying there, wrapped up in my duvet like a cocoon, I felt perfectly contented. Working on the diary pages, even if not very prestigious, gave me the opportunity to take part in all sorts of interesting happenings in London.

That day, rather untypically as I was now trying to steer clear of the prison label, I was going to cover a conference at which one of the speakers was the governor of Grendon Prison, the psychiatric prison whose threshold had beckoned but, for one reason or another, never received me. I would try to talk to him privately and perhaps get a good sensational quote about a dangerous sex offender. ' "Giving a twice rapist freedom is a calculated risk," says prison governor.'

I would probably stick out the conference till lunch and

then go on to the Savoy where I had been tipped off that a prominent union member would be entertaining a 'good friend'. After that there was an interview with a gay American priest, followed by a party at the London Library.

With that sort of day ahead, it would be sensible to wear a suit and tie. I unrolled myself from the duvet, stretched a few times and went to see if there was anything in the kitchen which might serve as breakfast.

∞　∞　∞

THE CONFERENCE was held in a large circular hall, built in the nineteenth century as a meeting place for the hierarchy of the Church of England. Around the domed roof was painted in large ornamental lettering 'UNTO US A SON IS BORN.' A huge cross was suspended from the centre of the dome, giving a somewhat Sword of Damocles effect.

As usual, I had feared being late, and arrived early. The girls working for the charity were accustoming themselves to the layout of the hall, pinning on their badges. When I told them who I was, they were very pleased and said they always set aside seats for the press and usually no one turned up. 'If you want something to drink,' one girl offered, 'there's a special room up the stairs and to the right. The speakers will gather there as they arrive.'

So I wandered upstairs where parties of school-children were beginning to jostle along. Although I was only ten years older, I felt as alien from them as if they were my grandchildren. Their faces, receptive to each other, seemed utterly closed to anything or anyone outside their immediate circle. I wondered how they would react to information from a woman who killed her husband. Would that cross their barriers?

The room was an endless space of beige carpeting and banana-coloured walls. There seemed to be no windows. At one end stood a small table with a couple of Thermoses and some cups. I was just pouring myself some tea when three more people came in. The director of the charity, a jovial man, introduced himself and his two companions, one as the governor of Grendon psychiatric prison and the other as Nan Bentall, the woman I wanted to interview. I had learnt one rule about being a journalist: pounce whenever you get the chance.

'I'd very much like to interview you.' I separated Nan, fixed her in my eye-line. She had short, greying hair surrounding a determined triangle of face. She put her hand on my arm and I could sense she was glad I was a woman.

'Fine by me,' she said. 'How about right now? We've got twenty minutes.'

Twenty rushed minutes was not nearly long enough and, besides, I wanted to hear her talk first. 'The break would be better. I'll see if I can arrange a private room.' We can do business, I felt her thinking, talk straight. Perhaps she would even explain to me what it felt like to have killed your husband. More likely, she would describe prison conditions.

Now that I had made my arrangements, there was no need to stay so I put down my cup and left the room. As I pushed out through the swing doors, a group of four men came towards me. Two were old, one small and dark and the other young and fair. I passed by and joined the crowds of school-children now pouring into the hall. I don't like sitting in press seats, it makes me feel set apart and uncomfortable, so I joined a crowd of girls, one of the few groups in uniform and sat among them.

Soberly anonymous, I opened my pad and started scribbling a few questions I might ask Nan.

∞   ∞   ∞

THE CHURCH Hall was a gloomy place or it would have been if it hadn't been filled with school-children, pushing and shoving. At least half seemed to be Asian, another quarter black and the rest an indeterminate mixture. It said a lot either about the racial mix of state schools in Central London or about the sort of school that sends their sixth form to conferences about prisons. I arrived a quarter of an hour before it started, in time to have a word with all the speakers. 'I'd very much like to visit Grendon,' I told the governor.

284

'We have to get Home Office clearance,' he answered, friendly enough. 'There'll be no problem. It just takes time.' Miles Gordon blinked a little warily. I realised I would have to give the governor my real name so that he would, inevitably, discover my prison record. Not now, though. 'What paper did you say you were from?' I told him again. 'I was just introduced to another reporter from your paper. A woman.' He looked round. 'She was here a moment ago.'

I remembered the tall, slim girl in trousers I'd seen passing along the corridors.

'Bit of a waste of labour, isn't it?' the Governor asked. 'Sending two reporters to the same place.'

'I'm from the diary, she might be from another part of the paper. What was she called?'

'Lily Kirk. Writes under the name of L. L. Kirk, she said. Attractive girl.'

So L. L. Kirk was here too. I turned away. It was time to go into the hall. I joined the two or three other reporters and went with them up to the gallery where a row of seats had been reserved for us.

∞   ∞   ∞

THE GOVERNOR of Grendon spoke first, followed by Nan who leapt to her feet and, without notes, began describing, with great passion, stories about her years in prison. This was not what really interested me. I wanted to know how she felt about herself as a murderer, how she managed to live with herself. But her stories were so horrific I could hardly help becoming involved. She told us about the woman in a psychotic state, who was stripped and left naked in the cell and yet even so managed to pull out the stitches in her arm with her teeth and dig a deep enough hole in her blood vessel to kill herself. There was the woman who half escaped over the wall and then impaled herself. There was the common practice of shoving heads down well-used lavatory bowls and pulling the flush. Around me, the school-children chewed gum and whispered.

Just before eleven, I slipped out of the hall so I could divert Nan before she was captured by other journalists.

I heard the clapping from seven hundred dutiful seventeen-year-olds, imaginations unstirred, as I reached the swing-doors. As I'd hoped, Nan was out remarkably quickly afterwards, escorted or, at least, chased by the director.

'You were tremendous,' I said.

She looked at me ironically. I understood she'd taken in the children's response. 'Thanks.'

'I've found a room this way.'

It was another big bare room into which I'd imported two stack chairs. We sat facing each other.

∞ ∞ ∞

THE EX-CON, Nan Bentall, packed a powerful punch. Before the meeting started, I had written her off as one of those bitter old lesbians, but she enjoyed life. She enjoyed telling us her gaol nightmares. I liked that and wanted a few words more.

'She was whisked off by your colleague,' the director told me as if it were a huge joke.

That figured. I might as well meet the famous L. L. Kirk now as any other time, I thought to myself a little belligerently. 'Where are they?'

'Down the corridor. Third door on the right.'

∞ ∞ ∞

THE DOOR opened abruptly and there was this young blond man staring at us. I guessed he was another journalist so I smiled charmingly, 'Give me another ten minutes,' I said. 'We won't be long.'

But he came on in. 'You're L. L. Kirk, aren't you?' he said. He was very handsome and clean cut in his dark suit and tie. 'I'm Miles Gordon. An admirer.' I realised he was one of the men who'd passed by me in the corridor.

Nan looked curiously from one to the other of us. 'We're from the same paper,' I explained.

'That makes you big rivals?' she asked.

'We've never met before.' The man looked around as if he wanted another chair.

'I don't think we need a threesome.' I was firm. He was far too dominating, too good-looking, too masculine.

'OK.' He capitulated quickly. I watched him go to the door. He didn't turn but went straight out.

'What's the matter?' Nan stared at me. She was used to something being the matter.

'I just thought I did know him for a moment, that's all. I can't think from where.'

Nan smiled. 'You certainly tread on each other's toes.'

'He's on the diary pages. I don't know what he's doing here.' I became businesslike again, keen not to be too late for the next session.

∞   ∞   ∞

It was a peculiar sight, those two women sitting facing each other in that huge featureless room. I thought that was why the image stayed in my memory, although it was the face of the famous L. L. Kirk that was most vivid. I felt as if I'd seen it before. At any rate, I left the conference, dashed back to the office and scribbled off a piece about the vile conditions of women's prisons (which I was sure wouldn't be used with Kirk covering it too) and then made a beeline for the Savoy. While I was waiting to catch my lecherous prey, I had a large vodka and tonic at the bar which was unusual for me on the job. The result was the wily union official made his escape through a back exit. So I missed my man which was unusual too.

I decided to go back to the office and work out what was bothering me.

∞   ∞   ∞

I spent all day at the conference. I like doing that, immersing myself, making no judgements until I sit down later with a pad and pen. But that day I felt curiously removed, as if only one part of myself was able to concentrate. The other part seemed to be somewhere else which was connected with Miles Gordon's face because it kept reappearing in my imagination. I even wondered if I had fallen madly in love – a grand obsession – but I did not feel the sort of tingling happiness that I assumed should go along with love. I felt more of a dizzy excitement and fear as if I were about to make a great leap into the dark.

At five o'clock I went back to the office, determined to conquer this strange mood and write up my piece about Nan while it was still fresh in my memory.

∞   ∞   ∞

I DID my interview with the gay American priest but my mind wasn't fully on it. I thought about Nell's family and how they were agonising over the slowness of the annulment. The priest seemed sincere enough but more concerned about his own problems than his flock's. He was a political priest, I suppose, and I wasn't in the mood for politics. 'I am a priest first, a human being next, a man after that and a gay man last of all,' he told me.

This seemed good copy so I wrote it down. But the only reason I was interviewing him was because he was gay. 'What do you think of annulment?' I asked him.

'The Catholic church uses annulment as if it were divorce.'

We were sitting in the bar of Brown's Hotel and I suddenly felt an intense dislike for him. 'Do you not think it self-indulgent to spend time talking about yourself and your views?' I asked. 'As a priest, first.'

'I have a duty to my fellow gays.'

He was not to be drawn. I had come to the conclusion that my reaction to L. L. Kirk had been mostly jealousy, but I noted that her face was still appearing now and again between the cold eyes of the priest.

'Do you think ordinary Catholics are ready for your message?' I asked.

'The message that priests are human too? They've been getting that since Peter denied Jesus three times over.'

'But he tried to do better. You're not trying to change yourself. You're saying, this is how I am and this is how I'll stay.'

'It is not a sin to be gay.'

Well, there we were. Not much more to be said after that. We were both glad to escape. As he shook my hand with warm professionalism, he looked into my eyes. 'Don't murder me,' he said. 'I'm not worth it.'

'I'm not in the murdering business.' I smiled and once again I saw Kirk's rather hunched shoulders and the long wavy hair falling forward round her face. The image gave me a slightly sick feeling in my stomach, although I still could not tell why.

I went back to the office for one more time and wrote a virulent attack on the priest. By now it was after six and time for the party at the London Library. I needed to wash and clean up so I went out into the corridor towards the lavatories. Half-way along, a woman suddenly backed out of an office door and bumped into me. She turned round and our faces came very close. She screamed, dropped the pile of folders she was carrying and ran away.

I stood where I was.

∞ ∞ ∞

I RAN into the lavatory and locked the door. I don't know how long I stood there, shaking, not thinking. Not thinking was the best part. When I came out there was a man looking at me oddly so I realised I was in the gents but I hadn't even strength enough to say, I'm sorry. As soon as he'd gone I slithered down on the floor and put my head on my knees.

∞ ∞ ∞

WE HAD recognised each other from our meeting in the Cutting Edge, not from our subsequent court appearances. Over the years our bodies had gradually returned to something quite near the healthy young specimens we had been then. There was an irony in that somewhere.

CHAPTER
FORTY-FOUR

I TOLD no one about my meeting with Patrick William Downes. I recovered enough to go home and spent all evening and throughout the night thinking what to do.

The next morning I went into the office early and button-holed the editor's secretary so I could get to him before anyone else. 'It's so secret I can't tell even you.' I smiled at her, knowing she would think I was onto an important story.

I had dressed carefully, wearing my most tailored trouser suit which would make me look as little like an hysterical girl as possible. The editor was on my side, I knew it. He had chosen me and would understand my feelings.

Despite my efforts, it was ten thirty before he had time to see me. I could see he felt he was doing me a favour already just by squeezing me into his already impossible schedule.

'Well, Lily, you've got something good?' He was standing by his desk, hand on the telephone. This was all wrong. I floundered.

'Yes. No. It's something . . .'

'Sit down.' He relaxed a little, took a chair, himself. He had remembered I was his protégée. 'Now tell me.'

So I did. 'Seven years ago I was attacked and nearly murdered . . .' I went on from there, trying to keep it brief and factual. He listened attentively, although I could still feel his urgent need to get on to the next meeting. It made me nervous, picking wrong words, becoming emotional however hard I tried not to. I reached the end, the climax I suppose. 'And now that man is working here. He was called Patrick William Downes but now he's called Miles Gordon.'

The editor got up, squeezed my shoulder. 'That's terrible, Lily.'

I said nothing, waited.

'It explains a lot to me. About your writing, I mean. That's a terrible story, Lily. Or should I say Lydia?'

I couldn't wait any longer. 'But he can't work here with me! You'll have to sack him!' My control burst open. 'He's a murderer! A murderer!' I was screaming into silence.

He turned away from me. 'We have to think about this very carefully. I'm very sympathetic to your position, to your feelings. But we have to think about this very carefully. He has rights.'

'Rights! He forfeited all rights . . .' He turned round again and, with a great effort, I managed to stop. 'I'm sorry.' This was all going wrong. Why was I apologising?

'He served his sentence.' He spoke in a quiet, steady voice.

I could not speak because I would probably start screaming again and that would do more harm than good. I looked down at my hands and mumbled, 'Yes.' I wanted to say what a ridiculously short sentence it had been but didn't dare start on that.

'It's most unfortunate he came to this paper. As you perhaps know the deputy editor is very keen on him. On the other hand, he's only here on trial. If you leave it, he'll probably move on anyway.'

I understood his point of view. He wanted the problem, so almost unbelievable, to disappear, and me with it. Besides, I could see he was getting anxious about time again. While we had been sitting there, the orange light on his telephone had been flashing every few seconds.

'I'll see if I can think of a way out.' He was on his feet again, once more squeezing my shoulder in a fatherly way. 'You know how highly I rate you as a writer,' he added. I knew this was true, but how long would he consider to rate me if I made too much trouble?

I was out of the door, shaking, having achieved nothing. Or so I thought.

Later that day, I received a memo. The editor prided himself on acting decisively. 'Why don't you consider doing a report for us to be published in paperback? Suggested title: "The victim's role in society".' I understood from this that he was thinking of ways to keep me working at home. I went back to my flat and thought a lot more about what I should do. Then I began to make telephone calls.

∞　∞　∞

I DID not go into the office the day after I met Lydia Kremachowski. I only had a kind of temporary desk. No one would miss me. Her real name had never meant much to me and I had to ring up Ruth to find it out.

'What bad luck,' she sympathised when I told her the story.

'Yeah.' That was about the sum of it. Try as I might, I couldn't think it out much further. It was up to Kirk. Perhaps she would let it lie but somehow I didn't think so.

Ruth and I met after she finished work and had a drink in a pub. 'What's she like?' she asked.

'Controlled. Energetic. Not very like the girl I stuck a knife into.'

'Don't talk like that! You're not a child.'

'What do you want me to say? That this is the girl whose life I ruined? Well, she doesn't seem very ruined to me. She's got a better job than I have. She's physically all right, too, as far as I could see.'

We both drank too much and then I insisted on coming back to Ruth's flat.

'I don't want to sleep with you,' she protested as I put my arms round her. 'You're all churned up. It has nothing to do with me. I'm not going to be used by you.'

'You didn't mind me being churned up before.'

She sat on the sofa. I stood. 'That was before. That was different. You needed me.'

'I need you now.'

'Not really. Anyway, I feel differently. I don't want to get involved between you and this girl. You must work it out for yourself.'

She turned me out so I bought another bottle of vodka and went back to my flat. It seemed very like a cell that night. At about three or four in the morning just when I'd fallen asleep, one of my flatmates came back with a girl and their energetic activity made sleep impossible for the rest of the night.

The next day I went into the office early. It was no surprise when I was told the deputy editor, my friend, wanted to see me.

His office was not very splendid and not very private. People passed backwards and forwards in front of the glass walls and the phone rang continuously. He was speaking on the telephone when I came in, sounding irritable. 'Gossip is what you're talking about. Simple old-fashioned gossip.'

'That's you I'm talking about.' He put down the receiver and turned to me, still with bad humour.

'My secret's out.' I tried to be coolly ironic. I sat down, although he hadn't asked me to. I felt calm suddenly, not even angry with L. L. Kirk (I preferred thinking of her by her journalist's name). It was quite understandable she would not want me in the same offices, just as it was understandable that I would not go without a fight. This was my life.

'I gather you nearly murdered Lily?' He said it as if it were an absurd exaggeration. People find it very difficult to believe this sort of thing close to home, despite what they read in the papers. Or, in his case, write in the papers.

'Correct. I was tried and convicted and served a prison sentence. I've been out for over four years now.' I've never seen a man look less pleased with a bit of factual information. 'There it is,' I added. 'If I could change, I would. But that's the story.'

'So what's your real name?' He became belligerent, my friend.

'Pat Downes.'

'You don't look very Irish to me.'

'I can't change that either.' We sat there looking at each other. I could see he was wishing he hadn't suggested I came down from Manchester. I wasn't that good a journalist. But he had, and I wasn't budging. If I had to shout stupid things like 'I've paid my debt to society' then I would.

'She's telling everyone,' he said eventually.

'That's my bad luck.' I looked him in the eyes. He might as well be perfectly certain that I would not go away.

'I see. So you think you can face it out?'

'Why not?'

'But what about her?'

'That's her problem.' That was a mistake. Despite his manner he really was on my side but now he began to feel I was being too cold-hearted. He looked through the glass walls and tapped his pen on the desk.

'You don't take any responsibility for her feelings, then?'

How could I answer that? 'I did a shocking thing.' Perhaps that would satisfy him.

'It's all very difficult.' He sighed.

I relaxed a little. 'I had to work very hard to get onto this paper,' I said. I wanted to appeal a little. 'It wasn't easy from where I started.'

'I know. I know. I'm fighting for you.' The telephone rang. 'Yes?' He listened for a moment. 'Hold on.' He waved his hand at me. 'We'll talk later. Just keep out of her way for the time being. Out of everybody's way. Go home, best of all.'

I went. Dispensable, that was me.

FORTY-FIVE

I DON'T know when I decided to ring Larry. I suppose it was at the back of my mind all along. I had wanted to make contact again when I could boast about the dizzying heights I'd climbed but now it would have to be a 'Help! Save me from falling.'

It was not too difficult to track him down. He still lived in his old flat and a woman's voice, presumably Helen's, speaking on an answering machine, gave me his office number. There, his secretary informed me that he was at the pub.

'What pub?' I asked. It was ten o'clock in the morning, the day after I'd seen the deputy editor, and it seemed an odd time to be drinking.

'The pub he's turning into offices,' the girl explained obligingly. So Larry was moving into property development. I wondered briefly if he still owned the kitchen-equipment shop.

The pub was set back from a pretty tree-lined avenue in an expensive part of Notting Hill Gate. The scaffolding made it easy to find. 'I'm looking for Larry Purley,' I told the first helmeted worker. He pointed upwards and there, indeed, was Larry, high up on the top layer of scaffolding, resplendent as always, although this time in a shiny yellow helmet.

'Hey, Larry!' I shouted and eventually he looked down. 'It's me, Pat. I was just dropping by for a drink and a chat.'

He smiled, only now realising who I was. I was glad he smiled and glad to think I'd changed so much. Nevertheless he took his time reaching ground level. 'Get that,' he said when we were face to face, 'the prodigal son returns.' I decided to believe this was a friendly overture.

'Yeah. I've been in London a few months now.'

'I know. Ruth told me. Doing all right, she seemed to feel.'

I had forgotten Ruth was Larry's solicitor. She had hardly mentioned him when I weekended at her flat. 'I do have a problem now.' There seemed no point in delaying the confession.

He seemed to hesitate and then took a breath. 'Treat me as family.' That made me feel better still. He was my only family and that remained absolute, however we'd quarrelled.

He led me to a downstairs room in the pub, being used as an office. Winter light eased through the dust-caked window. We found two plastic chairs and Larry poured us each a cup of coffee from a Thermos.

'So you're not throwing things any more?' This was less encouraging. Perhaps he wanted an apology.

'I'm sorry about that. Post-prison anger, I suppose.' There was a pause.

'Helen and I got married.'

'Yes, I know. Congratulations.' Ruth had told me that.

'She's going to have a baby. Me. A father!' He looked amazed and delighted but I felt put off my stride.

'It's not so good with me now.' I forced a firm tone.

'Oh.' He looked away. I saw I was still not his favourite person.

'If you don't want to listen?'

'No. No. Go ahead. Police-type trouble?'

'No.' Didn't he realise I was not that sort of person any longer? 'It's sheer bad luck. Fucking bad luck. The girl, the woman who got in the way of my knife, your knife actually . . .' I paused, not liking the expression on his face and the way he had not bothered to take off his yellow helmet. 'She turns out to be L. L. Kirk.'

'Who's L. L. Kirk?'

'Lydia Kremachowski.' Now I had his attention. He stood up, took off his helmet and put it on a table.

'So what's Lydia up to?'

'She's a successful journalist called L. L. Kirk on the same paper that's giving me a chance and she's telling everyone about me in the hope she'll get me thrown off.'

Larry sat down. I noticed how he had aged in the years since I'd seen him. His yellow hair had grey threads, his skin was no longer shining and golden but dusty as if he spent too much time on sites like this. 'She must be pretty angry. After all these years.' He appeared to be thinking.

'I guess that's the explanation.' I wanted him to wave a wand, not make sensitive deductions, particularly not about Kirk. I was beginning to be pretty angry with her if it came to that. 'She has no right to wreck my life.'

'It may not seem like that to her.'

'I wish you'd stop trying to see everything from her point of view.'

He looked up at me sharply but spoke meditatively. 'I used to like Lydia. Quite a clever, sensible girl in many ways. But hysterical when it came to talking about you. It sounds as if she hasn't changed. What do you want me to do? I'm not so big a deal in the newspaper world that I can ring up your editor and tell him he can't sack you or I'll bring the crushers in.'

I didn't know what I wanted him to do. So I kept quiet.

'I could talk to her. I used to talk to her a lot. Years ago. She wasn't so successful then.'

I knew what I didn't want. 'I don't want you to talk to her.'

A workman came, interrupting my intensity, telling Larry the architect was waiting for him. When he turned back to me, he'd already lost some of his interest.

'You know I only have three papers,' he said, 'the shiny freebie, edited by a chap called Herbie Watson where Lydia used to work, and a couple of specialist jobs based outside London. If the worst comes to the worst, you can always work on one of those.'

'If the worst comes to the worst,' I squeezed out the words bitterly, this was not how I planned to tell him, 'I can work on my own paper.' He listened more attentively as I described my success, my move to the Manchester paper and finally what seemed like the great leap to London.

'That's terrific. A chip off the family block, after all. I'd say you don't need me.'

Perhaps he was right. He wanted to think so. He suggested, after a pause, that one way out of it would be to clear off back to Manchester until things calmed down.

'But it's not "things".' I saw the flaw now in the way he was talking. 'It's Kirk. She doesn't want me in the world. Her world, that is – which also happens to be my world.'

'Look, I've got to go.' Larry stood up. He had obviously decided my credentials as a victim were not too strong. 'Call me at home. I'm sure Helen would like to see you. She always took your part, asked after you. Drop by. We can talk more then.'

He went, clapping me on the shoulder, hugging me a little, as if restoring me to part of his bosom.

∞   ∞   ∞

EVERYBODY I spoke to on the newspaper was horrified. Literally no one thought William Patrick Downes should be allowed to stay another minute at his desk. They told me he was out of the office so I even nobbled his fellow workers on the diary. I should have been embarrassed by all this self-exposure but I was so convinced by what I was doing that nothing could stop me. I even leaked a sensational story, 'Journalistic colleague murder attempt,' which was run by the *Evening Standard* and picked up by a couple of national tabloids. I wanted Downes dead. Dead to *me*.

There were only two people who didn't seem totally convinced by my mission: my editor and my father.

On the third day I received another memo. 'Have you thought more about my suggestion re book idea? It might be the project to advance your career on this newspaper.'

Was this a threat? I sat in my corner of the office and the telephone rang. My father had never rung me at the office before and failed to recognise my clipped 'Kirk here.'

When we'd cleared that up, he announced he was coming to stay that night. I reacted with my usual combination of, 'You're very welcome,' with the sub-text of 'And I know that means you're seeing your girl-friend of which I thoroughly disapprove.' But he didn't immediately ring off as I expected.

'So how do you feel about being in the news?' I heard the rattle of paper as he found the place. ' "Lydia Kremachowski, alias L. L. Kirk describes what it's like to bump into the man who tried to murder—" '

I interrupted him. 'I can't have him working here, Papa. You can see that.'

'So you're going along with all this publicity? Washing your dirty linen in public, they used to call it.'

'I'm not going along with it. I'm making it happen. I want Patrick William Downes to find whatever black hole he crawled out of and crawl back in!' I was shouting.

'I see. Well, I'll be at the flat about ten.' He rang off leaving disapproval buzzing louder than the telephone.

'No. I won't give an interview,' I told the next reporter who rang. 'And I certainly don't want to have my scars photographed!' I should have laughed.

It struck me that you can start a story running but it's not so easy to direct its course. 'I go in fear of my life' was one newspaper headline. Was that the truth?

The next person to call me was Herbie. He seemed full of admiration. 'Let's have a celebration lunch,' he suggested.

'What are we celebrating?'

'You coming out of the victim closet.'

'OK.'

The new (not so new now) glamorous Herbie only ate at the most fashionable places. This time it was the Groucho Club. 'You're the most famous person here,' was the first thing he said to me. 'For today.'

I thought he had called me out of the remembrance of our old friendship, wishing to give sympathy. 'You're just a star-fucker.' I tried to be bracing in order not to be dismal.

'That's my job. Like to give me an interview?'

'For your vapid estate agents to gloat over? Certainly not. You should know I'm not their type.'

He laughed and I looked away. He was not prepared to take me seriously. I would eat my lunch and leave. It was as I took this decision that I realised that the one person I really did need to speak to was Larry. At least Herbie could be useful for something. 'Give me Larry's number, would you?'

'Home or office? He's married now, you know.'

'Both.' Holding that number in my hand gave me a new sense of confidence.

Nevertheless I did not manage to get hold of Larry for a day or two. His secretary said he was out on a 'site' and his wife only seemed to exist on an answering machine.

Finally, I reached him on his car-phone number. He couldn't hear me very well. 'Who? What's your name?'

I realised I had been saying 'Lily Kirk'. 'Lydia Kremachow-ski,' I bellowed. Luckily, I had returned to the flat for the afternoon.

'Lydia. Oh, Lydia.' There was a longish pause. 'You'd better come and talk to me.'

'I'd like to. That's why I rang.'

There was another pause, more like a break in contact. I waited. 'Come to my flat tomorrow evening eight o'clock.'

He gave me the address, miles away on the Isle of Dogs and rang off.

∞   ∞   ∞

WHEN YOU really need sympathy, you find yourself most isolated. That evening I came back to my stinking little flat and not one of my flatmates was in. When the telephone rang, I jumped to answer it. I was holding my second can of beer in one hand. 'Downes here.' I wanted it to be someone who cared about me. A voice said, 'You're a murderous bastard. Cutting off your balls would be too good for you. What I'd do is get a mincer . . .' Since he seemed prepared to continue making free with my body, I put down the telephone. I had that bit of sense. I drank two more beers and telephoned Ruth.

'It's me. Pat.' I had to say this because she sounded as if she didn't recognise my voice.

'Yes. I know.'

'Can I come and talk to you?'

'I don't think that would be a good idea.' Her voice was cool, if not frigid.

'Ruth, have you seen what they're writing in the papers? I've been having anonymous phone calls. Threatening phone calls!' I appealed to her pathetically.

'I'd call the police.'

I began to get angry. I had never been so cruel to her that she had to treat me like this in what I saw as my hour of need. 'Everything's collapsing! Just because of that fucking girl—'

'Why don't you telephone Marion?' She cut me off, seemed ready to put down the telephone. I realised it was true what they say about a woman scorned.

'Marion isn't my solicitor.'

'If you want to talk to me as your solicitor, telephone my office in the morning and make an appointment.'

'After all I've been through—'

'You're not the only one who goes through things.' She cut me off again and this time did hang up. When I redialled

300

the phone was engaged. So I took her advice and tried Marion but there was no answer there. Bed and a progression from beer to vodka seemed the only answer.

It had become dark when the telephone rang again. The voice was indistinct, a woman's.

'Who is it?'

'Nell.'

'Nell?' This was a voice from another era. In my emotional drunken state, I pictured her as the girl who had comforted me after my parents' death.

'Oh, Nell. It's all such a fucking mess.' I was piteous, weeping.

'I know. I know. I saw about it in the papers. My husband said it served you right and if they mentioned me or Bruno, he'd kill you, but I couldn't help feeling sorry.'

'Oh, Nell.' Someone felt sorry for me. It was incredible.

'I've crept downstairs. But I just wanted to send my sympathy and hope it works out.'

'Nell. Nell.'

'My father died, you know. But my mother and I spoke. She's sorry too. Think about it, Pat. Call Larry.'

I really was crying now. Far beyond words. I wasn't even capable of saying thank you or goodbye before she put the receiver down. I crouched in the little dark sitting room and stared at the wall for a very long time. I couldn't pull out the threads but I knew they were there, my childhood, the thing that had happened with my mother, my parents' death, Nell, the attack.

∞   ∞   ∞

My FATHER came round to the flat almost as soon as I was back.

'I thought you were coming at ten?' I was exhilarated by my actions. I felt like an avenging angel, at last free to run my sword through the guilty prey. I could feel the electricity in my hair, the glitter in my eye. His dour solidity did not suit my mood. I wanted to shout, 'I'm going to get him! After all these years!' I thought these things but since I was also tired, I bowed to my father's implacability and sank into a chair.

'You can't go on like this,' he began the moment I had settled.

'Don't tell me that. Just don't tell me.'

'Your mother agrees with me. It will do you no good.'

'You mean I should face him every day?' I roused myself enough to shout. 'Is that what you want!'

'You're doing yourself far more harm than him.'

'Rubbish!' Earlier that day I had been forced to hear my erstwhile psychoanalyst saying much the same thing. It seemed that none of them could understand that this was the first time in the seven years since I had been attacked that I was really being true to my feelings. This was the real me. This was my rage, my vengeance, my life.

After my father stopped talking and I had thrown into the wastepaper basket the crappy tabloids that were still telling my story (not because I was ashamed of them but to stop him waving them in the air) I went and cooked us both some supper. We ate it quietly.

CHAPTER
FORTY-SIX

I WENT to see the deputy editor again. He seemed to look at me with distaste, although that might have been my imagination. 'You're still here,' he said, as if hoping for thanks. 'Are you filing stories for the diary?'

'No. I—'

'You mustn't lose your nerve now. You wanted to stay. You have stayed. So, file.'

He was right. My nerve was nearly broken. I drank too much, couldn't sleep, couldn't look anyone in the eye, least of all myself when I saw my unshaven mug staring back at me in the newspaper's washroom mirror.

After the deputy editor's words of advice, I was galvanised enough to go out and cover a race between two paraplegic boys who had just been presented with new super wheel-chairs. It was a publicity stunt, arranged to raise money for two chairs rocketed along a path in the middle of Hyde Park. Leaves, blown down from the trees above, scattered round their wheels. Low autumnal sun sparked off the chromium, competing with the flashlights of the cameramen. One of the boys – he must have been sixteen or seventeen – had hair as fair as mine which was thick and long and stood out behind him. I wondered how he had broken his body so badly and imagined a motor-cycle flying through the air and a figure somersaulting upwards and then tumbling down, cracking against the hard ground. I turned away and found, to my disgust, that my face was wet with tears.

I walked all the way back to the office, most of the way through the park. The steady pace and the absence of anyone who might know who I was calmed me. The sun stayed with me, also doing something to counteract the effects of the last few days. I remembered, with a sense of hope, that Larry had said I could stop by for supper that evening.

∞   ∞   ∞

MY DESK was an absolute mess. I said to the girl who sat next to me in the office, 'It looks as if someone's been stirring up my papers with a spoon.'

'Oh, no one's that interested in your affairs,' she replied sharply.

I started to explain that I was not imagining spies but she turned back to her screen. I understood that what she had only partly said was true: no one wanted my affairs to domi-nate life in the office for ever. They were ready to get on with the next story. I saw it in the way nobody particularly talked to me, although they did not avoid me either. I had had my time as a freak show, and, as far as I knew, Patrick William Downes was still somewhere in the building.

Telling myself to stay calm, stay gripped, I put up onto the screen a story I was working on about the Isles of Scilly.

As I re-read my own descriptions (culled from books) of bracken-covered cliff hardly trodden by man, I had a traitorous longing for escape from the battle. But that was not the way, I told myself. 'The men can find work on the land,' I tapped out firmly, 'but, without tourism, the women must leave to find employment on the mainland.'

∞   ∞   ∞

I TOOK a boat as far as I could to Larry's flat. It was expensive, a pound a stop, as we zig-zagged down the Thames. There was only a handful of other people aboard and it was beginning to grow dark. By the time we reached the last two stops there was only myself and the two boatmen. They ignored me, talking to each other about a mutual friend who seemed to have every vice. 'He didn't just drink whisky, nor even gulp it, he swilled it, SWILLED it, swilled it down.' They seemed to like the word, repeating it with relish.

I found it soothing, like an incantation which, combined with the rocking movement of the boat, made me feel sleepy for the first time for days. When one shouted, 'Isle of Dogs,' I felt extremely disinclined to move. I might even have made the return journey and given up all idea of seeing Larry, but they were stopping here for a while, I gathered, visiting a favourite pub where they expected to find the man who 'swilled' whisky. I could see they were excited at the prospect.

They stayed just long enough to give me directions to Larry's block of flats and then I was on my own in the soft autumnal evening.

The block of flats was built right on the river but I had to walk along the large inland road. Sooner than expected, I began to recognise where I was. This was the road down which the policeman had driven on Christmas Day. Such a thing could not happen to me now. I was a successful magazine owner and emerging journalist. But the memory unnerved me, throwing me back into that self who had stood outside the respectable world, peering in bitterly and hopelessly.

304

I reached the bottom of Larry's block and stood in front of the long row of bells. I was about to press 'Purley' when Larry himself pushed open the door, knocking me backwards with the force of his arrival.

'Sorry, Pat! Helen's gone into hospital. Here, take the key. I'll call you as soon as I know what's what.' He was off.

On the whole I liked the idea of having the flat to myself for a while. I went upwards calmly. If Helen had started the baby, Larry might be away for some time.

The flat was smaller than I had remembered. I suppose coming straight from my prison cell had given me a different perspective. It was still a large room with a glassy uncurtained view over the river but not an endless space. I poured a beer, promising myself to make it the only one, and sat down in one of the wide leather armchairs. I felt too sleepy for any occupation.

∞   ∞   ∞

I ARRIVED at Larry's flat on the dot of eight as he'd said. I had taken a taxi for the last bit of the journey and when it left I felt curiously isolated on this far reach of the Thames. The darkness was soft and unthreatening enough but there was something about entering his territory which unnerved me. When Larry and I had met regularly, it had always been in hotels or other anonymous settings. Reminding myself that his wife, Helen, would also be there, I rang the bell.

∞   ∞   ∞

THE DOORBELL woke me up. Assuming it to be Larry, I pressed the release to the outside door and, then, leaving the flat door open, returned still half asleep, to my chair.

∞   ∞   ∞

LIKE A child, I counted the floors as the lift carried me slowly upwards. One, two, three . . . Larry lived on the twelfth floor. I wished he had at least greeted me as I stood outside.

305

I felt uncomfortably hot and tense. The lift jerked to a stop and I stepped out onto the cheaply carpeted corridor. There was a window over the river which drew my attention for a moment and then I saw the door open at the end of the corridor.

It was like a dream or a nightmare, I suppose. As I went through the door, the little hallway and into the wide sitting room he was sitting there, smiling a little, waiting for me. I wanted to scream and run but I was so overcome by terror that, as at the newspaper, my body lost all its strength and I sank down on the floor. Without analysing why or how, I was certain that he was there to finish off the job he'd begun all those years ago. Although weak with terror, I did not faint and watched him intently. This time I would not turn my back.

'I . . .' He started to speak. The smile had gone the moment he recognised me and was replaced by a white rigidity. He opened his mouth again but did not seem able to make any words.

Nothing lasts for ever. Something has to happen. One of us had to move. I watched as he got up slowly from his chair and walked towards me. When he was within a foot of me he held out his hand, still without saying a word, although his face was moving. The sight of his hand, pale and broad, covered with blond hairs, gave me the impetus to struggle up.

I realised he was watching me with the same intensity as I was him. He pushed a chair closer to me and then retreated back as far as the window. I understood he was giving me space, but my fearfulness made me feel like a wild animal being stalked by a would-be captor. If I sat down, the net would fall.

I stood by the chair, leaning on it for support. Gradually my strength was returning. In a few moments I would be able to run out, take the lift, plunge freely into the street outside.

He had now turned his back on me and was gazing over the river. The curtains were not drawn and there was a wide expanse of black, decorated by a line of glittering buildings on the other bank of the river.

'I am not going to hurt you.' His voice was soft and pleasant, but it set up a reaction in me as a dog's hackles rise at an enemy. This made me less frightened and more angry. I glared at his back.

'I don't know why Larry has done this to us.' He sounded exhausted and what he said started my brain going again. Had Larry deliberately brought us here together? Would he have done that if he thought I would be in danger?

He turned round suddenly and I jumped back. This seemed to confuse him. 'Sorry. I told you I won't hurt you.'

The 'sorry' sounded loudly in my ears. I wanted to speak now. But not to him. I wanted to tell someone about all those years when no one had said 'sorry' to me, when everyone told me to get over it without actually dealing with the 'it'.

'Don't go.' He said that. 'Don't go.' I looked at him amazed. He came back from the window and sat down again in the chair where he'd been when I first saw him. I continued to stare. He was tall, broad-shouldered, he had fair hair, unwashed, regular features, and he looked as if he hadn't shaved for several days. There were dark puffy circles under his eyes which made him look older than I knew he was. He was wearing a dark T-shirt, brown leather jacket, well-worn jeans and trainers. His legs were very long, sticking straight out in front of him. I found I wanted to sit down too and I realised I wasn't so frightened any more. I believed the man in the chair. He wasn't going to hurt me.

∞   ∞   ∞

As soon as she sat down, I felt as if I'd stopped holding my breath. Neither of us spoke. I felt too tired to make anything else happen. We were there sitting together in the same room. That seemed enough for the time being.

∞   ∞   ∞

I thought he had gone to sleep, he was slumped so deeply

in the chair with his eyes half closed. This did not suit me as I was beginning to feel more alert, more talkative. Casting myself in the woman's role, I eventually got up, 'I'll make us both some coffee.' He blinked up at me. His eyes were the blue of children, trusting and naïve.

When I came back with the coffee he pulled himself up a little and took the cup with a hand that trembled.

'A baby is being born now,' I said.

'I don't understand.' He looked at me blankly. His exhaustion spread through the room. I sat up straighter.

'What's your name?' I asked him. I wanted to hear him pronounce those words I'd heard in my head for so long.

'What?' He was bewildered.

'Tell me your name,' I said a little impatiently.

'You know it. Them. Both my names.'

'I want you to say out slowly the name you were given at birth, first name, middle name and then surname.'

'Why should I?' He wasn't as totally lacking in energy as he looked.

'Because I'm asking you. Please.'

He said it then, 'Patrick William Downes.' I made him say it again and again. As he spoke I watched his mouth and the expression on his face. At first the words seemed to be only an echo of those in my head but gradually they began to come out of his mouth and then they were being delivered by this man about my age, very tired, anxious, unhappy.

∞   ∞   ∞

I THOUGHT she must be crazy when she made me pronounce my name, slowly and clearly – she stopped me if I went too fast – over and over again. No one had told me L. L. Kirk was crazy, but perhaps that explained her wild determination for vengeance.

'Thank you.' She signalled I could stop. I felt that she was more relaxed and dared to look at her face. It was strong-featured with long nose, pointed chin and wide-apart very dark eyes. Her skin was not very good as if she didn't bother much with fresh air or healthy eating. She was very thin, dressed in corduroy trousers cut like jodhpurs and an expensive-looking jacket. She was dressed to be successful and on guard. I wondered if she wore something less powerful when she interviewed all those weeping women which had become her speciality.

'Would you have recognised me?' Her voice had regained what I assumed to be its natural tone, clear and strong.

'What do you want me to say?'

'Actually, I know a whole lot about you.'

'You do?'

'Larry told me. Years ago. When you were in prison. He wanted us to meet even then.' As she talked, her face which had seemed to me quite plain, even ugly, became brighter and more appealing.

'He used to tell me about your parents dying and your marriage, the baby. He tried to explain things to me but I wouldn't listen. Then when you came out of prison he told me you weren't worth bothering about after all.'

'He told you that?'

'Yes. After which he dropped out of my life.' She stopped abruptly and looked away from me.

'What's the matter?'

'Nothing.' But her voice was harder and colder. 'Do you know what I'd like to do?' She sounded so fierce I was prepared for anything.

'No.' Actually, I was unprepared for anything.

'I'd like to show you my scars. That is your scars. The scars you made on my body.

The situation was ridiculous. I tried and failed to smile. She was beyond me. She wanted to bring back that person who had attacked her. She wanted that hysterical boy back in the room.

'I want you to see the closed mouths of the wounds you cut with your knife.' Her voice had risen with determination.

'Please.' I found my fists were clenched tight. I forced them open and held them up defensively.

'I need you to feel them, to know how they feel!' She was like someone drunk, impervious to anything but her own voice. Was she really planning to take off her designer jacket

309

and protective jodhpurs so I could place my fingers on the unnatural creases in her skin? My face became hot and my head started to swim round as if I might faint.

'I can't,' I said, deciding to take her seriously.

'But you must.' She stood up and came over to me. 'They're your scars. You made them. They belong to you. You put them on my body but they're not mine. I never wanted them. You put your mark on me so I could never be wholly myself again.'

Once again, I told myself she was crazy. 'Please, no,' I repeated pathetically. But she was strident and bullying and I was weak.

Slowly, I got out of my chair.

∞   ∞   ∞

WHEN HE got out of his chair and put his arms round me, I stood absolutely still. I let him enfold me with his body so that there was no corner of me unprotected. He held me there tightly so that I could feel his warmth and the trembling of his limbs. After a second or two I allowed myself to cry but he held me still. We were locked together like the closest of lovers.

FORTY-SEVEN

IT WAS an effort to hold her. I had to make the effort but I was desperate for the moment to end. When she began to cry, I held her still and, at last – it seemed like an age – she moved slightly and it was possible to lead her to the chair and let her slowly down into it. I hovered by her indecisively. As the tears slowed down and dried away, I saw her face was transfigured with happiness. When she looked at me, I saw immense gratitude.

I went back to my chair and sat down. I was glad she did not speak because there was a hard argumentative voice inside me which was ready to spoil everything.

Then she did speak. 'You've made me feel I exist again.' I knew I should respond, but the tightness inside me grew. She had her happy ending, best to leave me alone.

The telephone rang, startling us both. I got up slowly to answer it. The movement was a relief. 'Yes?'

'Pat?'

'Yup.' Larry seemed doubtful of my identity.

'I'm still at the hospital. The baby is taking its time.'

'How's Helen?' Helen had been wonderful. I remembered how wonderful Helen had been.

'She's doing fine. Pat?'

'Yup.'

'Are you on your own?' So he knew we were here together.

'No. Kirk's here.'

There was a pause. 'Are you OK?'

'We're fine.'

'I'm glad. It was just one of those things, Pat.' He sounded ingratiating, apologetic, not as curious as I would have expected. I suppose his mind was on the baby.

'Don't worry about us, Larry.' I looked towards Kirk. She was smiling.

'I'll see you later then, Pat.'

'Good luck,' I replied, putting down the receiver. I stood up and went over to Kirk. 'I think we should eat,' I said. The conversation with Larry had changed my mood. I still had that nasty hard knot but I was released into action.

So we cooked together in the kitchen where Helen and I had made supper all those years ago. We made spaghetti and a sauce and grated cheese to go with it.

'Comfort food,' commented Kirk, smiling. 'My mother always made it for my sister and me when we were cross. She believed being cross was the same as being sick. All the same, she didn't like cooking.'

We were on to family reminiscences. Hers. We drank beer, she told me about her Catholic mother and sister, her Polish father and how happy her sister was now with her husband

311

and baby. She told me about her father's need for a mistress and how when one had fled he'd merely allowed a decent interval to elapse before finding another younger model. She told me all these things as if I should feel a part of them. She moved onto her career, her ambitions and how hard she'd worked and still worked. She told me about her psychiatrist, her boy-friend called Herbie who was no longer sympathetic and her American friend who had gone back home to die of cancer. Then she talked about her mother again. Or perhaps I thought she did.

She talked for hours, laying her life in front of me. We moved back from the kitchen and found our chairs again, moved from beer to whisky. I realised she was talking me backwards, retreating inexorably to that point when I had entered her life.

'You want me to explain, don't you?' I interrupted her suddenly. 'You think if I go through it with you, sitting here cosily side by side, it will work like an exorcism.'

Stopped in mid-sentence, she stared at me with flushed, lively face. The flow of ideas had filled her with vitality. Then she spoke soberly. 'Is that possible?'

'I don't know.' Her eager expectant face made me both frightened and angry and I turned away.

'Words are nothing.' She was smiling again. 'That's the conclusion I reached after a bit. All the words in the world don't add up to an explanation.'

But I had spent the last two hours listening to her happy family stories. She saw my expression and thought she understood.

'They're necessary, of course, but just to get them out of the way.'

Why was she acting so superior? I stood up. 'It's after midnight.'

'Do you want to go?' Her voice was smaller at once, less self-confident.

'I can't give you what you need.' She should have heard the change in my voice.

'It's not like that.' She was huddling down in the chair.

Now I was standing over her, I realised the enormous

pressure that had been building in me as I sat there endlessly listening, listening. 'Do you know what,' my voice had changed again, hoarse and strained, 'I think we should re-enact the whole disgusting scene!' I took a stride or two towards the kitchen. 'I go and get a nice sharp knife while you hang about here all unsuspecting.'

∞   ∞   ∞

WHEN HE went into the kitchen talking about a knife, I couldn't take it seriously. Since our quiet embrace we had spent hours together. We had eaten a meal together, I had told him my life story. It was impossible I should think of him any longer as the youth who had nearly murdered me. He was someone else, tired, depressed, silent. I had turned him into my closest confidant and support. I had acted on the basis that our lives were linked indissolubly together. My past took our lives back to where they had first come into contact.

'Please, Pat,' I called after him as I had heard Larry do all those years ago, 'please, Pat, you don't have to say or do anything.'

But the kitchen door which was on a swing had shut behind him and I could hear nothing. Nothing in the evening, no flicker of aggression in his face, his movements or his speech made me feel the slightest bit on guard. I was filled with gratitude to him for allowing me to forgive. I trusted him. I was prepared to love him.

Then he came through the door holding a heavy-handled carving knife. I still was not properly frightened. His face was intent but not angry as a man who planned to use the knife.

I stood up and went towards him. 'Pat. Tell me what's wrong.'

He said nothing, came very close to me, took hold of my shoulder, gently but firmly. He put me into the curve of his arms. As a lover might, he cradled me. Then he raised the knife and held it across my neck. It pushed my head up high so that I was staring up to the ceiling.

313

'I'll tell you,' he whispered. And he began talking. Talking, talking, talking. In a terrible tortured voice. On and on and on. At first it was about prison. He kept repeating how he could never get over it, never. I can't remember anything in much detail for as soon as I realised that he was planning to replay his attack on me, my brain seemed to block.

I know his parents came into it, his mother, her beauty, her coldness, his love for her, their absence, their death. He was very agitated at this point, hardly able to get out the words. Then he talked of his wife, 'the whore' as he called her, 'the harlot', then his child, 'poor little bear', his solicitor friend Ruth, his friend Marion who was 'fat, disgustingly fat'. The names repeated in my head but there was no thread to catch hold of unless it was his unhappiness. Then he got on to Larry and Helen. She was good, the only good woman he had ever met, Larry was bad. Gradually, I realised that he was actually trying to give me what I had given him, his life story.

But he was doing it with me a captive, a knife at my neck. The voice talking behind me, into my ear. The arms trembling but still holding me like a strait-jacket. I've no idea how long it went on, perhaps as long as an hour or more. I had no thought to struggle. In fact if anything I became more passive, even partly unconscious. I did recall, once or twice, that other time. That horror.

I was brought to life again by a sharp click. Pat did not hear it. He was too deep in his own world. Besides, his back was to the hallway. Over his shoulder, I saw Larry come into the flat. He was so tired that it took him a second or two to take in what he was seeing; the knife dropped a little from my throat but still held as a threat. In that moment Pat sensed a third presence and, without letting go of me, turned his head.

Larry, a formidable man, big and strong and fit, sprang forward.

I screamed. The knife quivered at my throat. I managed to swivel from it. That was brave. All this seemed to be happening at the same time, fast motion, slow motion – it was hard to tell which. And Larry was almost on him.

Then Pat and I were separated by a shattering shrieking bellowing noise. I was thrown on the floor where for a second I didn't understand.

When I looked up I saw a splintered and jagged hole in the picture window to the sky, like a star in the night, and saw Pat hurling himself towards it.

I screamed again. 'No, Pat! No. Please!' I pounded the floor.

I knew Larry was after him but the transformation had been so sudden that I could not believe he could catch Pat who seemed like a missile already launched into space. I put my face sideways to the carpet and shut my eyes.

∞　∞　∞

I WANTED to kill her, wipe her off the face of the earth. I felt that would make everything clean again. But there was something else. Something else.

I flung the knife with all my strength away from the girl, away from Larry. It went so defiantly through the glass. It flew from my hand, out into the night. Now I only thought to follow it, far from the agony inside my head. It seemed such an obvious answer, waiting patiently for me ever since I'd first noticed that window. I bellowed with exultation as I took a mighty dive.

∞　∞　∞

LARRY HAD him by the legs. He had caught him a foot or two from the window. They were on the floor, at my eye-line. Pat was thrashing about and yelling and I realised Larry was having difficulty holding on to him.

I found I could just manage to crawl towards them. Pat's arms were beating about so I was afraid to get too close. I did try ineffectually to grab one arm and then Larry shouted, 'Get me something to tie him with!'

It took me ages. On my feet again, tottering like an old lady. Eventually, I brought him a dressing-gown sash. I watched as he bound Pat's ankles together. Pat was still thrashing about but he was silent now and when Larry moved up and sat on his chest, he became completely quiet.

'Get something to tie his arms,' said Larry in an utterly exhausted voice. This time I found Helen's sash. Soon Pat was as neatly trussed as a chicken.

Larry crouched back on his haunches. I was standing above him. Behind us I could feel cold fresh air blowing in from the broken window.

Larry was breathing heavily. He pushed back his hair and rubbed his sweating face. He swivelled round so he could see me. 'God, I'm sorry. Are you all right?'

I stared at him. There was a look of Pat about him, more than just the blondness. I had somehow never totally believed they were first cousins but now I could see it quite clearly.

I looked at Pat's face. He was sweating heavily too and his blue eyes were open, staring blindly. I crouched down beside him. He was completely still, almost as if paralysed. I stroked his hair away from his face. He blinked but did not look at me or seem to object.

So I sat there with him, stroking his face, and gradually it softened a little and his eyelids drooped more naturally.

'I'll ring a doctor.' Larry stumbled to his feet.

'Did Helen have a baby?' I asked him softly.

'Oh, yes. A boy. A lovely boy.' Despite everything, he half smiled.

I continued to sit with Pat.

I heard Larry talking to a doctor and realised he was objecting to coming out at four in the morning.

'He'll come round at seven,' Larry said. 'He's got to find a hospital to take him.'

'You go to bed.' He looked as if he might fall over at any minute. 'I'll watch Pat.'

Just before he went, I said, 'He tried to commit suicide, that's all.'

Larry was too tired to argue. 'I just couldn't believe he was insane.'

It was cold under the window so I found a spare room and took off all the bedclothes. Then I put them over Pat and came and lay down beside him. He was breathing quietly but I didn't know if he was asleep or awake for he had closed his eyes. After a few moments, I rose again and turned off all the lamps except for one. I was calm, strong. Then I lay down with him again.

I spent the hours that followed wide awake. They were truly the most important in my life. I realised that for all the years since the attack I had thought that what I most needed to survive happily and healthily was for Patrick William Downes to be wiped out of existence. I had wanted him dead preferably, if not dead, as far away from me as possible. But now, lying next to him, as close as we could be, I felt the first real sense of peace since his attack. It was a most extra-ordinary sensation. Indescribable.

When the absolute black outside began to thin to a greyish mist, I went and made us both a cup of tea. But he was 'asleep so I drank mine alone. I took it to the window where the air smelled saltily as if the sea was out there instead of a sluggish city river. I stood by the jagged hole, breathing deeply.

'I always meant to curtain that window.' Larry had come silently from his bedroom and now stood looking at me. 'You OK?'

'Yes.'

He bent down and looked at Pat. 'He's wet himself.'

'That must have been since I left him.' I came over and took Larry's arm. 'When the doctor comes, I shall go to the hospital with Pat in the ambulance.'

'Don't be a fool, Lydia. A man nearly kills you for the second time.'

I cut him off. 'I'm strong now. You should go and see Helen and the baby.'

I did not try to explain to him how I felt.

PART FIVE

FORTY-EIGHT

Lydia used to worry that being in a mental hospital would make me think I was back in prison again.

'You are not being punished,' she was at pains to point out. 'You are being helped.'

Such niceties were far above my head in the first weeks when I was so heavily drugged that I could have been in Disneyland for all I cared. Actually, I was in a ward of a National Health hospital in South London. I had been brought in by ambulance and not, as again Lydia insisted, by the police but once I had arrived Larry, as my nearest relative, had set in process that I should be sectioned. 'For his own protection,' he had told Lydia but she was not convinced. That was why she kept reminding me I was not in prison, because, in effect, I was and she felt guilty.

But, as I have said, none of this worried me because I lay, filled with lithium, in my little bed and slept for twenty hours of the day and spent the other four eating, washing or defecating.

By the time I was starting to take notice of my surroundings, I had been moved to another hospital on the outskirts of London where the windows showed large squares of sky and trees and grass. Although I was locked into the ward as securely as any prison I now had a private bedroom, with curtains and wardrobe, which was nothing like a cell, and I could move freely between that room, the sitting room with television, the dining area, kitchen, billiard room and anywhere else on that floor. Although there were patients there as violent as any prisoner, they were given the freedom to be human beings. It was in these surroundings that I began to come alive again.

You see, I had not killed her and, better than that, I no longer wanted to.

CHAPTER
FORTY-NINE

IT WAS lucky I was a journalist otherwise my visits to Pat would have ruined my career.

When he was in the Maudsley it was relatively easy. The number eighty-eight bus went all the way and, although it took over an hour, I trained myself to read and even write on it. I sat on the top, at the front, sailing along to my destiny.

My destiny at this point was a poor thing. I was his only visitor because Larry, having made sure he was securely put away, washed his hands of him. He had his new little baby, of course. Perhaps he thought some of Pat's disorder would enter his sunny nursery. Or perhaps he just couldn't take it. A lot of people are afraid of the contamination of the insane.

My own family worried that I, too, was losing my marbles. Echoing Larry on that chaotic night in his flat, my mother wailed, 'But, Lydia, Lydia, this is a man who has twice nearly killed you' – the fact that he held a knife at my throat had emerged (although not to the police) despite all my efforts – 'How can you want him in your life?'

Only my father saw that it was precisely because of what he had done to me that I had to have him in my life. Even Charmian, so capable of forgiveness, could not quite see things from my point of view. But she had two babies to look after now.

Nothing was more necessary than my presence, sitting reading by his bed, talking sometimes to the other patients, talking most of all to the nurses. 'He may not seem aware of you,' they said, 'but we can tell the difference when you're here and when you're not here. Even if he doesn't exactly

322

converse' – he never spoke at all – 'he knows you come and that's very important.'

The days I visited Pat were special. I would start work very early, before it was light, and then catch my bus around two o'clock. I spent the afternoon in the hospital and then came back, always buying myself a treat, a pineapple, a hard-back book, a tape, before I re-entered my flat. Once when Pat had put out his hand to me, I bought a little bottle of champagne. These were prizes to myself for surviving another visit. They also said this had been a good day. Look, you have not only seen Pat, who held out his hand to you, but you have progressed a little further in an article and now you have come back to your flat, still active. On those evenings I didn't want to see anyone.

But when he was transferred to Bethlem Royal, things changed. First of all, the journey now required a tube ride, a train journey and a taxi. It could not be fitted into my working schedule. It was a day out. Then he began to come alive and I was required to be more than a merely passive presence. He would be waiting at the locked door, pacing a few steps back and forth as if he had been standing there some time and could no longer keep still.

'You're late.'

'I had to wait ages for a train.' I had never told him I would arrive at any particular time but he had fixed on eleven thirty and if I came before or after informed me firmly, 'You're early,' 'You're late.' Then he would take my bag in one hand and my arm in the other and lead me quickly to his room. He looked neither to right nor left but escorted me anxiously, afraid that my attention might be diverted by another patient or a nurse.

It was true that the other patients did try to take a bit of me for themselves but I made sure that was not until later. In Pat's bedroom, we sat side by side on the bed and he looked in the bag to see what I had brought him. He liked grapes best and fizzy drinks and, although he could not yet concentrate enough to read, I sometimes brought him a newspaper to give him the idea. As the weather became colder, I bought him a sweater and then a scarf because he complained that he liked to sit by his open window but it made him shiver.

He was a reduced human being, but I didn't mind. I talked to his doctors and they told me he needed this period of blankness; it was a necessary part of the healing process, and that already they were cutting down his drugs. They told me, 'Just hold his hand', meaning it metaphorically, although I held it in reality too.

After he'd examined the contents of my bag, he would take me the rounds of the rooms, offer me a coffee, suggest a game of billiards, check out for my entertainment what was on television. As the day wore on, his jealousy of me would lessen and he would let me talk to the other patients, listening with a kind of pride, as if my health and capability resounded to his credit.

'This is my friend, Lydia,' he introduced me. 'She is very clever. She works on a newspaper.' He turned to me. 'Lydia, show them that piece you wrote on badgers in inner London.'

He was always interested in my latest piece and as he didn't seem able to read them himself, I got into the habit of reading them aloud. Quite often he surprised me by his useful criticism so sometimes I brought an article I was still working on. At least it passed the time.

'I wish you would come more,' he would appeal to me at intervals throughout the day.

'You know I can't. I'm working.'

His blue eyes, so trusting, filled with tears, like a child. I thought to myself that I could organise it so that I came once during the week and once during the weekend. For a couple of weeks this seemed to satisfy him and then he started again. 'I wish you would come more. The other days are so empty.'

It was early December now but bitterly cold with the grass bent stiff and white in the mornings and my journey, in and out of different forms of unheated or overheated transport, very tiring. I asked to see the consultant who looked after Pat.

324

'He is so dependent,' I told him. 'I encouraged him but now I'm afraid I cannot satisfy his need.'

The consultant remained unworried. 'What do you talk about?'

'Nothing much. Trivialities. We pass the time of day.' I knew he meant did we talk about his attacks on me but if he wasn't going to refer to it directly then neither would I.

'I see, then he probably isn't ready. Why are you his only visitor?'

I was taken aback. 'I don't know. I mean, his cousin . . .' But the doctor knew about Mr Purley. He wanted to hear about others.

'There is his solicitor, a friend.' I was doubtful.

'Good.' The doctor became cheerful. 'And what about his wife?'

'His wife?' Now I was really taken aback. 'But they've been divorced for ages. She's even remarried.'

'All the better. There's a child too, I believe. Of course she may not wish to see him. But some do. Quite a lot find they have it in them to help. Even the most cruelly used.'

He looked at me meaningfully. I wondered why I disliked the thought of his wife visiting. Was it jealousy? But how absurd! And the boy was his child. 'Perhaps the child doesn't even know he exists,' I suggested.

'Perfectly possible. More than likely. See what you can do. You're absolutely right. He shouldn't be entirely dependent on you.' Was there no one else who could probe for further visitors?

I would have done nothing. Then, just before Christmas, Pat took me into his bedroom with particular urgency and told me to sit down. Delving in the back of his cupboard, he produced an envelope and inside was a Christmas card and inside the Christmas card was a photograph.

'It's from Nell.' He was so agitated that his speech had become slurred again as when he was on heavy drugs. 'Look, look, the photograph of the little boy. It's my son.' He paused at the word, as if amazed, and then continued in a rush. 'It's of Bruno, that's what he's called. He's seven now, nearly eight. Such a big boy. What do you think, Lydia? What do you think? Is he handsome? He's smiling at someone, I guess. The person taking the photograph. Perhaps Nell.'

He thrust the photograph at me, for my inspection, my approval, I didn't know what. I found tears had come into my eyes. 'He's beautiful, Pat. He's a wonderful little boy.' What I didn't say was that he looked just like his father. But he did, floppy fair hair, over wide forehead, blue eyes, broad cheekbones.

But Pat was still upset. He gripped my hand and stared closely into my eyes. 'Can you tell? Can you tell? Is he happy? Do you think he looks happy?'

He looked very obviously happy, well cared for and smiling but I was fascinated by Pat's intensity. 'Why shouldn't he be happy?'

He let go of my hand and fell back against the wall behind the bed on which we sat. His eyes avoided mine. 'I wasn't happy,' he mumbled. 'When I was a little boy like that.'

Now I understood. I took hold of him and made him lean against me. 'He's the jolliest little boy I've ever seen.' I was decisive but he still held himself rigidly and spoke with his face turned away.

'I couldn't bear it if he was unhappy. I couldn't bear it. I couldn't bear it to happen all over again.' His intensity, tears in his eyes, was agonising.

'It won't, Pat. I promise you.' This was himself we were talking about. At last. I found I was holding my breath. 'His mother loves him. You can tell that.'

'Yes. She loves him.' He repeated my words but still distractedly. 'I didn't want him to be born, you see. It terrified me.'

'Perhaps,' I took a gulp of air, 'perhaps you would like to see Nell,' I pronounced her name carefully, 'and hear how well he is from her.'

This idea astonished him. Sweat started on his forehead and his eyes opened wide. I told myself it was his doctor's idea, not mine. But I had underestimated him. After a pause while he calmed himself, he gave a kind of half smile. 'It would be unfair to bring Bruno to this place but if Nell wanted to come I would be glad.'

'She did send you a Christmas card,' I pointed out, feeling like a social worker.

'Yes. Now we've talked about it, I'll put it up on the shelf.' Carefully, he placed the card, but not the photograph, I noticed, where he could see it from his bed.

It struck me that since he was now being so sensible – more sensible than I felt – it might be a good time to raise the question of other visitors.

'Is there anyone else you'd like to see? Larry mentioned your solicitor was a friend.'

He stood with his back to me, looking out of the window. 'Ruth probably won't come. Not Marion. Nor Helen. But I wish they would. I like women, you know, they're kinder than men.'

CHAPTER
FIFTY

IN THE New Year, Lydia, my Lydia, wrote to Ruth and Marion and Nell and Helen and suggested that they come to visit me. She also approached the deputy editor of the paper which had employed us both and still employed her and suggested he came to see what a mental hospital was like.

It was a strange time. My doctors had decided I was no longer suicidal or violent so, except that I was still in a closed ward, I could make of my day what I would. I had group therapy twice a week but there I found keeping quiet the best policy.

My true therapy was Lydia.

Then I was faced with these other visitors. First Ruth. She arrived without warning at the end of the day, when I was sitting watching a television soap. She stood in front of me, blocking the screen. Perhaps it was just nerves but she seemed aggressive. I gave up trying to look round her and stood up too.

'We could go to my room, if you like?' I suggested politely. I wanted to be polite but I was frightened of her. 'I'm afraid I'm not very good company,' I added as we walked through the cream-painted corridors.

'It's nice to see you.' She followed me silently till we reached my room.

'I have a window.' I showed her the window. 'And a basin,' I showed her the basin. 'But I'm afraid we'll have to sit on the bed.'

'That's all right.' She seemed to be avoiding looking at me but eventually aimed her face roughly in my direction. 'I can't stay long.'

I realised she was shocked by my bland, drug-filled appearance. I had never known her so quiet. 'Would you like me to make you a coffee? I can do that in the kitchen.'

'No. No. I just came to wish you well.'

'That's kind.'

She sat clasping her knees tightly together.

'My only other visitor is Lydia.' I spoke proudly. It was the only thing I had to be proud about.

'I know. She rang me. She thought you might like to see me. She said you're getting better.'

'I do and I am.' I sat down beside her but stood up again as I felt her shift away a little. I could hardly blame her.

'I'm so sorry that it all went so wrong for you.' This is what she had come to give. Sympathy. I felt pleased. I tried to show it with a smile. She looked away. Did I look so dreadful?

'Shall I show you round?'

'I'd like that.' We were both standing again and she remembered an outsize bar of Toblerone she'd brought me.

'I love Toblerone,' I reassured her, enthusiastically.

After I'd shown her round we poised awkwardly at the door while she waited for a nurse to unlock it. She seemed depressed. I tried to make conversation. 'I expect you're working hard. It's very kind of you to make this long journey.'

'I wanted to come.' The nurse was approaching, pointing the key like a gun. Ruth became suddenly animated. 'I'm seeing William again, you know. Inevitably, I suppose. But it made me realise I shouldn't blame you too much. We were both using each other. That's what I wanted to say.'

'Thank you.' The nurse came between us. I put my hands out to Ruth as she slipped towards the door. 'Come again when you can.'

'I will.' She smiled, I believe for the first time. People who visit mental wards fall into two categories. Either they don't smile at all or they smile the whole time.

Nell wrote to me. The letter arrived soon after Christmas, a flowing letter, filled with emotion. I carried it round for several days before I dared open it. It was very long and referred twice to my 'breakdown'. This was why her 'husband', another powerful word, had consented she should write to me. He was a 'good' man. It was no wonder that the letter took some time and energy (of which I had little) to digest. I showed it to Lydia, of course, and since she was not struck hammer blows by those powerful words she got on with it much quicker and in some ways seemed to read a different letter altogether. She found a proud mother's description of her son.

'Read it aloud,' I begged. 'I'll understand it better if I can hear it in your voice.'

' "Bruno is now the eldest of my three children." ' This was enough to make me gasp. My son was part of a real family. But that was hardly the start of it. ' "And since Tom had two children already when we married, he is quite sandwiched by brothers and sisters. Elsa and Johnny are eight and six, Bruno's in between, then Ricky and finally little Debbie, who is only one. As you can imagine," ' I couldn't but I tried, how I tried! ' "Johnny, Bruno and Ricky form quite a gang in the middle there. Sometimes they quite wear me out but I love them all so much. Even on a GP's salary. It is just what I always wanted. And I have to say that, after all these years, our time together seems like a bad dream. I don't blame you. I never really did. But . . ." '

'Don't read any more.' I did not want to hear 'breakdown' read out loud.

Lydia was finishing the letter. 'I think she's probably telling you that Bruno is part of that family she describes now. Perhaps he even thinks Tom is his father.'

I made an effort to be sensible. 'He was so young when I left and even then he only saw me a few times.'

'I don't expect she'd want to disturb him. Look, there's another photograph.'

She emptied it out of the envelope. It was a group photograph, a group of children who had been told to smile for the camera and thought it funny to pull faces and shut their eyes; in the middle this blond boy who I recognised as being part of me grinned madly. I handed it back to Lydia quickly. 'That's all right, then.'

She didn't question me further.

Perhaps she knew what I meant. But the next time she came, she had brought her mother.

This was a shock. She should have warned me. I turned my back on them and went and sat alone in my bedroom until I felt calmer. When I came out they were drinking coffee in the living area, trying to make sense of a severely depressed girl who thought she was telling them her life story but was actually only managing a few disconnected words.

The moment Lydia's mother spotted me, she was on her feet, nervously talking. 'I told Lydia she should have warned you. But she's so obstinate, will have her own way. Shall I go now? Not bother you any more? I'd hate to be a bother.'

'You're not a bother . . . It was just the surprise.' I gave Lydia, my kind Lydia, a dirty look . . . which she didn't deserve.

'I've driven in from the country, you see, coming in, as it were, the other way from London . . .'

It seemed I had to put her at her ease. 'Shall we go for a walk?' I suggested. 'The sun is shining.'

This was new, this going for a walk. It was a heady pleasure for me, an unsteadying sense of space which made me look for an arm. I walked between Lydia and her mother in the garden and after a bit none of us felt the need to talk too much.

'Well.' Mrs Kremachowski came close enough, as she was about to leave, so that I could see that her eyes were the same colour as her daughter's. 'It was kind of you to have me here. I understand more about Lydia's feelings now and I wish you luck.'

We shook hands. It was a serious moment but Lydia was moving from foot to foot in the background. If they hadn't left together I'd have told her she looked like a child not a tough journalist.

FIFTY-ONE

IT WAS warm by March. Pat and I sat on a bench under a magnolia tree. He said I was like a light in his life, like a glowing candle, like one of the magnolia flowers above our heads.

'You're a romantic,' I told him. 'I'm hard and dry and my skin is not at all like a waxy petal.'

'Your skin is smoother than a waxy petal.' He ran his fingers up my arm under my sleeve. 'It's far more delicate and, now I come to think of it, not like a waxy petal at all. In fact I eschew waxy petals!' Bending over he pressed his lips onto my forearm. They were warm, firm, masculine.

No one, no man had kissed me anywhere on my body for so long. I looked at him. His face was beginning to come into shape again, the puffiness receding, the blue eyes focused and aware. I looked away. Had I expected this? Did I want it?

'Yesterday I was told I could go out in the daytime. In a month's time, if all goes well, they say I should go out altogether. For good. That's what they said, go out for good.'

He was facing a future. I began to gabble. I talked about

the deputy editor who'd written and said he would take him back on the paper when he was ready. I reminded him that my mother had now visited him twice and would expect a return visit. Indeed, my whole family were prepared to welcome him as my friend. I had been fighting off my sister's husband, Joseph, for weeks. He was just longing for a meeting. I said that Helen and Larry's baby was more than six months old now and that, even if Larry still found the situation difficult, Helen had always been on his side and would soon win her husband round. I talked about everything except us.

I'd run out of steam. He picked up my right hand and silently traced the filigree of scars on its back. They were no longer sensitive and I did not even think them ugly. 'You don't have to go on being kind to me when I come out. I shall find somewhere to live. I shall find a job, although I don't think I can go back to journalism. If I'm quite lonely for a while, that will be all right.'

CHAPTER
FIFTY-TWO

I HAD fallen in love with Lydia. When I told my doctor he gave me a long lecture about Lydia's role as a kind of lay analyst and that I was transferring myself onto her and that I would probably feel quite different once I got into the real world and took up the threads of my old life. That was a laugh. The last thing in the world I wanted was to take up the threads of my old life.

I didn't bother to try to convince him. I was too certain for it to matter whether he believed it or not. When I met her, thought of her, talked about her, I was swamped by a warmth of well-being. It was trust, security, joy, excitement, all the things I'd never felt in my life before. Strangest of all, I felt it without needing her to love me. Certainly I needed her affection, her kindness, her confidence in me, but I did not expect love. Not at first. Her existence was enough for me. Sometimes I tried to stay awake at night so I could spend peaceful hours thinking of nothing except her. Of course I was too happy and fell asleep after a mere half-hour or so!

∞   ∞   ∞

HE TOLD me he loved me the day he came out of hospital.

Since I could not drive, I had ordered a mini-cab to pick up him and his possessions which, in fact, were almost non-existent. I had thought it best he should not live with me or go back to his own flat and it seemed a lucky chance when my father told me he was renting a flat in London where Pat could stay.

Of course, I assumed the flat would include a girl-friend but it seemed to the contrary – she had left him. He was determined to make a go of it with my mother but four nights away would put less of a strain on their marriage. He needed a flatmate to help pay the rent. Pat had instructed Ruth to sell *The Global Philatelist* so had more than enough money to keep him going, even without a job. He said he would not work with me on the paper.

The flat was above an antique shop in Pimlico. It had small rooms with large elegant windows which reached the floor. I was reminded uneasily of the window in Larry's flat when I first saw Pat standing silhouetted against one in the living room.

'You'll be fine here.' I tried to convince myself.

'I'll settle in, then.' He seemed to be trying to get rid of me. Although the flooding light behind him made it impossible to see the expression on his face, I sensed a blank rigidity descending on his body.

I felt a need to make contact, to break the spell of the glassy wall to the road behind him. He didn't answer.

I took a step closer, tempted to touch him, but he held out a hand not in invitation but as if to ward me off. I hesitated, telling myself that I must encourage any signs of independence. But it was then that he spoke. 'I love you, Lydia. I

333

don't expect anything more from you than you already give me. But I want you to know. I love you for ever.'

I felt the echoes of his words. A child telling his mother he loves her, a lover with conviction but no hope and that window reminding me that this was the same man who had held a knife to my throat and then tried to throw himself into oblivion.

'Come away from that window,' I said. He glanced over his shoulder, unaware, apparently, of where he stood.

I wanted to respond but the threat of the past held me tight. Then I remembered how he had hugged me that evening. It had been a torture for him, the way he was then, but he had nevertheless done his best to respond. I took a step forward once more and this time he opened his arms to me eagerly.

We stood together for several seconds and gradually my memories were submerged in the sensation of being close to his body. Although I was supposed to be the strong one, he was holding me as if I needed protection. Our hearts were beating so loudly and close to each other that I could hardly tell them apart.

After a while I slipped from him and left the flat.

∞   ∞   ∞

WHEN I left hospital, I found out love didn't solve all my problems. In the mornings, after Mr Kremachowski had left for work, I sometimes couldn't even find the strength to get out of bed. It was a little like when I first came out of prison, except that now I was not trying to forget. Nothing happened unconsciously any more. Every action came from the will of the person I was trying to become.

My doctor, who I saw once a week, told me that things would improve. Once I dared to visit the newspaper and viewed, down a corridor through a glass door, my beloved Lydia as the efficient and successful journalist. I had to be humble and not intrude. The experience made it clearer still that I could never work on that paper again. In the evenings, although I did so little, my utter exhaustion made me feel nothing but self-pity.

Mr Kremachowski found me in tears one evening and clapped me on the back. 'Where's the hardened criminal now, I'd like to know?' This was supposed to be a joke. We found our relationship testing.

One afternoon, returning from a half-hearted attempt to find a job as a librarian, I was struck by a new idea. Perhaps my love for Lydia, this great love I set such store on, was in fact a perversion, the other side of a passionate desire to kill her. I began to replay the knife thrusts in that fetid store-room, the heavy crash as the Le Creuset pan fell on her skull, my furious lunges at her already prone and nearly senseless body.

How could anyone but a monster act so unnaturally? How could such a monster ever turn back into a human being? My self-doubt began to turn into self-hate.

Lying awake at night, I knew that the only person who could answer me was Lydia but how could I ask her? I was no longer sick, in hospital. I was supposed to be making my own way. She was good to me, of course, spending one or two evenings a week with me and some time at the weekend but unspoken between us was the knowledge that now I had to prove myself.

Nevertheless one June evening when the air was so balmy that we had thrown up all the windows and sat close to a gentle breeze, I could no longer resist asking her, 'Do you think I could ever harm you again?'

She lay on the floor, her legs covered in her usual tight jeans, her long wavy hair spread back from her face. She was pale, tired, having just arrived off a flight from Paris where she'd been doing an interview. She half shut her eyes, didn't even look my way. Then she said softly, 'Kiss me, Pat.'

I crouched down and kissed her cheek, not knowing if this was a kindly response to my question or something more. Then she put her arms round my neck and kissed me on the lips.

So we made love.

CHAPTER
FIFTY-THREE

HE IS part of my life now. Of course he always was. Sometimes I even wonder whether he chose to attack me in that little boxroom because unconsciously he felt an emotional pull towards me. After all, there were plenty of people in and out of the shop all day but it was me he chose as his victim. Perhaps that's too fanciful. Or too morbid.

We are so close now. In the summer, August, I took a holiday from journalism – something I had literally never done – and we went to Italy. We had rented a villa, actually it was only a two-roomed peasant's cottage, in the wooded hills of Tuscany. We wanted to be alone together.

Under the hot sun, Pat took off my clothes and instructed me to sunbathe. He was disbelieving and quite cross with me when the scars stayed disobligingly white while the rest of me gradually turned a nice biscuit colour.

'Put more oil on, Lydia.'

'It's no good, Pat. They're much smaller now and, what's more, I don't care.'

The point was that he cared.

We stayed in that hot little paradise for four weeks and then decided to extend our time to another fortnight. We slept a lot, we ate a lot, we read a lot, we talked a lot, we made love a lot.

I wanted Pat as my lover but it took time for us to accustom ourselves to each other. He was not used to loving the woman he made love to. We needed all that time. We needed to be physically close during the day as well as the night. In the daytime Pat told me about his growing up, his marriage, his baby. It was as if the clear bright air, the sky so high and far away, made his feelings more bearable.

We had talked about these things before, when he was in hospital and in London, but it was only here that we became close enough to trust each other with everything. It was in Italy that he talked about his feelings for his mother. 'I loved her too much. I wanted her too much. She knew it. She

336

made me ashamed. She was disgusted by me. I hated her. I was disgusted by her. I was disgusted by all women. I hated myself.' It was a litany. repeated often and gradually, I thought, becoming less intense.

I took pride in the way I listened to him. I told him not to confuse me with his mother. He did not take much notice of what I said, but he held my body and looked at us happily as we lay together.

The house was about half-way between Siena and Florence and we had hired a Vespa so we could make cultural expeditions. After the first week in which we never moved at all, Pat woke early one morning and announced, 'Today I'm taking you on a trip.'

'As long as it involves buying some food. We're down to tinned tuna and stealing beans from the garden.'

'Nothing wrong with that. But I could do with some wine.'

'And I must have pasta.'

We set off down the rough track. Birds flew from the tangled brambles on which plumped-up blackberries had recently appeared. There was a strong scent of wild mint and pine from the trees climbing up the hillside above us. As usual the sky was blue and the only sign of another person in the world were occasional piles of logs stacked by a woodcutter at the side of the track.

We reached the village at the bottom of the mountains, did our shopping, then checked on the map for the right road. We even made it as far as the crossroads.

'I don't know,' he said, or I said. We were both thinking the same thing.

Back we went up the hill and after that we stopped pretending that we wanted anything except to be with each other as peacefully and tenderly as possible.

London was different. Is different. I like working hard. I always have. I was still living at my flat while Pat stayed with my father as before.

My father said, 'I don't understand you, Lydia. Do you want him or not?' That was after I had stayed away several days working on an assignment. I told my father, fairly politely, to keep out of it.

Then Pat got a job on a magazine. It was the Catholic magazine on which Joseph worked and it was he who had found the job for Pat. With some shame, I remembered how I had tried to patronise my brother-in-law. But that was a long time ago.

Pat was tentatively pleased. He said he knew the same amount about Catholicism as he had done about stamps when he started on *The Global Philatelist*. 'We'll celebrate in your flat,' he told me, 'next week.'

The evening we met for his celebration was very wet. Rain, unseparated into drops, poured from a silvery sky. Pat was late and I stood by my window waiting for him to appear at the corner of the street so that I could watch him walk towards me. I liked seeing him among strangers, testing always whether he would become ordinary like everyone else. He never did.

The rain had darkened his hair, flattening it to his head so that his face and shape of his head was more visible. At one point he looked up and, guiltily, I waved. But he didn't see me.

'I'm soaked through. Steaming wet!' He took off his clothes when he came through the door, throwing them in a sodden heap on the floor while I went to find a towel. I rubbed him dry like a dog. I could feel his muscles under the warm skin.

We made love, lying on my rug in the living room. He told me he loved me, he worshipped me, he adored me.

I knew what he wanted and I was tempted to say it, 'I love you. I love you, Patrick William Downes.' But instead I got up and made us toast and honey and poured us each a little whisky.

We had a picnic on the floor while he told me about the new job and the eccentricities of my brother-in-law who insisted on giving him endless cups of tea heaped with sugar, insisting, 'You must keep up your energy, Pat.'

He was so beautiful, sitting there on my rug, almost naked, his skin still a dark golden from our holiday and his dried hair bleached almost white. His eyes looked at me with that innocent, that imploring blue I had noticed after his second attack on me. I stroked his arm and back feeling the healthy

338

smoothness. I wanted to make love to him again, over and over again.

I clasped him fiercely and told him that I wanted him to be all mine. That perhaps very soon he should come and live with me here.

The rain which had been running noisily down a drain outside the window, fell silent. The night became blacker and quieter. The traffic stopped.

We moved to the bedroom and I told him that I could never look at another man. That we needed each other. That we could not exist without each other. In fact I told him all the sorts of things lovers tell their beloved, except the one he most wanted to hear.

CHAPTER
FIFTY-FOUR

SHE HAS never said she loves me. I know she does but she won't say it.

I have had the same dream several nights now, once when I was lying in her arms which surprised me. It's short and simple but when I wake I find tears on my cheeks. I see a boy of about six or seven, with fair hair and sturdy sunburnt body, running through a field of long grass, mixed with poppies and daisies. His arms are opened wide as if he is running towards something wonderful and his hair streams out behind him. On the edge of the field the sun slants brightly through the trees. He might be running towards the sun. That's all there is to it. A little boy running with his arms open.